CODE

Ron ... cated at St... rvard Business School and was admitted to the California bar in 1968. Since then he has practised law in the film, television and record industries. He lives in Southern California with his wife and daughter. *Code Name Emerald* is his third novel and is being made into a major film. He is at work on his fourth book.

RONALD BASS

Code Name Emerald

FONTANA/Collins

First published in Great Britain as *The Emerald Illusion*
by William Collins Sons & Co. Ltd 1985
First issued in Fontana Paperbacks 1986

Made and printed in Great Britain by
William Collins Sons & Co. Ltd, Glasgow

To Chrissy and Jennifer
for making my life into our life

ACKNOWLEDGMENTS

My gratitude to:

Jay Acton for his loyalty, wise counsel and tireless efforts over nearly a decade

Melinda Jason for her faith and optimism and energy

Jon Sanger for his confidence and courageous support

Hillel Black and Freddie Freedman for their roles in shaping the beginnings of this story

Pat Golbitz for being there

ONE

Walter Hoffmann was suddenly awake. His heart pounding, his thoughts too vivid and complete. It was as if the thoughts had been waiting. Perched like scavenger birds, staring at him as he slept. Waiting to say, I'm here. Still here.

And slowly, one by one, Walter Hoffmann dismissed each of his birds of prey. Except the last. The one that silently reminded him of Anna and her fever. Of that tender place in her poor side, under the ribs. The doctor had said liver, and there had been those four days when Hoffmann knew that she was going to die. And then, the miracle of the doctor being simply, blessedly wrong. Slowly, Anna's body had begun to heal itself.

He turned towards her now in the darkness, the last of his morning birds clinging to the shoulder of his mind. She was cool; there was no fever at all. He snuggled to her for a moment and felt the response of her hips softly warming his thighs. He pulled back carefully. He would let her sleep. And slowly, with an effortless flutter of its great wings, the bird of Hoffmann's blackest fear was forced to quit its perch.

Hoffmann padded down the hall to the bathroom, gathering his strength for the ritual of Monday morning. It was as if he had to turn some magic, primitive crank inside himself to get the banality started. To rid himself of perspective, that passion to view and analyze and judge his life. To immerse himself instead in manageable, life-sized problems that gave security to the basic boundaries of things. A shave, a cup of strong coffee, and he would be on mindless automatic pilot for the rest of the week.

Not exactly. Mindlessness was not a state to which Walter

Hoffmann could aspire. His mind had been his oldest, his only, constant friend. They had passed forty-two years together and Hoffmann's mind had never let him down. Until now, until Pursesnatch.

Hoffmann squinted into the mirror as the brush stirred his shaving cream. It was a gentle and human face. A friendly face. Lank black hair and finely drawn features. Intelligent eyes and thin lips that seemed at once playful and questioning. There was humour, there was compassion, and neither far below the surface.

Anna was safe. The dark birds of night were forgotten. But as he shaved and showered, Hoffmann's mind was spinning towards the riddle of Pursesnatch. Surrounding it, enfolding it, as if re-examination alone would supply the answer. It could not. Hoffmann knew that he was out too far for his mind to pull him back. His first failure was about to become his last.

Rudi was in the kitchen, standing on a spindly chair to reach the sink. He was seven years old and struggling to fill a large iron pot from the faucet. This was the water for his father's coffee. Rudi's proudest, most sacred task.

'Good morning,' Hoffmann said, as he would say the words to a man, to an equal.

'Good morning, Papa.'

Rudi somehow managed to step down from the chair, pot firmly in his small hands. Friday he had dropped the pot with a horrifying clatter. Rudi was not certain that he would ever be trusted again. He was watching now, fearing the slightest offer of help that would signify loss of his father's confidence. But there was none. His father stood with hands behind his back, smiling the smile Rudi loved.

'I was thinking about something,' Hoffmann said. 'I was thinking how good it is to have a friend like you.'

Rudi just smiled. He never knew what to say when his father said things like that. He only knew the warm way it made him feel. With all his strength, he reached up to place the pot gently on its burner. There was nothing in this world that could have made him drop it.

'I'll get the baby,' Hoffmann said, and made his way to Oskar's room.

Oskar was nearly four. He was blond and fat, like Anna, as fair as his brother was dark. He was awake in his bed, coverlet clutched up around his face, waiting for his papa. Without a word, Hoffmann swung the child up into his arms. As always, there was a gasp and then a giggle.

'Do you know what day it is?' Hoffmann asked.

'Thursday,' Oskar said with conviction, picking a day at random.

'It's Monday,' Hoffmann said in a tone that was more agreement than correction. 'Do you know what that means?'

'It means,' Oskar said, 'that you don't have to go to the office.' It was the same wish that Hoffmann heard every morning.

'It means,' Hoffmann said, 'that when I come home from the office, I get to have supper with you. And we get to play.'

Hoffmann kissed his son and trundled him off to the bathroom to help him pee.

It was seven o'clock. The three of them shared breakfast. Hoffmann slipped upstairs to finish dressing. He knew the car would arrive in fifteen minutes.

Back down the stairs, the black and silver tunic slung over his shoulder. He looked through the glass. The car was waiting. Hoffmann put on the tunic, buttoning it as he said good-bye to his sons. They were to play quietly until their mother awakened. She was feeling much better, but she would still be tired.

He fastened the collar button. He bent and kissed each child on the lips. Rudi opened the door for his father. It was a crisp April morning and the air was wonderfully clean. Hoffmann skipped down the steps, turning at the usual place to wave. The sun shone on the silver lightning bolts at his collar. Rudi, his face very serious, waved back.

At the kerb, Hoffmann was greeted with a somewhat different form of salute. The arm of the young Sturmführer shot forward like a ramrod. It was a new driver. Hoffmann had not seen him before.

'Good morning, Oberführer,' the lieutenant said, a trifle loudly for Hoffmann's taste. There was a metallic timbre to his voice that seemed to violate the peace of the quiet residential street.

Hoffmann simply looked at the man. He did not look at him in any particular way. His gaze was bland and direct. Nonetheless, the lieutenant was suddenly unnerved. He began an explanation of how the usual driver had been transferred to the eastern front over the weekend. There had not been time to advise the Oberführer of the staffing change. This was not, of course, his personal responsibility, yet he found himself abjectly apologizing to Hoffmann's silence. The Oberführer, he had been told, appreciated surprises the way most men enjoy syphilis.

Hoffmann didn't know this particular SS lieutenant, but he was acquainted with the breed. He was wondering what Rudi would think of this man, of the carbon copies of this man swiftly multiplying among the normal population. Wondering if Rudi could, by any horrifying configuration of circumstance, be turned into something resembling this man. Hoffmann took the luxury of a full moment's silence to rid himself of that particular fear.

'Well,' Hoffmann said to the man's eyes, 'thank you so much for helping us this morning.' As if the man had done him a personal favour. But there was also the faintest hint that the favour would be accepted for this morning only, that the lieutenant might find himself transferred to God-knows-where by noon.

'What route would the Oberführer prefer this morning?' It was April 6, 1944, and the lieutenant was asking whether Hoffmann would order a circuitous route to avoid passing the more unsettling consequences of recent bombing raids on Berlin. This had been phrased in the interrogative only as a matter of courtesy. Each SS officer for whom the lieutenant had driven, without exception, had insisted on being spared exposure to any sights that could encourage negativism or defeatist thinking. They were a most positive group.

'The direct route,' Hoffmann said.

Hoffmann settled into the rear of the car. His face assumed the mask he would wear for his journey from Zehlendorf to SD headquarters in the district of Charlottenburg.

TWO

Hoffmann's driver swung north and east, away from the Havel River. To travel from Zehlendorf to Charlottenburg they would have to pass through the Wilmersdorf district. The damage was extensive in places, but altogether random, as if the whim of a great malevolent fist had chosen to crush this dwelling, this shop, and leave its neighbours untouched.

To the eyes of the driver, the devastation evident in some quarters of Berlin was in no way cause for alarm. This was merely the price of destiny. It fuelled dreams of vengeance which sometimes took the form of disturbingly vivid personal fantasies. These thoughts did not make the young lieutenant feel abnormal, because they were shared in great detail with like-minded colleagues of the SS. He and his fellows had become a group apart, a colony within the heart and bloodstream of metamorphosing Germany. A colony aware that it would soon become more than model. Its character was to conquer the existing cellular structure of its host people and become Germany itself.

As with most organic parasites, the inception of the SS was humble indeed. The Schutzstaffel had begun in 1923 as the protection squadron of the Nazi party – a small band of thugs mainly serving as Hitler's personal bodyguard. Under the leadership of Reichsführer Heinrich Himmler, this uniquely adaptable organization had blossomed to encompass secret police, slave labour management, savage front-line fighting troops, and the operation of complex and ingenious facilities for the slaughtering of human beings. There seemed no limit to the growth of the organization's scope, no boundaries other than the imagination of its leadership. And these were men of considerable imagination.

In 1932, the SS had spawned an embryonic unit designed to alert the Nazi party to threats against its security. This was the Sicherheitsdienst, the SD. It began simply as the security service of the SS. The SD expanded under the vision of the flamboyant Reinhard Heydrich, one of the most volatile and charismatic figures in the Reich, until his assassination in June 1942. Heydrich had built his own empire within Himmler's. If the SS was to become the body and bone of the New Germany, the SD was to be its nerve centre.

By 1939, Heydrich had transformed the SD into the security service of the entire German nation. It was now officially the RSHA (Reichssicherheitshauptamt), the Reich Central Security Office. The RSHA was organized into seven departments, all but one of which occupied the enormous headquarters at Prinz Albrechtstrasse 8, in the Tiergarten district at the centre of Berlin. Departments I and II were personnel and administration. Department III dealt with domestic intelligence. Department V, with detectives. Department VII, with ideological research and evaluation. But it was Department IV that remained the soulless heart of the organism. For this was the Gestapo, the ultimate mutant produced by the breeding of force into policy, of will into law.

Off to the west and south of the Tiergarten was the neighbouring district of Charlottenburg. There, at Berkaersstrasse 32, stood a building that seemed anything but majestic or imposing. Only four stories, its brick façade gently curved at the corner of Hohenzollerndamm. Flower pots stood on many of the window ledges. It had been built in 1930 as a Jewish home for the elderly. In 1941, the last remaining department of the RSHA commandeered the building and removed its inhabitants. This was Department VI, SD foreign intelligence. It was towards this building that Hoffmann's driver proceeded, muttering and cursing as piles of rubble and convoys of military trucks slowed his progress.

SD foreign intelligence was separated from the rest of the RSHA by more than the distance between buildings. The SS uniforms were the same and sometimes, only sometimes, the hearts beneath the skin were the same as well. But these were Hitler's spies. They were, unavoidably, a mixed bag. Political orthodoxy and racial purity were required, of course. But sometimes, only sometimes, talent was necessary as well. And talent had to be seized where one could find it.

Walter Hoffmann lived and worked within this hybrid of men and monsters. He had developed his own personal rating system for each of his colleagues. So many parts human, so many parts beast. Hoffmann checked himself against that standard on almost a daily basis, as a hypochondriac ceaselessly searches his own skin for the shiny black spot of a melanoma.

The head of SD foreign intelligence these past three years had been SS Brigadeführer Walter Schellenberg. At the age of thirty-one, this pink-cheeked boyish unknown had manipulated the great Heydrich into entrusting him with the leadership of the department. His enemies speculated that it had been his pretty face and plump figure that had mesmerized Heydrich. Hoffmann knew better. If Schellenberg was not a master spy, he was certainly a Machiavellian politician with few peers. The years after Heydrich's death testified to Schellenberg's genius, as his power consolidated, even expanded.

Schellenberg's effete manner, the soft pretensions to refinement, the devotion to physical luxury, could not conceal from Hoffmann the man's essential nature. The fates of other men, from the lowliest Jew or Pole to the Führer himself, were of no real concern to Schellenberg one way or another. Schellenberg was at his core flint-hard and merciless on one issue only, the advancement and protection of Walter Schellenberg. It was a cause Hoffmann had successfully made his own. Until now.

Schellenberg had tapped Walter Hoffmann for glory. Had placed him at his right hand, given him the rank of SS Standartenführer, the equivalent of a full colonel. Hoffmann had not disappointed. The more authority placed at his disposal, the better Hoffmann used it. Schellenberg proclaimed him a jewel in a field of cow droppings. In an amazingly short time it seemed that Schellenberg could trust no one else. All decisions of consequence gravitated to Hoffmann's desk, while Schellenberg found himself freed to ply his skill at court politics.

After an obscenely brief interval, Schellenberg had forced upon Hoffmann a promotion to SS Oberführer, a rank midway between colonel and general. This was done in disdain for, or perhaps largely to incite, the fierce envy of some rather ambitious subordinates. As Schellenberg had predicted, the effect had not been to place the staff at Hoffmann's throat, but rather to position them closer to his boot – in kneeling posture with tongues extended. The competition had been ended almost before it had begun. The only way up now was through Hoffmann's good graces, and he had become the beneficiary of a level of cooperation that bordered on reverence.

There was, however, the matter of Pursesnatch.

And so as Walter Hoffmann stepped from his car, as he was escorted through corridors and elevators to his office, his mind relentlessly turned in upon itself. Sifting, probing for the answer that could not be there.

It was held as axiomatic among certain elements of the German High Command that only one real test remained. The summer and fall of 1944 must pass without a successful Allied invasion of the continent. By the spring of 1945, Germany's hold on Europe would congeal and harden into everlasting fact. The Atlantikwall, Hitler's formidable line of defence, would face one desperate, conclusive assault within these next few months. There were but two questions. Where and when.

Despite the almost unimaginable strength of Hitler's

forces, 302 divisions, ten million men under arms, the truth was that the line had been stretched perilously thin. There were 179 divisions committed to Russia and the eastern front. This left only 40 per cent of Hitler's strength to face attack from the west. And where would it come? Hitler had deployed 26 divisions in the Balkans, 22 in Italy, 16 in Scandinavia. This left only 59 divisions for France, for a coastline stretching from the Pas-de-Calais, westward to Normandy and Brittany, then south to the Bay of Biscay. The Allies nurtured a single hope, a single chance. That in Hitler's frenzy to be strong everywhere, he would not be strong enough at the one place, at the one moment, that truly mattered.

Pursesnatch was the code name for a combination of stratagems designed to kidnap a Briton or an American who knew the secret of that place, that moment.

The idea had first taken shape in the private thoughts of Heinrich Himmler. There had followed the fateful night of Himmler's visit to Schellenberg's drawing room. Over brandy and fine cigars, the ballet had taken place. Schellenberg had been cautious at first, but as the evening progressed the message became all too clear. Himmler intended to report to the Führer that Pursesnatch was a reality. That his chief of foreign intelligence had personally assured Himmler of its impending success. If Schellenberg was not prepared to accept that responsibility, it might be best to consider posting him to duties for which he had more enthusiasm. Himmler was keen on enthusiasm. None of the foregoing was stated aloud, of course. All of it, including Schellenberg's intense enthusiasm for the plan, passed between the two men as easily and comfortably as a chat about the wine or the weather.

The conversation was replayed the following morning between Schellenberg and Hoffmann. Pursesnatch was placed firmly on Hoffmann's desk. He was told that funds and personnel in any quantity necessary would be at his disposal. Schellenberg did not ask for Hoffmann's enthusiasm. He required only that Hoffmann deliver.

That had been in January. In the next three months,

plans had been drawn, agents dispatched, large amounts of money in an assortment of currencies had changed hands. Two men had lost their lives. Spring had arrived. The prisoner, Himmler's prize, had not.

Hoffmann sat in his comfortable chair, in his oversized office, and stared at the neat pile of backlogged paperwork. His mind was meticulously churning the most recent fiasco of Pursesnatch's five consecutive failures.

There was a knock. Hoffmann said, 'Come,' and Ritter entered. Ernst Ritter was Hoffmann's immediate subordinate. He held the rank of SS Obersturmbannführer, the equivalent of a lieutenant colonel. Ritter bore the broad and handsome features that could easily grace any party poster. The dead, pale eyes. The grip that took private pride in being stronger than a socially proper handclasp.

Ritter's psyche was straight Gestapo, where, in fact, he had been posted for several years. He was, however, blessed with an IQ some sixty points higher than that of his colleagues, and this had been his ticket out and up. Hoffmann relied on Ritter's intellect for the more exacting staff assignments, largely because rational thought had become a commodity in increasingly short supply. Still, Hoffmann knew that Ritter was never to be trusted. For at his centre, Ritter was a man thrilled only by strength, by the scent of power uncontrolled.

Ritter now sat unnaturally still, his powerful hands clasped firmly in his lap. It was evident to Hoffmann that Ritter was particularly tense, that he was having difficulty broaching the true purpose of his visit. Hoffmann listened patiently as Ritter ran through a litany of reports on minor matters. When Ritter had talked himself dry, Hoffmann remained silent.

'We must,' Ritter said at last, 'accept the reality of our situation.'

'And what is that?'

'Our operation has failed. Schellenberg's relations with Himmler have been strained to the point that he fears his position will soon become untenable. We have to draw the line on this. End the operation and take corresponding necessary action.'

Ritter's panic was complete. He had hitched his wagon to Hoffmann's rising star from the first. Now, Hoffmann's destruction would be his as well.

'Corresponding action?' Hoffmann repeated with the playful smile that always infuriated Ritter. 'You mean suicide?'

Ritter's great shoulders twitched beneath his tunic. He was in no mood for gallows humour, or any humour for that matter. To him, Hoffmann was like Schellenberg. Brilliant foxes who would slip away from any catastrophe, leaving Ritter and the other plough horses to take the fall. Their collective futures were about to evaporate, and Hoffmann was either too foolish or too wise to believe that he would join the ranks of the obsolete.

'I mean only,' Ritter said, 'that we must do whatever is necessary to clarify for all concerned the true reasons for this failure.'

Hoffmann nodded, his smile dwindling to the barest wisp of irony.

'And who,' Hoffmann asked politely, 'is our scapegoat?'

Ritter bristled at the indelicacy of the phrase. Nor did he appreciate the accusation implicit in Hoffmann's tone. Self-righteous, judgmental sonofabitch. He had known Hoffmann long enough to know that he was not above making the best of a bad situation. And situations never came any worse than this one.

'There cannot be,' Ritter said, as calmly as he could manage, 'the slightest doubt that the SD and the Reich have again been victimized by Abwehr incompetence. Perhaps treason.'

The Abwehr was the foreign intelligence service of the German military. They were, simply put, the competition. Or at least they had been, until February. For decades, the Abwehr had monopolized German espionage. Formed from all three branches of the armed forces, the Abwehr had earned its reputation as a truly professional intelligence service. While the SD could never claim to match the Abwehr's expertise, its trump card remained its unquestioned devotion to Adolf Hitler. Over time, there had been episodes linking high-ranking Abwehr officials with the Schwarze Kapelle, the secret group of military leaders disloyal to the Führer. On February 12, Hitler had announced the formation of a unified German intelligence service, which would be entirely under SS control. The assimilation of the Abwehr by the SD was to take four months, and was still in progress. As elsewhere, the Führer was increasingly willing to sacrifice competence, even in vital areas, for the assurance of political reliability.

'And whom precisely,' Hoffmann asked, 'are you nominating for hell?'

'Jürgen Brausch, of course,' came the response.

Jürgen Brausch was an aging Army colonel who worked in Abwehr I, the branch responsible for recruitment, insertion, and control of spies abroad. He had run all German agents in the British Isles for more than a decade. Under the reorganization, Brausch's unit would be coming under Hoffmann's authority, but the fact remained that Brausch had been permitted to maintain his control of agents already in the field.

'There has been only one reason for the failure of Pursesnatch,' Ritter said. 'It has been Brausch's inability . . . perhaps even unwillingness . . . to provide crucial data from his precious agents in England.'

Hoffmann's eyes were cold now, but Ritter could see that the mind behind the eyes was at work. That was all he needed.

'I have taken the liberty,' Ritter added, 'of preparing a paper for your review, detailing the results of my inquiry into Brausch's role in this matter. The research is incomplete, of course, but the conclusions speak for themselves.'

'I'm sure they do, Ernst,' Hoffmann said quietly, intending the use of Ritter's first name to be taken as a sign of softening. 'Well, I shall, of course, give your paper the courtesy of some careful thought. Why don't you send it 'round to my home this evening.'

Ritter nodded with unspoken satisfaction. He was certain that Hoffmann had, on his brief moment's reflection, already made a favourable decision.

But Hoffmann's thoughts had taken a different tack. He had no desire whatsoever to destroy Jürgen Brausch. He would much prefer to use him.

THREE

A garden party in Hampstead, just north of London.

It was a spring afternoon of clear sunshine, and the guests were strolling the lawn among the colonel's perfect roses. A striped canvas of butter-yellow and lime had been stretched above the refreshment table, shielding the sandwiches and cakes. Its edges fluttered softly in the breeze.

These were military men with their ladies. Crisp uniforms, erect carriage, gallantry. The balancing of teacups and banter. To the eye of a casual observer, of which there were none, these officers could have been infantry, artillery, indistinguishable from their fellows in uniform. In fact, however, this was a most select gathering.

These men shared membership in MI-5, a particularly obscure branch of British military intelligence. Such glamour as there was to go around and, even more unfortunately, such funding as well, was invariably preempted by their brothers in MI-6. The boys of MI-6 were assigned to the gathering of foreign intelligence. They were the spies, foraying abroad with their disguises and wireless crystals, their forged papers and tiny pots of invisible ink.

The MI-5, however, was the stolid home contingent assigned to counterespionage. They were the defenders of the homeland against the treachery of enemy agents. By

April 1944, the popular view at Whitehall was that these boys had done such admirable work in tracking down Jerry that they had pretty well performed themselves right out of a job. The accepted belief was that any German agents left in England were either under close and constant scrutiny or had actually come over and were working for the Allied cause.

Colonel Basil Nicholas of MI-5, host of the afternoon's festivities, took pointed exception to this complacency. It was always a thankless task to prove a negative. Meaning, of course, that the only spies left who could hurt England were the ones they had not found as yet. His position, while theoretically unassailable, was deemed by His Majesty's Government to be understandably excessive caution. Nicholas was tolerated as a good soldier who had done his part. Such limited funds as were available would go elsewhere, to uncompleted tasks.

Alicia Nicholas came down the stairs and into the sunlight of the garden. Alicia was seventeen and sexy, a wild little flirt and clearly more than her father, the colonel, could handle. Her hair was dark honey and fell in loose ringlets across her shoulders, jiggling with the rest of her as she bounced into the midst of her father's guests.

Alicia wore a thin cotton dress with nothing of consequence underneath. The sight was made for sunlight, but the admiring glances of the officers present were kept to the quick and furtive. Whether they feared their ladies or their colonel, Alicia was a dangerous package with her open stance and the sun knifing through her dress.

Alicia was quite unconcerned, however, with the lack of overt attention to her entrance. She was looking most carefully for someone in particular.

He was standing alone. Tall and slender with hair of pale gold. Green eyes with blonde lashes any woman would envy. His uniform was that of an American Army captain, perhaps the only Yank on the premises. To Alicia's eye, he was set apart even more clearly by the quiet grace of his movements. His long fingers curved about the stem of his glass as he sipped. He stood so easily, so comfortable in stillness. Alicia saw him as more than beauty. He was a man in control, a man at peace with himself.

She paused for a moment before heading towards him. Her nervousness was uncharacteristic, and disturbed her more than a little. Angry with herself for her sudden cowardice, she circled around and approached him from the rear. Too late she realized that she was simply standing there like a puppy dog, looking up at him and waiting for him to turn around. She cleared her throat delicately. So little sound came out that she could scarcely hear it herself. She tried again, absolutely detesting herself and the way she had bungled everything. He turned, and the green eyes found hers.

'Hullo,' she said. It seemed somehow inadequate. 'I'm Alicia Nicholas,' she added. The following silence was not more than an instant, but for Alicia it was an unbearable void. She filled it with, 'And you're Gus Lang.'

Gus' smile flashed quick and boyish, as if he had been thoroughly charmed.

'Don't let me interrupt,' he said. 'You're handling both ends of this conversation beautifully.'

It might have been the sudden smile, or the form of the word *beautiful* but Alicia flushed all the way down to her ankles. She felt suddenly and entirely naked. She would never forgive herself for standing in the middle of this garden with so little on.

'Why don't we take a walk?' he said. 'You can show me your father's roses and tell me all about myself.'

He put down his glass and offered her his elbow. She slipped her bare arm through his and instinctively brushed her shoulder against his side. It wasn't nearly a cuddle, not yet, but a necessary prelude.

They turned down the path of enormous orange and crimson blossoms. Her eyes locked on the dirt before her.

'You are Augustus William Lang,' she said. 'You are a captain of the OSS . . .'

He gave her arm a little squeeze.

'Hey,' he said, 'I was only kidding. Actually, I already know that stuff.'

'Shall I talk about me?' She turned her cinnamon eyes up towards him and, to her thorough humiliation, actually found herself batting her lashes.

He just smiled down at her. It was an awfully friendly smile and terribly sexy, but there was just the first hint of older brother in it. She wasn't handling this well at all.

Then his stare lingered for a moment and the heat flashed through her.

'Stop working so hard,' he said gently. 'I already like you. Just give me a chance to do a little of the flirting.'

'Sure,' she choked, and her eyes locked on the path again, her arm crushing his into her breast as they walked.

'You're thirty-one,' she said, resuming her lecture with burning cheeks. 'Your father is an industrialist of German extraction. You live in New England. Connecticut. You attended – '

'Wait,' he interrupted, 'let me guess this one.'

'Yale University,' she continued, beaming. 'You speak six languages beautifully.' She leaned on the word.

'You've been eavesdropping on Daddy,' he said.

'Listening to Daddy,' she corrected. 'He says you have unique talents. You are a gifted young man. The only Yank he'd steal for MI-5 if he could swing it.'

She permitted a moment's pause, before the clincher. 'He also said you were single.'

They walked on.

'Boring stuff,' Gus concluded. 'Daddy wouldn't tell you anything little girls shouldn't hear.'

They had reached the end of the path. There was a manicured field beyond the back gate. Nestling her cheek against his shoulder, she pushed open the gate and walked him through. Hidden from the others by a tall hedge, they were very much alone as they set out across the field.

'He told me that the OSS posted you to MI-5 as a counterespionage liaison. You were too valuable to be left unused, and have been assigned to Double Cross Committee, tracking German agents.'

Gus was silent. Even his gait became tentative, signalling to Alicia that he had been impressed by her knowledge.

'Any agents in particular?' he asked.

There was not a moment's hesitation.

'The one the Germans call Treasure,' she said, 'and the one they call Emerald.'

Gus stopped in the middle of the open field. He put his hands on her shoulders.

'Someone has given you some very wild stories,' he said, leaving enough of a beat before his denial to convince Alicia that her information must be absolutely correct.

'Of course,' she nearly whispered, 'they aren't things I'd repeat to anyone.'

Of course they weren't. And to the extent that they were, Gus thought, so much the better.

'We should get back,' he smiled. Warm and very intimate. They had stolen away together.

As they turned back, she hesitantly slipped her arm around his waist. Gus gave her a strong hug in return, then gently pulled her arm away, closing his fingers warmly around her hand. His movement was so spontaneous and affectionate that the impact of the rejection was largely masked.

Gus had no intention of massaging anything but her ego.

'I think there's someone else we should talk about,' he said, slowing their steps.

She squeezed his hand tightly, but she had received the message.

'What does she look like?'

'Blue eyes and a sad, sweet face,' he lied. There was no one, had been no one for a very long time. 'She's honest and funny. You'd like her.'

They walked a little further.

'She's far away,' Alicia announced in a small voice.

'Except,' he said, 'for the part of her I brought with me.'

Gus stopped, took both her hands. They were still behind

the hedge. He gave her the look she would need for consolation. The look that said he wanted her.

'It's a promise I want to keep,' he said. 'No matter how much I might also want something else.'

His fingers added extra pressure. Her eyes were moist, a thing that did not usually happen to Alicia Nicholas, but she was too preoccupied to be embarrassed.

'Some people value promises,' she said. 'Some people value experiences even more. Especially when no one's hurt.'

'I think,' he said, 'that's the kind of person you've been wearing around the outside of you. But that's not how I see you. Everyone's hurt when you break a promise. I think you understand that. I think you understand things pretty well.'

Alicia couldn't feel the dampness in her eyes. She just gave him a little hug and led him back through the gate to her father's garden.

FOUR

Hoffmann had decided to pay a visit to Jürgen Brausch. He could have summoned him to Charlottenburg. Could have sat behind the authority of his grand carved desk and shown Brausch his place in the new order. That was how Ritter would have handled it. Ritter was burdened with the Gestapo view that all forms of intimidation, including humiliation, serve to enhance fear.

Hoffmann understood the workings of fear more clearly. The point, of course, was not simply to induce the maximum sensation of terror. The goal was rather to create an atmosphere in which fear would become the catalyst for the desired action or response. This meant introducing fear in a purposeful way, in a manner calculated to minimize the subject's defences.

And so Hoffmann's car proceeded to the Tiergarten on a diplomatic mission of mercy.

Brausch still maintained a suite of offices in the old Abwehr headquarters at 76/78 Tirpitzufer, adjoining the former home of the German High Command at the corner of Bendlerstrasse. The Abwehr quarters had been called the Fuchsbau, the Fox's Lair. It was a block of elegant townhouses on the north side of the Landwehr Canal, converted for the use of the elite spy corps.

A year earlier, due to Allied bombing raids, the Abwehr had officially moved from these comfortable surroundings to share the protection of the new Army headquarters at Zossen, twenty miles south of Berlin. Brausch and a few of his fellow fossils preferred to linger in the ambience of the Fox's Lair whenever possible.

Hoffmann entered the drawing room of the old townhouse, which had served as a reception area. The offices were former bedrooms, maids' rooms, even kitchens. Although the remodelling had been spare, the effect of these incongruous quarters was stateliness combined with warmth.

Hoffmann remembered the first day he had set foot in these rooms. A young lieutenant with an even younger wife. No money, high ambition. He remembered the sense of tradition that nearly overwhelmed him, that seemed to bleed from the walls and the furniture. He remembered the pride of realizing that he had become part of the Abwehr. A society of wizards and artists. Magical soldiers performing legendary deeds with a nonchalance inaccessible to mortals.

What Hoffmann certainly did not think of was the day, years later, when he was summoned to the massive RSHA monolith on Prinz Albrechtstrasse. When he sat with his heart in his belly, in the office of that Gestapo thug Kaltenbrunner, whom Himmler had made chief of all the RSHA. Sat while a fresh-faced child named Schellenberg raved on to Kaltenbrunner of the brilliance of Hoffmann's Abwehr record. Heard, as if it were a death sentence, the magnanimous 'offer' of promotion and opportunity.

Hoffmann made his way in the creaking old elevator to the fourth floor. This was the floor from which the almost-mythical Admiral Wilhelm Canaris, the Fox for whom the Lair was named, had masterminded the Abwehr until his fall. It finally had been suspicions, correct ones, as to Canaris' personal loyalty to the Führer that had been the catalyst for the February directive, placing the Abwehr at last under SD domination and resulting in Canaris' own dismissal and demotion. It was a testament to the old admiral's mystique that he had not only escaped arrest, but actually had been appointed to a comfortable, if less sensitive, new post.

Hoffmann found his way to Brausch's office. To enter was to go back in time to the first day he had nervously stood waiting for Brausch to look up from his reading. Elegant furniture from another era. Desk at an oblique angle so that the colonel could look out the window to the canal below, to the chestnuts of the Tiergarten. And on the desk, the three brass monkeys that were the insignia of the Abwehr. One cupped his ear to hear clearly. One looked over his shoulder to watch behind him. The last held his hand before his mouth.

That first morning, Brausch had watched Hoffmann staring at the monkeys. He had said to the boy, 'Hear all evil. See all evil. Say nothing.' In eight words, Brausch had given Hoffmann the gift of a golden rule from which all training developed as mere elaboration.

Hoffmann now looked across the room. Brausch was speaking softly into a scrambler telephone called an A-net. As he had long ago, Hoffmann folded his hands before him and waited patiently.

Brausch was a round-shouldered giant. He had the long, sagging face of a hound. There was a moustache that seemed, like his honour, a remnant from another era of German Army. There were tired old eyes, whose sixty-three years seemed to have seen a hundred.

The word *abwehr* meant defence, and it was to the defence of his country that Brausch had dedicated his life.

He had left the Humanistic Gymnasium in Wiesbaden before the turn of the century to join the 15th Field Artillery Regiment. He had begun World War I on the staff of the army group of Crown Prince Rupert of Bavaria. He had ended the war among the kaiser's finest, the 9th Potsdam Infantry Regiment. Paul von Hindenburg was his colonel in chief. From there he had gone to Fremde Heere West, the Army's intelligence-gathering and evaluation agency. And untimately, Canaris himself had tapped Brausch for the Abwehr.

He was the last of the dinosaurs, there was no doubt, and Hoffmann could not believe that he was now this man's superior officer. That by June 1, in less than two months, Abwehr I would become the military department of RSHA VI. Jürgen Brausch would, in effect, end his career in the service of the SS.

Brausch put down the receiver and smiled up at Hoffmann. Never, in any setting, had Hoffmann felt so much the intruder. Brausch stood to his full, shambling height. His arm extended, welcoming Hoffmann to the seat of honour, an overstuffed chair in a faded print that had been imported from Holland long ago.

'The place is deserted, Jürgen,' Hoffmann said softly. 'Shouldn't you be at Zeppelin?' This was the code name for the new headquarters at Zossen.

'It is good to see you too,' Brausch smiled, reproaching Hoffmann for his failure to offer a greeting. 'As for Zossen, I am happier to remain in Berlin. It keeps me closer to my new masters. The better to serve you, Walter.'

'Helga is well?' Hoffmann asked. 'and the children?'

Brausch nodded absently. His eyes looked to the packet in Hoffmann's lap. The glance seemed a directive to come to the point.

Hoffmann stood and brought the envelope to Brausch's desk. With a heavy sigh, Brausch took out his spectacles and began to skim the twelve-page document.

'This report,' Hoffmann said, 'was prepared by an officer named Ernst Ritter.'

'He is on your staff,' Brausch said without looking up. 'He is an Obersturmbannführer. Whether that is an officer . . .' his voice trailed off as he read. His face betrayed not the slightest emotion. When he had finished, he looked at Hoffmann.

'And what does Brigadeführer Schellenberg say to this report?'

'I pray God,' Hoffmann said, 'that he never reads it.'

Brausch wondered to which God precisely Hoffmann would be praying.

'And what will happen, Walter, when he does?'

'Schellenberg is frenzied,' Hoffman said calmly. 'You must know what has happened here. Himmler promised a prisoner to Hitler before Schellenberg even heard of this madness. Hitler was told that Schellenberg had already guaranteed success.'

Brausch nodded as if only confirming the obvious.

'If it had worked,' Brausch said wearily, 'the plan was Himmler's masterstroke. Since it did not, it was Schellenberg's failure to execute. Poor fellow,' Brausch added dryly, 'it all seems so unfair.'

Hoffmann conceded a small smile to Brausch's sarcasm. There was undeniably a touch of grim humour in watching rats caught in their own trap. Even though Hoffmann was one of them.

Brausch spread his large fleshy palms.

'I mean, what did the Brigadeführer expect, Walter? And yourself? Why do you children think you were promoted? Did you believe that a shark invites you to his waters because he needs swimming companions? You are lunch, nothing more.'

'Save your irony,' Hoffmann said gently, 'for when you are in shallower waters yourself, Jürgen. If the SD is to be lunch, the Abwehr is, at best, a canapé.'

Brausch's eyes said that this was very clear.

'Schellenberg will savage you, Jürgen. You have committed treason. It is his only chance. Your agents have deliberately denied the Führer his prize, because you and the

Abwehr and half the Army would rather destroy the party than save our homeland. Is there the smallest doubt in your mind?'

Brausch's eyes were locked into middle distance, as he made the necessary choices in his mind.

'Whatever becomes of Schellenberg,' Hoffmann continued, 'the Abwehr will be gone. It will be the gravest tragedy for Germany, Jürgen. Your people are the only intelligence professionals we have. To lose them on the eve of the Allied invasion . . .'

'How much time,' Brausch interrupted in a very quiet voice, 'before you show this to Schellenberg?'

'You have to give me something, Jürgen. Something now. A tale for Schellenberg in lieu of the report. And we would have to pay it off in, I would say, three weeks. Four at most.'

Brausch looked at Hoffmann with the mix of contempt and compassion felt by a father for the crimes of a wayward son. Hoffmann had indeed been a prodigy, and Brausch had shared with Canaris and others the pride of responsibility for his flowering. He recalled their assignment in Oberursell, a village just north of Frankfurt am Main. It was the site of Dulag Luft, the Luftwaffe's transit camp for captured enemy flyers. Brausch had been sent to train Luftwaffe interrogators, and had brought Hoffmann as his aide. He remembered Hoffmann's intuition, his light touch, his extraordinary creativity. He was the most instinctive, the most innately acute interrogator Brausch had ever trained.

In Brausch's eyes, Hoffmann had been seduced into the SD with promises of a skyrocketing career. To Hoffmann there had been no alternative, for to have rejected Schellenberg would have brought his career to an end. Brausch knew better, knew that there had been a choice. There was always a choice.

'There is something,' Brausch said at last. 'One last run I had hoped not to discuss at such a premature stage.'

Hoffmann's eyes narrowed slightly in silent, respectful attention.

'I have an agent in London, in MI-5,' Brausch said.
'Emerald,' Hoffmann said. 'American.'

Brausch's eyes registered no surprise that Hoffmann had found his way to that information. Though how and where, Brausch hadn't a clue. This was a dossier he had not intended to relinquish to the SD until certain precautions had been taken.

'We have long believed,' Brausch said, 'that the Allies will be forced to hold some form of rehearsal for the invasion. Exercises with their landing craft, most probably in Channel waters. On such boats would be several of the men you are seeking.'

Outwardly, Hoffmann appeared intent and polite. Within him, he felt the bands around his stomach loosen for the first time in months.

'From Emerald's position within Allied counterespionage,' Brausch said, 'he is spinning his web towards gaining the time and site of such an exercise.'

Brausch permitted himself a slowly emerging smile. This had its intended effect of increasing Hoffmann's excitement.

'He reports that he is very close,' Brausch said.

Hoffmann nodded as his long tension gave way to inner elation If Brausch admitted they were close, then they were closer.

FIVE

St James's Park in the chill of a Sunday morning. Gerhard Tessin made his way down a path of willows and flowers, looking for a man on a bench.

He walked with brisk, clipped stride. A scrawny fellow with sharp little features and eyes that were never still. Wispy orange hair in all directions, billowing like a saffron aura about his head as he walked.

Tessin was an Abwehr pimp, one of Brausch's best. He recruited and supplied. He had won a few and lost a few in his time, but at the moment his star was in the ascendant. This was due to his current stable of four agents, whom he alternately pampered and prodded according to his master's orchestration.

Tessin had been discovered in the Harvesthude section of Hamburg, working in the Ast outpost there. Ast was short for Abwehrstelle, or Abwehr post, and this was District X, the Abwehr regional office primarily in charge of working against the interests of Great Britain. Tessin had been graded a Specialist in Group I espionage, one of only seven so honoured out of three hundred men. He had visited England in the thirties under several assumed names, usually posing as a representative for the I. G. Farben pharmaceutical plant that produced Bayer aspirin.

Tessin's English was unaccented, his memory keen, and he had proven virtually fearless where mercenary gain was in the offing. As controller of the funds used to pay and supply his agents, the Abwehr pimp was rumoured in certain quarters to deduct a businesslike commission. Such incentives were frowned on by many seniors of the Abwehr, but Jürgen Brausch had happily proven more interested in results than in imposing his personal standards of integrity onto others.

If Brausch found Tessin's manner fussy, that manner made him appear all the more British. If Brausch found Tessin thoroughly venal, such venality made him all the more dependent on his superior's generosity and discretion. In short, a match made in heaven.

At long last, Tessin had been awarded the ultimate prize among espionage paraphernalia, a forged British passport. There were amazingly few of these in existence. The paper had to be made to rigid specifications. It was cooked in large tubs in a paper factory at Spechthausen, near Berlin. There were special teams of engravers, armed with rubber stamps and gold seals, meticulously plotting exit, entry, and visa stamps with appropriate dates and places.

Before Tessin could finally be placed, he was issued an accompanying array of forged letters, photographs, receipts, even a birth certificate. There was enough clothing of British woollens, buttons, and thread to get him started. There was also, of course, plenty of money. Pounds, gold, and even a small number of raw gems to be sold off in desperate circumstances.

There was one thing more. It was called an Afus, short for *Agentenfunk*, meaning agent radio. The radio, a hand-keyed apparatus tuned by quartz crystals to a single preset frequency, was the size of a small suitcase. It was easily Tessin's most precious tool, and was smuggled separately into Bristol with the cargo of a Spanish trader. It was to this radio that Tessin hoped to return, at the prearranged hour that evening, with a message that would forever solidify his position with his colonel.

Tessin had received the young agent's call only hours before. The call had been placed from a public phone booth, and the terse message was coded and proper in every way. Yet, there was a tantalizing air to Emerald's tone that quickened Tessin's step along the path. True, Gerhard Tessin's calling card within the Abwehr was still the fabled Treasure, the most productive and highly placed German agent in the history of the service. But Tessin had high hopes indeed for the young man who awaited him. For Emerald was a comer, a rising star.

At the far end of the path, Tessin saw Emerald alone on a bench, watching swans arc through the shadows of a rippling pond. To the Home Office files this man was GV-8635, the initials standing for *Gegen-Vertrauensmann*, or contrary agent.

Emerald watched Tessin approach. Tessin moved too crisply for his taste. Too evident a sense of purpose for what should be passing as a pre-church stroll. But then, he had never exactly admired Tessin's tradecraft.

Tessin arrived and took a seat on the bench beside him.

'Heil, Hitler,' Gus Lang whispered, and watched the little man fairly vibrate with irritation.

'I suppose,' Tessin said in theatrically hushed tones, 'this grotesque sense of humour is what you call flair. I will never understand why you feel compelled to deliberately breach every precept of secure contact.'

There was not a living soul within two hundred yards.

'You're right,' Gus agreed. 'Let's just keep our chat to the weather, shall we? Bit of a bite to the breeze this morning, wouldn't you say?'

Tessin shot him a murderous look.

'Catch the American ball scores?' Gus asked cheerily. 'Those Red Sox, boy, I don't know.'

Gus thought he could hear all of Tessin's internal organs grinding against one another. He had stopped searching for Tessin's redeeming qualities long ago. He was forced to admit that he simply found the little weasel personally repellent, and that was all there was to it.

'I've got some pretty good stuff for you this morning, Gerhard, but you're not getting off easy. Gonna have to say "pretty please."'

Tessin suddenly understood, for Gus had reached the man at his own level. Tessin's shoulders visibly relaxed. Extortion was something he knew how to handle, meaning he yielded to it, since it was Brausch's money anyway.

'This is an awkward moment,' Tessin said, 'to renegotiate one's arrangement. Home Office discourages blackmail.'

To Gus, this was the equivalent of a blank cheque.

'Nonsense,' he said, 'they think they invented blackmail. Shows initiative, sense of purpose, and most importantly, exquisite timing.'

Tessin scowled. No sense in letting the price get out of hand. Might be harder to save oneself a slice in the middle.

'Out of the question,' came Tessin's opening thrust.

Gus stood.

'Lovely to see you. Let's chat again real soon. Call you Thursday.'

Gus watched for a millisecond, just to make certain Tessin's eyes were watering, then turned on his heels and stepped away. Tessin cleared his throat with enough violence to shatter windows all the way to Buckingham Palace.

Gus took a few more steps, then stopped. He turned his glance slowly over his shoulder to see Tessin on his feet, hands clutching each other uselessly at his chest.

Gus assumed the face of a petulant child and scraped the dirt path with his toe. Slowly, he trudged back to Tessin's bench and sat beside him.

'I'll accept a donation,' Gus said, 'for my favourite charity in the amount of four thousand pounds sterling.'

Tessin's lips went white. He didn't know which of them Brausch would kill first. Gus figured he was having a stroke. It was probably more money than Tessin could get, even if he gave the whole bundle to Gus.

'Gerhard, you disapprove. Every farthing goes to widows and orphans, cross my heart. We've rendered these poor folk homeless with our senseless bombing raids, and we must do the right thing. Appeal to the colonel's sense of responsibility.'

Tessin simply fought to control his pulse rate.

'This is not a complex decision,' Gus said. 'If you say yes, you will hear an interesting story. If you say something stupid, such as "three thousand" or "three-five," you will spoil my mood entirely.'

It was not very long before Tessin's lips formed the word, 'Yes.'

The smile faded from Gus' lips. He gave the little man a look so hard and flat that Tessin was suddenly afraid Gus was about to up the price.

'There will be an exercise,' Gus said evenly, 'in Lyme Bay on the south coast of Devon.'

Every duct in Tessin's body slammed open to release a flood of adrenalin.

'I don't have the names of the landing craft,' Gus said, 'or their precise number. Probably not more than two or three. They will leave from Torbay at approximately twenty hundred hours and proceed south towards Prawle Point.'

Tessin simply shook his head in wonderment. This was

it. Lyme Bay on the Devon coast, somewhere between Torbay and Prawle Point.

'I would think,' Gus said, 'that one of our E-boat squadrons based in Cherbourg would do rather nicely. There will, of course be Overlords aboard.'

Overlord was the term that Gus had previously revealed to Tessin as the Allied code for those with knowledge of D-Day. Tessin struggled to maintain his composure, but Gus could see the thrill surging through him. The quality of Emerald's product had invariably proven letter-perfect.

'Always a pleasure,' Gus smiled, 'to cook for a man who's so easily satisfied.'

'The date,' Tessin said.

Gus' smile went away.

'When I see my money.'

'Would thirty minutes be inconvenient?' Tessin asked. For this, he would dip into his private stock.

'I can see,' Gus said with his smile returning, 'I've sold myself cheap again. Live and learn.'

Tessin stood, smoothing the wrinkles from his trousers.

'There are stories,' he said, 'that you have *befriended* your colonel's daughter. Could this have any relation to your source?'

Gus was not quite certain why the remark was so irritating. Since the rumour of his relationship with Alicia was one that Gus had helped to spread, he did not understand why Tessin's slimy tone on the word *befriended* made him want to squish the little man against the underside of their bench.

'Shall we say,' Gus offered, 'that you are curious?'

Tessin nodded.

'Shall we also say,' Gus put in the same tone, 'that you are repulsive?'

Tessin seemed offended, if such a thing were possible.

'If you think,' Gus said quietly, 'that Basil Nicholas would confide the secrets of an invasion rehearsal to his seventeen-year-old daughter, you are a greater moron than I have ever given you credit for being.'

That was insufficient, however, to wash the anger from Gus' system.

He stood, threateningly close now to Tessin. Since Tessin was no more than a parasite living off the genius of his agents, there was not the slightest fear of speaking plainly. In fact, occasional flare-ups usually helped keep the little weasel in line.

'The price is now five thousand pounds, Gerhard. And there's a reason for it. The lady in question is close enough to being my friend that I take a personal revulsion in hearing a reference to her pass your lips. She is a human being, Gerhard. A species you know very little about. Consequently, a subject on which you should learn to become silent.'

Gus watched the man's eyes widen, then turned and left before the impulse to touch him grew any stronger.

SIX

Gus entered the small cluttered room. Charts, discarded coffee tins, a whiff of human closeness that would proudly represent any locker room. There were no windows, of course, since they were thirty feet beneath the rest of London.

This was the office of Colonel Basil Nicholas of MI-5. A man whose simple task these past six years had been the tracking, catching, turning, and playing back of German agents.

For more than three years now, Nicholas had been a member of the XX Committee, a consortium of MI-5 officers and Foreign Office personnel. Called the Twenty Committee or Double Cross, the XX Committee made a specialty of double agents. Their interrogation centre was a place called Latchmere House, a former convalescent home for Army officers in Surrey. It was a working clinic for spooks, and attracted the best available.

It was at Latchmere House that Nicholas had first met young Captain Lang, shipped to England straight from the American OSS, the Office of Strategic Services. Gus had seemed a perfect fit for Double Cross, since he had been an integral part of the corresponding X2 counterintelligence group at the OSS. He had begun his intelligence career as a Yale senior cooperating with the FBI, infiltrating subversive German-American organizations. His success was phenomenal. When he ultimately entered the Army, he joined the OSS with the blessings of the Abwehr, since they believed he was now their man inside American intelligence.

Gus had become the rarest of the rare, a well-placed triple. More precious than the emeralds for which the Germans had named him.

'Enjoyed the party,' Gus said. 'Thanks for having me. Made me feel family.'

Nicholas was a square little man, with powerful hands and arms. His eyes were usually merry, but there was a weakness around the edges as he accepted Gus' gratitude.

'Hope,' Nicholas said as casually as he could manage, 'you found a moment to chat with Alicia. She'd been on and on about wangling an introduction.'

Nicholas had not missed an instant of Gus' time with Alicia at the party. Had stared at the garden gate through their absence until the moment of their return.

Gus just looked at him.

'Eighteen months I know you, Basil.' He never called him Basil. 'Eighteen months, never offered one opinion on your personal life. Ears open?'

Nicholas looked back and smiled.

'Ears and mind,' Nicholas said.

'There's a warm, gentle place in your daughter,' Gus said softly. 'It's a part of her you'd like very much. You'll never see it if you don't look.'

Nicholas was more than touched. Not knowing what to

say, he swallowed and said something foolish. 'Should count yourself lucky the girl didn't fairly attack you. Must be quite the burden, being so dashing and all.'

This was said with a red-faced grin that Gus accurately interpreted as gratitude.

'She's still a young girl,' Gus said. 'She still needs her father's love. She needs a friend, Basil, not a judge.'

Nicholas could remember only the sight of his daughter clinging to Gus' arm as she led him through the gate. He appreciated that the boy had the sensitivity to lie about her character. In fact, he appreciated everything about Gus.

'Pleasant stroll in the park this morning?' Nicholas inquired. Alicia was once more set aside to a rear compartment of his mind.

'I told Gerhard the tale,' Gus said. 'He drooled all over the bench. I even picked up five thousand Nazi quid for the War Relief.'

Nicholas' eyes popped open.

'Five *thousand*?'

'Should've asked for five million,' Gus grinned. 'I swore it was going to widows and orphans, but I'm not absolutely certain he believed me.'

Nicholas was greatly amused.

'I just hope we've done the right thing here,' Gus said.

Nicholas looked puzzled.

'Slipping them a sour one,' Gus explained. 'We've worked so damn hard setting Emerald up,' he said, speaking of his Nazi persona in the third person.

This was true, of course. An enormous effort had gone into establishing Emerald's credibility with the Germans. Nicholas had always seen to it that the information passed by Gus to Tessin was reliable and useful. More than once, this had cost dearly.

The most effective stratagem had been created by Gus. He and Nicholas managed to convince the Germans that MI-5 had assigned Gus to track Emerald. The assignment of tracking oneself is the ultimate cover for any double agent, and hugely increased Gus' value in the estimation of the

Abwehr. Nicholas had leaked Gus' 'assignment' not only to Alicia, but as widely as discretion permitted, counting on loose lips to provide Tessin with independently derived corroboration.

Nicholas' eyes had looked away. His fingers drummed the top of his desk. Gus had asked why they were jeopardizing Emerald's credibility by sending the Nazis on a wild-goose chase after some phantom Channel exercise. Now Nicholas' silence sent a chill straight through Gus. He understood, even before the words came, that the exercise was not a phantom at all.

'Fact is,' Nicholas said, still looking somewhere else, 'we're going to give them a boat. Two, actually. Not real LSTs, of course. Something smaller and less sophisticated, so that Jerry will underestimate us when the drop comes.'

Nicholas looked warily to Gus' eyes and found there precisely what he expected. The uncompromising, uncomprehending moral judgment of the young.

'Of course,' Nicholas added, 'there will be no Bigots aboard.' Bigot was the true code name for those who knew the secrets of D-Day. It had been derived from a reverse spelling of 'To Gib,' short for To Gibraltar, the code established for top-secret material during the African campaign.

To Gus, the men aboard these boats might not be Bigots, but they would be men. Men he had apparently condemned to death in his little chat with Gerhard Tessin. An E-boat squadron, Gus had said, should do rather nicely.

Gus felt the same sinking knot as the first time he heard of Coventry, Churchill's sacrifice of a city to protect a code-breaking machine called Ultra. This was the first time Gus had heard the words *necessary price*. He heard them again in March, when a major air attack over Stuttgart was tipped to the Germans to reinforce the credibility of a Double Cross agent.

He sat now and numbly heard Nicholas speak once again of the necessary price, of the millions of lives at stake in the overall war effort. Gus was not buying. The sacrifice of other men's lives came too easily and often. There should always, almost always, be another way.

'I'm watching your eyes,' Nicholas said. 'You're being unfair.'

Gus bit his lip.

'I'll tell you,' Gus said, 'exactly when I'll start listening. When you tell me that you know, personally, even one man who'll die on those boats. His wife. His baby riding a toy horse around the lawn. You come back to me when you have one scrap of human reality to balance all the bullshit.'

Gus was standing. It seemed a day for being angry.

'Just don't tell me that you made a goddam "decision," all right?' Gus wasn't shouting, but he was plenty hot. 'Just don't tell me that you "accept responsibility." Because you don't know what the hell you're doing. You don't even understand that it's *you* who's killing those men. You think it's the Nazis, or the war, or no-goddam-body at all. It's you. You stop this, they don't die. You stop it right now, maybe a hundred babies get to grow up with their fathers . . .'

At these last words Gus could see his friend's eyes start to crumble. Gus' voice instinctively softened, but the words kept coming.

'You don't know who these men are or what kinds of lives you're taking away from them. You don't know what happens to the people who loved them and needed them. So *don't* tell me how necessary the price is, because you don't know the first god-*dammed* thing about what your little tea party is going to cost.'

Nicholas just stared up at him. Strange as it was, Nicholas could think of only one thing. How much he wished he had a son like this.

'Will you sit down,' Nicholas said at last, 'if I tell you that you're right?'

Gus thought it over. He sat down.

'I chose to be where I am,' Nicholas said, 'and who I am. I chose to be the man who makes the decisions I make. And I chose to stop understanding what they cost. Because I didn't want that pain anymore.'

There was a sudden, absolute stillness.

'I'm guilty,' Nicholas said.

'Me too,' Gus said quietly. 'That doesn't mean I forgive either of us.'

Then Gus smiled with a corner of his mouth and watched the tension ease a little from the colonel's neck and shoulders.

'I can't call off the tea party, Gus, and I'm not at liberty to tell you why. But it doesn't have a damn thing to do with fooling Jerry about the size of our ships.'

Gus knew that if he sat still enough, stared long enough, he'd get a bit more than that.

'Do you play cards, Gus? Every other Wednesday now, I sit with some Yanks and they teach me stud poker. I've learned what it means to have an ace in the hole. Very precious. Under the right circumstances, perhaps I should say wrong circumstances, you'd do almost anything to protect it.'

This of course, told Gus nothing, so he kept sitting and staring. Nicholas understood that the silence was a question, but he shook his head.

'I *am* sorry,' he said. 'It's an ace I can't show even to you.'

SEVEN

It was Friday night on the docks of Plymouth, and the scene at Chelsea's Pub was rowdier than usual. The regulars had been pushed to the dimmer recesses of the place, away from their accustomed positions near the polished cherrywood bar. They nursed their pints and whispered together in twos and threes. They had no doubt that something was surely up.

It was not just that the place had been overrun by Yanks, since the sailors had been around for a while. No, it was the influx of infantry that made tonight's scene the cause for hushed speculation. They were new in Plymouth, a couple of thousand at least, and they were blowing off nervous energy as if something big were coming soon.

The regulars were right.

In twenty-two hours, six LSTs would slip into Plymouth Sound, heading south and east toward Prawle Point. Then northward, into Lyme Bay. They would anchor eleven miles offshore of a place called Slapton Sands, a spot chosen for its topographical resemblance to a stretch of French coastline that had been code named Utah Beach.

This was Exercise Walrus. In early-morning darkness, the first dress rehearsal for H-Hour would take place. The men doing the drinking, giggling as they made a botch of an impromptu darts tournament, were high indeed. The thrill of anticipation was unclouded by fear. For this one last time, there would be no enemy fire when they hit the sand.

The powers at SHAEF, Supreme Headquarters Allied Expeditionary Force, had guarded the secrecy of this one amazingly well. In truth, too well. There was no coordination with any nonessential units. Loose lips and all that. They were damned tired of leaks among the British, and more than damned tired of having Ike chew their butts about it.

To clear the way for Exercise Walrus, SHAEF had planned to cancel all overnight patrols in Lyme Bay. To protect Walrus secrecy, these other operations would be cancelled only at the last possible instant. There would be no exceptions and no explanation of any kind.

Among the various operations to be terminated would be a small patrol ordered by Basil Nicholas of MI-5, about which SHAEF had been told next to nothing in the first place. Goddam Limey spooks always fed them some full-of-baloney cover story. Thought they were running their own private little war.

Alone in the noise and beer of Chelsea's sat a small shy man, composing a letter.

Andy Wheeler had rimless spectacles partway down the

slender bridge of his nose. It was a boyish pleasant face, seeming younger than its twenty-seven years. He had lost several pounds from an already scrawny frame, and the uniform seemed at least an awkward size large.

Andy easily could have been the least conspicuous soldier in the unit. But the collars framing his smooth cheeks bore the oakleaf clusters of a major. Andy Wheeler was not, in fact, an ordinary dogface.

From his earliest childhood, Andy's mind had set him apart, isolated him from other humans. He had begun high school in Yelm, Washington, at the age of twelve, a frightened little boy, surrounded and ignored by adolescents. Two years later, Andy entered MIT. The consequences were precisely what anyone should have expected. Andy excelled in every area of the intellect, and withdrew from the parts of life that could not be controlled by his mind.

Andy's special genius was electronics. He was of necessity a Bigot, a man with the priceless secrets of the Normany invasion. For in nine weeks, Andy, who had difficulty communicating with nearly everyone, would be responsible for all communications coming in and out of Utah Beach. Andy would not be landing at Normandy, of course. He was far too valuable to risk. He would, however, be going ashore tomorrow in the exercise at Slapton Sands to show the wireless boys how to set things up.

Andy sat now, oblivious to the frenetic pitch of the horseplay around him. He was finishing his nightly letter to Stephanie.

Stephanie had been a single exception in the world of Andy's loneliness. They had met during his last summer at home. She was a shop clerk in Seattle whose eyes had been too timid to meet his across the counter. Barely nineteen, Stephanie worshipped Andy's mind and saw the gentle soul within him. To Andy, Stephanie was not a plain little girl alone in the world. She was a sweet and delicate creature who needed his love. With her alone, intimacy was possible and tenderness came easily.

Andy's letter was mostly about the invasion. It was not fact, of course, but feelings. He was trying to share with her his sense of awe about the boys around him. These boys he had watched drinking and scuffling, joking about girls and Krauts and Limeys, staring silently for an eternity at a single page of a letter from home. These boys would actually die. They would trade their whole lives, everything the next fifty years would have brought them, for a patch of sand on a beach no one had ever heard of. They knew this, didn't know it. It was no matter. They were going.

There was no way Andy could express his wonderment at their sacrifice. Or his guilt at not being among them. Andy rarely held a kind thought for himself. He could not deny that he possessed integrity, the strength to stand firm for principle. But to Andy, courage meant a great deal more. It was bravery in the lion's cage, facing the moment of losing everything. It was a moment Andy had never confronted and doubted that he could.

And if Andy could have told his heart at this moment to a stranger named Gus Lang, he would have found that Gus shared the same doubts about his own character. But there was a difference. Gus understood his own humanity. He could forgive himself. Andy's forgiveness was only for others.

EIGHT

It was nearly midnight. The German E-boat squadron had been prowling the waters south of Torbay in vain for hours. Nine swift torpedo boats, the only German craft still able to ply the Channel since the decimation of Germany's submarine fleet.

The lieutenant once again stepped to the side of his commander, quietly urging that they return to Cherbourg.

Many of the officers had heard the same rumour – that this operation had been prompted by SD intelligence. This alone was sufficient to convince them that the mission was worthless. They were in dangerous waters, pursuing some SS fantasy. These wild men had imposed their insanity on the conduct of the war, spending the lives of good sailors as small coin.

The commander understood all this. He understood that there would be no Allied assault ships rehearsing in Lyme Bay tonight. But he understood one thing more. The political muscle of the Kriegsmarine was no match for the SS. If he returned to Cherbourg without engaging the enemy, with half the night still before him, the admiral could never protect him from SS retribution.

He had no choice. He would roam the waters of Lyme Bay until two hours before dawn. He would pray to God that he did not stumble into something he couldn't handle. That the lives of his men would not become the price of his cowardice.

On the deck of the commander's ship was Wolf Müller, a boy of nineteen from the Ruhr, Germany's industrial heartland. He was a virgin, the veterans' term for boys who had not yet been in combat.

This was Wolf's fifth mission without seeing action. With his fellow novices, he had grumbled nightly in Cherbourg's bars about the frustration of all the waiting. They shared their bravado and then each returned to his bunk to wonder how it would be. It was the thought that each waking moment lingered on. In one way, Wolf was anxious for the first fire to come, so that the wondering would be over. In another, he lived in a dreamy unreality that it might never come. That such a thing could never really happen to him.

Standing on deck, Wolf watched the low-riding quarter moon. He was thinking of his mother, and of the package she had promised in her last letter. There would be cakes, made just for him, with real sugar and butter that she had hoarded from the rest of the family. Wolf thought of his tiny sister Gertie, and how strange it seemed that only now was he beginning to realize that he loved her. He thought of eggs. Fresh eggs in an iron pot with Mama's butter.

And as Wolf stared into the darkness, the huge black shapes glided slowly, amazingly, across the moon. Six ships. five thousand tons apiece, in single file.

Wolf was still as stone, mesmerized by the eerie beauty of the scene, and the juices of combat now pouring into his belly.

If he had thought of it, Wolf would have realized that he expected some form of slow-motion tableau. He was waiting for the battle to unfold for him with the clarity and detail of a well-produced film.

As in a dream, Wolf saw the torpedo, followed it off into the blackness. For an instant it was gone. Then the flash. The sound of the torpedo hitting LST 239. Then the incredible sound of fuel tank explosion. From first moment to last, thirty-eight seconds.

Wolf could not see the men, but he knew. There, across a calm stretch of Channel water, men were being flung into the sea. Men were being torn to pieces. There was a very good reason for the wetness that had come to Wolf's eyes. He did not know yet whether their deaths were signalling his own.

In the icy waters, Andy Wheeler clutched his bit of floating wreckage. The coldness was terrifying, beyond belief, and his heart pounded wildly against it. His rimless spectacles were grasped in his hand, as a lost child would cling to a stuffed toy, his only link with the world that had abandoned him.

There were no thoughts of home or childhood, no life passing before his mind. There was nothing that was not of this unspeakable moment. Before Andy's blurred eyes, men were burning, shrieking, drowning. Andy could not help them.

It was a form of horror that one imagines could not maintain its intensity for more than a few moments. It lasted, at full heart-stabbing pitch, for more than an hour.

And then, as if adrift, a single E-boat floated silently through the wreckage and agony, its searchlight moving over the water. This was Wolf's task. Although he could never know it, he was manning the light in search of Himmler's prize. The light that fell on Andy Wheeler.

The beam crossed Andy's eyes, searing, blinding. Andy's numbed fingers tore at the oak leaves, ripping them from the cloth. Slowly, drifting downwards in the blackness, the oak leaves slipped to the bottom of the Channel.

NINE

It was a sharp stab of light. In his sleep Gus threw up a hand to shield his eyes. When they opened, Basil Nicholas was standing over him.

Gus had never seen quite that look on a man's face before. There was an overload of grief and loss that was clearly more than Nicholas could even assimilate, let alone cope with. Gus fully expected to hear that Nicholas' entire family had been killed in an air raid.

'Please get dressed,' Nicholas said, in a miserable imitation of a man under control, 'I need you.'

'The decoy run,' Gus said.

Nicholas sucked in some air between his teeth. 'SHAEF cancelled our decoy.'

'Then I don't . . .'

'Cancelled the decoy and, without explaining a bloody thing to anyone, replaced it with something called Walrus.'

Nicholas' voice was steel stretched thin. He was a man whose world had unravelled.

'Walrus,' he said, 'turned out to be a secret bloody rehearsal for the landing at Utah Beach. An exercise, no less, with exactly one British corvette for escort.'

'Oh my God,' Gus breathed, not hearing his own voice.

'Well,' Nicholas went on, 'when Herr Tessin's little E-boat squadron finally decided to pick up jacks and go home, we had an LST at the bottom of the Channel, two more disabled, and three hundred Yanks dead or missing.'

Gus' face was frozen, his eyes utterly disbelieving.

'You crazy bastard,' Gus whispered, 'you . . . you never told them. You never told SHAEF what you were doing . . .'

Nicholas' face was jelly. 'You seem,' he said, 'to ignore the fact – '

'That *they* were assholes,' Gus shouted, 'for not taking *you* into *their* confidence? They're in command, Colonel. That's why we call them "Supreme." What I'm losing track of here is why we call MI-5 "intelligence."'

There was nothing Nicholas could say. Gus watched his agony and felt like an assassin who had twisted the knife.

'I'm sorry,' Gus said. 'Forgive me. I can see what you're going through. I want to help.'

There was sweat coating Nicholas' forehead now.

'You're not the one who needs forgiving,' he said. 'You haven't heard the worst of it. There were survivors who reported that some of the men in the water were picked up by Germans . . . We're going to get you dressed. We're going to get in the bloody car and drive to bloody Devon. And I'm going to pray every inch of the way that Jerry hasn't landed himself a Bigot. The boat that went down was crawling with them.'

The ultimate nightmare, and he was responsible for it. It was amazing the man could stand upright.

Nicholas looked down at Gus, half-naked in his bed.

'That is,' Nicholas said weakly, 'if you're up to the trip.'

'Well,' Gus said, 'I'll have to cancel my tea with the Duchess of Windsor . . .'

And miraculously, he drew a smile.

'I'll have the palace send your regrets,' Nicholas said reassuringly.

Gus reached out and squeezed his friend's arm.

'It's happened,' Gus said, 'it's over. We start fighting

back from here. You just clear your head of everything else.'

'We couldn't tell SHAEF, Gus. We couldn't face any questions about our ace in the hole. There are exactly four men in England who know and one of them is named Churchill. This was the one that couldn't be leaked, Gus, I beg you to believe it.'

Gus smiled the smile that said he believed.

'I'm bringing you along,' Nicholas said, 'for more than moral support. Whatever has happened here, whatever we want to tell Jerry about it, I'm going to play our story back through Emerald.'

'Always a pleasure,' Gus said, 'to be of service.'

TEN

Less than six hundred miles to the east, Walter Hoffmann was also awakened in the darkness. He dressed quietly and slipped down the front steps to the waiting car, its engine rumbling softly, exhaust condensing in the predawn chill.

Ritter was in the rear seat, affecting a cool and professional air. To Hoffmann, it was evident that the man was positively giddy.

Ritter's call had been terse and precise. 'I'm happy to tell you,' he had said, 'that our meeting is confirmed for tomorrow at nine-twenty.' With that, Ritter had hung up the phone..

Since Hoffmann's home telephone did not have a scrambler, Ritter had used a simple but effective code. The reference to 'happy' meant that the mission had succeeded in taking prisoners. 'Nine' had been the signal that Hoffmann's presence was immediately required, and that Ritter would bring a car for him. 'Twenty' was the number of minutes preceding Ritter's arrival.

The driver eased off into the night. He did not turn north towards SD headquarters, but rather south and west, heading for an exclusive residential section of Zehlendorf near the Grosser Wannsee.

As they rode, Ritter told Hoffmann of his report to Schellenberg. Four men had been recovered – all Americans. They would be held at Cherbourg pending further instructions. The car was on its way to Schellenberg's home, because Hoffmann had been summoned to bask personally in the Brigadeführer's delight and appreciation.

Hoffmann was less than elated. As to the operation, there was no indication that any of these four men was an Overlord. As to Ritter, one fact was disturbingly apparent. Ritter had reported directly to Schellenberg rather than to him. Perhaps Ritter also reported directly to Schellenberg on other subjects, such as Hoffmann's own political reliability. It was not the first time that Hoffmann had reached this disquieting conclusion.

The car turned from Potsdamerstrasse onto Dreilindenstrasse, the Street of the Three Lindens. Finally to a quiet side street. An elegant townhouse with a single light beaming.

'Well,' Hoffmann said, 'shall we get to our cognac?' He offered a friendly smile that he hoped would pass for at least partially sincere.

'No.' Ritter shook his head with a broader smile of his own. 'The Brigadeführer wants you alone, Walter. This is your night. Congratulations.'

If he were a paranoid man, which he was, Hoffmann might have suspected that Ritter's toothy grin was sending him off to slaughter. Since, however, he was also a realistic man, his wiser nature discounted such a fear. For the present.

'Congratulations to us all,' Hoffmann said, forcing himself to clasp Ritter's shoulder with the warm grip of friendship. 'It was your report that made me realize how vulnerable Brausch might be to more assertive pressure. That might have been just the kick in the pants he needed to get his boys in England to take a few risks.'

Ritter waved his hand, modestly dismissing his own contribution.

'Nonsense,' Hoffmann said reassuringly. 'You go back to bed. I'll go to work on his lordship in there. By the time you wake up in the morning, I'll be stone drunk and you'll be Standartenführer.'

Hoffmann knew that Ritter's promotion to full SS colonel was already closer than Ritter realized. With tonight's success, and Schellenberg's evident fondness for Ritter ever more apparent, the promotion was a certainty. Accordingly, Hoffmann might as well take the credit.

Ritter's eyes seemed overwhelmed with gratitude. Since greed was one of the man's only two or three honest emotions, Hoffmann was inclined to accept Ritter's appreciation at face value.

'Only the next step,' Hoffmann assured him warmly. 'More to follow.'

For a nauseating moment, Hoffmann suspected Ritter might actually kiss him. Mercifully, he settled for a bone-crunching handclasp.

Hoffmann climbed the steps to Schellenberg's door and was met by a uniformed servant. Not the cushiest of jobs, Hoffmann noted, since the hour was well past four in the morning.

Schellenberg received Hoffmann in a silk dressing gown, offering the inevitable cognac in his private study. The Brigadeführer's slightly feminine elegance was never in fuller flower than during a triumph. One look at the expression on his face told Hoffmann that the mission had been more successful than Ritter had realized. Or, perhaps, revealed.

Born thirty-four years before, the son of a Saarland piano manufacturer, Walter Schellenberg had always possessed an instinct for the essence of things. He had realized in his youth that there was only one institution in Germany worth joining. This was the NSDAP, the Nationalsozialistsche Deutsche Arbeiterpartei, or National Socialist German Worker's Party. It was, in plainer terms, the Nazi party, and was of course not an institution at all. It was a man. The first evidence of Schellenberg's ability to select the right man. Years later, in his career-making adhesion to the skyrocket of SD founder Reinhard Heydrich, Schellenberg parlayed that talent into the power and luxury he richly deserved.

'Welcome,' the young general said expansively. His plump fingers cradled what was clearly not his first brandy of the evening.

He threw his arms around Hoffmann to evidence his appreciation. Hoffmann returned the embrace as best he could.

They sat facing each other on matching brocaded sofas.

'I have just received,' Schellenberg beamed, 'a personal call of congratulation from Reichsführer Himmler. Not only is he sleepless with the joy of tonight's events, but he assures me that the Fuhrer is as well. Of course I told him, Walter, that the glory is your's alone.'

Of course he did.

'You are far too generous', Hoffmann conceded modestly. 'Without your leadership, the project was stillborn.'

'We have the first reports from Cherbourg,' Schellenberg said. 'Four men captured, three clearly from the rank and file, doubtful to possess classified information. Ah, but the fourth.'

Hoffmann knew that his place was to say nothing and sip his brandy.

'The fourth man,' Schellenberg said, 'has refused to offer either name or rank. Shocking breach of etiquette in these matters.'

Here, Hoffmann's place was to offer an understated smile in appreciation of his superior's wit.

'One of the other prisoners,' Schellenberg continued, 'has already revealed under private interrogation that this man's name is Wheeler. He is a major, no less, and a wireless expert without peer.'

Hoffmann had to admit that such a man offered possibilities.

'This man,' Schellenberg concluded, 'is without the slightest question our Overlord.'

Overlord had been the false code name passed along by Gus and others in order to protect the secrecy of the code name Bigot. Actually, Overlord had been the original code name for the Normandy invasion itself, until it was discarded in September 1943 with the adoption of the code name Neptune.

Hoffmann knew that Schellenberg's conclusion was wildly premature. He also knew better than to contradict that conclusion, now or ever. Major Wheeler had been designated an Overlord, and an Overlord he would stay. Truth was far less important than triumph, and the capture of an Overlord was triumph indeed.

'I have advised Reichsführer Himmler that you will personally take charge of the interrogation of the Overlord,' Schellenberg said proudly.

A mixed blessing, to say the least. If Wheeler was indeed an Overlord, and if Hoffmann could manage to extract the truth from him, the rewards would be immeasurable. If the results were otherwise, of course, Hoffmann did not want even to think of the consequences. Clearly, Hoffmann would choose to pass up his chance at the golden ring in order to protect the downside. If he still had a choice.

'Technically,' Hoffmann said carefully, 'this interrogation is still under the jurisdiction of Oberst Brausch. The reorganization of foreign intelligence won't be completed until June.'

'As you suggest,' Schellenberg answered, a bit too quickly for Hoffmann's taste, 'a mere technicality.'

This was going to be straight uphill.

'It was,' Hoffmann said evenly, 'Oberst Brausch's agent, a young man called Emerald, who provided the key information for the raid.'

Hoffmann had not suggested anything. He just let it sit there for a moment.

'And your point?' Schellenberg asked, confident smile still firmly in place.

'Brausch and his staff are skilled professionals,' Hoffmann said quietly. 'They are the finest interrogation team available to the Reich. This will be the most significant intelligence product of the war, and I know that the quality of that product is your paramount concern.'

Schellenberg's fingertips tapped against his glass, his thoughts masked by a bland smile. He knew, of course, that if he scratched the average SD officer, he would find three-quarters of a Gestapo thug. He also knew that the intelligence skills of the Abwehr were unmatched. This is why he had raided Hoffmann from their ranks in the first place.

'I understand,' Schellenberg said, 'and I fully sympathize.' His voice had changed completely. He was abandoning his customary tone of pretension to address Hoffmann as an equal. 'But we cannot duck this one, Walter. It's Himmler's show. That makes it ours.'

Schellenberg's fingers had travelled to the left side of his chin, to the horizontal scar he had received in a duel of honour long ago.

'It would be splendid,' Schellenberg said, 'to have the Abwehr take the fall for us if things don't work out. You are free to manage something along those lines to the extent possible. But the reality is that we simply don't have the room to fail. If this product doesn't prove out, it is the end for us, Walter. We may as well commandeer the limelight.'

Schellenberg's gracious smile accompanied his raised glass in a toast to Walter Hoffmann.

'You're in the saddle,' he said, 'and Godspeed.'

ELEVEN

The little village of Torcoss, just to the south of Slapton Sands, was closest to the spot where LST 239 had settled to the bottom of the Channel.

The poor folk of Torcoss had been inundated by an invasion of brass they could neither understand nor service. More senior officers from more units than they ever knew existed had converged upon this spot in less than twenty hours. Each with support staff and equipment, each making competing demands on the meagre resources and facilities of the village.

The most maddening aspect of it all was the absurd posture of these intruders that nothing of any consequence was really on. They would have the villagers believe that all the hysterical activity was merely a routine investigation into the sinking of a rather small and insignificant boat. It was like a policeman standing next to the smoking, twisted wreckage of a twenty-car pile-up blandly saying, 'Move along, folks; nothing to look at.'

Certainly the most frustrated individual on the premises was one Mr Barnaby Snively. He owned a pub on the docks, named, with admirable simplicity, Snively's. It was in fact the only pub on the docks. 'A virtual monopoly,' he was forever fond of saying. The problem was that two and one-half hours after the arrival of the initial assault wave, Mr Snively was totally out of beer and bitter. Less than an hour later, the ale followed suit. A broken man, he wandered the docks, explaining to any who would listen, 'If they'd only *told* me they was comin'.'

All humour disappeared in the presence of the frogmen. Faceless forms in deep green and black, there were only occasional glimpses of them to be had. Sometimes the curious could get close enough to see them with their bundles. Two of them might be struggling with either end of a sack, and it was clear that what was inside used to be a human being. Sometimes one of them would be seen climbing off the dinghy with a smaller parcel, all the more grisly as one imagined what part of a man it contained. And sometimes, most often actually, there was nothing at all to see. For they had been able to retrieve only a dog tag.

Gus and Nicholas stood shivering in the bitter air of the water's edge. Clutched in Nicholas' hand was a single sheet of yellow paper. Names had been written in pencil and then carefully crossed off. Almost all of them. There had been eight left the previous night. There were five just after dawn. Then four.

Of all the officers and cleared civilian personnel on the beach, precious few could have known that this sheet listed the Bigots of LST 239. Indeed, Gus and Nicholas made very little impression of any kind on their peers as they stood in woollen sweaters, looking for all the world like quiet and respectful tourists.

They stood as the morning passed into hazy midday. The ensign who had been assigned as their runner came less frequently now, and Nicholas' eyes were always straining up the beach watching for him.

Gus was concentrating on another man. A civilian, he moved constantly on the periphery of the area, his gaze often focused on Nicholas. He was a small man with a round, pasty face and eyes that were level and piercing. There was something unmistakably menacing about his silence and his presence. Nicholas identified the man only as Mr Peters.

'He is here,' Nicholas had said, 'for Sir Geoffrey.'

Nicholas was speaking of Sir Geoffrey Macklin of LCS, the London Controlling Section. This was the organ ultimately in charge of coordinating all Allied intelligence efforts, its membership as secret and as powerful as any ever assembled for such a purpose. Sir Geoffrey represented the final authority in Nicholas' world, and the colonel seemed altogether intimidated by Mr Peters. On the few occasions when Mr Peters circled into Nicholas' line of sight, Nicholas would clumsily look away.

'Does he make you nervous?' Gus would ask.

'Who?'

'The little guy who's terrifying you.'

'He's only doing his job,' Nicholas would answer. 'Take no notice.'

His job, apparently, was to 'appreciate' the situation for Sir Geoffrey. If a man's career were hanging in the balance of such an 'appreciation,' Gus would have thought that the evaluator might wish to actually speak to those being evaluated. Mr Peters, however, spoke to no one at all.

There was something dead in the centre of Mr Peters. Gus could feel it from fifty yards. He had taken an immediate and growing dislike to the man.

It was coming on towards dusk and the orange sun seemed to hesitate, gathering courage for the final plunge. Nicholas' list had shrunk to two.

The ensign appeared one last time. In his hand, the dog tags of a young captain. The captain had been a meteorologist and an expert in charting currents and tides. Had been a softball player. Semipro, third base. Had been husband and father. Had been many things that were no more.

For Nicholas, the young captain was a line through a name.

And the list had been reduced to a single word. *Wheeler*.

TWELVE

The car turned onto the Berkaerstrasse and pulled to a stop before the curved brick building on the corner. The young Sturmführer leaped from behind the wheel to help his passenger extract himself from the rear seat.

Jürgen Brausch had been summoned to SD headquarters, a place, strangely enough, he had never visited before. Hoffmann's call had been warm and respectful. Still, the message had been clear. Even though Emerald had produced Himmler's prize, this had not purchased any slack for the last days of the Abwehr. A car had been sent. His presence was required. The grasp of SS authority was tightening.

As the young lieutenant led Brausch through the reception area and into the corridors, heads turned to see this huge man in Army uniform among the black and silver. Brausch had the unmistakable feeling that he was the lieutenant's prisoner. A feeling which, on reflection, he concluded was not far from right.

The Sturmführer escorted Brausch into a large outer office. Waited, ramrod stiff, as a pretty secretary breathed their arrival into the receiver. She motioned with her eyes, and the Sturmführer went through the door, arm shooting straight out in salute, feet stomping together crisply.

Brausch entered behind him, filling the doorway as he moved through it.

'Jürgen,' Hoffmann said warmly, and rose to greet him.

Brausch looked back at the Sturmführer, his arm still straight before him.

'That salute,' Brausch said, 'somehow always reminds me of an erection.'

'How pleasant at our age,' Hoffmann said, 'that we can still be reminded of such things.'

Even in a joke, Hoffmann was instinctively gracious enough to say 'our' age, although he was more than twenty years Brausch's junior. It softened the point nicely, but Brausch detected the trace of a *leitmotiv*. His era was passing into impotence.

Hoffmann stood in full uniform, crisp and sparkling. It seemed a further symbol. The grand office, the uniform, the comprehensive trappings of dominance.

Brausch spread his arms.

'Walter,' he said, 'you are resplendent. I can't recall ever seeing you in full costume.'

Hoffmann's pleasant smile never flickered. He turned slowly in a circle, arms away from his body, as if giving Brausch a better look.

'It's the only reason,' Hoffmann said, referring to the uniform, 'that I left the Army.'

Brausch was grinning in spite of himself.

'We have a whole new line coming in next month,' Hoffmann said, resuming his seat. 'Designed by Goering.'

As Brausch chuckled, Hoffmann finally dismissed the

lieutenant, who had been forced to witness the entire performance.

Brausch was not deceived by the display of humour and humanity. It was another softening, a relaxant, but the spine of the message was pure steel. Hoffmann had commanded him here, to this place. That was the essence of this meeting. Brausch could only wait for the next command.

'Can I get you anything?' Hoffmann offered.

Brausch sighed. 'A new government would be nice.'

Hoffmann pursed his lips and nodded.

'Ludwig Beck's department,' Hoffmann said, referring to a general widely rumoured to be among the leadership of the Schwarze Kapelle, the cabal of senior officers dedicated to Hitler's demise. 'I'll refer your request.'

Brausch cleared his throat politely.

'I think,' Brausch said, 'that we should declare opening pleasantries to be officially concluded.'

Hoffmann seemed to agree.

'Brigadeführer Schellenberg,' Hoffmann said, 'has insisted that I convey to you his personal commendation and gratitude for bringing Pursesnatch to its triumphant conclusion.'

'Please convey to the Brigadeführer,' Brausch said with a perfectly straight face, 'that my gratitude for his gratitude exceeds his gratitude for my brilliance. I am forced to admit, however, that I could not have achieved this without the aid of many lesser figures. Among them, Walter, I would single you out for your role in holding the gun to my head.'

Hoffmann's finger traced the edge of his leather desk blotter.

'Jürgen, the Brigadeführer has assigned me to take personal control of the interrogation of the Overlord.'

'A perfect choice,' Brausch conceded. 'You are most deserving.'

Hoffmann looked up with a half smile.

'I take your meaning,' Hoffmann said, 'and I probably agree.'

He placed his hands flat on the desk.

'Nonetheless,' Hoffmann said, 'I have decided to leave this matter in the hands of the Abwehr.'

Brausch grinned broadly.

'Does the Abwehr really need more rope to hang itself even higher?' he asked.

Hoffmann's eyes grew cool and flat.

'I do not mean that you are to be used as a scapegoat,' he said. 'Unfortunately, I cannot accomplish that. Believe me, I would if I could.'

Brausch believed him.

'Jürgen, this man has been presented to the Führer as an Overlord. There remains only the insignificant denouement of extracting this man's knowledge from his skull. This accomplished, we will crush Churchill at the applicable beach and live merrily ever after. It is a straightforward scenario.'

Hoffmann clasped his hands before him.

'If you and I fail to hold up our end,' Hoffmann said simply, 'neither of us will be having pleasant chats in tasteful surroundings. Our throats are on the butcher's block, Jürgen. We have no choice but to succeed.'

With a wry grin and a wave of his fingertips, he appended an afterthought.

'As added incentive,' he said lightly, 'this will probably decide the outcome of the entire war.'

'You said, Walter, that you wish to leave this matter in the hands of the Abwehr . . .'

Hoffmann nodded. 'I am offering you *de facto* autonomy. That is an entirely self-interested offer. Everything depends on the accuracy of this product. You are, in my estimation, the single most able man available to direct such an effort.'

'This is . . . acceptable to the Brigadeführer?'

'Candidly, no. I must appear to supervise the project to placate Schellenberg.'

'Ah,' Brausch said knowingly. His fingertips tapped together as he reflected for a moment.

'You appear,' Brausch said at last, 'to be asking for my help. Why not simply order me to do as you wish?'

'Because I want results, not lip service. I am concerned only with the quality of the product. If your heart isn't in this, Jürgen, the Abwehr can go directly into hell or history, I don't care which, and I'll simply have to find another way.'

It was a poetic choice Hoffmann offered, hell or history. Brausch had the distinct impression that he was lurching towards both simultaneously.

'Let me tell you,' Brausch said slowly, 'what will happen. You offer me control of this interrogation. I don't care whether you are quite sincere or quite otherwise . . .'

'I'm somewhere,' Hoffmann interjected, 'quite inbetween.'

And hearing his own words, Hoffmann was forced to smile. 'Quite inbetween' was becoming his permanent residence. They should start posting his mail there.

'A refreshing instant of candour,' Brausch admitted. 'You constantly remind me, Walter, of how pleasant it would be to work with you again. I think this is a project that would be the supreme test for our combined talents, and I wouldn't give a damn which of us made the decisions. We would make them together, Walter. We always did.'

Hoffmann was not ready to smile yet. There was obviously more.

'The problem is,' Brausch continued, 'I would not be working with you. I would be working for Walter Schellenberg and Heinrich Himmler. These are capable, intelligent, energetic servants of the state. Unfortunately, they happen to be vermin. Consequently, I despise them.'

'Consequently . . .?' Hoffmann asked calmly.

'Consequently,' Brausch said, 'before I can be ordered to the contrary, I hereby resign my commission. I've played this game too long, Walter, for my country. Too long to begin playing it now for the SS. There is a cottage in the Rhine Valley. There is sunshine. There are grandchildren. Helga and I invite you down to see us when press of duty permits.'

He shook his head with what seemed most honest emotion.

'Duty . . . ,' Brausch repeated, and let the word hang forever in the stillness between them.

Hoffmann wore a smile that was very grim.

'That is the maddening thing about him,' Hoffmann said. 'He knows us.'

'Who?' Brausch asked.

'Hitler. He knew that the weak would be co-opted. And that the strong would withdraw.'

Brausch could only admire the accuracy of the shot.

'If our best souls,' Hoffmann said, 'shrink away to sunshine and grandchildren, it is easy to understand why Heinrich Himmler sits where he does. The more pervasive their brutality, the more Germany needs a counterweight of reason and humanity.'

It was a perfect moment. Brausch could display a slow smile of what appeared to be grudging agreement. 'This man Wheeler,' Brausch said, 'could be meaningless. Or, he could be the turning point of this war. I would accept nothing less than the best chance of extracting the truth from this man.'

Hoffmann read the thaw in Brausch's eyes. He did not care whether it was spontaneous or premeditated.

'You spoke,' Hoffmann said softly, 'so lovingly of duty. I am somewhat more nostalgic about truth. Do you remember truth, Jürgen?'

Brausch remembered it very well.

'I am distinguising real truth from political truth,' Hoffmann said. 'From the systematic corroboration of some cretin's personal preconceptions. This will be one interrogation where the report won't be written before we meet the prisoner. Unorthodox, I admit. A throwback, to be sure. It's the first piece of work that's excited me in years, Jürgen. I want you with me.'

Brausch parted his lips for a single word.

'Paris,' he said.

Hoffmann did not understand.

'That is my price,' Brausch said quietly. 'We conduct our interrogation in Paris. Unless you remove the process from

Berlin, you will have only a farce, choreographed by Himmler every step of the way.'

Hoffmann gave this a moment's silent reflection. Brausch was correct, of course. Hoffmann contemplated Schellenberg's reaction. Politically impractical, he concluded.

'Unrealistic,' Hoffmann said evenly.

'Politically unrealistic,' Brausch corrected. 'And it will be politics before truth at every turn. It took you less than fifteen seconds to prove that.'

Hoffmann's smile was genuine.

'No one said, Jürgen, that this was going to be easy.'

'Do it in Paris,' Brausch said, 'or do it alone. It is what we used to call in the Army an ultimatum, before the SS pre-empted exclusive rights to the word.'

But Hoffmann was looking at Brausch's eyes. They told Hoffmann that Brausch was in. With or without Paris. And Hoffmann was wondering why.

'We mustn't threaten each other,' Hoffmann said gently. 'It makes us sound ridiculous.'

Hoffmann eased back in his chair.

'We will do this thing together, Jürgen. We will make all the decisions together, the way we always have. And I will fight to get you everything you need. Including Paris.'

THIRTEEN

The endless inscription on the building read: THE ROYAL VICTORIA PATRIOTIC ASYLUM FOR THE ORPHAN DAUGHTERS OF SOLDIERS AND SAILORS KILLED IN THE CRIMEAN WAR. Gus referred to it as the Royal Asylum. In reality, it was the MI-5 interrogation and security clearance centre at Battersea.

Gus entered Nicholas' office. Despite its greater size and

somewhat more luxurious appointments, the disregard for order recalled the cramped quarters of Nicholas' underground bunker.

Nicholas fidgetted behind his desk. In the corner, perched on a straight-backed chair, was Mr Peters.

Gus took his seat and was handed a sheaf of papers.

'These are background materials and psychological profiles on the four captured men,' Nicholas said, 'including Major Wheeler. The information is completely accurate. All of it is to be given to Herr Tessin.'

Gus stared at Nicholas for a moment, then quickly skimmed the dossier on Andy Wheeler.

'I don't understand,' Gus said slowly, his eyes passing over the last of the materials. 'This will indicate that Wheeler might well be a Bigot.'

Nicholas sighed. His hands folded calmly together.

'Unfortunately,' he said, 'the Germans already have the important clues about Major Wheeler. This will tell them nothing new of any importance. It will, however, reinforce your credibility for the role you will eventually play.'

'They know about him?'

'They are not certain yet that he is a Bigot,' Nicholas said, 'but they know a great deal.'

'And how,' Gus asked, 'did we learn all this?'

Peters' voice attacked from the rear.

'We know,' he said abruptly, with the finality of a command to inquire no further.

Gus turned to look at Peters. It was a vacant face, Gus thought. An assassin's face.

'And what,' Gus asked, 'is this role I will eventually play?'

'You will play,' Peters said, 'the role you have been commissioned to play, Captain. You will receive orders when your superiors deem fit to issue them, and you will execute those orders. Will that be entirely satisfactory?'

Gus' eyes measured the man for a frozen moment.

'I'll let you know,' Gus said quietly.

The little man stiffened.

'And exactly when would you intend to let us know, Captain?'

'When I'm good and ready.'

Peters' jaw hardened. His eyes unblinking and thoroughly hostile.

'Don't pout,' Gus said. 'I'm already good, so you're halfway there.'

With a final glare, Gus' eyes returned to the dossier. Peters needed him. The less shit Gus took at this point, the better his meagre chances of establishing some spine to his position.

In absolute silence, Gus carefully reread the materials. Six pages of Andy Wheeler's life. There was an image in Gus' mind of a shy, wondrously brilliant boy who had been thrust into a strange and confusing world. There was a quick surge of feeling within Gus, admittedly with little rational support. He liked this man.

Gus looked back up at Peters.

'What kind of fellow is Wheeler?' Gus asked.

'A pansy,' Peters said flatly. 'The worst kind of risk in this situation. An introverted little intellectual who could crack at the slightest pressure.'

Gus wondered how anyone could assess the character of another man so clearly and so harshly. He felt his own emotions leaping to Andy's defence. Nonetheless, it was clear to Gus that Peters' condemnation would be the party line.

Gus thought for a moment.

'In that case,' Gus said at last, 'I would recommend one addition to this dossier. A medical condition. Maybe heart-related. Something obscure, difficult to confirm by medical examination. But deadly enough to indicate that the stress of torture could kill him.'

Nicholas was already nodding.

'I like it,' Nicholas said to Peters. 'I think we need it.'

Peters was thinking, weighing.

'Don't you feel, Captain,' he said at last, 'that would sound just a trifle suspicious?'

'Certainly,' Gus answered, 'suspicious as hell. But the Nazis can't take the chance that it might be true.'

And slowly, Peters nodded.

'No,' he said, 'I suppose they couldn't.'

Gus' smile was matter-of-fact.

'It's your call,' Gus told him. 'But if you're certain Wheeler can't hold up under torture, we'll have to take some chances to keep him off the rack.'

FOURTEEN

The swans were feeding at the far end of the pond. A sailor and his girl had brought the better part of a loaf of dark bread, a rare treat for swans in time of shortages. St James's Park was lazy and warm. It was the kind of Tuesday afternoon to make one forget that a war was in progress anywhere. When life seemed simply life again.

Gerhard Tessin sat on his accustomed bench, slowly turning the pages of a paper he was not reading. Emerald was very late and Tessin had been sitting for nearly an hour. Still, the euphoria of these past few days had imparted an uncharacteristic capacity for patience.

Tessin folded the paper and watched the swans, white backs and throats gleaming with the sun. They honked and squabbled over the largest morsels of bread. So graceful and regal in outward appearance, but underneath, no less grasping than their fellow creatures. The swiftest were getting the best of it, and this was not lost on Gerhard Tessin, who just now was doing splendidly in his own little pond. He knew how much he owed to Gus Lang, and so young Emerald could be as late as he damn well pleased. Tessin was confident that Gus would deliver.

So far from remaining angry at Gus' outburst of the

previous week, Tessin had become anxious to regain Emerald's good graces. More than once Tessin had seen an agent become a star and promptly request a change of pimps. He had decided to buy Gus a little peace offering, and had begun inquiries towards purchasing a small emerald, if a stone of suitably clarity and reasonable price could be found.

Gus arrived. He took his seat beside Tessin, placing a small packet between them on the bench. The dossiers would remain when Gus departed.

'What news,' Tessin began, 'of our Major Wheeler?'

The tone was proprietary. An owner confirming the racing soundness of his prize thoroughbred. Bad news was off the list of indicated responses.

Gus gave it his best look of genuine concern.

'Well,' he said, 'we can't rule him out yet. But I don't think he's our man.'

To say that Tessin bristled would be considerable understatement. Apparently, hope had already solidified into irrevocable conviction.

'This is not a subject, or a moment, for humour', Tessin announced.

'I think,' Gus said gently, 'that our enthusiasm for the major's prospects arises from the fact that he's all we've got. He's a quiet little fellow who knows electronics. That doesn't mean Eisenhower tells him where he's going to land.'

Tessin evidenced a clear preference for terminating this direction of conversation.

'He is a quiet little fellow,' Tessin corrected, 'who has been presented to our Führer as an Overlord.'

Brick wall. There was going to be no chance whatsoever.

'Nicholas doesn't think he's an Overlord,' Gus said solemnly.

'He told you that?'

'He seemed immensely relieved to find that Wheeler was the only officer captured.'

'He wouldn't lie to you?'

'No,' Gus said. 'I would say pretty close to no chance at all.'

'His superiors wouldn't lie to him?'

Gus stopped for a moment, as if giving the question some thought.

'I doubt it. If an Overlord went down, they'd need the cooperation of all intelligence branches. Nicholas would know.'

Tessin's face flickered into a vague, almost disoriented expression. A child trying to recall something lost and long forgotten.

'The Führer,' he said, and paused. 'The *Führer*,' he repeated, as if to be absolutely certain Gus knew just whom they were discussing, 'has been told that this man is an Overlord.'

'That may have been unwise,' Gus said quietly.

'That,' Tessin said with sudden irritation, 'has *happened*, my dear boy.'

Gus shrugged, but kept his expression sympathetic.

'If someone up the line has painted himself into a corner, that's not my problem. Or yours.'

Tessin's lips curled in astonishment.

'I'd give anything,' he said, 'to be that young again. Do you really think, dear, dear child, that Berlin would absolve either of us in the name of, what, fairness? Is that the world inside your pretty head? Absolutely charming.'

Gus stared at his eyes. His voice was soothing.

'You're overreacting, Gerhard. We gave them six boats. Overlords crawling over them like roaches. We can't help what they pick out of the water.'

Tessin shut his eyes tightly in exasperation. When he opened them, Gus was somehow still there, his face offering the same calm, rational comfort. It was infuriating.

'If that man,' Tessin hissed, 'is not an Overlord, then *we* have sold Berlin damaged goods. Believe it!'

The implications for the war were entirely out of mind. This man had a *career* on the line. Gus realized that Tessin's reaction would be duplicated all the way up the chain of command. As he had warned Peters, this tack would be hopeless.

Gus sagged back against the bench. His eyes seemed to finally accept Tessin's cynical cosmology.

'They'll never know,' Gus said at last, 'whether he's an Overlord or not. They'll only know the Gestapo couldn't beat the truth out of him.'

Tessin gavc him a strangely blank look.

'You're on the team,' Tessin said.

Gus did not understand.

'The interrogation team,' Tessin said. 'You're going to the Continent to help question the Overlord.'

Peters. The role you will eventually play. Adrenalin surged through Gus. Ice at his wrists, acid winding through his intestines. How in the world had Peters made this happen?

'The assignment,' Tessin said with a weak smile, 'is a great honour. You will portray an American prisoner and gain Wheeler's confidence. Berlin views this as one of the most important phases of the interrogation.'

In agency terms, Gus had become a player.

Fear was instantaneous and almost overpowering. Astonishing in its physical, chemical force. Gus had not signed on to be a hero, had never considered himself one. Now, for the first time, there was a thought of his life ending that had become more than thought. From the instant of Tessin's disclosure, it had become a knowing. Denied, struggled with in a burst of overlapping rationalizations, but still a knowing. A sinking awareness of loss, for decades of moments that would never be. For a suddenly detailed portrait of the future that Gus had never known was in his mind.

And still, as Tessin spoke, an undeniable excitement was rising in Gus. He would not claim this feeling as anything noble or courageous. Rather, it seemed purely the thrill of being thrust into the centre of it all. To be the man who could somehow make the difference.

All the anger of these past weeks came rushing back to Gus now. Into his mind, behind the eyes that calmly listened to Tessin's details. There was a sudden and complete understanding of just how much anger Gus had been carrying with him. This had not been a pattern of Gus' life and mind before London. The anger was very new. It was the frustration of being a captive witness to horror and failure. And now, fears and all, he was a player. He would act. The anger was suddenly gone. No, stored away for future use. Everything in Gus' mind was sorting now, preparing him, almost automatically, for the dramatic reversal of his role.

As Tessin finished his proposal, Gus's eyes were calm. He was more in control than he had felt in a long time.

'You will . . . ,' Tessin said haltingly, 'you will . . . go . . . won't you?'

Gus smiled, aware of Tessin's abject terror that he might refuse the assignment. Agents, particularly mercenary non-Germans, had a disturbing habit of resigning in the face of complication or danger. If Wheeler might not be an Overlord, would Emerald be willing to participate so directly?

'A chance,' Gus said, 'to earn so much glory for us both, Gerhard? How could I refuse? You would never forgive me.'

Tessin looked at the green eyes. At some level of consciousness, he sensed something different. A subtle change of tone that made Emerald seem quieter and stronger. As with a slight shift of air pressure, the difference was unseen, but somehow distracting.

'Seriously, now,' Tessin said, 'you will go?'

'Shall I,' Gus asked, 'tell Nicholas that I've decided to take a spring holiday in Berlin? The linden trees are lovely this time of year?'

'A trifle,' Tessin assured him. 'Your cover is already in progress.'

Tessin's tongue moistened his lips. He was still not entirely certain that Gus would cooperate.

'The Funkabwehr,' Tessin said, referring to the wireless intelligence service, 'has been playing back a double-wire for the past three days.'

Occasionally, the Germans were able to capture an enemy

agent with his ciphers and code keys intact. They continued wireless communication with London, impersonating the agent and passing false information. With skill and luck, a double-wire game could last for months.

'This particular double-wire is from a captured SOE operative in France.' Tessin was referring to the Special Operations Executive, British agents assigned to organize and supply the Resistance.

'We are telling MI-5 that the German agent Emerald has been called to Paris. We are asking that you, the man who has been tracking Emerald for MI-5, be air-dropped into France. Supposedly, you will be advising an SOE unit who will be tracking and observing Emerald's mission there.'

It was a cover that could have been designed with equal ease by the Abwehr or MI-5 itself. Once more, Gus' mind turned to Peters.

Never had Gus so keenly felt the isolation and helplessness of the double agent. In Gus' world, information was the precise equivalent of power, and his information was carefully rationed to him by both sides. Controlled by everyone about him, the seen and unseen, Gus was alone.

FIFTEEN

Walter Hoffmann stood silently in the outer office. His full-dress uniform immaculate, his hat clasped firmly between his left arm and his side. He couldn't remember the last time he had taken the hat from its box in the closet. He hated the thing, its silliness and pomposity. Still, it was part of full dress, and this was an extraordinary audience.

Hoffmann was more than nervous. He had never met the man. He fought the impulse to fidget, for he was even now being observed by the young and hostile eyes of the outer-office staff, a group of the most beautiful young men

Hoffmann had ever seen. A strange choice of staffing for a man with an almost hysterical aversion to homosexuals.

Hoffmann stood erect and impassive. The perfect Aryan officer. At last, the door was opened. Hoffmann was ushered inside.

His right arm shot forward. Hoffmann gave the words *Heil, Hitler* the conviction and resolve appropriate to the occasion.

Across an ordered antique desk was Reichsführer Heinrich Himmler. A small man with closely cropped hair. The eyes of a reptile behind thick lenses. A playful, almost epicurean smile.

At such a moment, this man was neither butcher nor God. He was simply the man who held Hoffmann's career in his soft hands.

Himmler did not rise. He did not pause from his task of signing the stack of documents before him. He looked up, in fact, only momentarily.

'Oberführer Hoffmann,' he said in a voice so quiet as to seem deliberately irritating. 'Please sit.'

Meticulously, Himmler signed the balance of the documents, initialling each page, as Hoffmann sat in perfect stillness across the desk.

But when Himmler at last looked up, there was an unexpected light in his eyes. A slow, almost unnerving, smile of pleasure crept across his lips.

'It is a great pity,' Himmler said, 'that we have never met.'

A silence followed, while Himmler regarded him with the stare of a collector inspecting a newly acquired masterpiece.

'Walter,' Himmler said, referring to Schellenberg, 'had kept you hidden away, my dear Oberführer. His private stock.'

Hoffmann judged that no response was indicated.

'Well, we have followed your career, Oberführer, with interest and with steadily growing pride.'

'Thank you, Reichsführer.' Hoffmann's voice was simple and sincere. He seemed completely at ease.

'We overuse the word *destiny*,' Himmler said softly. 'We have leached the majesty from that most majestic of concepts. I know. But you must listen with fresh ears when I tell you that this truly is a moment of destiny.'

Hoffmann's eyes were clear and attentive.

'You,' Himmler intoned, 'have presented your Fatherland with the most precious of gifts. You have laid bare the throat of our enemy to the Führer's sword. Your achievement humbles us all.'

Himmler took a shallow breath.

'In these next weeks, as the interrogation of this man unfolds, your future and that of the Reich itself will intertwine. The moment that we have the truth from this man's lips is the moment that this war has ended.'

His voice lowered, as if suddenly imparting a confidence to be treasured.

'We will not move our strength to the invasion site immediately. The point, of course, is not to give Churchill time to cancel and regroup. We will see this assault launched and then obliterated with the greatest number of casualties possible. Particularly American. Humiliate Roosevelt with his electorate, force him to turn his remaining strength to the Pacific.'

Himmler's fingers waved in a gesture that said the rest would be obvious.

'This will, in turn, free us to look eastward. I should say we could then commit nearly two hundred and fifty divisions to the task of annihilating Marshal Stalin. Within one year, perhaps two, our control of the Continent will have solidified into everlasting fact. Europe will be Germany.'

The voice was now almost a whisper.

'This is the moment our people were spawned for. This moment. I salute and envy your role in these next few days.'

After a respectful silence, Hoffmann cleared his throat. 'My gratitude for the Reichsführer's confidence is truly inexpressible. That confidence will be my greatest resource as I address the challenge that awaits.'

The first trial balloon. A single word, *challenge*. It did not pass unnoticed.

Himmler's fingers moved to his lips.

'Challenge, yes.' he said. 'There are those who assume that your task is as good as done. I am not among them.'

A small piece of good news. Hoffmann would wait for the rest.

'Paris,' Himmler said, without further prompting. 'You have requested that this interrogation be conducted in Paris. Why?'

Hoffmann's eyes were earnest. He leaned forward slightly.

'I am not at all surprised,' he said, 'to find that the Reichsführer appreciates the difficulty of our assignment. More than any other of our nation's leaders, you have examined the problems inherent in extracting the truth from the mind of an enemy. It is the most critical, the most sensitive act in the conduct of warfare. And you have most eloquently reviewed what lies in the balance of this particular inquiry.'

Himmler largely discounted Hoffmann's praise as obligatory, or at least overly effusive. As was his habit, however, he was unable to permit any compliment to pass entirely unappreciated. Hoffmann had identified Himmler as the Reich's pre-eminent expert in the art of interrogation. This could only increase Himmler's respect for the man's judgment.

'I am not pursuing Paris,' Hoffmann said. 'I am pursuing a man. He is an Abwehr colonel named Jürgen Brausch, an ultimate intelligence professional. His technique, his insight, are without peer.'

Himmler seemed, for the first time, rather amused.

'I know something, of course, of Oberst Brausch. I had not understood, however, that he lived in Paris. Still, I imagine that our budget could find for him a rail ticket to Berlin.'

And as was Himmler's invariable custom, he permitted himself a modest smile in recognition of his own wit.

Hoffmann pressed on in a straight line.

'It is Oberst Brausch's urgent recommendation that this interrogation be removed from Berlin.'

Himmler's brows raised in the transparent pretence that he was hearing this for the first time.

'And why would that be?'

'He fears the possibility of political tampering or intrusion.'

Himmler shook his head slightly. He understood completely, but was astounded to hear such words spoken aloud.

'Does this mean,' Himmler said evenly, 'that SS oversight is to be seen as intrusion?'

Straight ahead, eyes glowing with honesty and directness. 'To this man, yes.'

It was so unusual to be told the simple truth that Himmler smiled in spite of himself.

'For me,' Hoffmann continued, 'the genius of the SS has always been its capacity to find whatever means is most suitable to achieving any desired result.'

Hoffmann was saying that Himmler was efficient, ingenious, and, above all, pragmatic. Himmler could only agree.

'This interrogation,' Hoffmann said quietly, 'requires delicacy bordering on artistry. Brausch is a master. His team is the finest. We are their conquerors, Reichsführer. In a month, their organization will become the military department of the SD. They fear us. They will perform more creatively and effectively if we permit them distance from the shadow of our strength.'

Himmler pressed his fingertips together before his lips.

'And is Oberst Brausch so indispensable to us?'

Hoffmann's smile was firm. 'No. He is most certainly replaceable. He is merely useful.'

It was an absolutely essential response. Himmler did not need this man or any man. He would use this man if it was his pleasure.

Himmler's eyes drifted off now. He had heard everything

he needed to hear. There was nothing that would prompt him to change the decision he had already made.

'Did you know, Oberführer, that in less than six months London will be entirely reduced to rubble?'

As he frequently did at such a moment, Himmler had changed the subject abruptly. This enabled him to savour his supplicant's anxiety as the decisive pronouncement was postponed. He watched Hoffmann's eyes for the inevitable display of tension that this gambit always produced. There was none. Hoffmann seemed as attentive as if they had been discussing this all along.

'What do you know,' Himmler continued, 'of the V-3?'

'Very little,' Hoffmann said. He probably knew as much as Himmler, but he was not about to deny the Reichsführer this opportunity to rhapsodize over his vivid fantasy of Churchill's destruction.

Himmler was, to be sure, a bit disappointed at Hoffmann's equanimity.

'They are called the London Guns. They are only now under construction at Mimoyecques, a small village just behind Calais. They are only a hundred fifty kilometres from London.'

Himmler settled back in his chair. His immense satisfaction was evident.

'Fifty guns,' he said, 'two batteries of twenty-five. Each barrel will be a hundred thirty-five metres long, set at a precise angle into concrete housings sunk into the earth. Only the mouths of the cannons will be visible. The shells will be twenty-five kilos of high explosives, and they will be fired by the ignition of explosive charges at various intervals along the length of the barrel.'

Hoffmann's eyes showed that he was suitably awed by the disclosure.

'In six months,' Himmler concluded, 'we should be able to commence. We will fire one shell every twelve seconds. We can do this continuously and indefinitely. Until there is not a single building standing in London.'

If, Hoffmann thought, our engineers are right for once.

And, more importantly, if we still hold Calais in six months.

'Should give Winnie the chance to spend more time at his country estate,' Hoffmann said.

Himmler's smile was almost childlike in its glee.

'I should think,' he responded. 'Since Parliament will need new quarters within five minutes after we commence firing, it may take the rest of day before they can gather to require his resignation.'

Hoffmann's smile was understated, as befitted his station, but he was clearly sharing in the Reichsführer's relish.

This accomplished, Himmler fell silent, permitting Hoffmann to replead his case regarding Paris. Hoffmann did nothing of the kind. He waited patiently, for whatever subject would be his master's pleasure.

Himmler cleared his throat. 'Well,' he said, 'to the question of Paris.'

Himmler paused once more, seeming to reflect on the decision which had already been made.

'Over Brigadeführer Schellenberg's objection, we will respect your judgment and your confidence in this man Brausch. The interrogation may take place in Paris. We will ensure that there is no interference from Berlin. Of course, it should be clearly understood that we would have offered you a free hand, Oberführer, whatever the site of this operation.'

Himmler waited for a smile of gratitude. It arrived on schedule.

'I believe in ideas, Oberführer. And in men. My confidence, and the Führer's confidence, rest in you. Whatever you need to accomplish your inevitable triumph will be provided.'

There was a slight, almost imperceptible, twitch at the corner of Himmler's mouth. It made the hair stand out on the back of Hoffmann's neck, even before Himmler's full smile would have warned a lesser man.

'To that end,' Himmler said, 'I am sending your strong right arm, Obersturmbannführer Ritter, to Paris with you. He will be promoted to SS Standartenführer, so that his rank will be comparable to that of Oberst Brausch. They will each be subordinate only to you. I know that the presence of Standartenführer Ritter will give you comfort that necessary security procedures will be in reliable hands though far from home.'

The leash might be a bit longer, but it would have little slack.

'I can only thank you,' Hoffmann said, 'for your insight in anticipating both my needs and my desires. With Ernst Ritter to complete our team, I do not see how success can possibly elude us.'

SIXTEEN

It was well past midnight when they brought Gus to Parliament Square and the fabled bunker at Storey's Gate.

He had been summoned from his sleep by two young British lieutenants. After disclosing that Gus' 'appointment was now confirmed,' a curious phrase for a command appearance at such a late hour, they were entirely silent for the balance of the journey. Still, there was an air of warmth and protectiveness about them. They looked almost exactly alike, and as Gus sat between them on the ride through the curfew-darkened streets, their eyes moved ceaselessly over the buildings and alleyways. Gus had the distinct impression that he was being escorted to Westminster by a perfectly matched brace of loyal attack dogs.

They arrived at Great George Street and Gus walked between the young officers, hearing the echoes of their footfalls in the emptiness of Parliament Square. The only light was the guard post at the entrance to the War Cabinet Offices.

One of Gus' lieutenants peeled off to deal with the guard.

They spoke in hushed tones, breath frosting in the coldness. The conversation seemed rather extended. Gus could see the guard retreating to a telephone, requesting clearance for their entry, which apparently had not yet been confirmed to him. Gus watched the face of his lieutenant. Courteous, controlled, yet tense enough to seem quite menacing. He had been ordered to fetch Gus without delay. He was not amused by the screw-up at the gate.

Gus stood with his other trusty Doberman, shifting his weight from one foot to the other in the cold. At last the guard's phone rang. As Gus and his escort were waved into the bunker, the poor guard was apologizing as fast as his tongue could carry him.

They crossed the lobby and headed down into the underground network of command posts, passing through a series of metal bulkhead doors. There were several checkpoints along the way, but each interior guard seemed fully prepared to nod Gus through. As they passed along the maze of corridors lined with steel and wooden reinforcements, the pace of the lieutenants quickened, as if they wanted to make up the time lost at the entrance.

At last they reached their destination, the area reserved for London Controlling Section, the supreme coordinating authority for all of Allied intelligence.

They passed a series of small antiseptic offices and came to the only closed door in the section. As one lieutenant stood sentry, the other ushered Gus inside. Surprisingly, the room was an oak-panelled study, lined with books and filled with soft leather furniture. Gus was led to a comfortable chair, given a large glass of port, and suddenly the lieutenant was gone.

Nearly an hour passed. The comic aspects of Gus' predicament were not entirely lost on him. Awakened in the middle of the night, rushed to the nerve centre of the war effort, then deposited in what could have been the private library of a Victorian schoolmaster, and promptly abandoned.

There he sat, cradling his goblet of port in his lap, feeling altogether ridiculous. After a while, he began to wonder whether anyone was coming for him at all. Perhaps this was just the way the British incarcerated their political prisoners.

At last his host appeared.

Sir Geoffrey Macklin, a cadaverous aristocrat, quietly entered and settled into an easy chair across from Gus. He was well past seventy, and his bones fairly seemed to collapse into a pile as the soft leather enfolded him. Gus could not remember ever seeing a figure so gaunt, so weary.

As a key member of London Controlling Section, Sir Geoffrey was a level of superior that Gus had never expected to catch a glimpse of. These were the boys who talked to Churchill.

Gus had done such limited homework on the man as was available, principally reviewing his write-up in *Kelly's Handbook to the Titled, Landed and Official Classes*.

Macklin had taken the right road through. He had entered St Mary's, the 'Blessed College,' at Eton in 1886. Master of the Eton College Hunt. President of 'Pop'. He had gone on to Christ Church, the richest college at Oxford, where he had somehow managed to excel in matters of the intellect without creating suspicion as to his discretion, breeding, or character. He rode at the Beaufort Hunt. He was a member of Brooks's, presently the most renowned political club in London. He was a Knight of the Order of St Michael and St George.

Of his professional career, however, little was known. This had been customary with men of his craft since the founding of the first clandestine intelligence service by Sir Francis Walsingham in the sixteenth century. The secret service recruited mainly from the privileged classes. When one joined, one's public career appeared to drop off the end of the earth. Chronicles such as *Kelly's Handbook* would have us believe that these men did nothing at all. Taking cover in an admiralty or military rank which always seemed to be without a command, or in shadowy liaison posts with the Foreign Office, the substance of their activities remained invisible to all but the most powerful of government leaders.

Sir Geoffrey Macklin was more visible than most. He had made his reputation in the service of Captain Mansfield Smith-Cumming, the first MI-6 chief to adopt the cipher 'C' as his code name. Macklin's achievements during the Great War were so extraordinary that in 1918 he was presented with the Ivory. This was an ivory plaque that historically permitted the bearer, in time of siege, to enter St James's Park through the Horse Guards' gate. It was given only to those whose presence in crisis would be essential to the monarch.

Sir Geoffrey and his comrades had watched in dismay as MI-6 was virtually dismantled after World War I, by the simple expedient of reducing its budget to humbling proportions. For nearly two decades they lobbied in vain, urging Whitehall to recognize the paramount necessity of maintaining vital intelligence services in time of peace. It had taken Adolph Hitler to resurrect Geoffrey Macklin and the MI-6.

Macklin sat now in his private study, deep within Churchill's bunker. His wrinkled face was in shadow, but the eyes shone through. They seemed to warm as they silently appraised the young man before them. It was a long moment before he spoke.

'My dear Captain,' he said at last. 'You have been called to Paris by the Hun to help examine his new bit of treasure. This, happily, places you in a position to be of unique service to your country and our cause.'

His voice had a soft crackling sound. The rustle of cellophane, the last moments of a dying fire.

'You have probably surmised that this is something more than glorious coincidence,' Macklin said dryly.

Gus had indeed.

'Basil Nicholas tells us that he has cryptically alluded to a certain 'ace in the hole.' I do not pretend to understand the game to which he refers, but I assume he speaks of the most precious, secret card of all. The one which must neither be played nor revealed until the precise instant of decisive action.'

The old man's eyes narrowed. It seemed that all the remaining force in his wasted body had been focused to laser clarity in those eyes.

'Our card is a German intelligence officer,' Sir Geoffrey said softly. 'He is not a traitor to his land. He is a patriot in the highest and purest sense of that word. He knows that the only catastrophe greater for his people than Allied victory would be Nazi victory.'

Macklin took a short breath as if, even now, his throat was hesitant to release this man's identity.

'His name,' Macklin said, 'is Jürgen Brausch.'

Images exploded in Gus' mind as a thousand moments from these past months tumbled swiftly into order.

'It is Jürgen Brausch who has made a place for you on the interrogation team. He will be in Paris with you and Major Wheeler. He will make it possible for you to complete the single most necessary assignment of this war. The assassination of the major.'

The blood in Gus' veins ceased to flow. His irrational identification with Andy Wheeler had blinded him to the obvious. They did not want Andy freed. They merely needed him dead. Quickly.

Incredibly, Gus heard words coming from his own lips.

'No,' Gus said quietly, 'if I go to Paris, I bring the major back with me.'

In the silence that followed, Sir Geoffrey's face was without expression. There had been sufficient conviction in Gus' voice to indicate that this was not an outburst of superficial gallantry. Macklin could, of course, solve the problem. His mind was selecting the most appropriate tack, gauging the consequence of each possible tone his response might take. He decided upon a middle ground between peremptory dismissal and a more detailed explanation sympathetic to Gus' feelings. The former might evoke stubbornness, while the latter might lend false encouragement that compromise was available.

'This, of course,' he said at last, 'would be both unnecessary and quite impossible. The security that will surround Major Wheeler will make escape unthinkable. However, you will have access to him. Private access. You need only present him with the cyanide capsule. The major should be relied upon to do what is necessary. Only if that fails would you be required to handle the matter in a way that would be more obvious.'

Gus had been doing some sorting of his own. Ordering the steps through which he would lead Macklin. Looking for the most logical progression.

'You said Brausch will be there,' Gus said slowly. 'Why not have Brausch do it?'

Macklin folded his hands. It seemed a logical question.

'There remains, of course, some risk of detection. Somewhat greater if Wheeler refuses the cyanide. We do not choose to risk Colonel Brausch in this regard. He is the greatest living asset to the intelligence efforts of this war. We prefer to risk you, truth be told. Nonetheless, I am hopeful that the risk will be minimal.'

True, Gus thought, but not exhaustive. There was a far more significant reason for not leaving Wheeler's death to Brausch. Gus would set this aside for a moment.

'What is your level of confidence in Wheeler's reliability?' As rhetorical a question as Gus had ever put.

'None,' Macklin said. 'We do not know the man.'

'What if he panics when he learns we'd rather kill him than help him? What if he'd rather talk to the enemy than be murdered by his friends?'

Sir Geoffrey paused only momentarily.

'Then perhaps,' the old man said, 'a quick bullet is the safest approach.'

Gus gave it a beat, appeared to be thinking it through.

'But if we kill him, we'll never know how much he told the Nazis before he died.'

This hung between them for a moment. There was an

obvious answer, with a less-than-obvious problem attached. Macklin, the chess master, was suddenly wondering just how many moves ahead this boy was working.

'Brausch will know,' Sir Geoffrey said very softly.

It was time for Gus to close that particular door.

'He would know,' Gus agreed. 'The only question is, how much do you really trust him? What if he turns out to be Himmler's ace in the hole? Surely that crossed your mind. Isn't that my ticket to Paris in the first place? Isn't that really why you haven't left this assassination to him?'

The silence returned. Gus was watching the old eyes in the dimness, and he had no doubt that he had struck a nerve. The greatest living asset to the intelligence effort of the war was still, after all, a Hun.

'Impossible to free him?' Gus repeated.

Macklin was looking at the young man a little differently.

'Put it out of your mind,' he said.

'Then we'll have to play him in place,' Gus said.

Macklin gestured for Gus to proceed.

'Make Andy Wheeler our ally instead of our victim. Give him a decoy scenario for the invasion and let him feed it back to the Germans.'

Macklin sighed.

'Please believe that this thought, too, had crossed my mind,' Macklin said. 'It's a splendid notion. But only if it works. Neptune will land only eight divisions. Three more will follow within eighteen hours. Hitler has something over three hundred divisions, by our reckoning. If he gets enough of a sniff at the truth to put even five per cent of his strength in the right place at the right moment, it would be the most humiliating bloodbath Britain or America has ever endured.'

Gus smiled sympathetically.

'None of our alternatives is entirely appealing,' Gus agreed. 'Still, we have to choose one. Killing Wheeler is pointless unless we know what he's told the Germans. If you're willing to risk the entire invasion on Brausch's loyalty to you . . .'

Macklin's bony hand massaged his brow. He was tired.

'You will be on the team,' Macklin said. 'You can make your own appreciation of what the major has disclosed.'

Gus shook his head.

'We keep coming 'round to the same problem,' Gus answered. 'If Brausch is deceiving you, then every Nazi on his team knows exactly who I am. All they'll tell me, all they'll show me, is whatever they want me to play back to you.'

'It is a dilemma,' Macklin said, 'which affects your proposal as well. To guide Wheeler in a decoy situation, we would have to initiate you as a Bigot. You would be given all truth and all lies in perfect detail. You would then become as dangerous, if discovered, as Wheeler himself. If Brausch were Himmler's triple . . .'

'He'd have no more,' Gus interrupted, 'than he has now. I can't blow this thing any higher than Andy Wheeler already can.'

Gus took a deep breath.

'Look,' he said, 'at some rapidly approaching point, Neptune is either on or off. You want the answer quick, but you need the answer right.'

Gus knew that SHAEF had to be shrieking for a decision, that Macklin must be scrambling frantically to buy time. It could be that Gus' little trip was Macklin's only defence against an immediate pulling of the plug. If so, the old man would have to let Gus write some of the rules.

'It can't be a matter of guesswork,' Gus continued. 'Not if you're facing the most humiliating bloodbath in your nation's history. You need to hear me sound an all clear. I can't do that by guessing about the loyalties of a German double. I can only do it by working with Andy Wheeler. He's not a professional liar. I'll know if he's told me the truth.'

Macklin's nod was short and sharp. An executioner's blow.

'At which point,' he said, 'you will eliminate the major?'

Gus eyes were clear and direct.

'At which point,' he said, 'I will appreciate the situation. If Wheeler and I can sell them a decoy, we could turn this whole thing around for you. At the first sign that it can't work, I will take action appropriate to the circumstances.'

Macklin's lips pursed in thought. He was weighing his growing respect for Gus against his own better judgment.

'You don't have to tell me,' Gus said evenly, 'how many lives are at stake. If the situation requires eliminating Wheeler, or myself, I couldn't do anything else.'

Macklin believed one thing clearly. This was a young man who was going to do precisely as he wished.

'Leaves things,' Macklin said, 'a bit loose your end. I'm afraid my people are habituated to traditional notions of control. They prefer to have some idea of what an agent intends to do before he actually does it.'

Gus smiled.

'Takes all the sport out of it,' Gus said.

'Sadly, yes. I know that Yanks are fond of surprises. There is something to be said, however, for the old-fashioned notion of obeying a direct order from a superior.'

Gus' eyes became cold and flat. This was the clincher and he knew he really had to sell it.

'Being a Yank and all,' Gus said slowly, 'I would feel compelled to discuss any direct order with General Eisenhower's staff.'

The old man's eyes stiffened. Gus had hit more than a nerve. Nicholas said only four men knew about this little ace in the hole. Gus was betting that they were all British, and that Macklin would like it to stay that way. SHAEF had never heard of Brausch, and God only knew what Macklin had told them about Emerald and this mission. One thing was certain: Macklin was in too deep to start telling the truth, unless his wits failed to provide a more effective story.

'My last orders from OSS were to cooperate with British intelligence, but to rely on my own initiative,' Gus said. 'Unless you choose to contradict that, I see no need to speak with them further.'

Locked and bolted. The man had no exit. A Bigot was down; a fiasco caused by British intelligence keeping secrets from SHAEF. MI-6 was running a highly placed German double, again on the quiet, in fear that a SHAEF leak would blow Brausch away. Now London Controlling was trying to clean up its own mess by sending its triple into the lion's jaws, again with something less than comprehensive disclosure. If I were Sir Geoffrey, Gus concluded, I would be ready to stop giving orders and start looking for help.

Sir Geoffrey was ready.

'There is an odour,' Macklin said with a faint smile, 'to what you may be implying. It is a scent with an unpleasant name.'

Gus raised his brows.

'Blackmail?' he said, hurt and wronged. 'To suggest that London Controlling execute its charter by acting in full concert with my government?'

And now the old man's smile was very warm indeed.

'Blackmail,' Macklin said, 'is such a crude and unforgiving term. Shall we instead say "benign extortion"?'

'I'm the only man you can get onto that team. If you don't send me, you're risking everything on Brausch. You can trust your agent or theirs.'

Macklin folded his hands and licked his lips. He was sorry to admit it, but he hugely liked this boy. Fifty years ago, he'd have done the same and he knew it.

'You have a gift,' the old man said, 'for presenting choices so clearly that one cannot help but put one's foot to the right path.'

Mackin was only restating a primary canon of Gus' training. Manage things so as to offer no choices at all.

SEVENTEEN

The noise was deafening. As Gus sat, hugging his knees, it seemed that the tiny plane was about to rattle apart, rivet by rivet. It was astonishing that any sound so violent could seem so tentative. Every other moment brought a hitch or sputter that assured Gus of instant fiery death.

Gus sat with the heavy canvas pack strapped across his shoulders. It had looked so inadequate when they first handed it to him. Now it felt huge and impossibly awkward.

He was purely terrified. In a few minutes he would step out into nothing, fall about a million miles, pull a cord, and hope that a silken bedsheet would magically unfold over his head.

Of all the things his mother did not raise her boy to be, this was top of the list.

Gus' misery was compounded, of course, by the irony of the situation. Although Macklin knew the Germans were waiting for Gus, he could not permit them to suspect that he knew. There was no choice but to send Gus into France with the customary parachute drop, even though everyone on both shores of the English Channel knew Gus was coming. It would have been ever so much more congenial to have simply taken a ferry from Dover.

Willoughby, a rugged Special Operations officer with an auburn brush for a moustache, watched Gus' wretched condition with great amusement. Willoughby was eating an orange with obvious relish. He was crouched over a great rucksack, from which he kept producing a seemingly inexhaustible supply of fruit. His eyes were small and olive-coloured. They kept darting up to Gus with a firm defiance that suggested Willoughby would protect his fruit from all attack. Gus didn't doubt it for a minute.

'Well,' Willoughby drawled, 'y'could say you're a very lucky man.' The way he rolled his words, Gus supposed there was more than a little Welsh in him.

The broad features smirked down at his orange. There was a tight little Welsh secret about to be told. Exactly what Gus needed during his last moments on this earth.

'And why is that?' Gus asked. He was suddenly imbued with a hunch that he really wanted to hear this after all.

Willoughby held his tongue for a moment, deciding whether Gus had asked prettily enough.

'They told me somethin' about ya, young Captain.'

The round little eyes looked up suddenly, almost fiercely, despite the lightness of his smile.

'They told me,' his drawl came very softly, 'that th'Germans think you're one of theirs.'

Dandy. Just terrific.

'And why would they tell you something like that?'

'T'save your pink little ass, m'son. They've leaked to th'Germans where we're droppin'. The Nazis know our route t'Paris. They'll be watchin' over us, protective-like, so y'don't get shot up by one of their own patrols along th'way. London Controlling had t'let me in on th'joke, so's ah'd know not t'free-lance. Take th'right route and all.'

And so now there was one more man who knew Gus to be Macklin's triple. Only this one was dropping into France right alongside Gus, right where the Germans could pluck him out of the forest and lay him on the rack.

'I'm a lucky man,' Gus said joylessly.

Willoughby had caught his tone. A slow grin emerged. The empathy of a rational man.

'Stupid sons of bitches,' Willoughby muttered in concurrence with Gus' unspoken judgment. 'Soon as ah'd kissed y'goodbye and sent y'down the Rue de Rivoli, some lads in green suits might pop out of th'bushes t'ask me a wee question about ya.'

The large hand reached out to Gus. In it was maybe a third of the orange.

Gus' stomach was up around his Adam's apple at this

point. He had been close to chucking for the last twenty bone-rattling minutes. Gus took the orange with a silent nod, wolfing it down with the eagerness that the offer commanded.

'So like y'said,' Willoughby grinned, 'you're a lucky man. Because we're droppin' someplace else. We're takin' a route ah'll make up as ah go along. And by th'time y'see Sacré-Coeur, m'son, ah'll be ear-deep in Frog pussy a hundred miles away.'

Nausea notwithstanding, Gus managed a smile.

'That's their genius, don't y'know,' Willoughby said. 'These boys in London don't know which end of their pants t'climb into. But they do know how t'do one thing right.'

He punctuated with a wink.

'They know,' he said, 'which men to send to th'field.'

Apparently, the wink had included Gus within the class of the field-worthy. A dizzying accolade from a man who dispensed praise as closely as he did fruit.

Willoughby was in the branch of the Special Operations Executive known as F Section. His simple responsibility was finding, organizing, training, and equipping the guerrillas of the French Resistance. It was a task that the world later assumed had been performed spontaneously and skillfully by the fierce souls of freedom-starved France. General de Gaulle's feelings on the matter notwithstanding, this was not quite the case. For sheer heroics, for the kind of raw risk-your-guts-daily courage that Anglo-Saxons thrill to, the field officers of F Section were unsurpassed.

The SD's going rate for a live F Section officer was currently the equivalent of six thousand pounds sterling. By the end of April 1944, there were some folks in Europe who would have sold family members for less. Willoughby chose his allies carefully. Gus figured the list was probably blank.

The little plane shuddered again and, for what seemed the longest trembling moment, the engine was silent. On a whim, it coughed itself back to life.

'Your people from Wales?' Gus asked.

Willoughby nodded and kept nodding.

'And Skye in th'north of Scotland,' he said, 'and York. Ah'm all-Britain, don't y'know. Bit of a mongrel.'

His hand was in the rucksack again, rummaging for more fruit. He came up with a pear, brown and only slightly withered. Gus was in awe, not only of the man's appetite, but of his resourcefulness in finding all this stuff. These things were jewels on the black market, either side of the Channel.

'Y'like the Froggies?' Willoughby's eyes were still down in the sack, taking inventory.

'Should I?'

Willoughby looked up. The grin was on crooked.

'They're a piece of work, those Froggies. No mistake.'

Willoughby's eyes returned to the sack.

'May of 1940,' he said, 'life was very chic in gay Par*ee*. Elegant supper parties. Th'opera was full. Business was good. This thing, this war, goin' on somewhere to th'east. Why, that was th' *drôle de guerre*. Y'speak Frog?'

'A little.'

Willoughby nodded, his eyes a bit vacant.

'S'pose y'd do at that,' he said. 'Yanks love th'Froggies. Well, *drôle de guerre*, th'funny war. Th'Germans attacked on May th'tenth. In four days, in *four days*, they had broken both th'Second and Ninth armies. Th'French government responded by attending mass at Notre-Dame, and trotted out th'holy relics. "In God we trust," is that th'phrase?'

'Old Yank phrase,' Gus confirmed.

'So all th'little Froggies wet their pants. They ran south, like Hitler couldn't find his way to Bordeaux. Burned all their little secret papers. Crated up everything in their grand museums and carted it off. Even killed th'cats and dogs they couldn't take along, so they wouldn't starve slow. Animal lovers, th'Frogs are.'

Gus smiled just enough to keep the story coming.

'Th'eleventh of June, th'Germans roll tanks through Paris. Half th'city is abandoned, th'other half is hiding under th'bed. Hitler shows up, makes them sign in th'same railway car where th'Germans surrendered t'Foch in th'last war. Total humiliation. Got th'picture?'

Gus had the picture.

'Only while th'Froggies are grovelling around his boots, Hitler sizes up th'situation. Y'see it's one thing t'conquer th'little snivellers. It's another t'run their whole bloody country for 'em, when y'haven't a man t'spare. I mean, someone's got t'grow and process and ship th'damn food, so Hitler can steal half of it for Germany and feed th'Froggies with th'scraps. Someone's got t'man their factories, push th'paper, run th'traffic at th'corner. Hitler's boys are stretched all along that Atlantikwall.'

Once again, Gus had the picture.

'All th'Froggies had t'do, y'understand, was just lie down. Thirty, even twenty, per cent of 'em lie down, Hitler's in serious trouble. I mean, y'can't shoot 'em all.'

There was a terrible smile of grim amusement.

'Hitler had 'em figured for cowards. Figured if he gave 'em half an alibi, they'd go right on grovelling. Sure enough. Once th'merchants saw that th'Germans were payin', they were welcomed into th'shops. Police demonstrated their sense of duty by stayin' on th'job. Hotels treated th'Germans like tourists. Socialites competed t'get the highest ranking Krauts t'tea. In a few months, it was all th'normal, permanent way of life.'

Willoughby's face had taken colour.

'Well, what goddam excuse have y'got for these people, Captain? Y'tell me why they deserve t'live.'

This was an interesting man.

'You've been jumping out of aeroplanes,' Gus said evenly, 'blowing up bridges and crawling through the cold marsh on your belly for these people. I've been lying on my ass in London, largely ignoring them. Why don't you tell me?'

Willoughby just buried his moustache in the remains of the pear. Gus thought he was maybe masking a grin.

'Petain!' Willoughby exploded. 'National bloody hero. Demigod, he is. Tells 'em collaboration is preserving national unity. French way of life. Which is an in-ter-esting way t'look at slavery.'

'They're people,' Gus said quietly. 'They were humiliated. Degraded, helpless. They thought it would last forever, and maybe it will. They don't want to die or to suffer. They don't want to think of themselves as slaves or whores. They want to think they're making the best of it. Isn't that human?'

Willoughby wiped the moustache with the broad back of his hand. The sly grin had some bite to it.

'Human t'be a coward?' he said. 'Is that how y'fancy us all?'

'Human to have weakness,' Gus said. 'Human to have fear.'

Willoughby nodded slowly, his eyes playing again.

'And what do y'fear, young Captain?'

Gus' eyes flickered. His face became flat and very cold for the briefest of moments. Then, the blinding smile.

'I'm afraid to die,' Gus said softly. 'And I'm not afraid of you.'

But Willoughby had seen that chilling instant before the smile. He had been meant to. It was a look down into a depth he had not sensed was there. In that single flash, he saw Gus as a man who could kill. As a man who could be alone. It was a glimpse that brought a sense of kinship, a lingering taste of something fraternal.

'You're right on both counts,' Willoughby drawled.

The plane, as if yanked by a giant cable, suddenly jerked upwards. Gus knew that they had reached the coast. The usual procedure for an airdrop was to fly as low as possible over the Channel, then soar as high as possible at the coastline, since this was where the heavy aircraft guns were fixed. Once past the coast, they would cut back the engine, dive to maybe two hundred metres. They would stay low as long as possible, then climb again to sufficient height for the jump.

Willoughby sat hugging his knees, his unblinking eyes fixed on Gus. Willoughby's body leaned gently into the plane's mad climb, as if he was instinctively anticipating each moment's change in angle. Gus was grabbing everything in sight, trying to hold his balance and his supper at the same time.

The plane righted itself. A minute passed in silence. Gus was just working on slowing his heartbeat, getting the air in and out of his lungs. It was one of those moments when nothing in one's body could be trusted to work without intense personal supervision.

Gus had all but forgotten about the plunge. It came, of course, as abruptly as the ascent. A power dive that picked up speed so resolutely, Gus figured the pilot was trying to see if he could ram this thing all the way to the centre of the earth.

The levelling out was smooth and sudden, and brought Gus' bowels all the way up to his eyeballs. All this fun, he thought, and there aren't even any Nazis yet.

Willoughby was sitting as before, his eyes searching Gus for something. For confirmation that Gus' moment of steel and ice had really been there. Like Macklin before him, Willoughby had so little time to measure this man. This man who would mean so much to them all.

They flew for a long while in silence. At last the gentle, final climb began.

'Let me tell ya,' Willoughby said slowly, 'what kind of an animal is a Frenchman.'

His eyes, however, were not on Gus. They were staring over Gus' shoulder, as if watching a bug on a wall. Willoughby stood, stepped to one side of Gus, and with a single motion opened a doorway in the side of the plane. Freezing air blasted in past Gus' right shoulder. The world outside the plane was utter blackness, but Willoughby kept staring out into it as if he could actually see something.

'So,' he said, still staring out at the night, 'what kind of creature is a Froggie?'

Slowly, he backed away from the open hatch. He took his seat again and his eyes returned to Gus, fierce and focused as ever.

'A Frog,' he said, 'is a wee beast that creates somethin' called the Milice. D'ya know that one, young Captain?'

Gus didn't know much.

'They're Frog storm troopers,' Willoughby drawled extra slowly. 'Volunteers. They're trained and equipped by th'SS. They operate totally outside any law but their own. They inform on their own people. Participate in torture and murder. We don't know how many of them there are, but Frogland is entirely infested with 'em.'

His eyes returned to the darkness beyond Gus' right shoulder. Suddenly, they snapped back to Gus' face.

'Ah'll tell ya,' he said, his voice now a low growl, 'one number we do know. It's an official Nazi statistic one of th'boys picked up.'

The smile flashed dark and dirty.

'Ninety-two thousand,' he said. 'That's th'number of illegitimate children that th'Frenchwomen have borne t'Nazi fathers. D'ya think those were all rapes?'

Casually, Willoughby climbed again to his feet. Towering over Gus, he peered out into the blackness beyond the hatchway. If this man does not get to Paris, he had been told, there was no invasion this year. It was all he knew.

'Remember,' he said, looking out at the night, 'all that Daddy has taught you. If you forget t'pull th'cord, Ike will have t'scrap his whole bloody D-Day and Churchill will be personally cross with me.'

Gus began thinking of the best way to tell this lunatic that he was not jumping out of the plane.

Willoughby looked at Gus for a second, a crazed smile on his puss. He reached down, as if to adjust Gus' shoulder harness. His massive hands closed around the straps. Just as Gus was trying to form the thought that Willoughby might actually do it, Willoughby lifted him straight into the air and threw him out of the plane.

There was a shock so powerful that it overrode even terror. Gus had always thought that air was empty, nothingness. This was like being thrown into a brick wall.

Once he was outside the plane, the night no longer seemed as black. Gus could see moonlit trees and fields. At first, the ground didn't seem to be coming any closer. Then, it rushed towards him. Suddenly he was upside down, watching Willoughby seeming to float in midair somewhere above his outstretched toes.

Gus noticed that some part of his brain had calmly counted to eight and was suggesting to his fingers that they pull on that funny little ring.

When the 'chute snapped open, Gus was certain that it had dislocated both of his shoulders.

He floated glumly down towards the moonlit clearing, waiting with resignation for the shock that would surely snap both his legs.

EIGHTEEN

Once on the ground, Willoughby was pure jungle cat. There was a reliance on instinct and physical senses that Gus had never seen in a human.

They would be sitting in a clearing, chewing on the dried garbage that Willoughby told him was portable food. Willoughby would be droning on about one of his many mongrel ancestral homelands, Ardvasar on the Isle of Skye or Llandudno in the north of Wales. Suddenly, he would stop in the middle of a guttural oath. His nostrils would flare and his eyes would sweep every rock and tree. It was a performance that never left Gus in doubt that death was less than a twig snap away.

It was two days before they arrived at the farmhouse just outside the village of Eragny. Gus had no idea, but they were less than ten miles from the outskirts of Paris. Willoughby sat in the tall grass and watched the farmhouse through an hour of twilight. When it was dark, he climbed to his feet and simply walked to the front door.

A young girl received them. Gus could only guess that she was fourteen or fifteen. She kissed Willoughby lightly on the cheek, but the pat that he gave to her bottom was more than fatherly. She blushed and slapped his hand, then held it all the way to the kitchen.

Her name was Charlotte. She had cooked them a large supper, which was waiting and hot. Fresh bread and soup and pork. She arranged the table for them silently. Poured red wine as if she were their waitress.

'Y'll have to excuse us this evening.' Willoughby winked at Gus. 'The girl usually sets a table somewhat more substantial.'

Charlotte apparently spoke no English. She stood and waited until Willoughby had tasted the pork. Until he turned and told her, with surprising gentleness, that the meat was very good. Then she left.

When they were alone, Willoughby gave Gus another wink.

'Y'll forgive me,' he said, 'if ah don't sleep with ya tonight.'

'She's a pretty girl,' Gus said, although she wasn't.

'She's been alone on this place for three months now. Her mother's dead. Her father's dead. Her brother's workin' for a *réseau*, in Chantilly.'

Réseaux were Resistance networks. Willoughby's voice had become flat Welsh indifference. As if the girl's circumstances were secondary to her pork.

Sure enough, his next words were 'Good pork, don't y'think. Froggies were born t'cook.'

Gus grinned.

'Somethin' amusing?' Willoughby asked.

'If y'told me y'liked her,' Gus said, imitating Willoughby's drawl, 'or even that y'were a wee bit worried about her, yer secret would be safe with me. Carry it to th'grave, ah would.'

Willoughby thought for a second, then laughed out loud.

'She's thirteen years old, man,' Willoughby growled.

'Stop bragging,' Gus said. 'She's fifteen if she's a day.'

'Thirteen last October. Y'don't think any th'less of me?'

And Gus' face slipped so easily into the frozen mask that Willoughby had glimpsed on the plane.

'I think you're filth,' Gus said quietly. Gus held the silence for a full five seconds before the giggle burst from him, red wine spilling down his chin.

Willoughby's grin split his face. He had to admit that something caught in his stomach when the glacier settled on those green eyes. It was a face few men could wear.

'When y'go to bed t'night,' Willoughby said, 'y'll never see me again. 'Less y'live t'buy me a pint in Cardiff.'

Gus nodded, and in his nod was the promise that he'd be there in Willoughby's chosen pub and he'd be buying.

'Charlotte will take ya in with th'horse and cart. She'll get ya before dawn. Y'ask her about th'Fritzes on th'way in. She'll tell ya some things t'remember.'

'Fritzes?'

'That's what they call th'Krauts in th'country. In Paris they call 'em *Haricots Verts*. Means green beans, y'know. Their uniforms are green.'

Willoughby put his grin on sideways.

'That's right,' he corrected himself, 'y'speak Frog, don't ya?'

He looked at his watch.

'Time for Charlie McCarthy,' he said. It was seven-thirty.

He disappeared and returned with a large radio. Setting it down carefully so as not to scratch Charlotte's table, he began turning the dial against the static.

'BBC,' he said absently, as if to himself, 'straight from Bush House in the Strand.'

And from the radio came the first four notes of Beethoven's Fifth Symphony. In Morse code, the cadence spelled *V. V* for victory.

'Good evening,' said a British voice in refined French, 'here are the evening's personal messages.'

There followed a fascinating string of nonsense fragments.

'The spotted rabbit licks the soft cheese . . . the moon smells sweetly of jasmine . . .'

Each phrase was repeated slowly and distinctly, so that not a word could be missed.

'These are the A messages,' Willoughby said. 'They alert th'Resistance t'prepare for a particular action. One means get ready t'blow up a train at such and such a place. One of 'em told Charlotte t'get ready for us.'

He flicked off the receiver.

'Then,' he said, 'when we're ready, we broadcast th'B message, th'action message. Tells 'em it's time t'execute th'previous order.'

'Does it work?'

Willoughby gave him the long stare.

'Used t'work. Before Starkey.'

Starkey had been the code name for a particularly elaborate and unsuccessful deception. During the summer of 1943, the Allies had attempted to persuade the Germans that there would be an autumn invasion at the Pas-de-Calais. A main objective was to draw the Luftwaffe into concentrated air battles, where it was hoped they would be decimated in preparation for the real invasion. The lure was unsuccessful. No major air battles developed.

'The boys in London,' Willoughby drawled, 'sent out th'A messages for th'Resistance t'get ready for th'invasion. So th'Froggies came out of their holes. Became more visible, took a lot of risks. London figured th'Germans would see this increased Resistance activity as a sure sign that Starkey was real.'

Gus understood. Another 'necessary' price.

''Course,' Willoughby said with grim eyes, 'they didn't let th'Froggies in on th'joke. Who'd trust a Frog t'risk his life just t'help cover a decoy?'

Willoughby shook his head slowly.

'Didn't tell most of F Section either. Ah guess they figured some of us were Frogophiles by that point. So we were trapped right along with th'Froggies. Necks stretched way out t'there.'

Willoughby paused for an emphasis that was not needed.

'Germans stepped on hundreds of 'em, like so many bugs. One of th'biggest *ratissages* of th'whole bloody war.'

Ratissages meant rat hunts, major campaigns to exterminate Resistance personnel.

'But then,' Gus said softly, 'they were only Frogs.'

There was a silence.

'It is,' Willoughby agreed, 'a bloody shame t'kill th'good ones.'

He leaned back and propped his feet gently against Charlotte's table.

''Course,' Willoughby said, 'if it wasn't for th'princely stipend, ah wouldn't have any truck with th'buggers.'

'You're in it for the oranges,' Gus said.

Willoughby chucked.

'Sometimes these Froggies do give one a smile. Ah mean, in th'whole bloody country, maybe only eighty thousand have any guns at all. Maybe ten per cent have ammo for more than one day's fight. So, they're out there puttin' sugar cubes in petrol tanks, turning signposts in th'wrong direction.'

He pointed a huge finger at Gus. 'Y'think I'm trainin' young bucks t'use automatic weapons? Ah'm teaching girls like Charlotte how t'short out a telephone cable with a thumbtack.'

And now Willoughby was looking at the ceiling and talking mostly to himself.

'Then there's the factions. Th'*Gaullistes* and th'Reds keep turnin' each other over to th'Germans. It's most remarkable. *Gaullistes* are a useless bloody joke altogether. Y'can't tell 'em anything.'

The eyes snapped back to Gus. The punch line was on its way.

'Prosper Network supplied sixty *réseaux*. Sixty. Germans worked a few doubles into th'right spots and th'whole damn thing collapsed. But th'Frogs blamed us for it. They thought we sold them out as part of Starkey.'

'How's that?' Gus' voice was calm and neutral.

'They figured we helped th'Germans catch all the Prosper Froggies, so that when th'Germans put 'em on th'rack . . . when they busted their guts open . . . why, they'd confirm the Starkey tale that we were landing at Calais.'

They just looked at each other.

'We'd have t'be pretty damn cold,' Willoughby said, 't'dream up somethin' like that.'

Gus stared straight at his eyes.

'Pretty damn cold,' Gus agreed.

'Bloody paranoid, th'Frogs are. Paranoid and cheeky.' Willoughby tried a small grin.

'They've got a hell of a nerve,' Gus said, 'mistrusting a guy like you.' Gus wasn't smiling at all.

Willoughby offered a rare and gentle smile, free from all of his usual defences.

'First thing t'know,' he said, 'is that there's no truth in it. Next thing t'know is that yer gonna hear this story. Yer gonna see it behind their eyes. Ah told London that Starkey was death. Y'start lying to these people . . . even once . . .'

'London told you,' Gus said, 'that it was your problem.'

Willoughby nodded.

'They're very predictable in that way,' Willoughby said.

Gus still wasn't smiling.

'You wouldn't,' Gus said, 'be sending me off to a Prosper *réseau* in Paris, would you?'

Willoughby shook his head.

'No, son,' he said. 'The idea is we want t'*win* this war. What's left of Prosper has more Nazis in it than Frogs. Ah'm sending you to th'best I've got. But they have ears, and ah'm afraid th'Prosper thing will have 'em a mite untrusting.'

And now the look that Willoughby had glimpsed on the plane settled over Gus' eyes. This time it had come to stay.

'I've got no time to watch my back for surprises,' Gus said evenly. 'When I tell these people to jump, they'd better hit the air two feet higher than they would for De Gaulle. And if you haven't got them ready for that, mister, you goddam well set them straight before you go ear-deep in Frog pussy a hundred miles away. Have you got that?'

Willoughby's colour was deep.

'Yessir, ah have.'

The green eyes kept bearing in, flat and level.

'Mister, I don't know what the fuck you do have straight. I am here because London screwed up so royally, we oughta take the whole lot out and shoot them. I am the Supreme Command in Frogland, mister. I *am* Ike and Monty and Winnie. Did they tell you that much?'

Willoughby nodded. 'They did.'

'I am going to be giving your Frogs some orders, mister. There isn't one inch of room for one Frog to have one second's hesitation about whether I'm selling out him, his kids, his dog, or the whole fucking Resistance.'

Willoughby cleared his throat.

'Y'll get cooperation. Ah guarantee it.'

Gus' eyes seemed almost to be glowing. It was goddam unnerving.

'Screw cooperation,' Gus said through his teeth. 'I'm talking about obedience. I'm talking about the whole fucking invasion going back to square one if any of *your* frogs blinks cross-eyed. Now, you get on your little radio, and you talk to your biggest Froggie, and you set him up to pee in his pants when he even thinks of my name.'

And Willoughby's mind turned to the square features and calm eyes of Armand Leclerc. This boy was right. It had been Willoughby's job to deliver Resistance support of unquestioning obedience. Instead, he was sending him to Armand.

Save some of that heat, he thought. Save a little for Armand, young Captain. But what he said was, 'I'll get the radio.'

Gus shook his head sharply.

'First,' Gus said, 'I want all your fucking little surprises. One at a time. Nice and slow.'

Willoughby swallowed. Gus' eyes were so hard, he thought Gus might come right over the table at him if he mouthed off.

'Y'want t'save some of that heat for th'Germans,' Willoughby said. 'Don't use it up on y'friends.'

'My friends are the guys who do their job right. So I can do mine. Now, you want to go in the next room and get laid, or you want to do your job?'

Willoughby was frozen solid. He wanted very much to do his job. Had from the first.

'Let me make it easy,' Gus said. 'You're sending me to the best you've got, because he's all you've got.'

Gus sighed wearily, because Willoughby's face was telling him that he was going to be right on all counts.

'It's not that the guy isn't competent,' Gus continued. 'He's smart, tough, experienced, and, most of all, very senior. I know he's good at surviving, because he's still walking upright after four years. His people worship him because he saw them through Starkey, assorted *ratissages*, and other potential mine fields. He has all their loyalty. Only trouble is, the feeling is mutual.'

Willoughby's eyes were very sad. They were telling Gus that Willoughby was sorry.

'Here's a guy,' Gus said, 'who only cares about *la France* and his people. He relies strictly on his own judgment and it's always worked so far. After Starkey and the Prosper collapse, he wouldn't carry out an order from a Yank or a Limey if he *agreed* with it. So this guy is gonna smile at my face, give me a snappy salute, and then go off and win the war by doing exactly as he damn well pleases.'

Gus took a very deep breath. At this point, he wanted only to crawl into a feather bed and sleep for a couple of days.

'The punch line,' Gus concluded, 'is that you knew this all along and were ordered by some imbecile in London to keep your mouth shut. Maybe this jerk figured that when I found out I couldn't trust my back, I'd walk off the job. Or do something really dangerous, like lose my intense faith in London and make some free-lance alterations in the game plan.'

Willoughby had to smile in spite of his misery. 'Y'wanna shut up for a minute?'

'No. You followed this fucking order because it was a fucking order. You didn't really want to send me over the cliff, because I'm such a good looking and wholesome youngster. Accordingly, your rampant guilt spills out in all these stories about Starkey and Prosper. You tipped me, mister.'

Willoughby was now grinning ear to ear.

'Now?' he asked.

'No. Just don't tell me that I'm right, okay? Being right in this war is taking me nowhere. Just once, let me be lucky instead.'

Willoughby leaned forward. He clasped his large hands together on the table.

'His name is Armand Leclerc . . .'

'Fine. He's out.'

It was a mark of Gus' persuasiveness that Willoughby actually considered this for a moment.

'Can't be out,' Willoughby said. 'This is Jade Amicol *réseau*. It's all ah've got in Paris. This is their man at my end. If ah ask to replace him, they'll refuse and y'll get total paranoia and hostility. And y'can't make it without these people. Someone's gotta work th'radio with London for ya. Someone's gotta get ya to th'Alps when it's over. Y'can't be naked in this.'

Gus' face was still, but the eyes were working.

'This man Leclerc is an enemy,' Gus said. 'It's a word that includes anyone I can't trust. Can I play him like an enemy?'

Willoughby thought it over.

'From what ah've seen,' he said, 'ah think y'can beat him. Don't reason with him. Out-strong him. Y've got t'be leader of th'pack. Give him that good strong stare. He'll growl, but he'll slink away.'

Gus shook his head.

'You can't beat a man who's behind your back. You can only play him.'

'Let's hear it,' Willoughby said.

'He's out,' Gus said slowly, 'but he doesn't know it. I whip him once, so he knows he's afraid to take me head-on. That's sound. But I can't leave him behind my back after that. I tell him I need to work with a go-between. Too dangerous to keep contacting him directly, and he's too important to the Resistance to be risked. Give him a face-saver to withdraw to supervisory status.'

Willoughby nodded. He liked it.

'Then,' Gus smiled, 'all I have to do is make the go-between more loyal to me than to him.'

'For a man of your talents . . .' Willoughby grinned at the craziness of such a thought.

'Piece of cake,' Gus winked.

NINETEEN

In the hour between the end of curfew and the coming of dawn, Charlotte had taken Gus in the horse and cart.

It was light when they arrived at the outskirts of Argenteuil, a suburb to the northeast of Paris. She had wanted to take him all the way in, assuring him that she was in no danger. He kissed her cheek and pressed a roll of bills into her hand as he climbed down.

Gus walked for nearly a mile until he spotted a velo-taxi, a small cart pulled by a young man on a bicycle.

'Arc de Triomphe,' Gus said. The 'driver' smiled pleasantly. Gus climbed into the cart and clattered off, a tourist taking his morning ride into town.

There were no checkpoints, no soldiers in the streets of Argenteuil at that hour. There was a sudden wild fantasy that Gus was entering a city already liberated. He had expected an armed camp, but Argenteuil seemed only a sleepy village, slowly awakening to another day of mundane commerce.

As they drew closer to the city, the signs of occupation began to reveal themselves. At first, there were small bands of German soldiers in their green uniforms and grey coats. They seemed improbably young, perhaps fifteen or sixteen, in some cases. A few carried arms as they stood sentry or marched in short columns. Others, off duty, carried cameras instead, giggling and taking snapshots like adolescent tourists.

Then, there was the banner. Stretched across the baroque façade of a large building, it said, DEUTSCHLAND SIEGT AN ALLEN FRONTEN. Germany Victorious on All Fronts. Welcome to Paris.

It was as if Gus had passed through an invisible border crossing. There was a sudden profusion of soldiers, of German banners and signs. And everywhere, now, the swastikas. The black emblem, encircled by white, on a garish field of brilliant red. It glared like obscene graffiti from shops and theatres and the balconies of hotels requisitioned for Nazi personnel. As if the hideous symbol had been created expressly to violate the grace and beauty of this particular city.

Paris was coming fully awake now, and there were convoys of German trucks, sounding their fearsome claxons. As one convoy passed a uniformed gendarme directing traffic, the French policeman shot an arm forward in the Nazi salute. Gus thought of Willoughby, crouched over his rucksack of oranges, muttering about the French way of life.

This was a city that was now accustomed to rising in the dark, since the Germans had brought the clock forward an hour to Greater Reich Time. Already, the queues of housewives had formed at the few shops where there was anything left to buy. Gus looked at these women as if he expected to see misery and anguish etched into their faces. Instead, he saw only the blank eyes of women embarking on another day's routine, so commonplace had their deprivation become. In a way, Gus found this all the more saddening.

It was strange to see women in pants, particularly in such numbers. This had become a convenient form of dress, since virtually everyone rode bicycles. There were no cars on the streets of Paris except those licensed by the Germans as 'public service' vehicles. Paris had become a city of two million bicycles and only seven thousand automobiles. The underground Métro, the horsedrawn cabs, and the velo-taxis struggled to take up the slack. Here and there were buses whose engines had been modified to run on natural gas. Petrol belonged to the war.

Some of the shops bore the rectangular yellow and black sign denoting a Jewish business. Most of these seemed long deserted, with broken glass or boarded windows. Gus scanned the people on the street, looking for a yellow star. He saw none. By April 1944, there had become increasingly few to see.

As the cart made its way to the centre of the city, Gus saw the poster for the first time. A beautiful German soldier, blonde and fearless, stared lovingly down at a small child in his arms. The words on the poster said, 'You have been abandoned. Put your trust in the German soldier.' Gus saw a second, then a third. A chill swept through him. This poster was not useless propaganda. It was the distilled essence of collaboration, the last defence of a helpless people. To release one's hold on reality. To believe that ceaseless rape had somehow become an act of protection and love.

They had arrived at the Arc. Gus stepped off onto Avenue Kléber. Once on foot, his perspective changed dramatically. The ride had been a newsreel, passing the crimes of the occupation in review. Now he was in Paris. Despite the overlay of Nazi ugliness, it was without question the most magnificent city Gus had ever seen.

He followed the curve of the pavement to the mouth of the Champs-Elysées. He stood, staring down its full length to the Place de la Concorde. The avenue was nearly eighty yards wide, lined with broad-leaved trees wearing their freshest April colour. Sidewalk cafés, dappled with clear sunshine, were filling with early-morning clientele. Could there still be coffee and chocolate for breakfast in this city? Mothers were pushing their prams and strollers. Businessmen were glancing at their watches, clutching leather cases. Even the bicycles no longer seemed symbols of deprivation, but graceful reminders of a more peaceful and lyrical age. The scene was a tableau alive with the most vibrant beauty.

Gus realized at last that he had been standing, motionless, for a very long time. He was living in a moment he didn't want to release. He smiled, thrust his hands in his pockets, and set off down the avenue. He was whistling as he strolled, giving himself willingly now to the giddy fantasy. He was a tourist. A free man in a free city. He had not reported to the Nazis yet. No one knew he had arrived, no one could locate him. He could rent a room somewhere, disappear. He could take a job, find a girl. He would not have to die.

Gus smiled at the solid, reasonable sound of the words in his brain. Fear of death creates its own logic, and never had Gus been more aware of that fear. Take a job, find a girl. The grin broadened as he savoured the sheer insanity of it.

He was in the avenue now, immersed in it. He had wrapped himself in its sunshine and colour and chestnut-scented air.

A fragment of his past came suddenly to him. It was not clear enough to be a memory. It was the resonance of a distant feeling. He had been alone and very small, but in surroundings of great beauty. The loneliness was all right, he had told himself, all right in this place. Because he was *with* the place, as if it were a wondrous and comforting friend.

But slowly, the odour of the occupation began to bleed back through the walls of his cocoon.

The finest hotels, the grandest of public buildings, had been requisitioned for an endless myriad of military, civil, and SS bureaucracies. Restaurants had been requisitioned as Army canteens called *Lokales*. He passed a cinema with freshly painted barricades. It had become a *Soldatenkino*, a theatre where only German soldiers were welcome. The theatre's programme was not in evidence, as the marquee had been given over to propaganda slogans.

Each swastika, each poster, now stabbed at the flesh of Gus' romance. This was his first morning in Paris, the only first morning he would ever have. They had poisoned his avenue and his sunshine, violated his morning. It was not murder, torture or enslavement, not a mind-numbing crime for the ages. It was, however, a hook on which Gus could hang a moment of purely personal hatred. He welcomed it, clung to it, as his heels clicked sharply along the pavement.

At number 52, he passed the headquarters of the Propaganda Abteilung. This was the organ in charge of censorship. Cinema, theatre, radio. Books and newspapers, even to rationing available paper supplies into the most cooperative hands. He passed Radio-Paris and Radio-City, both stations now organs of collaboration. Gus had known which of them was now the broadcasting home of Maurice Chevalier, but he had forgotten.

At 31/33 the old Marignan Cinéma housed Organization Todt, responsible for commissioning all construction projects needed by the German Army. They employed half a million French workers, all well paid for their contributions to the Atlantikwall, the airfields, the U-boat pens. If only 20 per cent had just lain down, Willoughby had said.

And as Gus walked on, two images grew to dominate his mind. There was the face of Willoughby and his crooked grin, trying to tell Gus of the grief and the madness and the shame that simple weakness had wrought. And there was the face from the poster, the loving German soldier, looking down at Gus now with inexpressible tenderness. You have been abandoned, he murmured. Put your trust in the German soldier.

TWENTY

By late morning, Gus had made his way to a block of exclusive flats on the Rue Pergolèse. He stood in the sunshine, slowly leafing through a morning paper. This was the last time he would be free of Nazi tracking, and therefore his one opportunity to do some tracking of his own.

Following an adversary, even on a recreational stroll, usually yielded something of interest – mannerisms, idiosyncrasies revealing a fragment of character. The real attraction for Gus, however, was the element of play. Free-lance tracking was mostly fun, and, after all, this was his day off.

Eventually, Armand Leclerc emerged from a doorway, looking passably like his photo. Well into his forties, a balding man with powerful shoulders. Hands that kept clenching and unclenching as he walked. It was an athletic stride. There was a broad, flat nose, but it was nonetheless a masculine face of considerable appeal. He was dressed expensively, as befitted the well-to-do collaborator, which was his cover.

Leclerc turned north onto Avenue de Malakoff and proceeded to the Métro station at the Porte Maillot. He skipped down the steps quickly. Gus was forced to draw a little closer than he might have liked, for fear of losing him in the rabbit warren of tunnels and stairwells.

Leclerc ducked into a hole marked Direction Vincennes. Gus followed and was relieved to see a fair-sized crowd on the landing. He hung back until the train appeared, then stepped to the opposite door of the car that Leclerc boarded. There was an angry knot of midday commuters at the doorway, but Gus managed to slip through with a smile and a little elbow work.

The train lurched off. Gus was careful to position himself close to his own door, so that he could match an unexpectedly quick exit.

Willoughby had offered a concise briefing on the *réseau* of Jade Amicol. It remained the last stronghold of MI-6 within Paris, encompassing over fifteen hundred agents, together with presumably trustworthy sympathizers. The beating heart of Jade Amicol was a Lazarite convent, Saint Agonie. The convent stood on the Rue de la Santé, under the walls of the lunatic asylum of Sainte-Anne. It was run with awesome precision by its mother superior, Madame Henriette Frede, and nine sisters of the order. In its spare stone cells the leadership of Jade Amicol met in candlelight. In the loft over the sacristy rested the radio transceiver that would provide Gus' sole link to London.

The train had stopped at Concorde station. Leclerc had not risen to join the mob impatiently crowding the door. As they departed, however, Leclerc stood and was through the door in almost a single motion. His movements were so fluid and unobtrusive that this was accomplished without seeming to be in any particular hurry.

And across the car, Leclerc's effortless disappearance was duplicated by Gus an instant before the doors hissed shut behind him.

Gus had managed it smoothly enough, but his pulse was pumping a bit as he watched Leclerc stride away down the tunnel. Gus gave him the slack of forty metres, and started after him at a mildly catch-up rate. Leclerc moved fast. While Gus usually discounted personality inferences from a man's walk, there was a decisiveness and self-possession to Leclerc's carriage that was difficult to ignore.

Leclerc entered the tunnel for the Porte de la Chapelle. The train was already waiting, and Gus had to hustle to make the opposite door of Leclerc's car.

As they rumbled through Madeleine station, Gus was debating the significance of Leclerc's rapid exit. Customary precepts of trade craft would, of course, insist that Leclerc believed he was being followed. Gus didn't think so. If Leclerc had wanted to lose a tracker, he had passed up much better opportunities in the maze of Concorde Station. Gus concluded that the exit had simply been a practised movement, executed by force of habit.

At Pigalle station, Leclerc stood and left the train in the fashion of a normal commuter. Unfortunately, the landing was virtually empty. Gus waited for the last moment, until Leclerc was already heading up the quay, and barely squeezed through the door in time.

Leclerc climbed to the street, and Gus emerged behind him onto Place Pigalle. Here was the sunshine of early afternoon, more liquid and diffuse than the clarity of light on his morning stroll. Montmartre was a quarter of intense colour and life, but the hardships of occupation were far more in evidence than on the Champs-Elysées.

Leclerc seemed too well tailored for this quarter. And as Gus followed him down the Boulevard de Clichy, it was evident that Gus had picked an interesting moment to refresh his tracking skills. Leclerc didn't belong in this place. Therefore, this afternoon's walk was a clandestine one. Like an off-duty detective on a busman's holiday, Gus' curiosity had been enticed.

Sure enough, Leclerc began a circuitous route, slipping down Rue des Martyrs, then doubling back to Clichy on Rue Houdon. This was not done with the swift, vanishing movements of a man who is being followed. Rather, Leclerc's switchbacks had the languid pace of an agent on his way to a private destination. Unruffled, but allowing himself the cover of a seemingly aimless stroll.

Leclerc looked every bit the part of an obscenely wealthy merchant. Which, in fact, he was. He had made himself invaluable to Das Deutsche Beschaffungsamt in Frankreich, The German Procurement Staff in France. Like hundreds of his fellow burghers, Leclerc had become a senior link between the Nazis and the black market. Jewellery, caviare, the finest Burgundies. Metals from gold to ball bearings, which were even more precious. Of course, the cornering of markets and consequent ballooning of prices were exactly the crimes that the Nazis had always attributed to the Jews. An irony which was somehow lost on loyal officers of the Reich.

There was a specific Nazi excuse for wallowing belly-deep in the loot of the black market. Since black marketeers frequently sold information concerning the Resistance, the Nazis were forced to lubricate these contacts in the struggle against terrorism. The fabulous private wealth accumulated along the way was to be regarded as an irrelevant by-product.

Leclerc turned down Rue des Abbesses and entered a large café. Gus watched from the street as a waiter brought

Leclerc a Campari and soda without having been asked to do so. Obviously, Leclerc was a regular here. This little jaunt was out of his way, to say the least, yet he made it often. The most logical explanation would be repeated meetings with a clandestine contact. This would explain the stroll around Montmartre, as he probably did not wish to arrive too far in advance of the appointed time. The contact could be Resistance, Nazi, or perhaps simply a lover.

Within a few minutes, Leclerc was joined by a companion. From her youth and appearance, Gus might have taken her for Leclerc's mistress. However, she was accompanied by her daughter, a ravishing child of two or three with strawberry-blonde hair.

Willoughby had said Leclerc was without a wife or any significant romantic attachment. From the look of it, Willoughby might have to revise his file.

The woman kissed Leclerc warmly. Her slender fingers covered his hand as she sat beside him. She was an astonishing beauty. Black hair spilling over frail shoulders. Huge eyes of pure, startling grey.

Gus' first thought was that Leclerc couldn't be the child's father, for the little girl was so very blonde. His next thought, however, was that the woman was simply the most beautiful creature – no, the most exquisite single thing – he had ever laid his eyes on. She was, in his first glance, the calling forth of ancient dreams.

It was a delicious sensation. There, full within him, was the first woman Gus had ever known as beautiful. She was a housemaid in a home they visited one summer. By a lake. A young woman, slim, with black hair and milky skin. He was eleven, and when she flashed that private, wicked smile at him, he could not name the warmth that coursed through him.

There came a vivid replaying of his earliest fantasies of Paris. To leave Connecticut forever and live alone in some rain-and-colour-drenched quarter. Paint and write and truly fall in love. To finally do, to finally feel, that right and perfect and joyous something that had to be waiting.

There were other distant images flickering now through his mind, but a single thought swept them away. Gus was searching for the last woman he had simply wanted at first sight. It was terribly sad and terribly funny to find that he couldn't remember one. Not with the head-snapping jolt that he wanted this one.

The smile that crept forth was reserved for those moments when Gus was laughing at himself. Where, he asked, have your values gone? Long fingers, a slender throat. Large eyes. She may be stupid; she may be cheap. She may, and now the smile truly widened, be a bad person. Doggies. His mind replayed its devastating imitation of his mother, referring to the sexual ecumenicism of Gus' father and other males. All of them, just little doggies. And Gus' sense of outrage that she had somehow excluded him from the class of the condemned.

Gus fought back the surge towards remembering exactly where he was. He owed the nameless Lady of the Grey Eyes a debt. She had given him a simple moment of feeling good. She had restored a tender fragment of his boyhood, and reminded him that there was past and flesh and more things to him than the work he had begun. There was no reality to her of any kind, and this had made his moment of staring through the glass all the more precious.

If he walked through the door and into that café, all spells would shatter. The three-day idyll that had begun with Willoughby and the tiny plane, that had brought him to a magical instant of longing and recall, would be ended. Reality would resume and, Gus knew with a sickening clarity of vision, would continue unabated for the few remaining days of his life.

Gus realized that his moment was the first letting go, the first of his goodbyes to everything he had been. Hands thrust into his pockets, he entered the café.

He chose a table, far too near them. He couldn't pretend, even to himself, that he was studying Leclerc. There was an attraction, a thrill simply to watch her, that was clearly obsessive. She was not of this war, and the sight of her was his only thread back to life.

She stood. Leclerc cuddled the child, kissing her full cheeks. Mother and daughter were gone.

Slowly, Gus walked to the table. He sat down across from Leclerc.

'My name is Lang,' he said in French, with an easy smile. 'Petals on a lake, swept before the wind. The cleansing breath of rain.'

Leclerc listened to the prearranged code words. He seemed composed. His eyes flicked across the room one last time. Perhaps this was as good a place as any.

They talked for less than five minutes. Essential information was exchanged in the tone of a pleasant business conversation. Leclerc promised a list of names, addresses.

'Nothing in writing,' Gus had said. 'Tell me now.'

Leclerc had complied, watching Gus' clear green eyes concentrating on each word.

'Your wife and daughter,' Gus said at last, 'are very beautiful.'

Leclerc smiled, but there was a moment before the smile. A moment of private feeling that Gus thought far more visible than professional competence should permit.

'Her name is Claire Jouvet,' Leclerc said, the smile belatedly relaxed and open. 'She is not my wife. Claire makes jewellery. She is also a forger for Jade Amicol. What you saw a moment ago was her cover. She poses as my mistress.'

He leaned on the word *poses*, as if to emphasize that her role was contrary to fact. To Gus' ear, this provided a reverse twist. Either the woman was in fact his lover, or Leclerc wished it were so.

'And her husband?' Gus asked.

Leclerc studied him for a moment.

'Little Amy's father is British,' Leclerc said. 'He and Claire never married. He has been sent to a concentration camp at Royal-Lieu. She loves him very much. She is devoted to him.'

It was said most convincingly. There was no discernible evidence of falsehood. Still, the man had answered a bit more than Gus had asked. Gus' doubt was only a sniff, but a strong one.

Gus nodded, his face a mask of discreet sympathy.

'And the little girl?' he asked in a neutral tone.

'Amy is bilingual, a very bright and sensitive child. She is her mother's only comfort.'

Gus didn't think or plan. The words simply came from him.

'Tomorrow morning, I report to the SD. From that moment, I will be under constant surveillance. There will be no opportunity to contact you or anyone like you.'

Leclerc's eyes were attentive. He had no real foretaste of where Gus was headed.

'Still,' Gus said, 'I will need to be in contact with London on nearly a daily basis.'

Leclerc still did not understand.

'Therefore,' Gus said calmly, 'I will arrange to meet Mademoiselle Jouvet socially. She will assume cover as my girl-friend for the duration of my assignment. She will be my link to you.'

Leclerc's face darkened in spite of himself, but his voice remained low and controlled.

'It is out of the question,' he said. 'I absolutely forbid it. I have a responsibility to protect Claire from anything so dangerous. I will not see Amy become an orphan.'

Gus was smiling easily through Leclerc's outburst, absorbing the hostility. Now, the smile faded. The icy glare locked into place.

'What,' Gus asked very softly, 'do you know about my mission?'

The question had come quite unexpectedly.

'Nothing,' came the response. It was an obvious lie. The beat, the eyes, the muscles of his face.

'The next time,' Gus said, and now the eyes were burning, 'that you lie to me, monsieur, you will never hear of me again. And that will be a sad day indeed for your people, monsieur, make no mistake. The saddest day you could possibly imagine.'

A moment of indecision washed over Leclerc. It was composed of calculation and emotion. But in the end, the fierce green eyes across the table counselled Leclerc not to escalate. Not for the moment.

'There is a prisoner,' Leclerc said evenly. He did not drop his voice, because they were surrounded by strangers, and nothing would attract attention more clearly than a sharply lowered voice.

Gus nodded for him to continue.

'The prisoner,' Leclerc said, 'has information concerning a landing. He must be eliminated.'

Gus held Leclerc's eyes.

'There *is* no landing,' Gus said quietly, 'unless I succeed. It will be scrapped, replanned. It will take more than a year. I want you to think about your people and the next twelve months under present conditions.'

The heat was slowly draining from Leclerc. He was starting to think again.

'Let me introduce myself,' Gus said softly. 'I'm your last chance. And I trust you a hell of a lot less than you trust me. Let me tell you something else. I'm the best there is. That's why I'm here.'

Gus watched the muscles of Leclerc's shoulders as they slowly released.

'I'm a professional,' Gus said, 'not a martyr. My life means more to me than you and your whole fucking country, monsieur. Bet on that. The first moment I sense something unreliable behind my back, I disappear. I'll watch the next twelve months from Switzerland, and you'll watch them from right where you are. Do you understand?'

There was a moment. Then a small grim nod.

As with Macklin, Gus was indispensable to this man. Gus knew that this would be his last easy victory, the final time he would hold the cards. He wanted only to end this cleanly, leaving matters in optimum position for what lay ahead. Gus sensed that nothing should undercut the clarity of his dominance.

'Every decision,' Gus said flatly, 'every detail, every

inflection is mine. If I tell you to kiss my ass on top of the Bastille at high noon, your only question is what colour lipstick.'

Now Gus was sifting through the resentment in Leclerc's eyes, analyzing for tone and colour. He searched for weakness, for the scent of envy that would signify submission to the new leader of the tribe. And despite the imperfect calculus of such a moment, Gus decided that he had seen enough. Leclerc would withdraw, would rationalize his obedience by the importance of Gus' mission.

The Lady of the Grey Eyes would now become Gus' lifeline.

TWENTY-ONE

Ernst Ritter glanced up from his desk. He couldn't deny that this was a most refreshing surprise. Before him was a proud figure of Aryan manhood. Golden hair swept back, standing tall and erect. This might be an Abwehr agent, but he would be magnificent in the black and silver of the SS.

'Captain Lang, welcome to Paris. Sit down, please. I expect that your journey has been an arduous one.' Ritter's English was accented and not entirely comfortable. Unsmiling, Gus responded in far better German.

'Thank you, Standartenführer. I am rested, fit for duty.'

Gus paused for a moment, as if not wishing to seem presumptuous.

'I understood that I was to receive my orientation from the Oberführer.'

Gus was still standing. Muscles taut, face correctly expressionless. Ritter liked that. His eyes moved over Gus. He liked the boy's German, an accent from the north. Ritter detested southerners, the Führer's heritage notwithstanding.

Ritter was tapping a pencil softly against the desktop. He was in no hurry to answer the question about the Oberführer. He would prefer to evaluate Gus' reaction to nonresponsive behaviour. Gus remained motionless, eyes clear and direct. Ritter released a smile very slowly.

'Please do sit down, Captain. Make yourself comfortable.' Ritter had returned to his native language. The balance of the interview would be conducted entirely in German.

Gus returned the smile.

'I am comfortable, Standartenführer.'

Gus sat. He said nothing further. Ritter had objected when Brausch added Gus to the team, but now the doubts were fading. Ritter was given to hunches, to reliance on first impressions. There was something in the bearing of this boy that was truly delightful. Something dead-centre right about him. The way he sat. Attentive, respectful, but still at his ease.

'There has been a change of schedule,' Ritter said. 'We have time for a chat before the Oberführer arrives.'

Gus understood that this chat would be an SS interrogation. Probably the first of many. He made no response to Ritter, for none was indicated. His eyes were calm and alert, his body quite still. All of this registered to Ritter's continuing approval.

Ritter offered a French cigarette. Gus declined. Ritter undid the top two buttons of his tunic and eased back in his seat. He was reaching for a tone of intimacy. To Gus, the effort was noticeable.

'Your people,' Ritter said with nearly a smirk, 'are from Bavaria?' This was a joke, and intended to be received as such. Obviously, Ritter would have read Gus' dossier, stating that his parents came from Saxony in the north. Gus had seen a profile on Ritter, and knew that he was from neighbouring Schleswig-Holstein. The 'joke,' therefore, revealed Ritter's prejudice against the south. Gus knew that this was common among northerners. It was also an opportunity for Gus to form a bond with Ritter.

Gus bristled for an instant, as if taking Ritter's question as an insult. Then he smiled, as if realizing that the remark was in jest.

'Why are you smiling?' Ritter asked innocently.

'I was thinking of Bismarck, Standartenführer. He said that a Bavarian was a cross between a man and an Austrian.'

Ritter snorted an approving chuckle.

'That would be a dangerous quote in Berlin today,' Ritter said.

'The Führer,' Gus answered, 'seems an exception to a great many rules. My father is a prejudiced man in such matters. I suppose I am, after all, his son.'

'You speak our language quite beautifully, for an American. I must tell you, Captain, that I have always held considerable respect for your people.'

Ritter watched as Gus' shoulders, the muscles of his throat, appeared to stiffen. The green eyes fought to maintain composure.

'Please know, Standartenführer, that I am German. From my earliest childhood, I have known myself to be a German living in a foreign land. Americans are a people I have never fully understood. I find them talented in many ways, but weak and self-deluding. I do not hate them. For me, they are simply foreigners.'

Carefully, Gus pulled from his breast pocket a neatly folded sheet of tissue copy. He unfolded the sheet and handed it across to Ritter.

It was an *Ahnenliste*, an ancestry list, tracing Gus' Aryan bloodlines back four centuries. Each party member was required to have such a genealogy, and Ritter had studied many in his time. Rarely had he seen one more extensive or meticulous.

He looked across at the defiant pride shining in the eyes of this young man.

'I have risked my life,' Gus said quietly, 'each day for these past four years. Because I am German. In that, I am the equal of any man who wears your uniform.'

The conversation continued for thirty minutes. Gus'

primary training had been as an interrogator. It was evident that Ritter was not a professional of this trade, was not skilled in the use of its tools. Especially silence. Professionals sculpted an interview from silence. The metre, the rhythm of speech, was as essential as the words themselves. Each pause, abrupt or lingering, created the seamlessly shifting tone that was the hallmark of Gus' craft.

Ritter was not a professional, and could never be accorded the highest level of respect. There were, however, certain turns of phrase, lines of association, that revealed Ritter as surprisingly intelligent. There was no temptation to underestimate this man. Ritter would be presumed dangerous until proven otherwise.

Eventually, Ritter turned to a proud summary of the security precautions in place at Château de Vincennes, the prison where the Overlord was being held. Ritter had been responsible for designing and implementing these security measures, and he reviewed in loving detail each triple-checked facet of the system.

It was immediately evident to Gus that any thought of escape would be ludicrous. It would be easier for Andy Wheeler to break into Fort Knox than to break out of Vincennes.

They chatted further. Ritter was lighting his fourth cigarette. A strange look came to his eyes. Fleeting, but so bittersweet that Gus' belly instantly tightened.

'What is your assessment,' Ritter asked slowly, 'of the Jewish problem in America?'

Gus' eyes were reflective, as if giving the matter serious thought. This line of questioning would clearly provide the turning point of the interview.

'I would say, Standartenführer, that I lack the knowledge necessary to form a judgment on this question.'

Ritter had hoped for something considerably more direct.

'What, then,' he asked, 'are your feelings about American Jewry? Surely you have feelings in the matter.'

'The Jews I have known in America, I tend to think of simply as Americans.'

Ritter formed a tight smile.

'Similarly, then, are German Jews simply Germans?'

'No,' Gus said quietly. 'What Jews are, what Americans are, I do not really understand. Germans are a people.'

Ritter filled his lungs from the cigarette.

'A race?' he asked.

'A people,' came Gus' answer. His eyes were firm and calm. 'Race is a question of science, and I am not a scientist.'

Ritter's tight smile returned. Was it playful? Gus sensed that it was not a smile at all, but a nervous reflex. A mannerism that defended against the revealing of an aggressive impulse. Gus took the smile as the warning rattle of a snake.

'The Führer,' Ritter said at last, 'teaches that *Jews* are a race.'

Gus logged this as reinforcing his theory about the smile.

'Perhaps he is right,' Gus said.

'Perhaps?' And now Ritter's smile had screwed itself into the rictus of a corpse. Frozen on his face, it had become the antithesis of a smile.

'Do you think,' Gus asked, 'that the Führer is infallible?'

Ritter did not respond.

'I think,' Gus said, 'that he is a man. A man who has accomplished something that no man has before. A man whose true teaching is what one single man is capable of achieving.'

Ritter's doubt, his tension, began slowly to release. The signs were quite minor, but perceptible.

'Human history,' Gus concluded, 'is strewn with gods. Such a man is rarer than any god.'

This was the clincher. It struck Ritter as at once profound and poetic. He made a mental note to appropriate the phrase for his own use.

Gus had passed his entrance exam. The chat wound itself down for ten more minutes.

Finally, the door opened.

Ritter was clearly taken aback by the figure of his

superior officer, who was dressed in a woollen turtleneck sweater rather than the black and silver of the SS. The man extended his hand to Gus.

'I am Walter Hoffmann,' he said. 'It is a lovely morning. Will you walk with me?'

TWENTY-TWO

Hoffmann led Gus back through the maze of corridors. In one arm, he carried a large sack.

'I had some sandwiches made,' he said in perfect English. 'There is some wine. I thought perhaps we could take our lunch in the park.'

He talked continuously in English as they moved through the building, pointing out facilities and personnel. Gus was given little opportunity to speak at all.

Hoffmann had designated English as the permanent language of their dialogue, quite as easily as Gus had imposed German upon Ritter. This was not simply a matter of Hoffmann's fluency, for there was a canon of craft involved. Gus had been taught always to force the use of his adversary's native language. It gave the man a subtly pervasive sense of being with his own kind. Hearing a foreign tongue, however, served as a constant reminder to keep defences at the ready.

The game of 'forcing the tongue' was usually the first round of battle between sparring professionals. If this precept was followed by the SD, and Gus had no reason to believe otherwise, it was a round that Hoffmann had instantly and effortlessly won.

Hoffmann led Gus down the steps to the sunlit boulevard. The SD, having requisitioned 72 Avenue Foch as its headquarters, had appropriated one of the most elegant addresses in the city. But Gus' eye was drawn not to the grace of the architecture or the expanse of the grounds, but rather to the waiting line of black limousines. In a city virtually devoid of automobiles, it was a display of power so conspicuous as to border on exhibitionism.

'You've noticed,' Hoffmann said, following his eye, 'that you're on the right side of this war after all.'

Gus smiled.

'Just resolved all my doubts,' Gus said, and Hoffmann smiled warmly in return. How easily, Gus noted, Hoffmann had dictated the ambience. Colloquial and entirely comfortable. Two like souls, discovering each other, drifting towards the beginnings of intimacy.

'Only the beginning,' Hoffmann said. 'We are kings in this city. Actually, we live more like Oriental potentates. I have a three-room suite at the Ritz, which is staggering in its opulence. Marble, antiques, exquisite Persian rugs. Yet my colleagues are mortified by my asceticism. They have taken entire homes in Garches and Marly. These places belonged to Jews or others who fled to the south.'

Gus watched Hoffmann's dark eyes as he spoke. They were telling Gus that, despite the lightness of his voice, Hoffmann found no pleasure in the situation.

'Ritter took a house in Neuilly,' Hoffmann continued. 'He has French servants in uniforms with white gloves. He eats with the silver and china and linen of some Jew who's locked in a camp at Drancy. He has black-market food and wine, and a most impressive gathering of Parisian society at his dinner parties.'

They just walked for a moment in silence.

'We are conquering Romans,' Hoffmann said quietly. 'We are Mongols. Which is to say, we are pigs.'

The dark eyes looked to Gus for affirmation. They saw only sympathetic concern for Hoffmann's own distress. Gus' personal feelings were not yet in evidence.

'If this occupation,' Hoffmann said, 'is intended to last for a thousand years, we've chosen a curious way to begin.'

'Are we talking about morality or efficiency?' Gus asked.

'We know everything about conquering,' Hoffmann said,

'and nothing about ruling. Sometimes morality is efficient, just because you're dealing with human beings.'

Gus smiled at the eloquence of Hoffmann's evasion.

'You should visit me on the Place des Ternes,' Gus said. 'It's a garret. Hot water on Thursdays. Four-flight walk-up. Exemplary austerity.'

The dark eyes studied Gus for an instant, and Gus was treated to his first wisp of the playful smile.

'It's the place that you always dreamed you'd have when you finally came to Paris,' Hoffmann said simply.

The accuracy was so precise and unexpected, Gus was nearly awestruck.

'Lifelong romantic,' Gus said with a boyish grin.

Again, the dark eyes held him for an instant.

'Calculating romantic,' Hoffmann corrected. 'You and I must be the last of the breed. Look, room wherever you like. It's a free country.'

Gus smiled in appreciation of Hoffmann's irresistible humour, his command of the American idiom. Inside, Gus was becoming a slowly clenched fist.

Gus had never been a man given to boasting, aloud or within his heart. Still, he had yet to meet an interrogator who he was certain could outsmart him. And now, from the first gentle smile and soft words of Walter Hoffmann, the conviction was rapidly forming within Gus that he had finally met just such a man. In fifteen minutes, Gus was as frightened of this man as anything he had faced in his life.

They strolled up the tree-lined Avenue Foch to the Bois de Boulogne. They sat on a thin cloth, under a tree. Hoffmann began each track from his personal experience. His wife, his youth. Days at the university. His children, his travels. Each line gently drawing Gus into sharing his own life, thoughts, emotions.

'My father . . .,' Hoffmann said at one point, and his eyes looked up through the broad leaves towards the sun. 'He was a quiet little man. A clerk. He worked with figures and he lived in his mind. He always wanted to travel, always . . . talked about it.'

Hoffmann grinned, shook his head.

'I don't suppose,' Hoffmann said, 'that he was ever more than two hundred kilometres from Bremen in his entire life. He was a man of values, you know. He knew the right of things. He knew the right thing was to give me love. He didn't know how to do it, of course. But he tried so damn hard, it was the same thing.'

And then Hoffmann just looked at Gus. Dark, liquid eyes so calm and so patient.

'Unfortunately,' Gus said, '*my* father is German.'

Hoffmann smiled. Unobtrusively, cooperatively. Coaxing the story on.

'Wealthy man,' Gus said. 'Clever, full of fun. On Sunday afternoons, if I was very lucky, I would be admitted to his presence. Usually, he preferred his mistress. Sometimes, he took me out with her. And while I was hating him, the sonofabitch would practically force me to love him. We had a hell of a time. We laughed. He could tell stories you'd never forget. He gave me a glimpse of everything delicious and thrilling in life. I saw it all there, right on his plate, in his eyes. In his arms.'

'Then,' Hoffmann said quietly, 'you would go back to your mother . . .'

'And she'd hold me,' Gus said, 'because she didn't have anything else to hold. There was nothing inside her but grief for her own walking death. She couldn't leave him and, God knows why, he wouldn't leave her. She wasn't a bad woman. But she was empty and shrivelled, and she was the one I was supposed to love. He was the guy I'd give anything to be, and then hated myself for feeling it, because there wasn't an ounce of character or compassion in his whole goddam gorgeous body.'

Gus looked across at Hoffmann, his enemy. They were playing the game. Baring their souls. Telling the truth, of course, because anything else would ring like stone on lead. But through it all, through whatever Hoffmann was doing with his mind, the miraculous, compelling, no doubt-about-it fact was that Hoffmann was actually listening. He understood. And in all his life, Gus could count those people on the fingers of one hand.

'My father,' Hoffmann said at last, 'always knew I was going to be a good person. Loving person. He didn't know it, of course, he just assumed it. Couldn't see me any other way. He only wanted one thing for me. He told me all my life. Told me from his deathbed. One thing that, strangely enough, never meant a goddam thing to me.'

And now, the playful smile again.

'He wanted,' Hoffmann said, 'for me to be rich.'

It was Gus' turn to understand. To feel the cord pulling him to this man.

'My father,' Gus said, 'made me rich whether I liked it or not. He never asked my opinion about that or anything else.'

'Was it so very terrible to have money?'

Gus smiled to himself, reached inside himself for the truth of that one.

'Yeah,' Gus said. 'In a funny way. If you have something all your life, you never notice it at all. It's air, it's water, it's just part of the natural world around you. The pleasure in something is wanting it badly, wanting it, wanting it, and then somehow making it happen . . .'

He stopped. There was a thought that had never been inside him quite that way. There was a flickering question as to whether he should censor.

'Love,' Gus said suddenly. 'I had to learn about love from feeling the lack of it. So I guess the old man left me one thing I still have to find on my own.'

And the dark eyes were there waiting. Acknowledging, affirming. Learning Gus with each breath.

'Well, said Hoffmann quietly, 'look at it this way . . . your father sent you on the better quest.'

They ate and drank. They watched children with their boats on the pond. Never had Gus felt his inner self being sucked from him so skilfully, so inexorably. His gut was one solid knot from the tension of his concentration, as the chat stretched to two hours, then three. Hoffmann's warmth seemed so genuine, his skill so natural and comfortable.

In another world, Gus would have given anything to be this man's pupil. To be his friend.

They walked through the woods, to the edge of Lac Inférieur. The French had to queue up to rent boats. Germans had priority, and asserted their privilege with deliberate arrogance.

Hoffmann and Gus watched the scene without speaking. The tears of a four-year-old as his father pulled him from the tiny boat, relinquishing their claim to an abusive young soldier. The German had a scrawny, dead-eyed French doxy and a small Gramophone with a crank. The girl took the oar, while the soldier lay back. The Gramophone rested on his belly and sent German music sweeping across the lake at an obnoxious volume. Germans would call raucously to each other from neighbouring boats.

Hoffmann turned to Gus, and his smile was more of pity than disgust.

'The master race,' Hoffmann said, and his eyes returned to the lake.

At last the music stopped. A sudden calm fell over the scene. Boats drifted noiselessly now, and Gus could hear the movement of the wind. He lay back in the grass, watching Hoffmann as if from a great distance.

After a while, Gus became aware that Hoffmann was now staring at something quite specific. Gus followed his line of sight. There were three girls across the lake. Arms linked, they moved purposefully along the path, eight, perhaps ten, years old. The linked arms did not seem a children's game. There was no bounce, no gaiety. They were simply clinging together.

'Jews,' Hoffmann said.

The tone was neutral, but the word sent a shiver through Gus that he couldn't blame on the wind. He strained his eyes at the figures. There was no way Hoffmann could see a star on their clothing at such a distance. Still, Hoffmann knew.

And as Gus watched, he imagined that he knew as well.

There was a terror and a defiance that Gus imported into their gait. They were lost children.

The girls rounded the far corner of the lake and disappeared. Gus never saw their faces.

Hoffmann was still staring after them.

'Did Colonel Ritter solicit your feelings about the Jews?' he asked.

'He tried.'

Hoffmann turned sharply to Gus. His gaze was level and more intense than Gus had yet seen.

'Now I'm trying,' Hoffmann said.

'How well do I know you?' Gus smiled.

'Not at all,' came the softly spoken answer, and the dark eyes softened with it.

Gus looked down at his hands, then back up to Hoffmann's eyes.

'I don't understand it,' Gus said. 'I never have. If some of them are criminals, they should pay. But an entire people . . .'

'It's a sickness,' Hoffmann said. 'Hating Jews, killing them, is a monstrous disease. It's highly contagious and hugely debilitating. No one who's caught it has ever been worth a damn again.'

They were amazing words. Words that Gus had no right to believe from the lips of an SS Oberführer. And yet, Gus more than half believed that Hoffmann meant every word. And the damnedest thing was, Gus still didn't know if Hoffmann was talking about morality or efficiency. He was beginning to sense that this was not evasion after all, but that Hoffmann had somehow fused the two in a synthesis that made the distinction superfluous.

'There is a board in Paris,' Hoffmann said, 'called the Commissariat Générale aux Questions Juives, the CGQJ. They have offices in the Place des Petits-Pères. And every day a line will form of frightened people trying to buy Certificates of Aryanization. Begging, bribing, whatever. Some are Jews, some are not. All huddled pitifully together. Finally brothers.'

'This board,' Gus asked, 'they are Frenchman?'
Hoffmann nodded.
'Very contagious,' Hoffmann repeated. 'We have brought the best of our German way of life to the heathen. We are in the conversion business, and business is brisk.'
Hoffmann smiled sadly.
'At first,' he said, 'it was simple and symbolic. Banning the music of Jewish composers in the cabarets. Renaming the Sarah Bernhardt Theatre. Then, Jews must ride in the rear car of the Métro. They could not use public telephones. Had to wear the cloth star over their hearts, and trade textile coupons for the privilege. They were banned from restaurants and cinemas, eventually all public buildings.'
And Gus was aware again that Hoffmann was reaching into his eyes. Reading, learning.
'There were exceptions, of course,' Hoffmann went on. 'Pétain drew up a list of *dérogations* for favoured Jews. Friends, some with royal titles. The Reich had its own exceptions. Jews who were "economically useful." Then came the Wannsee Conference. Have you heard of it?'
Gus had not.
'Two years ago, the leadership of the SS held a conference. They developed a 'final solution' to their problem. It was to be implemented by a man named Karl Adolf Eichmann, head of the Gestapo's Jewish Office. Do you know what that solution was?'
Final solution, he had said. Final.
'Kill them,' Hoffmann said. 'Kill them all. Kill every Jew on the face of the earth.'
Gus' eyes were uncomprehending.
'It is true,' Hoffmann said. 'It is policy. It has already begun.'
Hoffmann watched as the weight and depth of it began to bleed back to him through Gus' eyes.
'So,' Hoffmann said, 'there are still some questions to be settled about this Reich of ours. The German people still must decide what it is truly to be. And first, you and I are going into the dungeon of Vincennes prison to meet a boy

named Wheeler. You and I are going to win this war, Gus, you and I. And despite every feeling I have shared with you today, there is no weakening of my resolve. Do you know why that is?'

Gus knew. He surely did.

'Because,' Gus said quietly, 'the only alternative to winning this war is to lose it.'

Hoffmann nodded very slowly.

'Have you ever seen,' Hoffmann asked, 'a country after it has lost a war? Not like the French, not a swift and merciful surrender. Can you dream what it would be to lose this war to the Russians?'

Hoffmann's eyes were now very far away.

'You think of every village and every farm and every orphaned child,' Hoffmann said. 'Sewage in the streets. The splintered bones of old people. You think of the minds that will be shattered in one month of horror. Never to be mended. And if these are your people, *your* people, then you put aside the pigs like Ritter and the helpless Jews and the rest of it . . . and you go down into that prison and you make that boy tell you what he knows.'

TWENTY-THREE

One by one, Gus moved through the streets and alleys of the Saint-Séverin quarter, trying each of the places Leclerc had given him. From Rue Saint-Jacques to Rue Dante, to the Boulevard Saint-Germain.

At last he came to a self-service luncheonette near the Sorbonne. It was three o'clock and the place had nearly emptied. A woman sat in the window reading the German-sponsored magazine *Signal*. In the far corner, a boy in a smudged apron was beginning to stack chairs on tables. He moved with excruciating slowness.

Somewhere in between, Claire sat alone with her newspaper and tea. Three tables away, Amy was standing on a chair, intently peering down at a red tablecloth.

Amy had poured most of the salt from its cellar onto the table, and her fingers arranged and rearranged the salt into various patterns.

Gus walked to Amy's table.

Staring only at the salt, he sat down very slowly. He was across the table, safely too far away to reach her. His hands were in his lap at first, so that he would appear as non-threatening as possible. His face was a portrait of concentration on the salt pile before him.

Amy watched with some uneasiness.

Gus chewed his fingertips in a pantomime of thoughtful anxiety. Amy giggled in spite of herself.

Finally, Gus picked up the pepper cellar. His hand moved slowly, slowly towards Amy's salt pile, his eyes growing wider and wider in anticipation. The closer he got, the slower he moved. Amy giggled again, her little hands flying up to her mouth, as if to stifle the sound.

Slowly, Gus poured the pepper from a great height down onto the salt pile, Grain by grain, little black snowflakes. Amy's fingers were twisting her blonde hair in utter delight.

When the pepper was gone, Gus reached over with one finger and traced it through the black and white pile again and again. Geometric patterns. A face. An indefinable animal with four legs and a tail.

For the first time, Gus looked up from the table. He found Amy's eyes, brown and grey and olive. Dark and altogether beautiful.

'Do you know what that is? he said softly in English. Leclerc had said she was bilingual.

'What?' she said.

'It's a big . . . mess!'

Laughter.

'No,' she said, 'it's a doggie.'

Gus looked at his design with renewed interest. He turned his head this way and that.

'Is it a pig?' he said at last.

'No, a doggie,' she insisted.

He nodded thoughtfully.

'What's his name?' Gus asked.

'I don't know,' she beamed to a singsong tune.

'His name,' Gus said, 'is . . . *doggie*!'

This struck Amy as one of the two or three funniest things ever said. She dissolved in giggles and mushed the salt and pepper around, making the doggie disappear.

Gus looked into her eyes very gravely.

'Are you a cowboy?' he asked.

'No.'

'Are you a big girl?'

'No, I'm a *little* girl.'

'I knew that,' he said.

A hand appeared at Amy's shoulder.

As Gus looked up, his heart was pounding full in his throat. He could hardly keep from laughing at himself, because his only thought was, She's actually smiling at *me*. She might as well have been Ingrid Bergman or Hedy Lamarr.

And she was indeed smiling. An easy smile of unexpected warmth. Grey eyes sizzling, without half trying.

'May I join you?' Her English seemed American, with only the softest trace of accent.

Gus looked back to Amy.

'Who's that?' he asked.

'That my mama.'

'Can she sit with us?'

Amy thought about it, but said nothing. Mama sat anyway.

'We were drawing a piggie,' he said to Claire. Amy squealed that it was a doggie, and laughed wildly at their private joke.

It was evident right off that even looking at Claire made it difficult to speak. For no good reason, he had imagined a demure porcelain doll. Here was a woman thoroughly at ease and confident.

Gus tried the closest thing to a winning smile that he could find.

'You're thinking,' he said, 'twenty-fourth guy this week trying to pick me up by making friends with the short blonde person.'

Her smile heated up a little. She tossed her head with a quick motion, black hair flying across her shoulder.

'Fifty-fourth,' she said. 'But you're the best at it I've seen in a while.'

Something, maybe in the voice. Something permitted Gus a moment's fantasy that she might be attracted to him. He fought this off as total insanity.

'Any chance at all?' he asked.

'I'm thinking it over,' she said. 'This is what I look like when I'm thinking it over.'

Her eyes were intelligent. They seemed very much in control.

He didn't know whether Leclerc had contacted her. With all his heart, he wanted nothing more in life than to be someone else. Never to tell her that he was Gus Lang.

'I'm Gus Lang,' he said.

The light slowly died away from behind her eyes. He had his answer.

'Look,' he said, 'you don't have to do it.'

The huge grey eyes, suddenly so cool and impersonal, flickered across his face.

'Armand said I had no choice,' she said quietly.

Gus looked at her for the longest moment, wondering what alternatives were left to him. She was perfect for this, beyond any plan or dream. Still, he would find another way.

'I changed my mind,' he said. 'That's all.'

She waited for the hook. There was none.

'And why did you change your mind?' she asked cautiously.

In answer, Gus' eyes looked to Amy, now intent on drawing her own doggie in the salt pile.

'Heartwarming,' Claire said dryly.

Now he was angry. The heat flashed straight up to his eyes.

'Is it okay if I actually *like* your kid, lady? Do you and your Armand have me all figured out, or are you gonna allow me one honest feeling?'

And once again, Gus watched what she looked like while thinking it over. Very slowly, her smile returned.

'If you play your cards right,' she said, 'maybe I'll allow you two.'

If there was flirtation implicit in the line, it had passed Gus entirely. He felt only relief that he was still in the running.

'My contact,' he said, 'has to be someone I can see every day. It could only be a girl friend. If the Germans object to my dating as an unwise distraction, and they might, I have to tell them that I won't give the girl up. My stubbornness is going to be less suspicious if my girl friend is . . . irresistible.'

There was no sound of flattery or calculation in his voice. Only the vulnerability of a man speaking the truth.

'I picked you,' he said, 'for that reason. You're the most beautiful woman I've ever seen.'

And her smile unleashed all of its dazzling power.

'Two,' she said softly.

He did not understand.

'Honest feelings,' she reminded him. 'You use them this well, maybe I'll allow you three or four.'

TWENTY-FOUR

The tracking had begun. The first shift was reading his paper in the lobby when Gus came down for breakfast.

Gus had moved from his garret to a room at the elegant George V. This was against his desires, but in accordance with his better judgment. The garret had been a conspicuous eccentricity which could only attract the wrong kind of attention.

The tracker sat as Gus finished his morning chocolate,

then followed him into the avenue at a respectful distance of forty metres.

Gus played tourist throughout the day. There were four trackers, on rotating three-hour shifts. Gus led them around carefully, testing the leash. Losing each man for a moment, then reappearing. The trick, of course, was to maintain the fiction that he was unaware of being followed at all. Within this framework, Gus was slowly learning each of the four, noting their patterns and individual weaknesses.

Overall, he had to admit that these guys were a little better than he expected. He assumed, therefore, that they were more likely SD than Gestapo.

Gus waited for the end of the day, until the fourth shift had just arrived for duty. The new man was powerfully built, looking slightly out of place in his neat business suit. He was given to quick, athletic movement, which contrasted perceptibly with the placid mask of his face. Apart from this, his clothing and demeanour were almost painfully bland. He was, in short, a man trying to hide in a crowd.

They were on Rue Saint Honoré. Gus entered a large men's store with several exits. The tracker was forced to follow him into the store, since he couldn't predict which exit Gus might wander out. Gus looked casually in the tracker's general direction. Instinctively, the man turned his back to Gus, fingering the nearest available merchandise.

When he turned back, Gus was gone. The man rushed to the street, the alley. Gus had vanished.

Fifty metres up the alley, Gus sat motionless in the shadow of a butcher's stairwell. He sat in perfect stillness for twenty minutes, then slipped down a side street and into the Métro tunnel at Palais-Royal.

Gus was not at all pleased that he had been forced to lose his tracker. One never knew when such an incident might trigger increased surveillance, perhaps two-or-three-man teams. Still, this evening there was simply no alternative.

Gus made his way to the Left Bank, to a small decaying hotel on the Rue des Écoles. Five-flight walk-up. He knocked at the door to number 47. Hearing nothing, he tripped the latch.

The slumped figure beneath the lamp was enormous in the smallness of the room. Jürgen Brausch seemed so weary as he studied Gus, his watering eyes resting on puffy bags of flesh. There was no smile, no reflection of any thought or emotion. Only pale, tired eyes absorbing what was to be seen.

'I apologize,' Brausch said at last, 'for not inviting you to my suite at the Majestic. It really is quite pleasant there.'

Gus looked around at the limited selection of seedy furniture. He pulled up a rickety cane chair and sat in silence.

It was Brausch's turn now to look about the room. He shook his head.

'Colourful surroundings,' Brausch admitted, 'but they do offer privacy.'

Gus still had said nothing. This struck Brausch as reassuring. Gus' ease in silence was accepted almost as the passing of a code word, the identification of a colleague.

'You seem younger than I had expected,' Brausch said.

'Clean living,' Gus said softly. 'Inside I'm old and very tired.'

Brausch settled back in his overstuffed wing chair. He had not actually smiled yet, but he seemed discernibly more relaxed.

'So,' Brausch said, 'two tired old men. Enjoying their moment of privacy.'

'It's like heaven,' Gus agreed.

And Brausch smiled. The smile was a reward, transforming his face into the equivalent of a comfortable leather chair.

'What,' Brausch asked, 'has the world told you about me?'

'Geoffrey Macklin thinks you're a patriot.'

Brausch shook his head very slightly.

'Sir Geoffrey *calls* me a patriot,' Brausch corrected. 'He doesn't know what to think of me. If I am as I present myself, I may be of use. If I am otherwise, I may be the greatest British mistake of this war.'

A trace of delight crossed the sagging eyes.

'Bringing you here,' Brausch said, 'was my idea, not Macklin's. That is what drives him mad. He cannot dismiss the possibility that I intend to use you against him. With a mind like Macklin's, it is difficult to sleep at night.'

Gus nodded.

'How do you sleep?' Gus asked.

The wisp of a smile returned.

'Like the dead,' Brausch answered. 'But then, I know who I am.'

He studied Gus for a moment.

'Fact is,' Brausch added, 'I know all the players present. With the possible exception of you.'

'I'll give you one question,' Gus smiled. 'No charge.'

Brausch's eyes lingered as they moved across Gus' face.

'The important question is,' Brausch said slowly, 'do you savour fine gin?'

Gus thought it over. 'Yes.'

With considerable effort, Brausch extracted himself from the depths of the chair. He opened the drawer of a warped little dresser. Inside were two glasses and a bottle wrapped in brown paper. He pulled off the paper, holding up a fresh quart of Booth's.

Gus nodded his approval.

Brausch turned his huge back to Gus while he poured at the sideboard.

'If I hadn't liked you,' Brausch said, 'I would have hoarded this for myself.'

He handed over a glass filled with close to four fingers. Gus raised it in a toast.

'To German hospitality,' he said.

Brausch acknowledged and took a deep swallow.

'This is not,' Brausch said, 'your first experience of our hospitality. I heard passing mention of your lunch in the park.'

'Cheese was fair. The wine was better.'

Brausch nodded as if this were quite responsive.

'And what,' Brausch asked, 'was your opinion of our Colonel Hoffmann?'

'I wish he were on our side,' Gus said.

Brausch let the smile slowly melt from his features. His face now commanded attention by its very stillness. The eyes said, Listen to what comes next, if you listen to one thing the rest of your life.

'He . . . is . . . not . . .,' Brausch said with chilling deliberation. 'Never, never let anything that may happen cause you to doubt that. It would be the end of you, the end of everything.'

A heavy sigh escaped, but his eyes still held Gus. They were burdened eyes. They had been rolling the stone uphill for a long time now. They knew what was required.

'I wish,' Brausch said, 'that I had a needle and a serum. To inoculate you against Walter. Against growing . . . fond . . . of Walter.'

There was something in the weariness of the man, a sense of dignity through exhaustion and despair. It impelled loyalty as clearly as Hoffmann's empathy and charm.

'Walter and his kind,' Brausch said, 'are the true causes of this war. For Walter is not a monster. And without Walter, the monsters would still be brooding in some beer hall in Bavaria.'

And, Gus thought, either you are telling the perfect truth or a perfect lie. It was at least as likely that Hoffmann and Brausch had created this scenario for Gus' benefit. Make Gus choose sides, so that in trusting one of them, either of them, he would become their pawn in a double-wire back to London.

The weight of Gus' aloneness now, the pressure of it, was crushing his bones as surely as if he were miles beneath the sea.

'You've hardly touched your gin,' Brausch said, and raised his glass.

Slowly, as if it were the most natural thing in the world,

Brausch began to offer Gus his life story. Childhood in Cologne. Travels, studies, heroes.

At first, the technique seemed a repeat of Hoffmann's approach. After a short time, however, one distinction became quite apparent. Brausch did not permit Gus to speak at all. As he talked, he merely watched Gus' eyes with a steady, penetrating gaze. Either Brausch was reading Gus at a higher, more intuitive, level than Hoffmann had been able to, or he was looking for something entirely different.

Whether it was the hour or the gin or the emotions growing within Gus, he was certain that he had now become the subject of the ultimate interrogation. A questioning in which the subject only listened.

Too, there was the fascination with the scope of Brausch's life. Heroic achievements were modestly treated as passing footnotes. From his days with Crown Prince Rupert to his service for Hindenburg. His adventures with master spy Wilhelm Canaris, the founder of the Abwehr. Brausch's life was a road map of German military intelligence in this century. Could such a man now be serving London? Yet, could such a man ever serve Hitler? Both seemed categorically impossible.

'There is no one,' Brausch said, 'who knows of my contact with Geoffrey Macklin. No one. I am friendly with many of the officers of the Schwarze Kapelle, men who plot to assassinate Hitler. They trust me with their secret, with their lives. I honour that trust. Still, I do not return it.'

That flat neutral look passed again over his eyes. It was a stillness that was anything but passive. It was the calm that revealed bottomless strength.

'I have trusted no one,' Brausch said, 'and I will certainly never trust you. Please accept that.'

Gus did. Every word.

'Neither will you trust me,' Brausch continued. 'Nonetheless, it will be our duty and our pleasure to work together. And at the end . . . lose our lives together.'

This was said without drama. It was said as fact. A firm blow with a blunt instrument.

'I know you fear that I will ultimately betray you,' Brausch said. 'Hold onto all your fears. Identify them, understand them. Otherwise, you will be ineffective.'

He spoke the word *ineffective* as if it were a most contemptible sin.

They talked on. Time had ceased to be a matter for the clock, and was now measured in gin. They had talked another four fingers.

'Sir Geoffrey,' Gus said at one point, 'holds you to be a hero. He says you are his ace in the hole. The most precious card of all.'

Brausch looked at him for the longest moment. The strangest thing was that Brausch no longer seemed weary. He had somehow gained strength with the passing of time and the gin. He was fresh now and very vital.

'I am,' he said, 'a card that has already been played.'

Gus didn't understand.

'I created Emerald,' Brausch said. 'You are my agent. Do you think that you can kill Major Wheeler without implicating me?'

The heavy eyebrows lifted.

'Fact of the matter,' Brausch said, 'I don't know yet how it will be possible for you to kill him at all.'

Gus thought for a fraction of a beat. Go down the road for now.

'Sir Geoffrey spoke of a cyanide capsule,' Gus offered.

Brausch muttered something in German that included the word *einfält*, stupidity.

'Sir Geoffrey,' Brausch said, 'has been reading cheap fiction. Believe me, Standartenführer Ritter will have you subjected to a strip search so thorough you couldn't smuggle an aspirin tablet in there. They will shine a light into orifices you didn't even know you had. The same for all of us when we are to be with the prisoner.'

As far as Gus was concerned, this was so much the better.

Gus eased into his explanation of the decoy scenario, training Andy Wheeler to plant the tale of a false invasion. If Andy could not be eliminated, the only hope would be to use him to advantage. The plan had developed considerable detail and refinement since it was first exposed to Macklin. Only a part of this detail was now revealed to Brausch.

Throughout, Brausch listened attentively, his face thoroughly opaque. When Gus had finished, Brausch drew a heavy breath.

'Problem is,' Brausch said gently, 'that when decoys are finally discovered, interrogators have a tendency to read the scenario in reverse.'

Gus smiled.

'Ah,' Gus said, 'but there's a trick to it.'

'And that is . . . ?'

'Don't get caught.'

The shaggy eyebrows rose in mock astonishment. The old man was genuinely amused, whether by Gus' manner or stupidity Gus couldn't tell.

'Now,' Brausch said, 'that puts an entirely different light on the matter. Would you mind, Captain, if I bought you another drink?'

TWENTY-FIVE

Gus stood at the door. This was about as nervous as he could get without bursting major arteries. He had nothing to say. He should go home, write some things down. Unfortunately, he had already rung the bell.

Another minute took its own sweet time to pass. Gus stood clutching his bunch of violets and listening to a quart of blood go pounding past his temples and into his ears. It was just the kind of moment that usually found Gus able to laugh at himself. This, however, was an exception. A definite exception.

Without any decent form of warning, Claire opened the door.

There really wasn't much he could do except look at her and hold onto his violets. Black hair swept back behind perfect ears. Smooth, bare shoulders in a yellow sundress for the warm afternoon. A smile that flickered between shy and sexual, until it somehow fused both qualities into something more. Her eyes, clear and grey with the blackest lashes. Improbably, incredibly, the eyes were saying she was glad to see him.

She asked him to come in, and he stepped into a small but well-appointed flat.

'It's a beautiful dress,' was all he could say.

'I'm used to playing the mistress,' she said. 'Requires that you're always at least partially naked.'

He nodded.

'Fritz is on the street,' he said. 'He'll love the dress.'

'Fritz?'

'He's your audience,' Gus explained. 'A guy the size of a building. Follows me around. Walks like this . . .'

Gus did a pretty good imitation of Fritz' burly waddle, and got a barely suppressed giggle for his effort.

'And you actually know his name is Fritz?'

'Oh, no. I just had to pick my own name for him. See, it's impolite to introduce yourself. They like to pretend that they're unobtrusive.'

'They?'

Gus nodded. 'Fritz is the midday shift. The other guys we call Klaus, Hans, and Otto. Collectively, they are known as the Marx brothers.'

Now she laughed aloud.

'That explains,' she giggled, 'why you didn't name one of them Karl.'

Racing across the floor at full speed, loose blonde hair flying, came Amy. She toppled into Claire, clutching her mother's leg with both arms. Amy looked up at Gus. Squirming and beaming, she was the essence of flirtation.

'I thought,' Claire said, burying her hand in her daughter's hair, 'that we could bring Amy along. Give Fritz a sense that we're becoming family.'

Gus smiled approvingly. He remembered the violets, still clasped in a death grip, and handed them down to Amy. She hesitated for an instant, then wrapped both arms around the flowers, hugging them to her with mangling intensity.

'She calls you the Pepperman,' Claire said, 'because of the mess you made with the pepper.'

Claire tossed her head back and looked directly at his eyes.

'I told her,' she said, 'that you were going to be our new friend.'

There was no bitterness, no questioning, in the words. It was Gus' mind that supplied the images of what could happen to Claire and Amy. What Ernst Ritter would be more than capable of doing in the name of either leverage or retribution, depending upon whether Gus was still alive at the time. Trick is, Gus had told Brausch, don't get caught. Glib and light and reckless. And here was Amy, very real and alive, crushing her violets and grinning up at the Pepperman. Her new friend.

'I want a hug,' he said, because he did, very much.

Amy dropped the flowers. He lifted her gently and she wrapped her tiny arms around his neck, her cheek and hair tight against his ear.

He held her for a moment, then pulled her around so they were nose to nose. She giggled as he stared into her dark eyes from about an inch away.

'Do you want a ride?' he asked. 'Like an acrobat?'

She nodded furiously. He swung her up to a seat on his shoulders, legs straddling his neck, small fists tugging at his hair for balance.

Claire left to gather up their things as Gus went to a hanging mirror, bending slightly so that Amy could see herself atop her perch.

Flooding now into his mind was the fight with Basil Nicholas. If you personally knew, Gus had said, even one of the lives you're risking. One of their babies. He had no choice but to smile at himself. It was definitely more fun to set the standards of humanity when setting them for someone else.

He needed a contact. That was true. Whoever it was, there

would be a two-year-old or a seven-year-old or a crippled mother. That was logical. What he saw in the hanging mirror was neither truth nor logic. He saw a tiny person, sitting on his shoulders.

Claire returned, hooked her arm through his, and they headed down to the sunlight of Rue Montagne-Saint-Geneviève.

Fritz, of course, was waiting, scanning the inevitable newspaper. These guys had to wind up terribly well informed.

They walked up Saint-Germain to the Boul' Mich, Boulevard Saint-Michel. Gus was pushing Amy's stroller with one hand, making her shriek with surprise jolts and bumps.

Most of the grocers and bakeries were shuttered. A few were open and modest queues had formed. Gus asked if he should pick up something to eat in the park. Claire said no, the lines were too long, but there was a strange little smile that Gus noted and filed away.

As they started up Boul' Mich, Gus ducked into a tiny shop. In a moment he reappeared with a ribbon of black velvet. He knelt and tied it into Amy's golden hair, then held her up to the shop window so that she could see her reflection. She preened and arched her throat, as if posing for a photograph.

At Place de la Sorbonne was a huge poster of Marshal Pétain. He was praising Frenchmen for following Germany's crusade to stamp out bolshevism. How comforting. Gus preferred the poster of the loving German soldier. At least that was honestly insidious. This one simply made his skin crawl.

In the square was a German-language bookstore. Gus glanced towards the entrance.

'Want to pick up a little something to read in our masters' tongue?' he asked with a smile. 'Never hurts to brush up on your Jerry-speak.'

She shook her head.

'I get considerable practice,' she said. 'I'm starting to suspect that nothing is being printed in French any longer.'

She looked up at him.

'Here the blacklist is called the Otto List. It bans about a thousand authors.'

'Subversive authors,' he corrected. 'Jews and trash.'

She nodded.

'Very ecumenical list,' she said. 'Even bans some Germans. Freud, Einstein . . .'

'All the losers,' he noted.

'Anyway,' she continued, 'since we no longer need to waste time reading, we are free to pursue the more constructive aspects of French culture. You will find the races quite regular at Longchamps and Auteuil. Balenciaga and Dior and Cartier are in profit, thanks to our guests. Catch Mistinguett or Piaf on Radio-Paris almost any night. It's quite delightful.'

The edge was now rising to her words with surprising force.

'If you wish to go out and get drunk,' she said, 'you can have your choice of intellectuals as company. Colette, Cocteau, Braque. Simone de Beauvoir and Sartre drink with Picasso at the Café Flore, or the Catalan on Rue des Grands-Augustins. We'll go. No inconveniences but the curfew. You have to get drunk by eleven now.'

She was talking fast and walking faster. Amy's stroller clattered along before them. Gus held an image of Fritz behind them, trying to be inconspicuous while doubling his pace.

'Of course,' she said, 'basically I am a black marketeer's whore, so I usually drink with my own set at Le Colisée or Cercle Européen.'

He reached out and took her arm. He slid his hand into hers, grasping it firmly. Claire had slowed now to match his lead. She looked up at him, sorry for the outburst, but her eyes were still smouldering.

'I think I got the picture,' he said very gently. 'You're having a swell time here in Occupied France. It's truly a vacation paradise. That's why I saved up my pennies to be here.'

She grinned and returned the pressure of his hand very slightly. A wave of heat flashed through him.

'In case no one mentioned it,' she said, 'thanks for coming.'

He fought very hard to discount the intimacy in her eyes.

'Anyway,' he said, 'let's not blame the whole thing on Picasso. Christ, he's not even French. Seems to me those blonde guys in the green suits deserve at least some constructive criticism.'

Her smile was very tight now, her eyes moving over his face as they walked.

'I've noticed them,' she agreed. 'They're becoming tiresome.'

Claire looked back to watch Amy in the stroller. Her grip on his free hand now became interlocking and undeniably warm.

'What are you looking for from café society?' he said. 'Mass suicide?'

'I'm looking,' she said, 'for a little spine.'

Seemed fair enough to him.

'There's always Armand,' he said, and immediately wondered why. And, almost as immediately, knew.

She was thinking that one over, meaning she also knew.

'Armand has his moments,' she said with an elusive twist at the corner of her smile.

Not only was he jealous. Not only was he prying. Worst of all, it had snuck up on him from behind. Even worse than worst of all, she had read the entire thought and was teasing him for it. Armand was none of his goddam business, and if he could stop falling in love for ten seconds, maybe he could start acting like . . . like . . . a *mensch*.

He smiled now, remembering that word. It was a word his father taught him. It meant a real person, a decent person. It was a German word that had become a common Yiddish expression. This was funny enough coming from his father, the Hun. Funnier still because his father was as far from being a *mensch* as anyone Gus ever knew. Maybe that was why his father used a term popular with Jews for a concept he outwardly respected but inwardly despised.

Claire was looking at him now, seeing his eyes so far away.

'I just had an insight about my father,' he said. 'I hold you personally responsible.'

'The perfect courtesan,' she said. 'I also cook, cut your hair, and read your palm.'

They had arrived at the Luxembourg Garden. The air had sharpened since the morning. It held a freshness and a clarity that Gus had never tasted in New England or anywhere else.

The garden was large, but in no way comparable to the vast Bois de Boulogne, where he had strolled with Hoffmann. That had seemed an empty forest. Here, Parisians were everywhere. Children crowded about the fountain with wooden boats. Mothers chatted under broad-leaved trees and along shady gravel pathways.

The comfort level was inverse in proportion to the number of Germans present. Luxembourg Garden was on the Left Bank, much farther than the Bois from luxury hotels and the grander public buildings. Gus observed this as a curious twist on the spoiling of a neighbourhood, since it was the premium areas that were most infested with the invaders. The best place to be was now the worst place to be.

They found a private tree. Amy was meticulously arranging her dolls for a tea party a few metres down the hill.

Gus saw that Fritz and his newspaper were setting up shop on a bench well along the path. Fritz had turned his face to the sun and was doing more girl-watching than anything else. He had pulled some soft duty and was making the most of it.

'Wooden shoes,' Gus said, watching the parade of ladies at the fountain. 'Paris is becoming Holland.'

'Paris,' she said simply, 'is out of shoe leather.'

Gus knew nothing about the level of Claire's deprivation, and wasn't really certain how to ask.

'I wish I'd picked up some cheese and sausage for us. Starting to feel hungry,' he said.

As soon as he said it, he wished he hadn't. It was far too

close to her remark about running out of shoe leather. His line of association would be obvious.

When he looked over at her, the grey eyes were saying that she understood.

'We're all right,' she said gently. 'We have plenty to eat.'

He didn't bother to lie, to pretend that he had been misunderstood. He only returned her smile.

'Good,' he said, with a single nod.

'Sometimes,' she said, 'you have to work harder turning food down than you do finding it.'

He looked at her lovely face and found that quite believable.

'Unwelcome donors,' he said.

'You're the first man,' she said, 'to bring me flowers in the longest time. Mostly, they bring pork or a sack of rice.'

'Ah,' Gus smiled, 'romance . . .'

She nodded.

'It's a wonderful time,' she agreed, 'for men who like their women bought and paid for.'

She leaned back against their tree.

'The prettier ladies,' she said, 'eat as well as they're willing to. They don't see much genuine kindness.'

She bit her lip.

'So . . . thanks for the violets,' she said.

He really didn't know what to say.

'Anytime,' he said softly. 'Genuine kindness our speciality.'

She nodded without looking at him.

'Honest feelings,' she said, reminding him of that moment in the cafeteria.

They were quiet for a moment.

'Ration cards,' she said. 'I'm Category A. Amy is an E. When she's three, she becomes a J1. It's very scientific. She gets less bread than old people, but they get no milk. They started us off with three hundred and fifty grams of meat a week. It's been drying up steadily . . .'

Gus said nothing at all. His belly was starting to squeeze out something sour.

'Armand was very good to us. Very sweet. He'd tell me to take things for Amy, at least. He'd give things to me and I'd give them away to someone who really needed them. But I'd keep something back for Amy. Milk or fruit. Chocolate.'

Her eyes were wet now, there was no question in his mind.

'And I'd look at these . . . other people . . . mothers, whose children had . . . nothing at all . . .'

She stopped for a moment and he waited.

'I didn't know them,' she said. 'I just would see them in the street. And I would . . . dream about them. And I had to stop taking.'

She looked at him, grey eyes glistening.

'Because if I took anything at all . . . then *I* was doing it to them. Do you understand that?'

Yes he did.

'What did you do?' he asked quietly.

'I stopped my art. I used to paint. I was studying sculpture. But those things weren't selling. So I learned to make jewellery. Pretty little things. And I would barter. First for more materials, then for meat and vegetables. It works very well . . . in the summer.'

'They don't want pretty things in the winter?'

'The winter is another problem. You see, there *is* food, so you just have to find it. Heating oil is different. All the fuel goes to the Wehrmacht. Sunday morning is the worst, because the stores and buildings are closed. So you hide in bed, hugging your baby, wearing everything you have. Then maybe you join the crowd down in the Métro station, as far underground as you can get.'

His eyes were wet now too.

'Maybe Amy should have picked a smarter mama,' she said. 'There's always a gentleman somewhere with a nice warm flat. I'm sure some of them would even let you bring your baby.'

He reached out for her hand and she wound those slender fingers through his. They didn't say anything further. Just lay back on the grass, their fingers interlocked. She closed her eyes, squeezing the dampness from them. He lay with his wide open, listening to the wind and the soft sounds of Amy orchestrating her tea party.

For the moment, he had reached the worst part of the war. The heart of evil. Not simply to make people suffer, but to force them to change. To make honest feelings, even self-respect, a rationed commodity that few mothers could afford.

He closed his eyes now, giving his mind over to the images that were surging through it. He and Claire and Amy were a family, strolling and laughing in the streets of a liberated Paris. There were flashes, pictures, of a whole life together. A sunlit breakfast room. Amy, older, reading while music played.

And there were other images. Pictures that Gus knew as reality. Pictures of Walter Hoffmann, and the truth that Gus surely would be dead before D-Day.

There was one face that did not enter among the pictures. Leclerc's unnamed Briton, Amy's father, rotting away in a Nazi camp at Royal-Lieu. For this afternoon only, the man Claire loved did not exist.

And finally, Gus cleared his mind of all the pictures. Cleared his mind to make himself a promise. Whatever it would take, whatever he would have to bargain away, he would see that Claire and Amy were safe before he died.

TWENTY-SIX

Vincennes is and has been many things. It is a great wood off in the southeast corner of Paris. A forest dotted with many lakes, Lac Daumesnil to the west, Lac des Minimes to the east. There is the largest zoo in all of France. There is an exquisite floral garden. Even a racecourse.

But above all, Vincennes has been a fortress. Called the

'medieval Versailles,' its castle and château had been home to kings and cardinals until the early sixteenth century. Then, for nearly three hundred years, the towering, ominous keep was used as a state prison. While the rabble was consigned to the Bastille, the elite of Parisian convicts, royalty, and intellectuals, was housed in the great stone prison of Vincennes.

With its fortified walls, moat and drawbridge, the keep presented a model of the classically impregnable prison. Nearby, but still within the outer moat, stood the magnificently restored seventeenth-century buildings used by the Nazis for receptions and administrative offices.

It was to the elegant Pavillon du Roi, the King's Pavilion, that Jürgen Brausch had summoned the full interrogation team. All phases of preliminary examination had been concluded. Reports would be read and discussed by the entire team. In two days, the intensive phase of questioning the Overlord would begin.

Gus arrived alone at the walls of Vincennes. Alone, that is, except for Hans, who hung back on the Esplanade du Château. Hans stood at a great distance, his eyes fixed on the nape of Gus' neck, until Gus was admitted through the south portico and disappeared into the courtyard.

Once inside, Gus was taken quickly through the courtyard to the King's Pavilion. There were armed troops everywhere, almost as if the Germans intended to hold this place against a siege. From the look of it, they could have held out against Patton, Monty, and Genghis Khan.

Gus was led to the gracious appointments of a seventeenth-century drawing room, a startling contrast to the armed camp of the courtyard. Overhead fans, an anachronism in this elegant setting, stirred a gentle breeze. Two uniformed soldiers with white gloves moved silently among the seated officers, serving tea, sandwiches and drinks.

There were approximately fifteen present. All but Gus were in full uniform, about evenly divided between military green and SS black. Ritter caught Gus' eye immediately, waving him to a seat next to him on an ornately brocaded sofa. The furniture was arranged in a semicircle so that all present faced a single empty chair. It was into this seat that speakers would rotate as their reports were presented.

Next to Ritter's sofa was a heavy oak chair containing the huge figure of Jürgen Brausch. While the others chatted, Brausch was intent on a pile of dossiers held in his lap. Turning pages slowly, his concentration complete, he seemed so oblivious to his surroundings that Gus couldn't help but stare at him.

Conspicuous by his absence was Walter Hoffmann.

Gus talked easily with Ritter. Obviously, Fritz would have reported Gus' day in the park with Claire and Amy. He had no doubt that the Marx brothers reported directly to Ritter himself. Gus was waiting for some gentle question about how he had been spending these past three days, but the question never came. Ritter spoke instead of the weather, the eastern front, and a dinner party that Gus must attend at his place in Neuilly.

It could simply have been that, since Ritter was screwing half of Paris, he found Gus' romantic attachment less than eventful. More, likely, Ritter was displaying a highly professional level of patience. It would be more interesting to see how, and if, Gus introduced the subject without a naturally comfortable opening. Gus, needless to say, did not.

Walter Hoffmann had entered at the far end of the room. He was dressed in full black and silver and looked altogether dashing. His eyes swept the room easily. When they reached Gus, he locked into firm eye contact, smiling warmly as if relieved to find an old friend.

Brausch had not appeared to notice Hoffmann's arrival, indeed had not even seemed to glance up from his papers. Nonetheless, he cleared his throat authoritatively. With that single sound, the meeting had begun.

First to assume the hot seat was Hauptmann Trager, an Abwehr captain who was apparently Brausch's closest personal aide. A clear-eyed youthful sort, Trager seemed eager and competent. He had coordinated the preliminary phase of the Overlord's interrogation, and now offered a concise summary of these proceedings.

The Overlord had been interrogated on six to eight occasions each day, always at irregular intervals. The interrogations were conducted by rotating and comparatively low-level personnel. All procedures had been designed to disorient the Overlord in every way. He had been moved constantly from cell to cell. Sometimes in solitary, sometimes with a carefully selected cellmate. As with feeding, exercise, and interrogation, the intervals of these transfers had been kept irregular and unpredictable.

The Overlord had been thoroughly uncooperative, refusing to give even name and rank, either under formal interrogation or to cellmates. His anxiety level and related aspects of his demeanour under questioning, and when observed in his cell, suggested more than simple fear for his personal safety. They strongly indicated a man sitting on critical information. If this man was not an Overlord, he was doing the best conceivable impersonation of one.

The reports continued through the afternoon. Ritter seemed to have several questions prepared for each speaker. Brausch had still to say his first word. And as for Hoffmann, seated on the periphery of the circle, he had all but disappeared entirely.

The report that Gus found most interesting was delivered by a dark little man named Fröben, an Abwehr Oberleutnant. Posing as an Italian deserter, Fröben had been Andy Wheeler's cellmate for a twenty-hour stretch. Fröben had affected a heavily accented broken English for his role, and believed that Wheeler thoroughly trusted his authenticity.

'I think,' Fröben said, his eyes finding Gus, 'that this augurs well for the role that Agent Emerald will be portraying. This is an exceedingly immature fellow. He is very frightened, but this prompts him to be irresistibly drawn to anyone who is not German.'

A heavy sigh came from Ritter's direction.

'He told you . . .,' Ritter interjected, as though the little man needed prompting.

'Of his girl friend,' Fröben said, completing Ritter's sentence. 'She is a girl of nineteen named Stephanie. She lives in Seattle, in the northwest of America. Once he began to speak of her, he couldn't stop. He described her face, her gestures. He relayed long strands of personal conversation with her, as if I would be fascinated by each detail. And while he seems a shy man in such matters, he would lapse into the revelation of very intimate moments. It is all there, Standartenführer, in my report.'

'Would you say' – Ritter was leading his witness – 'that his discussion of this girl was his one true outpouring of human feeling?'

Fröben cleared his throat. Ritter was simply restating Fröben's words, as if offering a profound conclusion of his own.

'The girl,' Fröben said, 'is his obsession. At this point, he is clinging to her as he would to life.'

'Therefore,' Ritter said with a patience that more than bordered on condescension, 'you would advise Captain Lang to treat this girl as the Overlord's most accessible point of vulnerability.'

Once again, Ritter seemed to be appropriating the credit for Fröben's analysis.

Gus watched the little man's face flicker through an instant of resentment and distaste. Gus was guessing that Ritter inspired such feelings regularly. That Ritter must be accustomed to seeing that look in another man's eyes. To watching, as an irritated subordinate fought the impulse to say something he would regret. Ritter did not produce these reactions inadvertently. He enjoyed watching them.

'Yes, Standartenführer,' Froben said, having swallowed the impulse whole. 'I believe that would be a fair conclusion.'

The next report was from a round, soft-looking man with the oversized eyes of a baby deer. His cheeks were pink and smooth, and there seemed a perpetual twinkle just below the surface of his expression. He was one of the examining physicians, but he was offering a 'personality' report. To Gus' surprise, notwithstanding the Reich's reported opposition to psychiatry, this man was in fact presenting Andy Wheeler's psychological profile.

As the doctor spoke, Gus was struck by how clearly this picture of Andy squared with his own preconceptions. This reinforced the feeling that Andy was already an old friend.

There also emerged a contrasting image. Andy Wheeler had no friends, save the fantasy of his perfect love. Within himself, he had been alone all of his life. At this moment, he was surely as desperately alone as any man could ever be. Would his past isolation have given him the strength to hang on now? Gus was starting to fear that the reverse might be true. There were no reserves within Andy. No memories of love and comfort to draw on. This would explain his obsessive focus on Stephanie.

'As we move,' Ritter addressed the doctor, 'into the next phase of our mission, we will need to consider every option. One of these, of course, would be the possibility of more . . . intensive . . . interrogation.'

The round little doctor took Ritter's meaning perfectly. 'This man,' the doctor said, 'is not a good candidate for torture. He is unnaturally withdrawn. Wound tight enough to snap. Torture or threats thereof could cause him to lose his hold on reality entirely.'

Ritter accepted the words without a further question. His face, however, made it evident that this was not the answer he was hoping for. Ritter was obviously a man who preferred keeping his options open. Particularly that one.

Two more doctors, and finally the cardiologist, a frail man of over seventy, with watering eyes. He, too, had picked up the message of Ritter's continuing interest in conducting a more intensive interrogation. He directed his remarks solely to Ritter.

'The medical file supplied by Agent Emerald speaks of an elusive condition called cardiac arrhythmia. It is not a simple matter to explain to a lay person.'

'Try,' Ritter said softly. There was an intensity in his eyes that came very close to menace. The doctor seemed genuinely frightened. The stillness of the room was suddenly most uncomfortable.

'The heart,' the doctor said slowly, 'beats in response to electrical impulses. These impulses originate in the sinus node, from which they are transmitted directly to the atrial muscle. From there, the impulse spreads radially to the atrioventricular node, which continues as the atrioventricular bundle, sometimes called the Bundle of His. This bundle of tissue is the sole muscular connection between the atrium and the ventricle. It is the pathway, so to speak, for the electrical impulse . . .'

Ritter's eyes were no longer angry. They were flat and dead, yet staring at the doctor with such a perfect concentration that the old man seemed almost mesmerized. As a snake is hypnotized by a mongoose, the doctor could only stare back at Ritter.

'And so . . .' Ritter urged.

The doctor recovered his tongue.

'When there is an arrhythmia, there is an incomplete electrical connection along this pathway. The heart just stops. The patient might faint. The patient might die. It is unpredictable.'

'And the Overlord,' Ritter said, 'has such a condition?'

'The report which Agent Emerald took from the hospital files . . . this report says that the patient has suffered episodes of arrhythmia. He apparently fainted during an electrocardiogram. That is where it was discovered. They also found a family history of such episodes. Paternal grandfather, I believe.'

'All this,' Ritter said, 'from an American file?'

'British,' the doctor corrected.

'And, Doctor,' Ritter said very quietly, 'what has been *your* conclusion upon examining the prisoner?'

The old man cleared his throat with a sharp high-pitched sound.

'You cannot verify an arrhythmia on examination unless

an episode coincidentally occurs during an electrocardiogram. It is something that simply happens when it happens.'

'And is there anything in particular that could help it to "happen"?' The edge of impatience had returned to Ritter's voice. 'Such as fear or pain?'

'Oh, yes. Any stress greatly increases the risk of an episode occurring. The medical file shows that this boy would have been sent home, but for his apprently invaluable technical expertise. There were strict instructions, however, to keep him not only from combat, but from stress of any kind.'

Ritter nodded.

'And,' Ritter said, 'the prisoner could actually die from such an episode.'

'Most definitely. Suddenly and without warning.'

Ritter rubbed his large palms together. Gus watched the movement, struck by the man's ability to convey such potential for physical menace with the slightest gesture. There was an instinct for intimidation that was fascinating to observe.

'How exquisitely convenient,' Ritter said with a humourless smile.

Ritter turned his eyes to Gus. There was nothing sudden or dramatic in the movement. Yet Gus had the sensation of confronting an animal that had leaped down from a great height. Ritter seemed coiled to strike.

'And what is your view of the authenticity of these records?' Ritter asked.

Gus returned Ritter's unblinking gaze.

'I have no view,' Gus said. 'Obviously, the report could be a fraud. There were three days between the capture of this man and my locating these files. It would have taken some creativity and thoroughness to think of falsifying these records. More than I have observed among these people. But it is certainly possible.'

And from behind Ritter's shoulder came the rumbling voice of Jürgen Brausch.

'What do you say, Ernst? Shall we risk it?'

Ritter whipped around. He found Brausch waiting with a gentle, infuriating grin.

'Are you suggesting,' Ritter said, barely under control now, 'that I would act in a precipitous or irresponsible manner?'

Brausch's eyes and smile were clear. Only if you could get away with it, they said.

'I am observing,' Brausch said very softly, 'that you are slavering to put this boy on the rack. Since you are as aware as the rest of us that this is an unacceptable risk, I would also suggest that you are imposing on this gathering by venting your frustration at such ponderous length.'

Instinctively, Ritter turned towards the corner of the room where Walter Hoffmann sat unnoticed. Ritter's eyes demanded vindication from his superior.

Hoffmann tapped his fingers together. He stared at them for a long moment, letting the spotlight focus fully upon them.

'I think,' he said, 'that we have a larger issue in question. Medical reports aside, Ernst, I have never been an apologist for torture.'

And now the dark eyes found Gus. His silence commanded Gus' view on the subject.

'I would generally agree,' Gus said. 'What a man tells you under torture is only what he believes will stop the torture. It may or may not be the truth.'

Hoffmann nodded, his eyes very intent.

'More than that,' Hoffmann said. 'Torture dehumanizes everyone concerned. The victim and the questioner. We are human beings. What will bring the truth from a human heart requires that we remain aware of our subject's humanity. For everything rests on our ability to understand and empathize with that humanity.'

There was a gentle smile that seemed for Gus alone.

'This project,' Hoffmann said, 'will be more than the ultimate test of our craft. It will be the ultimate verdict on who and what we are.'

TWENTY-SEVEN

Once again, he stood fidgetting at the door. Gus had advised his stomach that there was no reason to be anxious. He massaged that particular line of constructive thought for at least fifteen seconds, then shut it off and just stood there, nervous as hell.

This would be a lot easier if he could shake the feeling that Claire really liked him. Come to think of it, that was pure bullshit. He couldn't think of one thing worse in the whole cosmos than Claire not liking him.

It came to him suddenly that 'nervous' was an imprecise description for the fluid that was surging through him. He was excited. He was more excited than he had been standing at any door, waiting for any woman, in his entire life. Now *that* made him nervous.

This engrossing internal monologue was ended by Claire's opening the door.

What Gus saw was Claire dressed for evening. A slinky gown, black as her hair. Her shoulders were bare once more. Always at least partially naked, she'd said. Smiling that shy and sexual smile of a thousand lights. She was beyond fantasy, beyond perfection.

She was much more than a woman to die for. She was a woman to kill for. That thought, that distinction, burned itself into Gus' mind with sudden clarity.

What Claire saw was Gus, clutching a dozen red roses, dressed in a crisp version of Parisian black tie. Claire executed a long, perfect wolf whistle.

Gus felt more than a little embarrassed. Actually, what he felt was more than a little aroused. He knew that he looked okay, God knows he spent enough time getting ready, but her whistle had caught him completely off guard. The Lady of the Grey Eyes was in control of this particular evening. He liked that very much.

On the street, Claire found that Gus had commandeered a limo for the evening. Sleek and black, complete with an Abwehr corporal behind the wheel.

As she slid into the back, she spoke to the driver in perfect German.

'What languages do you speak, Corporal?'

'German, madam,' he said. And after a long beat, 'I suppose a little French. Very little.'

'Can you be trusted,' she said, 'to speak no English whatsoever?'

The driver smiled.

'Absolutely, madam. Except *bathroom* and *whiskey* and . . . a word I can't tell you.'

'I'll use my imagination,' she said.

She turned to Gus. More than turning, she actually snuggled against him.

'Where is Klaus?' she whispered in English.

He put his lips to her ear. Warm and soft and perfect.

'Sixty metres down the road,' he whispered, 'in a Citroën, with the lights off and the motor running.'

'Where to?' she asked aloud.

He looked at her.

'Duck or veal?' he asked.

'Veal,' she said with a wicked grin.

He nodded.

'Obergartner,' he said to the corporal, 'please take us to Tour d'Argent. You know, Quai de la Tournelle. Where we took the countess last night.'

She was very amused.

'Countess?'

He nodded, modestly.

'Spirited blonde,' he admitted. 'She also likes veal.'

She tossed her head and the black hair spread across her shoulder.

'Well, I'm not sure I fancy being just another veal eater on the arm of an international playboy.'

'You're calling off our engagement?' he asked.

'No. I'm opting for duck.'

'Fine. Driver, Tour d'Argent.'

She giggled. 'Wait a second, that was your place for veal.'

'Also for duck,' he said, 'it's the only place I know. Look, you wanna go to Tour d'Argent or you wanna screw around?'

He hadn't meant it quite that way, but the spark in her eye was undeniable. It set every part of him on fire.

She held the silence forever. Her smile got tighter and tighter.

'For the moment,' she said at last, 'I'll settle for Tour d'Argent.'

Down the street, Klaus flicked on his lights and followed the limo off into the night.

Tour d'Argent, the magnificent restaurant overlooking the Seine, was filled with its customary blend of Parisian society and Nazi hierarchy. Even in this crowd, Claire and Gus made a smashing couple, and more than a few heads turned as the captain led them to their table.

Gus had reserved a place at the window, and Claire looked down directly onto the cathedral of Notre-Dame.

'I've never been here,' she said.

'A notorious woman such as yourself?'

'Such as myself,' she agreed. 'Armand used to take me to Laperouse and Marquise de Sévigné. A few other places in my notorious past. Never here.'

The captain was hovering conspicuously.

'Champagne of your choice,' Gus said to the captain. 'Dazzle me with your discretion. Menus to follow.'

Her eyes were disapproving.

'Hey,' he said breezily, 'you're going to accept an invitation to Tour d'Argent and then give me looks about overspending? I'm gonna load you up with a year's worth of guilt before dessert. Then we'll get gaudy. My favourite class at Yale was Intensive Cheese.'

She smiled warmly.

'I know this is all line of duty,' she said softly. 'Couldn't we fix things so I don't enjoy it quite so much?'

'How about if I insult you once in a while?' he offered. 'Or maybe just pick a crummy year for the Bordeaux.'

'I'm serious,' she said. 'It feels wonderful to be here. And it feels terrible. Down the *quai* and three streets over, children are starving. Because the only food the Germans haven't stolen is in places like this.'

He stared at her eyes.

'I know,' he said. 'That's why I fitted Paris into my busy schedule.

She nodded. He was right.

'Now,' he said, 'if you don't start looking a lot happier, the people in this restaurant won't realize how much you love me.'

On cue, she reached across the table for his hand, turning loose a smile that almost knocked him over backwards.

'Besides,' he said gently, 'I'm going to turn this tab in to the SD, the MI-6, and the OSS. Get paid three times.'

'What are you going to do with all that money?'

'Buy war bonds. I may be corrupt, but I'm still a patriot.'

Claire pulled a cigarette from her purse. Gus reached for a lighter, fumbling as he struggled to get the damn thing lit. Grinning like a little boy at his own clumsiness.

It was clear to her that Gus was no stranger to elegant surroundings. Still, his movements revealed a shyness that was altogether charming. She understood this as evidence that he was attracted to her. With other men, such knowledge had given Claire an unmistakable, if often unwelcome, awareness of control. At some dimly perceived level, Claire had resented the burden of that power and the men who so willingly forced it upon her.

With Gus and his green eyes, his puppy-dog charm and eagerness to amuse, Claire found the sensation to be somehow different. There was a resonance of a very old feeling. A feeling about men before there had been any men. And that had indeed been long ago.

The champagne had arrived. She raised her glass, and her eyes were shining.

'You first,' she said. 'You were born in poor, yet humble, surroundings . . .'

Gus sighed. His childhood was his least favourite story.

'I was born,' he said, 'if not stinking rich, at least stinking comfortable. Suffice it to say that I have been profoundly ungrateful for all of the advantages my parents lavished upon me in their spare time.'

'Spare time,' she repeated softly, picking out the only words that really mattered.

'The point is,' he said simply, 'that I'm a congenital ingrate.'

Her smile said she wasn't buying that one.

'I never learned to appreciate good luck,' he said. 'School was easy. People were easy. Everything was so goddam easy that it made me uneasy as hell. The smoother my life went, the more nervous I got. It's as if I've been looking for one good solid failure. And if I can live through that . . . then . . . maybe things will be all right . . .'

She raised her glass again.

'So welcome to Paris,' she said gently.

'You think that's why I'm here.'

Her eyes moved over his face.

'It's what *you* were thinking,' she said. 'And you looked like you'd never thought of it quite that way before.'

The lady could read like Walter Hoffmann. He should introduce them. And then, the way it often happened to Gus, a sudden and terrible flash of paranoia. The blackest, most chilling thought, always at the worst possible moment. What if the lady already knew Walter Hoffmann?

'Is that how you came to this line of work?' she asked. Her smile was understanding, genuinely interested. There was nothing behind it to connect with Gus' dark thought. Nothing he could see.

'It was sort of an accident,' he said. 'It happened to me step by step. Each step always seemed interesting. And, I guess, worthwhile.'

'Will you tell me about it?'

He was telling himself that there was no possible way that Claire was his enemy. But the irrational rigidity of his denial served as its own response. It was, of course, entirely possible.

Gus knew that fearing something, even very strongly, did not make it true. That fear created its own false sense of reality. As simple as this sounded, it had been the hardest lesson of Gus' training. Learning to will himself to trust, against that fear. The fear that, once it had crept within him, would never fully leave.

Although Gus knew nothing of the black scavenger birds of Walter Hoffmann's nights, this was indeed an agonizing way in which the two men were one. And if Hoffmann had been at Gus' shoulder, he would have smiled the playful smile. Professional hazard, Hoffmann would have said.

'Started at Yale,' Gus said easily, no trace in his voice of anything holding back. 'I had a friend who was helping the FBI on a project. He was working undercover, infiltrating an organization called Friends of the New Germany. He asked me to help. These people sounded pretty dangerous, pretty crazy. Next thing I know, I'm in the organization and I'm rising like a comet. It was . . . well, easy.'

She smiled. It made him feel better. He was fighting back towards her now. Back from his own version of Hoffmann's dark birds of prey.

'Finally,' he said, 'I was approached by some members in contact with the Abwehr. They thought I could be of service to German intelligence efforts. The whole thing fell in my lap.'

He smiled shyly. As if embarrassed by how effortless it had been.

'I remember the guy from the FBI, the night I told him. His name was Brewer. Didn't look like a Fed. Had these square little glasses, always pushing them back up his nose. He said if I wanted out, that was the night to say so. If I stayed in, they were going to back me with everything they had, and I was in for good.'

'Inspirational,' she said dryly.

'My thought exactly. I wanted to laugh in the little guy's face, but what stopped me was the realization that then it would be over. I didn't want that.'

The captain had returned with their menus. Gus' eye ran expertly down the list. This was something he was used to doing. A gift from his father, one of the few.

He glanced up at Claire.

'Order for me,' she said.

The green eyes just watched her for a moment.

'Please,' she said. 'It's a very rare offer. I only ask a man to take care of me about once every twenty years.'

'Keeps disappointments at a minimum?' he asked.

'Takes me that long to recover in between.'

Gus ordered and the captain left.

Crossroads. She had given him a comfortable path to change the subject. He could follow her line about men. It would flow naturally and give him time to reflect before discussing MI-5 and Emerald.

It was a decision that made itself. There was no reality in doubt and hedging. The truth was that he *did* trust Claire. It was essential for him to realize that, to give himself over to it. If he could not, if he would cling to his fear, then Claire could never be to him any of the things he needed her to be.

Slowly, meticulously, he continued his story. Enlistment in the Army upon graduation. The delight of his Abwehr contacts when he finally became 'their man' in the OSS. The transfer to London. The double cover he had worked with MI-5, convincing the Germans that he had been assigned to track himself.

He told her everything. Everything but Jürgen Brausch. It was one thing to trust her with his own life. There was no need yet, no right, to trust her with the life of another.

'It's a rather remarkable story,' she said. 'You sure know how to impress a country girl.'

Gus smiled ruefully.

'Hold your applause,' he said, 'until I sneak out of this particular assignment with all body parts intact.'

Her grey eyes were serious, caring. 'And what will that take?'

'Well, either I'll have to outsmart them . . . or I'll have to get awfully lucky.'

'Can you do it?' she asked simply.

Gus stopped for a moment and actually thought about it. He realized that he had only begun to discover the impossibility of it all.

'I guess,' he said, 'you can always get lucky. It's just that I've had so much good luck in my life, maybe it's been saving up to turn on me.'

'How about just outsmarting them?' she said.

Gus took that question to his portrait of Walter Hoffmann. To the little shrine he had begun to erect to Hoffmann's genius.

'No,' he said with strange conviction. 'There's one player involved I won't outsmart. I'm smart enough to know that.'

Her smile flashed quick and warm.

'How about *us*?' she said softly. 'Can *we* outsmart him?'

Her words were so suddenly and purely touching that Gus' eyes were damp. He hadn't realized just how alone he'd really felt.

'Maybe,' he said, and his voice almost broke as he said it. He caught himself and sent a brave smile. 'Maybe you and me and Amy will just beat the crap out of them.'

'Know what I think?' she said tenderly. 'I think your Nazi player is in over his head. Because I just don't think you know how to lose. Some people are like that. You've been trying to lose all your life and you haven't figured it out yet. I don't think you can do it.'

The food had arrived. Duckling in pear sauce, with firm fresh vegetables. The Wehrmacht might be shipping the sausages to the front, but the duckling was being saved for more refined palates.

With gentle prompting, Claire began the story of her childhood. Her eyes kept to the duck more often than they rose to meet his. This conveyed the feeling of a story she was not comfortable in telling.

Claire's parents had died. Papa had been a professor of European languages at the university in Bordeaux. Hence, her tongue-in-cheek reference to being a country girl.

Papa had always worshipped Claire's intellect. He dreamed that she would be a linguist or a mathematician. She, however, had always wanted to work with her hands. Watercolours, calligraphy, and finally sculpture. When she was sixteen, Papa bowed to the strength of her will. He sent her to a fine arts academy for young ladies in Baltimore, Maryland. If she was not to be a linguist, at least she could learn one language in the vernacular of a native population.

Every word rang clear and honest. There was, however, a self-protective absence of personal detail, which became more pronounced as her story continued.

'This isn't the easiest thing in the world for me,' she admitted at last. 'How am I doing?'

He smiled very gently. 'You're leaving out all the good stuff.'

'You mean,' she said, 'the stuff that's none of your business.'

'Exactly.'

She shook her head violently, like a playful schoolgirl.

'You first,' she insisted.

'There's no woman in my life,' he said openly. 'There hasn't been for a long time.'

Her eyes showed no reaction apart from intense interest.

'I don't think,' he said, 'I've ever been in love. There were a few times . . . a few women who were . . . close enough. I was just never able to return what they seemed to be feeling.'

'That sounds as if *she* broke it off,' Claire said. 'But I have the feeling it was the other way around.'

He nodded as if it were an admission.

'I'd always end up feeling guilty,' he said, 'because nothing ever seemed to be enough for them. Nothing honest, at any rate.'

She stared at him in silence for the longest moment.

'You are a man of principle,' she announced with only the softest irony.

'You mean I'm boring.'

'I mean you're a romantic. It's not quite the same.'

The champagne was gone. Gus turned the bottle neck down in the silver bucket.

'I went first,' he said.

She took a deep breath.

'Many men,' she said, 'starting very young. None I ever really trusted.'

She swallowed the last of her wine.

'That was Mama's advice when she first realized that I would be pretty. Mama said not to trust. I spent my life trying to disobey her. No luck.'

Her eyes drifted off now.

'Things were . . . not at all the same,' she said, 'when I was very young.'

She looked back at him, not really understanding what she was feeling.

'The past is a foreign land,' he said. 'They do things differently there.'

She smiled. As if that had resolved something for her.

'I didn't compose that,' he admitted quickly. 'I've even forgotten where I read it.'

'Man of principle,' she said, shaking her head in a gentle reproach. 'If you can use poetry that well, you're allowed to take credit for it. Do you have trouble taking credit?'

'Do you have trouble falling in love?' he said straight back to her.

Fair enough. It was still her turn.

'I've been in love,' she said slowly. 'But I suspect that we use the word a little differently.'

He wouldn't be at all surprised.

'Attraction and enthusiasm,' she said, 'can pass for love if you don't feel guilty about it.'

Gus shook his head.

'Passion is easy,' he said. 'Love isn't easy at all. I don't see how you think excitement can pass for the real thing.'

'Because,' she said, 'in the real world, sometimes it has to.'

'The real world,' Gus smiled. 'Another foreign land.'

She smiled back.

'That's right,' she said. 'And they do things differently there.'

He realized there was never going to be any better moment.

'I want to know,' he said, 'about Amy's father.'

Her face was not at all what he expected. There was no pain, no reaction of any kind.

'More disillusionment for the romantic,' she said. 'Amy's father was not a love. He wasn't even much of a boyfriend. Mostly, he was the man who made me pregnant.'

Gus repeated Leclerc's story. The Briton in the concentration camp. Claire's devotion to him. She smiled with understanding.

'Armand was being protective,' she said.

She knew that what Armand had been protecting was his own fantasy of a more intimate relationship with her. Still, he had been kind to her. She did not owe Gus any revelation that might embarrass Armand.

'He is British?' Gus was still on the trail of Amy's father.

'Yes, but hardly in a concentration camp. He turned out to be a collaborator. Living in Berlin now, I think. He's not a terrible sort. Just very pretty and very weak.'

There was a silence.

'And you don't love him?' Gus couldn't keep himself from adding.

'I said I didn't,' she grinned. 'You really are a very funny, old-fashioned sort of person. For an American.'

'For anybody,' he agreed.

'Does it matter if I'm in love? Are you really afraid of competition? I wouldn't have guessed you to be afraid of anything.'

Inside Gus, he was smiling at himself. Competing for her love. It had been on the table all night. But now that she had finally spoken the words, it felt like a shocking disclosure. He had been living in the fantasy that this was still a semi-professional flirtation. She was living in that foreign land called the real world, where people plainly saw what other people wanted. He *was* funny and old-fashioned.

There was a silence more tender than awkward. Claire was sorry for having teased him. She reached out and put her hand over his.

'Let's go home,' she said.

Gus called the captain and paid his bill. He would display his talent for cheeses on another occasion.

They arrived back at Claire's flat. She leaned through the driver's window and put her lips to the ear of the young corporal, so that Gus couldn't hear.

'Wait here for two minutes,' she whispered. 'Then go away.'

She held Gus' hand all the way to the door, long after Klaus could possibly see them. She opened the door and gently pulled him inside.

'Klaus will expect you to sleep over,' she said softly.

Gus still couldn't permit himself to realize fully.

She wound her arms around his neck.

'Klaus will expect it,' she said. 'And I will insist on it.'

The lovemaking was different from anything Gus could remember. No skin so liquid and yielding. No touch so peaceful.

When she drew him inside of her for the first time, there was a feeling he had never experienced at such a moment. Within his excitement beyond his excitement, there was an overwhelming sensation of relief. As if he were finally home from a lifetime's wandering journey.

When it was over, he wanted to ask her how she felt. But even more, he wanted to stay in her arms and say nothing.

TWENTY-EIGHT

They led Gus so far down into the earth that he stopped thinking of dungeons and started thinking of coal miners.

He sat alone on the floor of the cell in faded grey prison clothes. They had been pre-soiled for him and smelled very slightly of an unidentified animal. Gus preferred not to guess.

There was no furniture in the cell. Nothing at all but a sickly green light. The light was surprisingly strong, and Gus assumed that this was to facilitate observation through some form of peephole.

They had not told Gus about the peephole. They had told him only that they would be able to hear. As he sat, his eyes moved absently about the smooth walls of the cell. Now locked into middle distance, now moving again.

In ten minutes, his eyes had covered every inch of the cell. There were no holes. Gus concluded that they must be using the tiny air vent, where the wall joined the ceiling. Sitting in silence, he wondered which of them was actually watching.

After a while, and without looking up at the vent, Gus shifted his position. His face could still barely be seen from the vent, but by another slight shift of position, he would be able to turn his face entirely from view.

Twenty minutes passed.

The cell door opened. A guard led in a small man, arms folded tightly across his chest, as if clutching himself for warmth. He had rimless spectacles, but he was squinting. Andy Wheeler had been kept in a darker place.

It was not so much that Andy seemed frightened. It was more that Gus had never seen a man so alone in all his life.

Gus offered a smile and a little wave of greeting, but said nothing until the iron door was shut and bolted.

Gus's hands were clasped in his lap, his shoulders hunched

in the posture of someone trying to make himself as small and non-threatening as possible. Gus was recalling his first approach to Amy in the cafeteria. Andy Wheeler, too, would need a Pepperman.

'Gus Lang,' he said, softly and friendly.

There was a silence. Gus just kept on smiling.

'Hi,' Andy said at last.

Gus nodded.

'I know a guy named Hy,' Gus said. 'But he's Jewish. It's funny, you don't look Jewish.'

Andy was definitely amused.

'I meant,' Andy said, 'Hi, how ya doin'?'

'Oh.' Gus nodded in a pantomime of sudden comprehension. 'Never better. There's more sun on the Riviera, but you can't beat these prices.'

'You're okay?' Andy asked. The concern in his voice was so genuine. Where others had seen weakness, Gus sensed only innocence and warmth. A joke, a common fear, and the bond had begun. It had taken all of thirty seconds.

'Sure,' Gus said. 'No torture yet. Not the real stuff. You?'

Andy shook his head.

'Psychological,' he said, 'not physical.'

Although Gus knew this, there was still a strange wave of relief in hearing it from Andy's lips.

'Got a name, Admiral,' Gus asked, 'or do I just call you Nimitz?'

'Andy Wheeler,' came straight back to Gus. 'I'm from Yelm, Washington. I'm just a major.'

This was the first time that Andy had given his name or rank to anyone.

'I'm from Connecticut,' Gus said. 'New Canaan. I'm just a captain.'

Andy grinned once more.

'OSS,' Gus said, 'attached to MI-5. They picked us up in Norway, at a place called Rjukan. We were trying to blow up a heavy-water plant. The Krauts are using the stuff for nuclear fission experiments.'

Andy, the scientist, amazingly knew all about the Vemork plant at Rjukan.

'I thought,' Andy said, 'that we put them out of commission in February. We blew up a ferry, didn't we? Called . . . the *Hydro*. It was carrying nearly all the deuterium oxide.'

Gus nodded without missing a beat.

'Apparently their production capacity exceeded our estimates,' he said. 'If they stay on-line, they could make another shipment by winter.'

Andy shuddered at the thought.

They talked nonstop for more than an hour. In this phase, Gus kept it light and as funny as he could manage. Andy's own sense of humour came seeping in through the cracks.

Then, too, there was baseball. Andy had idolized Ted Williams, so Gus defended DiMaggio. Andy's command of statistics was little-boy perfect, and he obliterated Gus' arguments with an avalanche of percentages in categories Gus never knew existed.

Andy laughed. Andy was assertive. In a hole at the bottom of Vincennes prison, Andy Wheeler was having a hell of a time.

Gus watched with the patience that he knew would be crucial. He would have to wait until the grim pallor of aloneness had been thoroughly leached away. It was the only form of readiness he could offer Andy for the first step of their journey together.

When the time had arrived, Gus brought the conversation back to the question of torture.

'I wish they'd get started with it,' Gus said.

'Why?'

'Well, I have to let them take me a bit down that road before I can dump D-Day on them. If it comes too easily, they'll never buy it.'

Andy didn't understand.

Gus shifted his body slightly. Now the back of his head was turned squarely towards the air vent. If it was indeed a peephole, his face was fully hidden from view.

It was time for his test run. He was going to allow himself only one test for Andy, and he had his fingers crossed.

'The British have a code name,' Gus said, 'for personnel who know where and when D-Day is coming. They call us Overlords.'

As he spoke the words, Gus flashed Andy a broad wink and a huge grin. Andy's face froze slightly. The true code name, of course, was Bigot. If Andy couldn't catch on, if he corrected Gus' 'mistake,' Gus would have to tell the Germans that Bigot must be a new or somehow different code. There was no way to know how Hoffmann would take it. Still, Gus would count on Brausch to help him cover.

'You've heard that term, haven't you?' Gus said. Another wink.

'Sure,' Andy replied, and he nodded in recognition.

Inside his belly, Gus graded Andy with an A-plus. We've got a chance here, Gus told himself. A living, breathing, goddam hell of a chance. The adrenalin now was rushing through him. In the world of Gus' profession, this was the moment of combat. He was as ready as any foot soldier who ever fixed his bayonet to charge a hill.

Gus watched as Andy's muscles tightened a little. He may not know what the game is, but he knows the game is on.

'I was briefed by British Intelligence,' Gus said. 'If an Overlord is down, captured alive, they had to assume he will blow D-Day under torture. They figure the odds are four to five to one against any of us holding out, and they're not about to send our boys into Hitler's waiting arms.'

Andy nodded slowly, drinking it in.

'So there's no choice,' Gus said slowly. 'They have to switch the invasion to another site.'

Andy was searching Gus' eyes now. Gus was keeping his gaze strong and confident. Stay with me. Lean on me. Here we go.

'My orders,' Gus said, 'are to hold out as long as I can, then give them what I know. Give them D-Day.'

Another wink.

'If you make something up,' Gus said, 'the Krauts will

spot it. They're a lot better at watching you than you are at keeping a bunch of lies straight under torture. And if you make something up, you've only got a few credible scenarios to choose from. You might accidentally feed them the new invasion site.'

Andy now received a wink so hard that Gus felt as if he'd pushed his eyeball back into the middle of his brain.

Soundlessly, Gus' lips formed two words. *Calais. September.* His lips repeated the words a second time.

There was a drunken, swaying moment. Then, something in Andy's eyes showed the jolt of a connection.

Andy leaned forward. His voice became almost a whisper.

'You're actually gonna give them Calais?' he said in perfect imitation of disbelief.

Tears of gratitude and admiration flooded Gus' eyes. With everything Andy had been through, his performance was little short of a miracle.

'Not yet,' Gus said softly, his smile warm and loving, 'but when the time is right, Calais is what they'll get.'

Andy nodded slowly.

'September, too?' Andy asked. 'We're supposed to give them the real date? Shouldn't we push it back to October, give Ike more time?'

Gus' heart was pounding in his chest. He had never been so proud of anyone. Never underestimate an American, you bastards.

Gus turned his body slightly, so that his profile was now visible to the air vent.

'No,' Gus said. 'We stick to September. We stay with the real date . . . the one that used to be the truth. There are two other guys who went down with me, Andy. God knows where they are, but we're all giving the same story.'

He looked over at Andy, who was shivering. It was pretty cold in the cell, but Gus was guessing that it was more tension than chill.

'You all right?' Gus asked gently.

Andy was looking off into space.

'Sure,' Andy said after a long beat. 'It's just a shame I never got the same briefing you did.'

Gus could see Andy's wheels turning. Andy was trying to reach out to him. Past the unseen Nazis, in words that would be safe.

'Nobody thought,' Andy said, 'I'd be captured, I guess. I'm just a wireless guy. I was never supposed to leave England. You've gotta help me, Gus. Help me get everything right.'

Gus looked over at his new friend. A few feet and still a thousand miles away. Gus was overwhelmed by what he couldn't say, needed to say. He could only make a silent promise that he would never let this man down. If three people were to get out of this alive, Andy had just joined Claire and Amy on that list.

'We've got each other now,' Gus said aloud across the distance. 'That was their mistake. Together we're gonna be a whole lot more than they can handle. You start believing that, Andy. Start believing it now.'

TWENTY-NINE

A small room, deep in the belly of Vincennes. An oak table, a single lamp. Four glasses and a bottle of sweet heavy liquor.

Ritter was clearly elated. Brausch's gaze was reflective, but he seemed to regard Gus with new respect. Walter Hoffmann had slipped into his most pleasant and impassive smile. The four of them were alone in the world.

Gus' eyes were swimming with weariness. It was four-thirty in the dead of morning. He had sat on the concrete floor of that cell with Andy Wheeler for eleven hours of the most perfectly sustained concentration he had ever produced. And now that he was spent beyond exhaustion, the next step was about to begin.

As an added nightmare, this was the moment when he must forever incur the formidable hostility of Ernst Ritter.

The next step would be a war within a war. More accurately, a trial. Ritter would be his adversary, Hoffmann his judge. If Ritter prevailed, all the work of these past hours would be useless. Everything would be useless.

And yet, as Gus sat square in the path of Ritter's praise, hearing the lavish and slightly drunken compliments to his evening's performance, he was never more aware of how insidiously effective Ritter's subliminal intimidation had become. Gus' intestines were crawling at the thought of provoking this man. What was the fear? Find it, name it. That Ritter with his dead and merciless eyes would come straight over the table at him. That the massive hands would spring to Gus' throat and snap his neck like a dry twig.

Gus watched that fantasy in his mind, as vividly and with as much detail as he could create. He saw Ritter's lips part and curl with sudden fury. He watched the glint of light on the collar button of Ritter's tunic as he bolted from his chair with unstoppable force. He saw the powerful hands come towards him, Hoffmann and Brausch frozen in an instant of mesmerized horror.

As he sat and smiled and accepted Ritter's praise, Gus was a film editor, replaying that scene again and again. And slowly, finally, its reality had drained away. Fear was seen as only fear. Gus was ready.

Ritter is a classic SS personality, Brasch had counselled, who can respect only dominating behaviour. Best to establish yourself with him before a major confrontation. Provoke him subtly, Brasch had said. You have to dare his anger for him to sense you as a man. Remember, he will never ultimately respect your intellect. Only your will.

Ritter raised his glass in Gus' direction.

'To Calais,' Ritter said. 'September second.'

Gus' eyes were strangely cold in the face of Ritter's enthusiasm.

'The second?' Gus said and his voice bore a hint of

disdain. The shading was very slight, but Gus saw it immediately register in Ritter's eyes. The man was attuned to insult as a shark to blood.

'Yes, of course,' Ritter answered, the warmth fading ominously. 'Wheeler said, "September two."'

Gus' smile was unquestionably condescending.

'No,' Gus said. 'A little problem with your English, Colonel. Wheeler said "September, too, *too* as in *also*."'

Ritter's eyes had gone to that flat look of warning. Very thin ice, they said.

'And what,' Ritter said slowly, 'makes you so certain of that?'

Gus was shaking his head with maddening, taunting amusement.

'Just a matter of thinking it through,' Gus said. 'Your inference could scarcely be possible. How could the Americans choose a single exact date? They would need a range of several days from which to select the best weather.'

And now Brausch took his folded hands from his lips.

'Obvious,' he pronounced with aristocratic relish and precision.

Insolence from Gus was one matter. Ridicule from Brausch was quite another. Ritter wheeled on Brausch, instantly at his flash point.

'I'm sorry, Ernst,' Brausch said calmly. 'I hadn't meant to offend. We're tired. It's nearly dawn. We should be basking in triumph.'

As Brausch effectively defused the man, Gus was pondering the reason for Brausch's interjection. He concluded that Brausch had drawn Ritter's anger to himself because Gus was coming too close to the flame.

Ritter's expansive smile was more or less back in place.

'The triumph is all the more significant,' Ritter said, 'because Berlin seemed ready to lean in the wrong direction.'

Ritter glanced at Hoffmann, seeking permission to reveal this report to Gus. Hoffmann nodded very slightly.

'On May sixth,' Ritter announced with indelicate irony,

'General Jodl placed a telephone call to General Blumentritt. It seems that the High Command had determined to reinforce the coast of Normandy. They had moved the Panzer Lehr Division from Hungary, and the Twenty-first Panzer Division from Brittany.'

Ritter's glass was firmly raised.

'So,' he beamed, 'to Calais. To the month of September. To the Emerald product.'

Glasses clicked.

'I'm afraid,' Gus said slowly, 'that this is only the first page. Not the last.'

Ritter's eyebrows headed for his hairline. It was astonishing to hear Gus question his own achievement.

'You doubt the accuracy,' Ritter asked, 'of what we heard tonight?'

Gus sighed, but tried to keep it friendly.

'There are two distinct possibilities,' Gus said. 'It's true. Or it isn't.'

'Would Wheeler have lied to you?'

'I think he trusts me,' Gus said. 'I don't think he would have lied to *me*. But perhaps he thought he was lying to *you*.'

Ritter did not understand. Brausch did.

'You mean,' Brausch said, 'he might have suspected you were being overheard?'

Gus nodded.

'It's entirely possible,' Gus said.

There was a moment of stillness.

'A possibility,' Brausch said at last, 'which I fear must be examined. I think . . . Gus should get Wheeler off alone somewhere . . . a place where he could have no suspicion.'

'And where would the colonel suggest this be accomplished?' Ritter asked stiffly.

'Well,' Gus interposed, 'why don't I just take him to the beach for the weekend? Couple of broads and a case of beer.'

Ritter was so innately humourless that there was actually a beat before he realized Gus was joking.

Once again, Brausch's slow aristocratic smile.

'Impractical,' Brausch said drily. 'I would prefer a brief walk in the gardens here at the château. We can cordon off a large area. It would be perfectly secure. Out in the open air, Wheeler would know he was not being overheard.'

Ritter's palms were flat on the table. A sure sign that he was digging in.

'You are speaking,' he said, 'of an unmonitored interview. This is not in accordance with security guidelines. It is *not*.'

Gus looked Ritter flat in the eyes.

'You don't need a monitor, Standartenführer. I will tell you what the prisoner says. I have an excellent memory.'

Ritter's eyes were locked with his.

'You mustn't feel, young Captain, that you are mistrusted. Security is a matter of consistently applied procedures. Not individual decisions concerning personal trust.'

'Of course,' Gus agreed. 'It's just that I was somewhat curious as to where the Americans plan to invade this continent.'

Walter Hoffmann cleared his throat.

'At such an hour,' Hoffmann said quietly, 'my poor brain is even foggier than usual. As much as I relish friendly debate, I would prefer to devote such consciousness as remains to resolving our dilemma.'

Hoffmann pressed his fingertips together. He levelled his gaze at Gus's eyes.

'How essential,' he asked, 'is such a private conversation with the prisoner?'

'It's a question of just how certain you want to be,' Gus responded. 'If we're guessing, my guess is that Wheeler told me the truth.'

The dark eyes stayed on Gus. Stayed and thought.

'I think,' Gus added, 'that we'd only have to do it once. If Wheeler feared that we were being overheard in the cell, it's the first thing he'd tell me when we're alone.'

Hoffmann turned his eyes to Brausch.

'I know, Jürgen, that this is precisely the kind of conflict you feared.'

And as always, Hoffmann's mind remained for Gus a black and bottomless pool. Perhaps he had been truly persuaded. Perhaps he was offering Gus just a little more rope.

THIRTY

Gus was in his favourite place, at least so far in this particular lifetime. Claire's arms.

Amy had been fed and played with and kissed good-night. Gus had listened to the wireless reports and had given Claire the coded data Leclerc would send back to London.

Now was just being together.

Their talk drifted lazily, keeping to the present tense, always of the present moment.

Occasionally, there would be a slip.

'Someday we'll have a piano,' Claire said.

And in Gus' mind, 'someday' suddenly gave breath to a future beyond the first week of June. Beyond the day when, he hoped, a million Germans would huddle behind their fortifications in Pas-de-Calais. Waiting for an invasion that instead would come far to the west in Normandy.

There was no world that Gus could count on beyond that day. This was known, believed, and thoroughly rejected. Like fear, Claire's arms created a separate reality. A home so real in its presence that it turned all future into the cobweb dust of little lies.

'We'll be in the South of France, then,' Gus said, never having seen the South of France in his life. 'We'll live in a farmhouse near Aix. There'll be pigs and flowers.'

'And a piano,' she repeated softly.

'Amy will study the classics,' he said confidently, his eyes shut as she cradled his head against her breasts. 'But as for me, I expect I'll want to learn ragtime.'

She giggled.

'I think,' he said, 'I'll make inquiries. We'll have to import a teacher from Salzburg for Amy. And one from New Orleans for me. They could live in a separate guest-house and join us for breakfast. Maybe help feed the geese.'

'Couldn't we just have a piano?'

'Or,' he said, 'we could just have a piano. And live in Cleveland.'

She gently placed his head on the pillow and started to get out of bed.

'I have a surprise for you,' she announced.

His jaw slacked open in a burlesque of extreme astonishment.

'I bartered off the silver earrings,' she said. 'We're up to our ears in coupons.'

'Hey, we said we were keeping those for you.'

'Oh yeah?' She stuck out her jaw in her best tough-guy pose. 'Well, *we* don't pay us so good.'

His turn to giggle at her pseudo-Bronx accent.

'Real berries,' she pronounced as if declaring an end to the war, 'and real cream.'

She bounced the rest of the way out of bed and disappeared.

Once she was gone, Gus' mind slipped inexorably back to the tiny cubicle at the bottom of Vincennes.

Rote as a rosary, Gus retraced each syllable of his catechism on the danger of trusting Jürgen Brausch. The old man was in league with Hoffmann. They had brought Gus to Paris for fear of the very thing that Gus had told Andy. That the Allies would change the invasion site because of Andy's capture. Hoffmann could only triumph if he accomplished *both* of two objectives. The first, to break Andy. The second, to convince London that their secret was safe. Gus was, therefore, an indispensable pawn.

Brausch and Hoffmann could never dare to try a double-wire, disposing of Gus and sending messages to London in his name. Even if they could find and somehow break the code, which only Gus himself understood, they would know that Gus must have devised systems of triggers and checks. In one of these, Gus had arranged intentional misspellings of the third or sixth word of specific sentences. The absence of such triggers would alert London that Gus had been impersonated. No, Hoffmann would need Gus to remain alive and blissfully deluded, sending back his messages of comfort.

Until, of course . . . until D-Day.

Claire had returned with a single huge bowl, swimming with cream and berries dusted with brown sugar. There were two spoons.

'Start from one end,' she said, 'and we'll work towards the middle.'

'We should save this,' he said, 'for Colonel Ritter. Never know when I might need a quick bribe.'

She poked her spoon delicately at an especially plump berry.

'You said he rather liked you at first. How ever did you manage that?'

'Well,' he said, 'I told him that my bloodline was pure Aryan for a thousand years, *and* that this didn't necessarily make me a bad person.'

She smiled.

'You're really pure Aryan?' she asked, though looking at his face made it difficult to question.

'Don't rub it in,' he said. 'I feel bad enough already.'

She looked at him thoughtfully for a long moment.

'There is a man,' she said, 'I've decided to tell you about.'

'Ah,' he whispered, 'a man from the past.'

She responded with a smile of teasing delight.

'Exactly,' she said. 'The past.'

'Give it to me straight,' he grinned. 'I can take it.'

She was definitely teasing now. He was more than curious.

'All right,' she said. 'This man was not my lover. Not even my friend. In fact, I never knew him at all.'

'This has all the makings,' he said, 'of a very intimate revelation.'

She nodded vigorously.

'You bet,' she said. 'So intimate that I thought I was never going to tell you.'

Her eyes said she wasn't kidding about that. He was thoroughly stumped.

'I give up,' he said. 'You're having posthumous sex with Ulysses S. Grant during a weekly seance on Thursday afternoons.'

'Tuesdays,' she corrected. 'Actually, you are getting warmer because the man *is* dead.'

He took a deep breath and she held up a restraining hand.

'Don't guess anymore,' she said. 'Your guesses are too salacious.'

'If I can't be offensive, forget the whole conversation.'

She ignored this and plunged ahead.

'Anyway,' she said, 'this man lived and died in a village in Poland that I don't even know the name of.'

'This is a fascinating yarn,' he admitted. 'It's the richness of detail I find most irresistible.'

She nodded.

'It's about to get even richer,' she said. 'This man's wife and his children and his grandchildren all lived out their lives as practising Roman Catholics.'

'Absorbing,' he noted. 'And provocative.'

'But,' she said, '*he* was a Jew.'

Gus had run full force into a brick wall.

'He was your grandfather,' he said softly.

'Great-grandfather,' she answered.

Gus ran the back of his fingers gently across her cheek.

'And to *think*,' he said, with a pretty good imitation of Ritter's accent, 'that we *actually* made love.'

She nodded.

'You must feel unclean,' she said.

'Now, I will be forced to undergo the traditional purification ceremony required by these circumstances.'

'And what is that?' she asked, dutifully playing the straight man.

'I must,' he said grandly, 'have sex with an entire Hitler

Youth Club. They may be twelve-year-old boys, but at least they're racially pure.'

She laughed, but so quickly there was something else behind her eyes. Pain, guilt, something stabbing at her. He wanted to say something comforting, but her face was such that any words seemed almost an invasion of privacy.

Then, in the next moment, her eyes were filled with tears. All he could do was to take her hands and hold on.

'I'm so sorry,' she said through the tears. 'This is very unfair.'

He kept his grip steady and his mouth shut.

'You know how sometimes . . . a thought . . .'

'Sure,' he said. 'I know.'

She was shaking her head and the tears were now sliding down her cheeks.

'I never even asked his name,' she said.

He just waited. She gently pulled a hand free. She dried her face with the tips of her slender fingers.

'In July,' she said, 'two years ago, the Germans had what they called the *Grande Rafle*. The Great Raid. They sealed off a part of the city and they took all the Jews who weren't Frenchborn. They took them to the sports arena, the Vélodrome d'Hiver. It was monstrous. Mothers, in the streets, being hurried along by French policemen. Children clutching at their skirts, trying to keep up.'

She stopped to gulp for breath.

'You don't have to tell me this,' he said.

She stared at him.

'I have to tell you,' she said. 'We have to give him a name.'

He nodded, although he had no idea what she was talking about.

'They held these poor people,' she said, 'thousands of them. No food. No sanitation. Then they started taking them to Drancy. Do you know Drancy?'

'It's a work camp,' he said. 'Near the airport. Near Le Bourget.'

'It was an uncompleted housing project. They surrounded it with barbed wire. All the apartments around it can look right in.'

She had caught her breath now. There were no tears.

'By August,' she said, 'they had four thousand children in the camp. The oldest were twelve. Some of them were less than a year old. They had all been separated from their parents. All just dumped together in this big courtyard.'

'You saw this?'

She nodded.

'My girl friend was a Red Cross worker. The Germans were allowing them in at that time. She got sick and she called me. She begged me to go in her place. And I did.'

She shook her head, her mouth open.

'You couldn't believe the conditions. These babies slept in filth. They fed them soup – they called it soup. There were lice and skin diseases so horrible. Gus, they beat those babies. They beat them. And they robbed them.'

And now the tears came so suddenly and she was convulsed in sobs. He grabbed her and held her as tightly as he could.

'There was a little girl . . .' She was choking now, forcing the words from her throat. 'And she cried in my arms because they stole her locket. Her locket was all she had left of her mama. And they stole . . . one shoe. How could you steal . . . a baby's shoe . . . one shoe?'

She had pulled back now and was staring at him with the wildest eyes.

'So they were all there like that . . . in the courtyard. They were constantly in panic, just screaming all the time. And there were railway tracks. And this train pulls up with all these freight cars. And the soldiers, these German soldiers, are kicking the children now. Screaming at the big ones to carry the little ones into the cars.'

And suddenly, her tears stopped again. Gus saw that she had come to a grief beyond tears.

'I was holding this little boy in my arms. He was about four. And a larger child came and carried him to the train. So I followed. They pulled him up into the boxcar, and he held out his arms towards me, and he cried and he screamed.'

She looked down and shook her head. Then the grey eyes, wide and staring, shot back up to Gus.

'He said, "Let the lady hold me. So I can cry. The pretty lady. I want her to hold me when I cry."'

Her eyes were flooded again.

'And I walked past all those soldiers. I walked to the doorway of that freight car. And I took that baby in my arms. I told him that he was my little boy now. That I loved him and would always love him. I told him that no matter what happened, all he had to do was close his eyes and think of me. And when he did, then I would be thinking of him too. And we would be together.'

She cried until she was coughing uncontrollably.

'They took him out of my arms,' she gasped, 'and they packed him into that car with all those shrieking babies. And they rolled that door shut.'

He gently laid her back on the pillow. She looked up at him with eyes that were questioning.

'So that,' she said, 'is how I came to Jade Amicol. I learned to be a forger . . . and how to use a gun. But I'm really not a fighter. I just miss my little boy.'

'Martin,' Gus said with all the certainty and strength in him. 'Martin is his name. And Martin is all right. He's thinking of you right now. He's loving you for being his friend.'

She just kept nodding. Nodding with tears streaming down her face.

'Thank you,' she whispered.

THIRTY-ONE

Gus was back in the cell. There were two small cots now, rough khaki blankets draped across them in the eerie greenish light.

He lay on his back, using his hands for a pillow. His eyes were empty. They turned lifelessly, randomly, to every corner of the cell. Except the air vent. Behind the eyes, his mind honed itself with steady recitation of what lay ahead.

At last, they brought him Andy.

The sight of Gus made Andy's heart leap to his eyes. He hadn't known whether he would ever see Gus again.

'We'll have to stop meeting like this,' Gus said. 'Hitler's getting suspicious.'

Andy smiled so sweetly and openly that Satan himself would have softened. And to Gus' mind came a round-faced child he had never seen. A child he had christened Martin. You're my little boy now, Gus' heart told Andy. No one puts you in that freight car.

They talked, they slept. Fifteen hours.

A guard appeared. They were led through dark passageways, up many flights of ancient stone steps. They seemed almost guided by smell as they moved from rot towards the scent of something antiseptic.

Suddenly, a door was opened and there was blinding light. It was morning. This was Andy's first sense of time of day in nearly two weeks.

The guard led them through the courtyard, past the eyes of hundreds of armed soldiers and across the outer moat. They stood at the edge of a large wooded area.

The guard told them only that they were to be permitted an hour's stroll in the gardens. He showed them the path, and reminded them that the area had been thoroughly secured. Escape would be impossible, and the aftermath of any such attempt would be particularly unpleasant.

They began to walk together. Andy, still a little unsteady. They passed through a row of hedges. There were elm trees and roses.

They were alone.

They walked on in silence. Freedom so sudden had to be absorbed before it could be used.

'It is time,' Gus said softly, 'to clear your head of everything in this world. Everything but my voice.'

Andy nodded, his eyes on the path before him. They had issued Andy oversized prison clothes, to sharpen his feelings of smallness, helplessness. His sleeves and the cuffs of his trousers were rolled up in great bunches. He looked impossibly frail. A wave of discouragement swept through Gus, and he fought it back as if it were nausea. As if it were poison.

'You know,' Gus said, 'they can hear us in the cell. I think they can see us too. Through the air vent.'

Andy just nodded again. Eyes on his shoes. Concentration absolute.

'This may be our only time alone for a while,' Gus said. 'I'm going to give you all the truth there is.'

Gus took a deep breath.

'Andy, I'm not really a prisoner.'

Andy looked up at him sharply. Eyes clear. There was no anticipation, no judgment. He was listening.

'The Nazis think that I'm working for them under cover. That I'm tricking you.'

Andy nodded, as if such insanity made perfect sense. Something in his eyes reminded Gus just how fast Andy's brain could work. The discouragement flowed out of Gus entirely. He was drawing strength now from Andy's eyes.

'I'm trusting you with my life, Andy, by telling you that. If they pull it out of you, I'm a dead man.'

'You're telling me,' Andy said quietly, 'for a reason.'

Attaboy.

'I had to tell you,' Gus said, 'because we're up against an

SS colonel named Hoffmann. He is one damned smart sonofabitch. The day may come that he tells you I'm working for him. Proves it to you, somehow.'

'Why would he do that?

'Maybe my cover gets blown. Maybe he just gets suspicious and stops trusting me.'

The green eyes looked into Andy's now. Held them fast.

'But whatever he comes and tells you,' Gus said, 'whatever he uses, there's a world full of people back home that will be counting on you, Andy. Counting on you to do one thing. To trust me and nobody else.'

Gus stopped walking.

'You do trust me,' he said.

Andy's eyes said he sure as hell did.

'You trust me,' Gus smiled, 'because I'm such a damned handsome guy. Also, because I passed you the Calais in September story. I've been briefed, Andy. I know it's Normandy, fourth of June. The Germans, of course, think I don't know shit. If they did, they'd have me on the rack.'

Gus grinned down at Andy.

'You're not on the rack,' Gus said, 'because I phonied up some medical records about a heart condition.'

A light went on in Andy's eyes.

Andy told Gus about the German doctors. Electrodes, machines he'd never seen before. Lots of questions about his heart. As with all questions, of course, he had given no answer at all. Gus responded with the details of Andy's arrhythmia.

'For the Germans,' Gus said at last, 'the formal interrogation process is just a setup. They think the real interrogation is being conducted by me inside your cell.'

They were walking again, very slowly.

'So whatever you tell me in that cell,' Gus said, 'if you do it right . . . that's what these bastards are gonna believe.'

Andy was looking up at him now. Gus smiled with crystal-pure confidence.

'You're not gonna lose this war for us, Andy. You're gonna be more responsible than any man alive for winning it.'

Andy nodded slowly.

'You just tell me once,' Andy said. 'Tell me slow. I'll remember every word for the rest of my life.'

Andy looked a bit sheepish. He knew that he sounded immodest. Still, it was the God's truth, and Gus had to know.

'Okay,' Gus said, 'here we go. Now the beauty of this tale is that it comes from Ops B, Committee of Special Means. That's the SHAEF department responsible for all cover and deception. So we've been planting seeds of this stuff in phony documents and wireless reports for six months. When Hoffmann checks your story back to Berlin, he'll find plenty of corroboration from his own intelligence reports.'

Andy was walking a little faster now. Gus could see the juices flowing.

'Object of the game is to keep Hitler's Fifteenth Army, his strongest, pinned in Calais. Supposedly, the unit attacking Calais is called FUSAG, First United States Army Group. Actually, the unit doesn't even exist. We tell 'em it's got three US infantry divisions, one Canadian infantry, and one Canadian armoured. It's commanded by Patton himself. We've got eight more divisions of the US Third Army coming in a second wave. We've got fifty divisions more in the States. They'll be shipped at the last minute, and they'll pour over the Channel once FUSAG has its beachhead.'

'Now,' Gus said, 'the timing. We tell them that June and July will be preliminary thrusts in other directions. Give them Operation Fortitude as a coordinated attack on Norway. We're after the Petsamo nickel-ore mines. We'll use the Fourth Army and it'll hook up with FUSAG later.'

Gus paused again to give Andy a moment to absorb.

'I'm okay,' Andy said. 'Go as fast as you want now. It's all right.'

'We follow with Operation Zeppelin in the Balkans. We're going after the Black Sea coast, the oil fields at Ploiesti. That's a third of Hitler's oil.'

Andy was nodding again. More for Gus' comfort than anything else.

'You're going to complain about delays. SHAEF had given reinforcements of long-range bombers a higher priority than building up ground forces. Also, there are special landing craft that haven't tested well. They won't be ready until middle or late summer.'

They turned a bend in the path. A hundred fifty metres to the right, Gus saw two soldiers with rifles, Gus and Andy had wandered to the boundary of their open-air cage.

Gus stopped and waved his arms at the soldiers.

'Hey guys,' he shouted in English. 'How about we all meet back at my place for a beer?'

Andy giggled. The soldiers did not respond.

'Antisocial,' Gus yelled. Andy laughed some more, his tension mercifully finding escape.

'That's the trouble with a master race,' Gus said to Andy. 'They're snobs.'

Gus turned back, towards another bend in the path. The trees were shivering now in a sudden gust of breeze. All the colours of the world were triple-sharp. And Gus had only been locked away from them for fifteen hours. He wondered if there was a longer stretch waiting at the end of all this. No problem. Ernst Ritter would provide enough shrieking agony to blot out any sense of loss as to the colour of the leaves.

'Now, your big story,' Gus said, 'is the Russians. We all agreed in Tehran that we wouldn't invade France until after the Red Army launched its summer offensive. Obviously, this is because we want to keep sixty per cent of the Wehrmacht at the eastern front. The Russians had wanted to go in July, but they're hurting for ammo and their supply lines are all screwed up. They'll be lucky to launch in August, so that we can hit Calais start of September.'

They walked on. In twenty minutes, Gus repeated the bones of the story three times, adding more flesh with each telling.

'When you feed this stuff back to me in the cell,' Gus said, 'remember you're supposed to believe I'm an Overlord too. That I already know it. You can't appear to be teaching me.'

'Then how do I tell you?'

'As if we're rehearsing. I'll say it's time for us to tell them about June. You'll be scared. You'll ask me how to do it. I'll play Nazi interrogator and you'll practise giving answers. While you're practising, all this stuff will flow out very naturally. Just don't get impatient to say too much at once. Always follow my lead. If I cut you off, don't override me. There'll be a reason.'

Andy stiffened. Memorizing was one thing, acting was another.

'I'll do all the work,' Gus said. 'I'll start you, stop you, change course where we need to. Hey, you were perfect last time, and you didn't even know the score.'

That was true. The muscles of Andy's face relaxed a little. Gus looked awfully strong, awfully sure.

'Let's do one right now,' Gus beamed.

They tramped off through the woods. Gus doing his comic opera impersonation of Ritter, Andy pretending to be practising his answers.

'You're terrific,' Gus said at last. 'A natural. When this is over, I'm grabbing you for OSS.'

Gus was only lying a little. Andy was pretty good. If he could give eighty per cent of this performance inside the cell, it would be good enough.

'Can you keep your party funny,' Andy asked, 'even back in the cell? I think that would really help me.'

'We'll laugh our butts off,' Gus promised.

Andy's face had some colour now. This was as strong as Gus had seen him.

Gus' eyes held their twinkle, but seemed now to burn into Andy's. A firm hand grabbed Andy's shoulder.

'Look,' Gus said, 'I've had the same training these guys had. I understand what they're doing. They set everything up towards one objective . . . to make you think that they can read your mind. And you know why they do that?'

Andy shook his head.

'Because they can't,' Gus said. 'But if you think they can, then part of you gives up inside. Same trick we'd use on them in London, Andy. Same lie. They can't read your mind. They can only wait for you to give up.'

It was clear to him that Andy understood.

'I know people, Andy. I'm trained to judge them. You won't give up. You may think you will, fear you will. Everybody does that. I do, all the time. But you won't give up. Won't even come close.'

Andy's eyes were so grateful for those words.

'Here comes the first rule of intelligence work, Andy. It's your profession now, so listen up. The guy that wins isn't the guy with the guns or even the brains. He's the guy who has more information. That is the *only* thing that counts. They don't know what we're doing. We do. If we don't give up and tell' em, then we win. It is just . . . that . . . simple.'

Andy looked down at the grass, then back up to the strong green eyes.

'You know,' Andy said, 'when you told me you weren't a prisoner, that you were sent here by OSS . . . I figured, that's it. He's going to give me the cyanide. He's going to give it to me right here and now. And I'm going to die right here, in this garden. And I'll never, you know . . . say good-bye to my mom and dad. Or my girl.'

Gus started to try a joke, but he just couldn't. His eyes were flooded.

'I've got other plans for you,' Gus said softly, no trace of anything in his voice but deadly earnest. 'After we've conned these guys, you're going home. I am personally sending you back to the arms of all those people. Especially your girl. I'm going to make that happen, Andy. And you can depend on it.'

And now Andy was sobbing softly. Gus threw an arm around his shoulders.

'Hey,' Gus smiled, 'look at it this way. Have I ever lied to you?'

THIRTY-TWO

The spiral steps seemed endless. An SS Untersturmführer was leading the way with a kerosene lamp against the dimness. Gus followed, his head throbbing with a pain that seemed to split his skull, just behind the eyes. Migraine was an old enemy, choosing a dramatic moment to reappear.

The bottom of the stone stairwell. A long, impossibly narrow corridor, reeking of mildew, of every curse spawned by deprivation of air and sunlight.

Why were they taking a different route this time? Gus wondered if Hoffmann could have actually ordered such a thing. If this was a deliberate attempt to keep Gus from memorizing the pattern of Vincennes' underground maze. If so, did it indicate general precaution or direct suspicion? Then again, this might simply be the route most familiar to the lieutenant with the lamp.

None of this was helping the migraine one bit.

A door. A bolt thrown open. Light.

Here was the tiny room, the single lamp. The same bottle of thick sweet booze, just a little less in it. Three faces turned as one to observe Gus' entrance.

One friendly smile. It belonged to Walter Hoffmann.

'Pleasant day,' Hoffmann inquired, 'for a stroll in the woods?'

Gus took his seat. His eyes looked to the clear liquor in Hoffmann's glass.

'Drink that stuff before noon,' Gus said, 'it'll kill you.'

Hoffmann's smile was amused and comfortable. He waited just that extra fraction of a moment before responding, the beat that assumed authoritative command of rhythm and flow.

'That's schnapps,' Hoffmann said quietly.

'It's a German drink,' Ritter added, as if Gus wouldn't know much about Germans. He was drumming his fingers lightly on the oak table.

'Ah,' Gus said. 'And I thought you guys drank beer. Or maybe the blood of Englishmen.'

Ritter looked puzzled.

'It's a children's story,' Gus said, his mind working only a half step ahead of his mouth, 'called "Jack and the Beanstalk." A little fellow sneaks into a giant's castle. Sneaks out again with the giant's most precious possession.'

'Careless giant,' Hoffmann observed.

For the rarest of moments, Gus felt himself reading Hoffmann's eyes with almost magical clarity. He knew, somehow knew, that Hoffmann's mind was watching Gus climb the beanstalk, the spiral stairwell of Vincennes prison. Gus as Jack, the thief in the castle. Hoffmann as giant, protecting the prize.

Hoffmann had made the connection. Made it instantly. More quickly than would have been possible if Gus were not already under suspicion. Hoffmann *did* suspect. Had from the first.

Flying on guesswork passing as insight, Gus was nonetheless certain of his read. More, this was the first time he had been able to use Hoffmann's own quickness against him. That could build a fellow's confidence.

'Maybe too much schnapps before noon,' Gus offered.

Hoffmann nodded.

'A sleepy giant is a dead giant,' Hoffmann agreed.

Hoffmann's eyes were opaque once more. Had the window truly opened a crack in that moment? The glint Gus had seen could have meant a thousand other things, or nothing at all. Careless giant, Hoffmann had said. No. There had been a flash, all the way down to the bottom. In it, one cold and terrifying truth. A giant very wide awake. Hoffmann was Gus' tracker. Hoffmann was coming for him.

'Do you have a bedtime story for us?' Jürgen Brausch inquired.

'Wheeler,' Gus said simply, 'has no idea that we're being heard in the cell.'

Ritter stared at him for a moment.

'Perhaps,' Ritter said, 'he failed to speak of his fear because he mistrusts even you.'

Gus smiled and shook his head.

'In that case,' Gus said, 'he's the greatest little actor that ever lived. Colonel, this boy is lost and alone and absolutely certain that you're going to kill him. I am the only thing he has left in this world. When he sees me, his eyes light up like I was his girl friend.'

Ritter seemed to accept that. 'Were any substantive matters discussed?'

'Some,' Gus said. 'It's a tricky business, drawing out information he thinks I already know. I'm getting the hang of it. It's going well.'

'And in specifics . . .?' Ritter's impatience threshold had been reached and breached.

'I'm beginning to doubt,' Gus said, 'that he knows a great deal of detail. Apparently, there are various grades of Overlords, given different levels of information . . .'

'Why don't you tell us,' Ritter said much too sharply, 'what you *did* learn, rather than what you did not.'

Gus reached slowly for his glass.

'Your health.' He toasted Ritter, and took a small hit.

'Godawful stuff,' Gus complained, screwing his face into a grimace. 'After we overrun Britain, I'm gonna teach you guys to drink gin.'

Hoffmann's smile, the dancing eyes.

'Oberst Brausch already drinks gin, Gus. A very particular gin. Booth's. I thought you knew that.'

Hoffmann's eyes were daring Gus to take a step. Had Brausch betrayed his secret meeting with Gus? Had Brausch made only some harmless reference that they had shared a gin? Was Hoffmann simply guessing? Stop thinking, dammit. Way too long. Finesse it, fast.

'I drink Bombay,' Gus smiled. 'It's cleaner, sharper.'

'Less subtle,' Brausch drawled.

'Perhaps that's the difference between us,' Gus wondered aloud.

Christ that had taken far too long. Hoffmann had hit him with that gin thing and frozen him solid.

'If it wouldn't be too much trouble . . .' Ritter forced his way in, and Gus was never more grateful.

'Oh, yes,' Gus grinned lazily, 'my chat with what's-his-name.'

'If you please,' Ritter said.

Goddam that gin thing. Goddam it to stinking hell. Cool down. Use it. Parse it out, each step. It couldn't be a Brausch betrayal. If they were working together, Hoffmann certainly wouldn't have volunteered such a clue.

'Wheeler was going to coordinate wireless operations for part of the Calais landing,' Gus said slowly. 'He mentioned Canadians. I think some Canadian units will be involved in the assault.'

Right. The whole remark could have been innocent. But it wasn't. Hoffmann was probing. Still, for Hoffmann's style, the gambit seemed too obvious, too reckless. Unless. Unless he were after bigger game. Unless he were really after Jürgen Brausch. Unless he decided to take a little risk with his 'I thought you knew that,' hoping to push Gus into a response he could read. A defensive denial, an instant of visible calculation, anything to indicate a hidden tie between Gus and Brausch.

'There'll be some earlier thrusts before Calais,' Gus said. 'Something in the Balkans, that was clear. He said something about Italy, but I wasn't sure of the context. I was going awfully slow. Feeling my way.'

Hoffmann's eyes were locked to Gus' now.

'It seems,' Hoffmann said quietly, 'that your private chat was quite successful. Perhaps we should do it again.'

There was no doubt now in Gus' mind that there was a single purpose to this offer. To give Gus enough rope to hang himself, and maybe Brausch along with him.

'Well,' Gus said, 'he's tense in the cell. He's looser in the garden. They both have advantages. However, in view of

Colonel Ritter's aversion to unmonitored conversations . . .'

Ritter could not keep still.

'There is more involved,' he said unctuously, 'than security. No one's memory or powers of interpretation are infallible. Not even Captain Lang's. I would have to insist that we return exclusively to monitored situations.'

Brausch raised his heavy lids. 'Gus,' he asked, 'is Walter making sense here?'

The paranoia raging through and around Gus' migraine had obviously not spread to Brausch. Either Brausch had not picked up the danger signals, or he had disregarded them as trivial. Gus replayed the film in his mind. Careless giant. Hoffmann's eyes clicking through an association so clearly lurking at the surface of his thoughts.

'I'm getting what I want from Wheeler,' Gus said. 'I see no reason to upset Colonel Ritter. No reason to proceed in any way without full consensus. Let's keep it in the cell from here on.'

There was a hitch somewhere at the edge of Hoffmann's eyes. He had expected Gus to snatch the bait. It was Gus' turn to watch Hoffmann think for a moment.

'I don't mean to be difficult,' Hoffmann said with great deliberation, 'but I have the feeling that we might be losing a valuable opportunity here. Colonel Ritter is doing his job, of course. He does it superbly. But I sense, Gus, that you and Jürgen both feel that things might flow more . . . smoothly . . . if there were private strolls from time to time.'

Why was Gus so damn certain? Here was the chance for continuing privacy with Andy. It would simplify everything and do wonders for Andy's morale, yet, Gus was pulling away. Based on, he had to admit it, nothing more than a paranoid scent. But the harder Hoffmann pushed, the stronger it smelled.

'There is,' Hoffmann said, 'an artistry to what you do, Gus. I think your sense of things deserves our support in the final analysis.'

Gus stopped. Appeared to be considering the question as a minor one of incidental tactics.

'I appreciate your confidence, Oberführer,' Gus said. 'All the same, I'm quite comfortable with the cell. I think I can ply my art in close quarters.'

'Of that,' Hoffmann said softly, 'there is no question.'

But Hoffmann's face had clouded, ever so slightly. The bait had been left dancing on the hook, and the dark eyes had wandered into doubt.

THIRTY-THREE

Gus was sleeping deeply. Tangled in Claire, his breathing almost in rhythm with hers. There were no dreams of any kind.

At first, the sound was so far away that it was something akin to a dream. A slam, a pounding. Stopping again. So far away.

He rolled over onto his back. Pounding now closer. His eyelids fluttered. It was something on wood. It had stopped. Footfalls.

And suddenly he was awake as a deer locked in the eyes of a stalking tiger. Footfalls on the stairwell. Up the stairwell. His stairwell. Boots, a dozen, coming for him.

He lay on his back, Claire miraculously asleep beside him, and tried for a split second to will the sound away. There was a heart-stopping instant of silence, the great cat having leaped into the air. It fell against the door. An incredible, ear-splitting pounding at the door. Voices in German, shouting, cursing at the door.

He sat bolt upright.

There was no coldness in fear, was all he could think. Why did they always say cold fear? His skin and his belly were aflame. He was holding his breath, holding his very heartbeat.

And then, the instant he was never to forget.

The instant of realizing it was not Claire's door. It was another door. Another's death.

The instant, before the burning shame could follow, of thanking dear God that someone else was going to die.

Claire was awake now, clutching him.

He was springing from the bed, grabbing at his robe in the darkness. Jamming his fingers against the unseen armoire.

'Wait here,' he shouted as he tripped his way through the blackness, through the living room.

He fumbled with the doorknob. Suddenly, he was in the blinding light of the hallway.

They were SS. He could see four of them as they crowded together, three doors down. They had burst into an apartment. The door was in splinters. The cries of a woman from within were hideous, unimaginably piercing. Gus had never heard anything like those screams in his life.

Still, no other door on the landing had opened. No sound emerged from any other apartment. What prayer, what ritual against the dark, was passing through the hearts behind those doors?

Three more storm troopers emerged from the shattered doorway. One held an old man, flushed and quivering. Naked beneath his pyjama top, the man offered no resistance. He mumbled horribly to himself, as if his mind had already snapped. He was Claire's neighbour, Gus' neighbour now, but Gus had never seen him before.

It took two troopers to hold the old woman. Writhing, screaming piteously, her shrieks poured into the hallway and filled the stairwell. The troopers made no attempt to silence her. Their faces were neither amused nor angry. A night's work.

She was wearing only a thin, faded nightdress. Gus recognized her as Madame Sainte-Juste. They had met at the postbox two days before. She hadn't smiled. She disapproved of a young mother, such as Claire Jouvet, living in sin.

'Just a moment,' Gus barked in German, grateful to his toes that his voice had not cracked, nor his bladder emptied. Yet.

Seven troopers froze in astonishment at his presence. Even Madame Sainte-Juste stopped her wailing.

Gus' eyes swept the group. The most senior insignia was SS Obersturmführer. He looked no more than twenty. Gus outranked the boy, albeit in the wrong army.

'Who is in command here?' Gus insisted, eyes fixed on the boy.

From the stairwell, from the landing below, came the clearing of a husky throat. The lieutenant's eyes flicked to the stairwell in answer to Gus' demand.

Three pairs of boots climbed the stairs. A man in full-dress black and silver, strikingly handsome, led the way. He wore the insignia of Sturmbannführer, an SS major.

Gus stood erect as possible. His right arm shot forward.

'*Heil*, Hitler,' Gus said. His tone was calm, respectful of a senior's rank.

The major walked slowly towards him. Grey-haired, somehow tanned, the man was in his fifties. Blue eyes, so pale as to be nearly colourless.

'Who are you?' the major said quietly. The deadness of eye and softness of tone rekindled the fire in Gus' belly.

'I am Hauptmann Augustus Lang, Major. My permanent duties are with the Abwehr. I am in Paris as special assistant to SS Oberführer Walter Hoffmann.'

The man's eyes narrowed slightly. He knew Hoffmann's name.

With exquisite slowness, a smile crept across the major's lips. His right hand came forward, not in salute, but to offer a handclasp.

Gus reached out and took the hand, an unyielding metal vice.

'My name is Wilhelm Seitz,' the major said. But the man's eyes were now directed past Gus' right shoulder.

In a moment, Gus felt Claire wind her arm through his.

'My compliments,' Seitz said, 'to Oberführer Hoffmann. I trust, my dear Hauptmann, that we have not thoroughly spoiled your night's . . . sleep.'

The implication was leering, but the tone polite.

'If we had known,' Seitz said, 'that an officer was spending the night in this place . . . we would have postponed our duties.'

'Major Seitz, may I present Mademoiselle Jouvet. We live in this building.'

Seitz bowed slightly from the waist, his eyes glowing in Claire's direction.

'In that case, Hauptmann Lang, my compliments to you as well.'

'These people,' Gus said, his eyes flashing to the old couple, 'are our neighbours.'

'Ah,' Seitz said, with a smile of terrible amusement. 'Well, this is a police matter, Hauptmann. Do . . . not . . . concern . . . yourself.'

Advice given in such a tone was rarely disregarded. Seitz' eyes anticipated that this would be no exception.

'These people,' Gus asked in a tone of hushed confidence, 'are Jewish?'

'If they were Jewish, they would have been gone long before this.'

'And so . . .' Gus' eyes were clear and direct.

'A young savage killed an SS corporal in Montparnasse four days ago. Present policy is twenty lives for one. We begin with the killer's immediate family, and radiate outward. These people are great-aunt and-uncle.'

'I see,' Gus said.

'Theoretically,' Seitz continued, 'it makes the young hotheads think twice before they act. In practice, that's so much rubbish. It's all a dreadful nuisance. We take ten good men to collect Grandma and Grandpa here, because we never know what kind of armed resistance we'll meet from family or friends.'

Gus nodded. He was entirely sympathetic to the major's burden. 'Major Seitz . . .'

Seitz held up a hand. But he had stopped Gus' words even more surely with the steel in his eye.

'Hauptmann,' Seitz said, 'if you were to make an attempt . . . the slightest attempt . . . to intercede for these people, it would have to become the subject of an official Gestapo report. The report would also involve the young lady here.'

The eyes had become almost kind, in a robotic and inhuman way. Seitz was trying to help him.

'The report goes from Paris to Berlin in three days. There would then be an official inquiry as to why you had attempted to intercede on behalf of an enemy of the Reich. The . . . mildest . . . consequence for yourself would be immediate transfer from the occupied territory. The young lady's name would remain on file, and she would be subject to precautionary SD surveillance.'

Gus stared at the man and said nothing.

'The slightest attempt,' Seitz assured him again. 'Please abandon any fantasy that Oberführer Hoffmann would involve himself in your heroic display of gallantry towards your lady's neighbours. SD and Gestapo are fraternal orders to be sure . . . but each has its particular area of responsibility.'

Claire was squeezing his arm now. Her fingers saying what words need not. That there was no choice.

'These matters are most routine,' Seitz concluded. 'We no longer wait for public executions. These people will be dead before dawn, I assure you.'

Even at these words, there was no sound from Madame Saint-Juste. It took Gus a moment to realize that she spoke no German. She had yet to hear her own death sentence.

Seitz clicked his heels together. He bowed once more, slightly, in Claire's direction.

'And so,' Seitz pronounced with authoritative finality, 'good night and pleasant sleep to you both. Please do remember my respects to Oberführer Hoffmann.'

A wave of nausea swept so suddenly through Gus it seemed impossible to keep his stomach inside him. All of his muscles, so taut and attentive, had turned now to water. His mind raced wildly. It found nothing.

He stared at Seitz for what seemed a very long time. At last, his eyes turned to those of the old woman. Hers were pleading across the space between them. A thin ribbon of clear liquid was running, unnoticed, from her mouth and onto her nightdress.

Gus turned and took Claire back into the apartment. The scream of Madame Sainte-Juste followed them through the door.

He lay on his back, staring into the darkness. The scream stayed in his ears throughout his endless wait for dawn.

THIRTY-FOUR

There was a firm knock at the door.

'I'll get it,' Gus called back to Claire. He strode through the living room, adjusting his tie.

The door opened on Hoffmann's driver. A lieutenant, no less.

'The Oberführer presents his compliments. He hopes that he has not arrived at an inconvenient moment for you and Mademoiselle.'

Hoffmann had arrived, in fact, precisely on time.

Gus imagined the street scene in front of Claire's flat. Black limo with tiny Nazi flags fluttering above each headlamp. Small crowd from the neighbourhood beginning to gather, if they dared. Ritter, in full-dress SS uniform, tapping his fingers on his knee, impatient before the car had even rolled to a stop. Hoffmann, in black tie, sitting comfortably, gently urging poor Ritter to relax and enjoy the evening.

As Gus had instructed, Claire kept everyone waiting for a good ten minutes.

Gus and the driver sat in silence. The lieutenant was obsessed by visions of court-martial or worse as Ritter's retribution for the insufferable delay.

When Claire finally appeared, she was in a long, clinging gown of pure white. Her black hair was worn up, accentuating the bareness of her neck and slender shoulders. At her throat and wrist were delicate golden bands.

As the lieutenant saw her, the poor guy's heart almost stopped beating. He realized, finally, that while Gus had risen to greet her, he was still sitting and gaping. Humiliated, he lurched to his feet.

On the street, the effect was no less impressive. Hoffmann and Ritter were standing by the limo. They had never seen Claire, but the Gestapo report stated that she was quite beautiful. Nonetheless, they were somewhat unprepared for just *how* beautiful.

'Standartenführer,' Gus announced 'may I present Mademoiselle Jouvet.'

Ritter was beaming like an idiot. Taking her hand, he actually clicked his heels together. Just like in the movies, Gus couldn't help but think. Instantly, a colder association rolled through him. Just like Major Seitz.

'A great honour, mademoiselle.'

She smiled prettily.

'Well,' she corrected, 'at least a mild diversion.'

Hoffmann was thoroughly enchanted. He looked very dashing himself, in evening wear more elegant than Gus had pictured. His eyes were shining as he brought Claire's fingers to his lips.

Gus was counting on Claire *not* to deliver her promised opening line to Hoffmann of, 'Butcher's night out?' He was not disappointed.

'Far more than an honour,' Hoffmann said directly into her eyes, 'it is a pleasure.'

And now Claire's smile unleashed some candlepower.

'How enticing,' she said, 'to meet a man who delights in the ornamental. It's my favourite role, you know.'

Hoffmann shook his head slightly.

'I had not meant,' he said, 'to describe my pleasure as purely visual. If there is anything in this life more intoxicating than beauty, it is beauty combined with intelligence.'

She returned his gaze.

'An intoxicating combination,' she repeated, 'like barbiturates and liquor?'

'Like power and discretion,' he responded. 'Beauty *is* power. But so sadly wasted if not harnessed by a comparable intellect.'

She pursed her lips. 'You're very serious for such an attractive man. I've always felt that a girl can confine her intelligence to the decorative. If she applies herself.'

Hoffmann bowed slightly.

'We are all most grateful,' he said, 'that you have obviously never tried.'

Hoffmann's arm assisted Claire into the limo. They set off, gliding across the Pont Neuf, turning towards the Rue Royale.

When Gus had first told his colleagues that he was romantically involved, Ritter had been appalled. This could only affect Gus' concentration on the job at hand. The relationship must be broken off. Hoffmann's response had been the precise opposite. He proclaimed this a perfect release for Gus' tensions, and insisted that they meet the young lady socially at the earliest moment.

Gus took this as a further application of Hoffmann's theory: Give them as much rope as they're foolish enough to accept. Every aspect of human behaviour was to be encouraged. And observed. For in each component of his behaviour, the subject reveals himself.

They arrived at Maxim's and were treated to priority attention that bordered on the embarrassing. The headwaiter was a balding, lizard-like chap named Dietrich. He hovered, eyes and hands darting about suddenly as he commanded his minions to attend to the Oberführer's comfort.

'Maxim's,' Hoffmann explained, 'has been taken over by a famous Berlin restaurateur named Horcher. Dietrich knows me from the old days. Somehow, he clings to the notion that I am complimented by all this fuss. I suppose that's because I encourage it shamelessly.'

The evening continued in high spirits, with Claire the focus of all attention. She had asked Gus what was to be expected of her. He had answered, 'Charm, wit, all that stuff.' Claire was delivering.

By the time the fish course arrived, Gus' stomach was actually beginning to unclench.

'Now you must tell me, Colonel,' she said to Ritter, 'exactly what it is that you do.'

'Do?' he smiled.

'Yes,' she said. 'Whenever I ask Gus, he says that he does nothing at all. He says that he goes to an office and he waits for lunch. Mercifully, lunch ultimately arrives. It too quickly passes, leaving him with an even longer wait for supper.'

'It's a living,' Gus interjected.

'It is not a proper career,' she said firmly. 'Now be attentive, darling, and Ernst will tell us what you'll do when Walter makes you a colonel.'

Ritter was beguiled and more than a little inebriated.

'I do,' he said, 'a little of this and a little of that.'

'Aha!' she exclaimed. 'Ever so much more substance than simply waiting for meals. Now Gus can already do a little of *this*. Can he be a major until he masters doing a little of *that*?'

Ritter nodded.

'If you ask it,' he said, 'I'll wire General Eisenhower directly and recommend the promotion.'

Claire seemed genuinely puzzled, though not terribly disturbed. Gus had told the others that Claire knew nothing of his American Army status. The easier to avoid discussion of his double-agent persona.

'Oh, dear.' She turned to Gus. 'Are you with the enemy? How ungracious of you not to have mentioned. I'm enchanting entirely the wrong group of superiors.'

'You are enchanting,' Hoffmann observed, 'absolutely everyone.'

She looked at Gus directly.

'No,' she said, 'I'm serious. What did Ernst mean by that?'

'I'm here,' Gus said simply, 'to liberate France single-handed. To deliver your people from the cruel hand of the Nazi oppressor, and restore to you freedom and self-respect.'

She held his eyes for a moment. Then a giggle burst from her and she clutched his arm.

'You're such a good-hearted boy,' she said. She turned to Hoffmann's steady dark eyes. 'He's always doing things for others,' she explained. 'He's like that at home, you know.'

She looked back at Gus and her brow furrowed slightly, as if she still was not completely ready to let go of Ritter's slip. Gus thought this was a nice touch.

Hoffmann now stepped in to turn matters around.

'Actually,' he said, 'I would like to hear Ernst answer Claire's question. What is it that you actually do all day?'

Ritter, however, was still staring at Claire. Gus could only surmise that Ritter would have labelled his gaze seductive.

'What,' he said to her, 'would you think I do?'

She pursed her lips. The slip forgotten, she was back in the game.

'Oh, I should say that you sign many documents. On second thoughts, you probably only have time to initial them. Then . . . you chastize wrongdoers. Black marketeers, saboteurs, and such like. Then . . . the balance of the day is spent exhorting subordinates to greater heights of efficiency, loyalty, and creativity.'

Ritter was nodding very firmly.

'Remarkable,' he admitted. 'Except the part about initialling. Occasionally I am required to sign my full name.'

Hoffmann had summoned the girl with the flash camera. She took the group's portrait, fumbling a bit with the camera to assorted humorous remarks.

When she had finished, Hoffmann raised his glass.

'To Claire and to Gus,' he said. 'Now I will have a photograph to prove that I've dined with the handsomest couple in Europe.'

The sommelier appeared with their third bottle of champagne.

As the bottle progressed, resistance to the wine's effects began to deteriorate noticeably. To Gus' eye, Hoffmann only seemed more suave and romantic with each glass. He was either making a gentle play for Claire, or perhaps he felt that such attention was only a matter of common courtesy.

Ritter simply grew coarser, with alarming rapidity. At last, he sat mumbling to himself, poking at the remains of his venison.

'Standards,' Ritter said with booze on his voice, 'have all gone to hell. This meat . . . so tough, stringy . . . My God . . . you don't suspect that they're actually serving us roast Jew for supper?'

Ritter was suddenly convulsed in laughter.

'That Horcher was always a demon for controlling cost. Wouldn't put it past him.'

Ritter looked about to discover that no one was sharing in the hilarity. He tried to stifle his laughter, but a last drunken giggle escaped.

Claire arched her throat. She sent Ritter a smile of false compassion that was withering in its condescension.

'I think,' she said sweetly, 'that we have passed the colonel's bedtime. Shall we take him home and tuck him in?'

Ritter shook his sodden head. Still grinning stupidly, he lifted a limp finger in Claire's direction.

'Just a moment, young lady,' he said. 'Put all of your hypocrisy aside for a minute. Can you honestly tell me that you would sit down at this table with a Jew?'

Her smile grew even more cruel in its patronizing kindness.

'Please remember, Colonel, that you have invaded my country. If I'll eat with you, I'll eat with anyone.'

Hoffmann burst into instantaneous laughter. On half a second's bleary reflection, Ritter joined him.

The dessert had come, and with it, the Sauterne. Gus was starting to wonder whether Claire was too drunk to remember the writing sample.

She was not.

As the waiter passed, Claire lightly touched his arm. The man bent and listened attentively as she whispered into his ear. His face reflected that the requested task was a simple one.

'What's up?' Gus inquired as the waiter disappeared.

'I've sent for something,' she answered with a tight smile.

'How informative,' Gus observed.

'Woman of mystery,' she agreed.

The waiter reappeared with a pad of paper and a golden pen.

As the three men looked on in rapt attention, Claire carefully wrote a message on the top sheet. With a teasing smile, she slid the pad and pen over to Hoffmann. This evoked a most lascivious grunt from somewhere inside Ritter.

The note said: THANK YOU FOR MY EVENING, MY DEAR COLONEL. PLEASE KNOW THAT I FIND YOU TO BE ONE OF THE TWO MOST CHARMING MEN AT MY TABLE. AND IN THE REST OF PARIS AS WELL. CLAIRE.

A very slow smile crossed Hoffmann's lips. As Gus good-naturedly joined Ritter in demanding to see Claire's note, he was scrutinizing Hoffmann's expression. There was nothing lewd or sly in the smile. It was boyish, genuine and rather grateful.

Hoffmann picked up the pen and wrote his response: MY DEAREST CLAIRE. WHILE I CANNOT QUITE SAY THAT OUR EVENING HAS MADE THE WAR WORTHWHILE, IT HAS THOROUGHLY JUSTIFIED MY TRIP FROM BERLIN. I AM FLATTERED BY YOUR KINDNESS. BUT FOR MY LOVE FOR MY DEAR WIFE, AND MY GROWING AFFECTION FOR YOUR YOUNG MAN, MY RESPONSE MIGHT BE MORE THAN MERE APPRECIATION. WALTER.

And the longer Hoffmann wrote, the broader Gus' smile became.

THIRTY-FIVE

It was such a small room. Smooth walls, floor, ceiling. All painted a perfect stark white.

There was a desk with a Tiffany lamp. A crystal ashtray. Behind the desk sat Ernst Ritter. He shuffled papers absently. Perused a list. Apart from Ritter's desk and chair, the room held no other furniture.

On the wall to his right was a large portrait of the Führer. Next to the portrait, a mirror of equal size.

The mirror was two-way. In the adjoining room, larger and more commodious, the back of the mirror had become a window. Gus, Brausch and Hoffmann were settled comfortably. Each man kept to his own thoughts as he stared through the glass.

Finally, Andy Wheeler was escorted roughly into the interrogation room. As there were no chairs, the guard simply left him standing, facing Ritter at a distance of three metres.

Ritter never looked up. Utterly ignoring Andy, he continued to silently turn the pages of the dossier.

Five minutes passed.

Andy was now shifting his weight frequently, his hands folded tightly in front of him.

Gus hadn't seen Andy since their walk in the garden, but it was evident that he was thoroughly exhausted.

'He's tired,' Gus said simply.

'We've kept him awake,' Brausch remarked, 'for the past twenty-four hours.'

Gus kept his face impassive. He could feel Hoffmann's eyes.

'You have your function, Gus,' he heard Hoffmann say very softly. 'We have ours. We hope, our roles will be complementary.'

Gus turned to the dark eyes. They were indeed waiting.

'I understand,' Hoffmann said, 'your sympathy for the prisoner. It is entirely natural. And useful. One could not successfully portray a fellow prisoner without developing such an identification.'

Gus smiled slightly.

'I don't pretend,' Gus said pointing at the window, 'to understand whether all this is necessary.'

'Of course you don't. You are extracting information through kindness. Our task is otherwise. We must create a setting for Major Wheeler which has the sting of credibility. If we offer him a fortnight in the country, he could develop suspicions. We are, please remember, the brutal Hun.'

The brutal Hun. Major Seitz. The cold, irrevocable smile on Claire's landing. And yet, Ritter seemed more dangerous by far. The flash point, the free rein he gave to rage, would always be a wild card with Ritter. He nurtured his volatility with the conviction that it was a major asset. Ritter was more than the brutal Hun. A man so unpredictable in his fury could never be fully controlled.

If Andy Wheeler had to be locked in a room with that man, thank God Ritter knew that others were watching.

Another five minutes had passed.

Ritter at last put down his papers. He flicked a toggle switch and a bright light came on behind his head. The light shone directly into Andy's face, and he threw up his hands.

'Put your hands down, please,' Ritter said crisply.

Andy obeyed, squinting so hard he could barely see Ritter's form against the light.

'I am SS Standartenführer Ernst Ritter.'

There was silence.

'It is common courtesy,' Ritter said, 'to exchange name and rank with a fellow officer, my boy.'

More silence.

'Are you,' Ritter asked, 'a discourteous young man?' And the very lightness of Ritter's tone was more ominous than any overt threat could be. It suggested a man who was delighted by resistance. Because he so enjoyed overcoming it.

Ritter picked up the dossier. Scanned a page.

'Yes, yes,' he said. 'You have been a *most* discourteous fellow.'

Andy shifted his weight again. He was swallowing hard now. Trying to bring some moisture to relieve a throat dead dry and cracking from fright.

Gus watched with growing concern as Andy swallowed. It was the kind of unconscious gesture that Gus had seen followed by an involuntary emptying of the subject's bladder. Ritter had said nothing, done nothing, and Andy was already terrified by his mere presence.

'Do you know that it is against the Geneva Convention for you to deny me your name and rank?' Ritter asked.

Andy said nothing.

'Do *you*?' And the words rumbled from someplace low and dank. Someplace that offered a first hint of the stench of hell.

'Yessir,' Andy forced from his lips. It was a whine, high-pitched and pleading to be told how to surrender.

Gus held on. There was another part of Andy Wheeler. He had seen it in the garden. It was there. Andy would find a way to reach down to that part of him. Gus couldn't lose faith in Andy and expect Andy to keep faith in himself. He would sit there and goddam *will* Andy back to life.

'Shall we then,' Ritter said with the barest beginnings of a smile, 'discard the Geneva rules? Outmoded, are they? Naive. Inapplicable to men of the world such as ourselves.'

There was no response.

'Done,' Ritter said, in a soft clap of thunder. 'You see, we are a most accommodating band.'

Andy fought to focus his eyes. His pupils had now contracted to their limit, and he could see Ritter as more than a dark shadow against the sun.

Ritter had looked back to the dossier.

'You were interviewed by Hauptmann Trager. You were most uncooperative.'

Ritter was nodding his head slowly. He looked up with astonishing suddenness.

'Your rudeness caused Hauptmann Trager to be . . .

embarrassed . . . with his superiors. They felt he was not . . . firm . . . enough with you. Do you regret the trouble you've caused him?'

Andy shook his shoulders slightly. He reset them. More, he squared them. His knees straightened ever so slightly. There was no doubt in Gus' mind. Andy was coming back. Digging in.

'Well,' Ritter said flatly. 'Hauptmann Trager is, of course, in the Wehrmacht. They are a gentle, poetic breed. Filled with romantic fancies. Geneva rules and all. So you can imagine my pleasure in finding you to be a man more to my own taste. More . . . pragmatic.'

'Thank you, sir,' Andy said, not without an audible lacing of irony.

Ritter's eyes snapped open at the sudden temerity. His smile spread full length.

'Marvellous,' he said, and held the silence for a beat. 'Tell me, young man, what do you know about the SS?'

Andy thought for a moment. Gus watched and approved. Anything that showed self-possession could keep Ritter from the maddening scent of blood. The overdrive that Gus knew would kick in if Ritter felt everything in Andy suddenly let go.

'I've had no direct experience of the SS,' Andy said. 'I guess that means I know nothing.'

Ritter nodded very slowly.

'You shall begin your . . . experience . . . forthwith. You have just guaranteed that, my boy. Oh . . . and don't worry . . . you will not feel a thing.'

Ritter stood, pig-eyes gleaming.

'You think,' he said, 'that you have faced your fear. Lived through it. Seen the bottom of it.'

He began to gather his papers together. He looked up suddenly and watched Andy flinch. More than watch, he visibly savoured the moment. His eyes travelled Andy's full length and back again.

'Actually,' Ritter said, 'you have a great deal to look forward to. Oh yes.'

Ritter shook his head very slowly, in time with a distant secret rhythm. Perhaps the lashing of a naked back.

'There is a taste to fear,' he said. 'A taste capable of exquisite shades of refinement. More than food. More than love.'

He smiled. There was a terrible pleasure in the smile.

'To reach the pinnacle,' he said, 'one must be brought to the moment so carefully.'

He clapped the dossier shut and Andy flinched again. This time, Ritter did not even bother to notice. He walked directly to the door, then turned back.

'You will stand on that spot,' he said, 'until you have uttered your name and rank. If you sit down, if you so much as move or turn from the light, someone will come to remind you to do otherwise.'

And now one final smile. Evil, cunning, even sadism, all qualities overwhelmed by one alone. Strength. The man's smile said he had the strength to crush your bones to chalk dust. It said that impulse was never more than a hair trigger from instant, savage execution.

'While you wait alone,' Ritter said very softly, 'your first . . . experience . . . of the SS will be taking place without you.'

The smile died away, but the fierce light in his eyes remained.

Then he was gone.

THIRTY-SIX

An hour had passed.

Andy Wheeler stood on his spot, in agony obvious to those behind the glass. His legs shook in spasms from time to time, but he did not fall. His eyes were shut tightly against the light that Ritter had left searing his face.

What could not be seen were the jagged shards of consciousness piercing through Andy's pain and exhaustion.

There was an image from his childhood, a snapshot of a moment. He was propped in bed, reading. The book was *Billy Budd*. He couldn't see his mother, but he could hear the comforting sounds of her bustling about the kitchen. It was just before Thanksgiving and the cooking had begun. Outside, a sharp wind told him how lucky he was to be warm and safe in his bed. It was still only morning, and the hours of that day stretched before him as languid islands in an endless jewel-like archipelago.

And there must have been a thought, on that November morning. A thought that asked God if there were some way to strike a bargain. To trade the joy and pain and boredom of whatever lay ahead, and stay forever in this moment. For although it was not everything, it was enough.

The bargain had been rejected. Thanksgiving passed and Andy returned to school and to the rest of his life. His mind now reached back to that distant moment, desperately trying to exchange it for this one. To tell the lie that what had been once could always be again. Could be slipped on and worn like a coat. A cloak against the present.

The moment floated in his mind. Frozen, yet endlessly reappearing. Iceberg tips in an arctic sea. And bobbing between the peaks were the broken narratives of other moments.

Andy and Stephanie were picking their way downhill in the deep grass. There were trees, elm trees, with huge perfect leaves. The sun glinted and danced over Stephanie's bare arms and back. The clean scent of her chestnut hair came through all the wonderful smells of that place. San Juan Island in the centre of Puget Sound. Picking their way downhill towards an abandoned camp. British soldiers had once settled on this spot. Defending honour in some silly war over a stolen pig.

And although none of the men watching through the glass could know why, the thought of that pig, a war of gentleman against gentleman, had put the flicker of a smile to Andy Wheeler's lips. Gus saw the smile and realized that Andy was far away.

Stephanie had cuddled against him in the grass at the water's edge. It was just after dawn. He remembered that now. Stillness. Sun sliding across the surface of the water. Stephanie's throat, so slender and frail. Kissing her throat. This was a moment in which Andy had everything, yet would never have bargained for time to stop.. For it was a morning of knowing that life held so much more than one kind of everything. Life would serve everything to him in endless exquisite varieties. Stephanie would make that happen, easily, naturally. Inevitable as the sunlight.

There were other thoughts now. Ritter's eyes. His smile. Gus' arm around Andy in the garden.

The door opened.

Jürgen Brausch entered the room. He was alone, carrying a small folding chair.

Brausch opened the chair. Without a word, he motioned for Andy to sit down. Andy fell into the little chair and it nearly collapsed. He held it as if it were a life raft.

Brausch walked to the desk and flicked off the brutal light. He took his seat, waiting for Andy's pupils to dilate.

'My name is Brausch,' he said. 'I am a soldier, like yourself. I am an honest man. I am your enemy.'

Andy tried to study this huge figure, this kind-looking man who said he was an enemy. He was not Ritter. Was not SS. Beyond this, Andy could feel only the shrieking of his own muscles, released from their torment.

'In a moment,' Brausch said, 'you may go to sleep if you wish. That will be your choice.'

Andy had actually forgotten sleep. Forgotten that unconsciousness had ever been his. He wanted nothing else in the world now but that release from his mind and body.

'Would you like a cigarette?' Brausch asked.

Andy shook his head. The voice *was* kind. The man *was* kind. God had delivered him into the hands of a human being.

Brausch's heavy eyes were sad. They seemed to search Andy's before speaking again. A nurse, probing carefully for wounds.

'Do you,' Brausch drew the words carefully in the air, 'want to tell me something?'

Andy wanted to. He said nothing.

'I have been permitted,' Brausch said, 'to come here. To speak with you. Jurisdiction has now passed to the SS. You have met Standartenführer Ritter, I believe.'

Andy's brain said that this was a trick. But something in the tired eyes of this man said that Andy should believe him. A core of humanity was shining through those eyes. Humanity that monsters could not counterfeit.

Brausch shook his head into Andy's silence.

'Think hard,' Brausch said, 'before you reject an opportunity to talk with me. If you send me away without your name, you will never see me again. You would regret that decision. More than you could possibly know.'

Andy's heart was pounding in his throat once more. God help him, he believed this man. They knew his name, of course. Had heard everything in the cell. Ultimately, he would admit to his name, rank, and the whole fable of Calais in September. But only when and where Gus wanted. If he started to make independent decisions, he was lost. Everything was lost.

'You have been uncooperative,' Brausch said at last, 'with Standartenführer Ritter. Accordingly, there has been punishment.'

Has been punishment. Andy's mind couldn't wrap itself around the words. How could anything so paradoxical sound so menacing.

'The punishment for your behaviour,' Brausch said, 'has been visited upon an American Army captain. His name is Lang.'

The words were a sharp blow beneath the heart.

'He was very unhappy to receive this punishment. I was not present, but I am told that he cried before the punishment had been completed.'

The kind eyes reached out to Andy once more.

'He was told that you would receive comparable punishment if he failed to cooperate. He was most cooperative. Accordingly, you will not be punished. Do you understand what I have told you?'

There were huge tears in Andy's eyes. He was too tired to even notice them, and they began to spill down his face.

'You may go to sleep now,' Brausch said, 'in a very soft bed. With down pillows. While you sleep, Captain Lang will receive further punishment.'

Brausch's eyes pleaded for Andy to comprehend the inevitability of it all. The futility of accepting pain to no purpose.

'Or,' Brausch said quietly, 'if you choose, you may instead tell me your name.'

'Andrew Wheeler,' Andy heard himself say, choking back the tears. His voice sounded like something he'd never heard before. He was too tired to know what was real. Gus wasn't a prisoner at all. So this man must be lying. Then why was Andy crying?

The sun was setting now on their private spot, tucked away in the heart of San Juan Island. Stephanie's hand, small and white, clutched his for support as they climbed the hill. And he said to himself that nothing in this world, nothing that was bad, would ever happen to her. He would see to that.

The man was lying. Was not. It didn't matter. He would not risk causing Gus pain. He would give this man his rank, his unit. He would sleep. He would pray that they would give him Gus again. Gus would tell him what to do.

THIRTY-SEVEN

The cell.

Gus sat on his cot, hugging his knees. The vent was not working and the cell was hot. Smells of other centuries were bleeding through the walls of Vincennes' dungeon.

He sat and burned a hole in his stomach lining, worrying about Andy.

Gus had told Andy of his cover. He had not, however, advised Brausch of this revelation, fearing that Brausch would wrongly suspect his own cover had been compromised as well. This could result in Brausch wanting Andy Wheeler very dead very quickly.

It was now apparent, however, that not reporting fully to Brausch could have dangerous side effects. The surprise punish-your-buddy ploy must have left Andy scared and confused as hell. Particularly since Brausch sold it so well. Hoffmann was purely a genius. Brausch was more. Merlin. An ancient wizard, dwelling in timeless bemusement of lesser creatures.

In another world, Gus wanted Hoffmann for his brother. Brausch as father and eternal mentor. Andy Wheeler would be his son.

In this world, did he truly want Hoffmann dead? Perhaps the fear and admiration had worked their alchemy to produce a kind of love, even more compelling in a way than what he felt for Claire. And the moment he said those words to himself, he knew at last what he felt for Hoffmann. Why it was named hatred and love. He *was* Hoffmann. They were more than brothers, more than twins. Born into each other's world, he would be me. And I, him.

A chill flooded him, washed over him. He had to catch his breath until it flowed past. For Gus had taught himself a truth. And the moment Hoffmann learned this truth, he could read Gus' soul as if it were his own.

The door slammed open. Andy Wheeler was thrown through it. Thrown hard, to his hands and knees.

He didn't bother to pick himself up. He just curled his legs beneath him and sat on the floor, waiting for the door to clang shut behind him. Andy was grinning up at Gus. You could say he was happy to see him.

Still, Andy looked about a year older. Gus was thinking of Hoffmann's offer. More private strolls in the garden. No. He had done the right thing. Hoffmann had been deflected [illegible] had seen it. His twin psyche was tracking him now. [illegible] precious moment bought could be the one that [illegible] difference.

Gus smiled down at Andy, but he was truly s[illegible] himself. If he and Hoffmann shared identical souls, why had God gifted his enemy with the stronger intellect? At least he should have switched their birthplaces. Then maybe the right side would win this goddam war.

Of course, no one ever said God was supposed to be fair. No one who knew Him anyway. Being fair was man's job. Okay, right now we're not doing so hot, but don't kick a species when it's down. Not when it's this far down.

'What's so funny?' Andy asked, watching his eyes.

'I'm writing doggerel to myself,' Gus said. 'About God.'

Andy digested that for a moment.

'Do you believe God has power over things?' Andy's question was strangely and suddenly earnest.

'Almost God-like,' Gus answered.

Andy returned a very wistful smile. Not lately, the smile said.

'You look like they gave you a taste of the same thing they gave me,' Gus said.

Andy's eyes registered that he was back in the game. God was forgotten now. Just as well.

'They told me,' Gus said, 'that if I didn't cooperate, they'd hurt you. So, of course, I did. I just hope you had the good sense to do the same, before they put the screws to you.'

'Sure,' Andy nodded, a bit too quickly. It was painfully apparent that he didn't want Gus to worry.

'This buddy-torture thing is an old trick,' Gus said. 'Actually, I set them up for it. I showed them I liked you, felt protective. Worried about your health.'

Andy showed no surprise. He was listening, absorbing. His face reflected that level of purest concentration. Gus had little doubt that, in the right circumstance, Andy could outthink anyone. Maybe even Hoffmann. A shame Gus couldn't borrow forty points of Andy's IQ, just until he put H[illegible]mann away.

[illegible]his simplifies everything,' Gus said. 'Now we can give [illegible] D-Day a step at a time, without having to go through [illegible]re to make it credible. They'll just think we're trying to [illegible]tect each other.'

Andy beamed. His face said Gus was a genius. More than ever, Andy's hero.

The sweet Andy-smile couldn't hide the history of these past two days. He would need an extra jolt of something to bring him all the way back.

'Who did they use?' Gus asked, a conspiratorial smirk at his lips. Very light, very playful. 'Did they use Ritter? Big blonde guy.'

'Yeah,' Andy nodded. 'At first.'

Gus widened the grin.

'That guy is some pig,' Gus said. 'I mean solid pork from one ear to the other.'

Andy's eyes caught the spark.

'He's SS,' Gus said. 'Probably queer. I hear they all are.'

Gus threw a little bite into that one. He watched as Andy visualized how the scene must be playing in the next room.

Gus leaned forward with a steely-eyed imitation of Ritter's glare.

'I am SS Standartenführer Ernst Ritter,' he hissed in a voice that combined low comedy with a passable facsimile of Ritter's accent.

'And *you*,' Gus/Ritter rumbled, 'are in a lot of trouble, [illegible]nny. Do you know why?'

Andy shook his head, grinning like a child.

'Because,' Gus said, shading the accent towards the feminine, 'you are not pretty enough to merit . . . special consideration.'

He tossed a wicked leer and Andy broke up completely. Gus sat staring in mock icy rage at Andy's hilarity.

Slowly, Gus' brow furrowed, seemed to slide down over his eyes. His back hunched and his shoulders rolled forward, his arms now hanging loosely before him. Lips pursed into the pout of an angry ape, Gus had transformed himself into a Nazi gorilla.

He hopped off the cot and bounced around the room on his haunches, arms swinging wildly. With great whoops and screeches, Gus slammed into walls and cots, at last rolling over in a ball and coming up with a monkey version of the ramrod Nazi salute.

Andy was belly laughing now, so violently that he had to gulp for breath. Through it all, his mind had never stopped working. Never lost the picture of Ritter in his polished black and silver, listening nearby, defenceless against Gus' raucous insults.

For Andy, Gus' cocky defiance of those listening was more than a tonic. It was the living proof of what Gus had promised in the garden. The only real power is knowledge. The Nazis would be rendered helpless, because only Gus and Andy knew both sides of the game. It was happening right before his eyes.

'There is a *taste* to fear, you know,' Gus had trotted out the hissing Ritter one last time. 'An exquisitely refined taste.'

Gus tossed his head, becoming himself again.

'I mean,' Gus said, 'can you seriously picture that guy as the Marquis de Sade? Eighth-grade education, tops. Maybe, just maybe he knows two, three kinds of fear.'

Gus looked up at the air vent for inspiration.

'One, fear they'll run out of sausage somewhere. Two, same thing only with roast potatoes. Three, any phone call from Berlin.'

Both men were already at the edge of hysterics from Gus' monkey romp. A giggle from one would ignite a burst from the other. They would catch their breath, stare at each other for a half second, and the sillies would grab them again. It might not impress Noel Coward, but it was a high water mark for fun on death row.

Finally, Gus sagged back against the wall.

'Okay,' he said wearily, 'everybody out of the pool. Back to work, Andrew. Rehearsal time.'

Andy stifled one last giggle and put on his straightest face.

Gus would never get him looser. This was the moment.

'Give me D-Day,' Gus said, 'just the way you learned it in Plymouth. Give me Calais step by step. All the thrusts, the feints, the phonies. Italy, Norway, the works. Once straight through, then we'll chop it up and decide who gives them which piece when.'

Andy took a deep breath. He was beautifully relaxed.

Slowly, naturally, Andy began to spin the story of Calais. FUSAG, Patton, the way Gus had given it to him in the garden, only better. Better because Andy had spent each night building details, brick by brick.

The pompous little imaginary Scotsman who first briefed his unit. The sheaf of maps and charts with OVERLORD stamped in crimson ink. All the guys second-guessing Ike and Monty for picking Calais in the first place. Shortest route, it's just where the Krauts are gonna be waiting. Ah, the little and imaginary Scotsman says, that's the genius of it, boys. The deception of the obvious.

Gus just sat with glowing eyes. If he'd recruited from the whole damn OSS and FBI, his first choice would be the man sitting right there in front of him. Deception of the obvious, indeed.

THIRTY-EIGHT

Jasmine snuggled her back into the water. The tub was cooling now and she hadn't begun to wash. Jasmine had been thinking, only thinking, she didn't know for how long.

She was aware now of Simon, playing by himself on the floor in the next room. She called to him and he answered distractedly, intent on some unseen task. He was fine, Mama.

Jasmine lifted her brown leg from the water and ran the sponge along its length. The droplets seemed to quiver as they slid across her flesh. She watched them through the narrow focus of curiosity, as Simon would observe a bug. Anything to misdirect herself from her thoughts. Badger, ferret. The lily pond.

She stood, dripping, and reached for the towel. At twenty, her body was still firm. To some from her native land she was no longer a young woman. She still looked the same, though. The same dark, elusive beauty that the man had seen in her when she was sixteen.

Quietly, eyes locked into the distance, Jasmine dressed. Badger. Ferret.

She had been born in El Harrach, just southeast of Algiers. She had not been poor, had received education. Jasmine was far the brightest of her father's daughters. His jewel.

At sixteen she had met the man Duchez. She had loved him. No. If she had loved him, how could she remember so little of him now. As she buttoned her cotton blouse over her breasts, it seemed that she couldn't even remember the man's face. There were moments, though, when she would remember his touch.

Duchez was gone now. In his place there was Simon. Nearly three, with his mother's thick black hair and obsidian eyes. There was no mark of the man upon him. None that she could see. And to Jasmine, this was only right. Simon was hers alone.

She knelt with her son now. There was time to play bang-the-trucks for a while. The green one was missing two wheels. The red one, scarred as if it had been through some fiery crash.

She mouthed her way through the prescribed ritual. The barked orders, giggling but precise. The obligatory sound effects as the red truck plunged in slowest motion to excruciating annihilation.

In her mind, badger and ferret. The lily pond. The meadow, the copse, the glen. The squirrel. The falcon and the fieldmouse.

It was better, of course, that she didn't know the meaning of the words. Better for her. For Simon. But this couldn't stop the dancing of the words in her mind.

At two o'clock, she dressed Simon. The tightness already beginning in her belly, she set off with him down Rue de Vaugirard. She pushed his little stroller, for there were many blocks ahead. Jasmine knew that by the time she reached the park, her stomach would be filled with acid, her head swimming.

Still, she wouldn't forget. The mind that had been her father's treasure, the mind that the man Duchez hadn't paused to notice, still had never let her down. She would hear every word and remember.

Luxembourg Garden seemed nearly deserted. The sky had taken a turn towards the dark and overcast. There might be rain, but not within the hour. The weather wouldn't interrupt today's story.

She pushed the stroller along the gravel, her eyes scanning the familiar meeting places.

On a bench near the fountain sat a woman of great and fragile beauty. Hair as black as Jasmine's own, but softer in texture, framing the elegant bones of her face.

Jasmine sat at Claire's side. They kissed as if they were sisters.

Simon climbed from his stroller and raced to join Amy at the fountain. In his hand, a small wooden boat with a long string. The mothers watched them together. Simon was five months older, and very much the big brother, helping wrap the string around Amy's wrist so that their boat wouldn't sail away.

Their little faces were so intent, so earnest. The fountain and its ripples danced for their eyes. Lifted the tiny boat and set it down again. Tugged at the string, as Simon shouted for Amy to pull it this way and that. All their world was the here and now of that moment.

Jasmine could only envy their innocence. Could only pray that Simon would keep his heart and his eyes as clear as they were at this moment. That the horrible things of this world, the things that corrupt and compromise, would never find her little boy.

'Amy!' Claire called. 'Time for your story.'

It was time for Jasmine's story.

Without a word of protest, Amy reeled in the toy boat. Hand over hand, round little eyes focused only on the serious work before her. She turned and presented the boat to Simon, completing the ceremony. The two ran to join their mothers at the bench.

The book was open in Claire's lap. It was a book about fairies and dwarfs, but that didn't matter. Any book would do. The story had a life of its own.

Amy and Simon sat on either side of Claire, staring at the page for all the world as if they were reading.

Jasmine sat next to her son, smiling lazily, her stomach a thin and bitter soup. She would hear and she would remember.

'The badger and the ferret,' Claire began, 'met once more at the lily pond.'

Amy wiggled her rump, trying to get comfortable.

'The ferret told the badger a story,' Claire went on. 'It was the same story the badger had taught him in the thicket, just the other day.'

'Why?' Amy blurted very loudly.

Claire looked down at her daughter. Smoothed her blonde hair back behind her ear. She waited for Amy to finish her thought.

'Why he tell the *same* story?' Amy asked, looking urgently at her mother's eyes.

'Because sometimes I tell you a story. And then I like to hear you say the same story back to me. Just to see if you learned it.'

Jasmine heard and would remember. She would repeat the words later on command, but would live the balance of her life without ever knowing that the thicket was the garden of Vincennes. The lily pond a prison cell.

The ferret, of course, was the Overlord. And into Jasmine's ear was spun the story composed the night before by Claire herself. As she lay in the darkness of her bed, twined in the limbs of the sleeping badger.

THIRTY-NINE

The line began a short but respectful distance from the stone steps. It stretched along the Rue des Saussaies until it came to a tiny square leading to the Rue Cambacérès.

The line was broken, of course, at the intersection. As those in front were admitted up the steps, the others would dutifully close ranks. Those waiting at the intersection would be waved across to join the line at the other side of the street.

Peaceful, orderly. It was this way every morning at 11 Rue des Saussaies. A stranger might look at the queue and fancy this some sort of gigantic breadline. But if he looked at the faces, he would know better.

The people in this queue each carried a slip of paper. For some, the paper was tucked away in a pocket, yet seemed to be burning through the cloth into their flesh. Others clutched the paper as if grasping their own lives in their hands. This was a paradox. For the paper was anything but the gift of life.

The slip of paper was a summons. For 11 Rue des Saussaies, once the headquarters of the French Surêté, now served as the centralized bureau for each branch of German intelligence. The Geheime Feldpolizei, the military police, was here. The SD and other subdivisions of the SS maintained offices, archives, support personnel.

For the most part, however, those standing in the line of quiet submission were waiting to be admitted into the presence of the Gestapo.

Inside the giant complex, reality, or at least the surface patina of reality, did not match one's preconception of the Gestapo. Rather than thugs or scruffy alley brawlers, these were minions of a vast bureaucracy, moving efficiently among writing desks, card catalogues, shelves of documents. There was nothing in these faces to indicate darkness of spirit. Nothing to evidence a sudden impulse to brutality, a rapture in another's pain or fear. These were worker bees, processing the honey.

Sections of the building were given over to vaulted ceilings and cathedral-like quiet. One such hall, with its soft leather chairs, resembled nothing so much as the reading room of a giant library. In fact, this was precisely the case.

Ernst Ritter sat, file resting in his lap, slowly turning pages. The basic research had been done by others. Now, at the crucial moment, he wanted the final step to be his alone.

Next to Ritter was a sallow young man with dark, darting eyes. He had been watching with the attentiveness of a servant whose immediate future would turn on the pleasure or its opposite to be revealed by his master's next words.

Johann was not directly in Ritter's chain of command. Nonetheless, he was a boy of supple loyalties. He did not fully understand his mission. Nor did he want to. The Standartenführer had singled him out for his brilliance *and* his discretion. He would deliver both in full measure.

At last, Ritter had stopped scanning. He stared at a single page. Read it a second time, most carefully. And then a third.

Although Ritter's face remained entirely impassive, Johann discerned something in his eyes. Something had run deeply through this man to his core. Something intoxicating. Ritter's nostrils seemed to flare ever so slightly, as if he needed more oxygen to fuel the power surging through him.

And so Johann's excitement had already begun, resonating to those first tentative signs. And as Ritter's head began to nod, as his broad finger stabbed at the page in short, sharp thrusts, a form of ecstasy flashed through Johann. The intuition, the perseverance of his labours, would indeed be rewarded.

'This man . . .,' Ritter said, and tilted the file for Johann to see. 'This man is now – '

'In Hamburg,' Johann said instantly. 'He is decoding English-language intelligence for the Pers Z branch there.'

Ritter nodded. The pleasure, more than pleasure, was now flooding his eyes.

'What could you say,' Ritter murmured as if to himself, 'about this man's deportment?'

'He has been something of an embarrassment,' Johann answered, daring a grin that shaded towards intimacy.

'Something of a libertine?' Ritter suggested.

Johann nodded far too eagerly. He was fawning now, and he caught himself in mid-fawn. He must not impose upon a confidence freely granted. Must not cheapen himself, and thereby risk impairment of the Standartenführer's regard for his achievement.

'That would sum the man in a word,' Johann said soberly, his tone no longer intruding into Ritter's private reverie.

'But he is an able worker?' Ritter mused.

Johann cleared his throat. It was a high-pitched, unmanly sound that he instantly regretted.

'He is bright,' Johann said, trying to deepen the timbre of his voice, 'and his work product is well regarded.'

Ritter turned his face to the young man.

'This is splendid work, Johann. I am grateful.'

Ritter watched the boy's eyes, finding twice the reaction he had hoped for.

'Will you please see that this man is brought here? Quickly and without the knowledge of any nonessential personnel.'

'I will see to it at once.'

Ritter smiled.

'Would it be possible,' Ritter said, 'for the man to be here tomorrow?'

Johann's eyes said that he would move heaven, earth, and the rest of the solar system to make it possible.

'Tomorrow at four o'clock, then,' Ritter announced. 'Provide us with a suitable room, reserved under your authority. The use of my name in this affair . . . to anyone . . . will not be necessary.'

FORTY

Gus sat cross-legged on the bedroom floor, reading. There was a sudden knowing that he was not alone.

He looked up to see Amy, standing practically on top of him. She wore only cotton underpants and a dimpled, impish smile.

'Let's play,' she said boldly.

Gus threw his arms open and she charged wildly. He let the force of it bowl him over backwards, then dug his hands into her and started tickling. She dissolved into uncontrolled hysterics. Heartstopping screams, fat little legs flailing everywhere.

He held her upside down, then a spin in a tight circle, her blonde hair flying, whipping at her face. He dumped her on the floor and pounced. The rolled and tumbled until she seemed thoroughly exhausted, more by the laughter than the exercise.

Gus scooped her into his arms, and they held each other tightly until there was enough breath to begin a conversation.

'Let's play,' he said at last.

'Okay,' she answered, as if he had just come up with a good idea.

She ran-waddled off into the next room. She was his little girl. Claire might never belong to him. Andy surely never could. But Amy at twenty-seven months, this Amy, would be his forever. If he lived to be ninety-eight and lay dying on a beach in the Galápagos islands, that little face would look up at him with those round and ageless eyes. Let's play, she would say to him on his deathbed. And his eyes would be very wet, remembering the love of those tiny arms around his neck. How tightly, how honestly, she had held him.

Amy returned with an armful of books. Looked like enough reading for about two months. She set them down carefully next to Gus, as if they were Italian crystal. Without looking at him or saying a word, she dashed off again.

Gus understood. No point in running out of things to do.

She returned this time with her favourite doll and a small wooden dump truck. Again she placed them gently next to Gus and ran from the room.

Finally, she came back with a faded scrap of cream-coloured blanket cradled next to her cheek.

Amy was ready.

She walked up to Gus, turned her back, and slowly lowered her rump into his lap.

After a while, the rendezvous was interrupted by Claire. In a categorical tone that left no room for negotiation, she ordered her daughter to kiss Gus good-night, then lugged her off to bed.

When Claire returned, she was holding two pieces of paper. She curled up next to Gus as he examined them, looking slowly from one to the other.

The first was the note that Hoffmann had written to Claire at Maxim's. The other was her forgery.

The two were amazingly similar. His slow smile evidenced that he was truly impressed.

'I'm only about forty per cent of where I want to be,' she said modestly, pulling a strand of hair back behind her ear. 'Maybe another fifty hours to have it really flowing.'

He pulled her to him and kissed her gently.

'It's remarkable,' he said. 'It really is.'

She was clearly proud of herself.

'I'm satisfied with the progress,' she said. 'I just hope to God you never have to use it. These things never stand up to close analysis.'

Gus looked back at the paper.

'Can you tell something about this guy,' he asked, 'just from his handwriting?'

'Sure,' she said, cuddling closer. 'See that little loop right there? It means he has liver trouble.'

Gus was not asking to be ridiculed. He started tickling her in punishment.

'And he had a dog named Wilhelm when he was seven years old,' she gasped, trying to fight him off.

Unlike Amy, this one tickled back.

A truce was ultimately declared.

'If you really want me to figure Hoffmann out for you,' she said, 'I'd probably have to sleep with him.'

Gus nodded in a pantomime of total agreement.

'*Why*,' he wondered, 'didn't I think of that?'

'It would all be for the cause,' she teased. 'You can't tell me you'd be jealous.'

'Nah.'

'Would you shoot me?' she asked.

He thought it over.

'I'm more the type to shoot myself,' he said, 'and let *you* deal with the guilt.'

She was lying now with her head in his lap, her fingers playing with each other. It was clear that she was deciding whether to tell him something.

He waited.

'I've never been jealous before,' she admitted. 'You're the first.'

She looked up to gauge the impact. The green eyes were saying he liked being first.

'I think,' she said, 'that if you made love to another woman, I would just consider you a poor baby who was seduced.'

'Fair-minded approach,' he agreed.

'As for *her*, however . . . I think I would cut her into very small pieces . . . with a very dull knife.'

Gus stroked the softness of her cheek. It was his turn to smooth a black strand of hair from her forehead.

'Always the tough guy,' he said softly. 'Are you really such a tough guy?'

Her eyes were moving over his face now. Searching for something.

'No,' she said, and the grey eyes were suddenly brimming. 'Matter of fact, I'm scared to death.'

Her fingers closed around his hand and held on tight.

'Every once in a while,' he said gently, 'you're allowed to say that. It's in the rules.'

She looked at him and sniffled.

'Honest,' he said. 'I peeked.'

Claire took the deepest breath.

'There was never anyone to tell,' she said. 'Is that hard for you to imagine?'

He shook his head slowly. It wasn't hard at all.

'When Amy was born, I used to hold her in my arms and talk to her. For hours. All the things I never told anyone. I finally had my friend. And now I look at her . . . and she's so beautiful.'

She was clasping his arm now, tightly against her breast. The grey eyes were far away.

'I tell myself,' she said slowly, 'about thousands of lives, millions of lives. I tell myself that each one is a whole person with his own life, his own babies. But I don't belong to those people, Gus.'

He sure as hell knew what she meant.

'Amy is more important,' she blurted, forcing the words from her chest and through her lips. 'She is. I just know that in my heart. I know I'm doing a terrible thing.'

She was sobbing now and he just held her until she caught her breath.

'Do you ever think what will happen to that little baby if I'm gone?'

Martin. Martin was all he could think of.

'All the time,' he said. 'I think about all the terrible things that could happen to all of us. All the time.'

She sniffled and held him so tightly. Then she pulled back and the grey eyes were burning into him, begging in a way he'd never seen before.

'When she was born,' Claire repeated, 'she was my only friend. And if there is a God in heaven, I know what he wants me to do. He wants me to take care of that little baby, Gus. Don't you ever ask . . . ever . . . expect . . . that I'll ever do anything else.'

It was a plea. It was a warning.

For some reason, through everything of these last days, he had never loved her quite this much before.

'You hang onto that,' he said. 'No matter what. You've got the right idea.

FORTY-ONE

Thomas Waite Croffts sat on the edge of a small wooden chair. His long legs were crossed with aristocratic ease. His butt, however, was uncomfortable and the rest of him was more so.

Croffts was a fellow with an unusual, but scarcely unique, story. Life, since Croffts could remember, had been a dedicated and often pleasant search for places and ways in which to kill time. For the most part, things had wasted along rather nicely.

In the spring of 1940, however, the absorbing details of Croffts' revelry were intruded upon by the onset of a somewhat inconvenient war. He happened to be debauching in Paris at the moment.

Croffts vaguely realized, or rather was instructed by friends in communication with the real world, that his return to Britain, home of his youth, would mean immediate conscription. Or, he could just stay in Paris.

Mama hadn't raised her boy to be a soldier.

In fact, Mama had scarcely raised him at all. They had met, of course, on several occasions. None of them recent. Croffts was beautiful and wealthy, and there his good fortune had stopped.

Until now, it had seemed enough.

When the Nazis entered Paris in 1940, and both the strong and the weak of Parisian civilization trembled or fled, Croffts' continuous party suffered only a brief postponement. This was because he made a sincere, if clandestine, effort to determine how he could best be of service to his new masters. Croffts quickly found himself at the German Foreign Office, where it was determined that he indeed possessed useful skills and aptitudes.

His activities for the Germans remained secret for nearly two years. During this time, he continued to use his habitual cover of under-employed free-lance journalist. In public, he kept away from Nazis and notorious collaborators.

Near the end of 1942, a particular adroitness in cryptography earned him a promotion and a transfer to Berlin, which he was to find surprisingly to his taste. Before departing, he announced the fact of his service to the Reich to all friends and acquaintances who would listen. This to the amusement of some and the horror of others. Croffts moved in a wide and ecumenical circle.

The branch of the German Foreign Office dealing with code breaking was known as the Pers Z, actually the Z section of the personnel and administrative branch. They occupied a girls' school in the Dahlem district of southwest Berlin and specialized in the solving of diplomatic telegrams.

Nazi communications intelligence, as it turned out, was a competitive field. The Pers Z found itself elbowing other, often better financed, organs for the limelight. There was the Forschungstelle, or Research Post, which intercepted and unscrambled messages, including a rather famous one between Roosevelt and Churchill. There was Goering's unit, the Forschungsamt or Research Office, which intercepted radio messages and tapped every wire it could lay its hands on. The Wehrmacht, too, had its Cipher Branch. Indeed a growth industry.

Croffts excelled. Within four months he had intercepted and decoded seven messages that had earned the green F stamp as material important enough for the eyes of the Führer.

Ultimately, Croffts was rewarded with a transfer to a sensitive position in the key Pers Z branch in Hamburg. This was a city that he found even more to his liking than Berlin. The party continued.

Until Thursday.

Croffts had been startled by the rudest banging on the door of his flat. This was caused by two sizeable barbarians in black and silver. An SS summons brings horror to the soul of the bravest of men. For Croffts, the reaction was somewhat more intense.

He was taken to the train. He was roughly handled. His SS escort had refused to tell him his crime or his destination. He was told only that he would do well to cooperate. Now, here was a concept that Croffts had mastered. He lived for the moment when someone would tell him *how* to cooperate.

Croffts sat now, perched at the end of his hard wooden chair. Heart banging and bowels threatening to let go.

He wore a pathetic attempt to replicate the calm, easy smile that had always seen him through. He was miserably aware that he was fooling no one – meaning the man seated before him, quietly pretending to reread Croffts' dossier.

Ernst Ritter introduced himself. There was something very physical in the timbre of his voice. Croffts, in his panic, could scarcely take his eyes from Ritter's hands, which slowly opened and clenched in involuntary preparation for a savage mauling to come.

Ritter recited some of the more chequered details from Croffts' file. Stated that he found Croffts' cowardice and promiscuity to be personally revolting. It was a confirmation of the decadence of the Foreign Office that they would traffic with such trash. The SS, or even the military, would surely have squashed Croffts like a cockroach.

The tirade went on. A full ten minutes. Croffts could only wait for the punch line. He still had no clue as to why the black cloud had fallen over him.

'You have,' Ritter said at last, 'a child out of wedlock. A child named Amy Jouvet.'

Croffts nodded, eagerly confessing his sin. He had never denied the child. She was rather cute. Somewhere in the back of his mind, he had always vaguely wanted to see her again.

'That is a crime,' Ritter said.

'To have a bastard?' Croffts breathed in astonishment.

Ritter shrugged. 'A minor matter. Punishable by death,' he lied.

Croffts couldn't believe it. Still, he knew that truth scarcely mattered. Ritter could pull out that shiny black Walther pistol on his hip, blow Croffts' brains onto the wall right here in Gestapo HQ, and some little old French lady would bring in a mop and pail to clean up for the next interview.

'Tell me something about the child's mother,' Ritter said very slowly. 'Tell me something I would like to know.'

So that was it. Croffts' brain turned to vegetable soup. He had always suspected Claire of Resistance connections, which he found amusing and even somewhat attractive. Very spirited girl. He recalled his astonishment on the night she had announced her pregnancy, simultaneously declaring that she intended to keep the baby.

Brains and spunk. A little beauty, too, he remembered sadly. Sadly, because he was searching frenziedly for a way to barter her creamy white skin for his own.

Resistance contacts would be the key. There was, however, a problem. If he confessed that he had suspected her participation in the Resistance but had failed to disclose this previously, he would be shot as an accomplice.

After thinking it over far too long, Croffts shook his head.

Ritter smiled. The delay had been his answer.

'The lady,' Ritter said, 'is suspected of Resistance activity.'

Croffts was silent, waiting for a heart attack to end his misery.

'I admire gallantry,' Ritter admitted. 'Truly I do. But, surely, your overriding concern for the welfare of the Reich . . .'

Croffts' lips were twitching now, but he couldn't feel them.

'Perhaps,' Ritter surmised, 'you fear retribution for not having previously advised the Reich of her activities.'

Perhaps he did.

'Let me assure you,' Ritter said, 'that this will not be the case. You have performed valuable work, and we expect that to continue.'

Croffts took Ritter's heartfelt commitment at somewhat less than face value. It was, in fact, as obvious a lie as Croffts had ever heard.

Ritter rose and walked to Croffts' chair. He stood directly before him.

There was a sudden contortion of Ritter's mouth as if the muscles of his face had all twisted to one side. At the same instant, Ritter lashed out, slapping Croffts on the side of the head with such power that Croffts was sent flying out of the chair.

The pain was unbelievable. The taste of so much blood, the swallowing of it, terrified Croffts beyond anything he had ever known. There was no question that his jaw had been shattered beyond repair.

'Get up,' Ritter said quietly.

Somehow, Croffts struggled to his feet, lifting himself into his chair.

'The amnesty I have offered,' Ritter said with the same horrible calm, 'will be available for exactly ten seconds.'

Somehow, Croffts got his jaw to move.

'There was one friend of hers,' Croffts said, 'I had some question about. His name was Armand Leclerc. I never understood their relationship.'

'We know about Leclerc,' Ritter lied. 'It would be helpful, however, if other names occurred to you.'

Croffts' mind lurched desperately about, but there were no other names. In most ways, Claire was a woman he had scarcely known.

'I would . . . appreciate . . . receiving some fresh information from you, Herr Croffts. Did this woman, perhaps, associate with any Jewish persons?'

The light snapped on for Croffts. A last, miraculous chance.

'She's Jewish,' he said at once. 'Partly Jewish. There was a grandfather or an uncle. He lived in Poland, I think. Maybe Austria. A village.'

'You're quite certain?'

Croffts' pain had subsided considerably. It was now merely excruciating. Ritter was on the hook. He had a chance.

'She only told me once. She was very drunk, maudlin. But she told the story with considerable detail. Names and places. No question it was true.'

Ritter showed a smile of warm satisfaction. The irrational sense of hope flooded through Croffts, sweeping the pain aside.

'That is most useful,' Ritter said. 'Is there anything else at all?'

There was not.

'Then thank you, Herr Croffts, for your time.'

Ritter entered the adjoining room where Johann had been listening, transcribing the entire interview onto his pad with a most efficient shorthand.

Johann's eyes turned upwards, pleading to be of service.

'Question him,' Ritter said, 'about all of this. The man Leclerc. The Jewish ancestry. Anything else that presents itself.'

'Question . . . Johann repeated, the inflection requesting more precise instruction.

'Question him,' Ritter repeated patiently, 'by any means you deem suitable. Until you have everything.'

Johann nodded, his mind already clicking through the possibilities.

'When you are certain you have everything,' Ritter said, '. . . when you are certain enough to stake on it my . . . evaluation of your service . . . kill him.'

FORTY-TWO

It was not an unusual summons.

Brausch sat, sipping Armagnac, in Hoffmann's suite at the Ritz. The conversation had been uneventful, in fact, positively banal. There was nothing in view to cause Brausch the least alarm.

In short, something was up.

It wasn't that Hoffmann appeared particularly wary, or even alert. There was something, though. Barely discernible, like a minute change of air pressure in the room. Hoffmann seemed, Brausch would say, slightly more intimate in tone than he had been these past weeks. As if he were forcing it, ever so subtly, to defend against revealing that he suddenly felt more remote.

Something had happened. Something specific.

The conversation turned to business. This offered no

clue. Hoffmann was finalizing his report on the Emerald product. Berlin was pressing, understandably, for a final recommendation as to the veracity of the material. In truth, they had already begun to act on it.

As always, Brausch declined to take the lead. Perfect certainty, he concluded, was never attainable in any interrogation. Still, the Overlord's demeanour, the consistency and detail of his story, had left no doubt apart from the residue of standard professional reserve.

'We all believe it,' Brausch admitted. 'We are merely rehashing and observing as a precaution, until someone gets up the nerve to close the book.'

Hoffmann offered the smile of old and tested friendship.

'Why,' he mused, 'is it always so hard to close the book?'

'A human quirk,' Brausch answered. 'These are absolute stakes. One would hate to be wrong.'

'And still,' Hoffmann said, 'there finally comes a moment at which any further hesitation would indicate . . .'

'A want of leadership,' Brausch said, completing the thought.

Hoffmann nodded.

'Ominous word, *indecisive*,' Hoffmann agreed. 'Not many indecisive brigadiers.'

'I've met a few,' Brausch smiled.

Hoffmann's finger gestured to the black and silver tunic, hung neatly by the door.

'Not,' he said, 'in my branch of the service.'

They stared at each other. In their eyes, the warm comfort of shared minds, mutual trust.

Brausch's belly was crawling now. Hoffmann was constructing his silence towards an end. Brausch could anticipate this as clearly as the tumbling notes of a concert pianist signalled the onset of a cadenza.

'Well,' Hoffmann said simply, 'my book to close.'

Brausch nodded.

'Any last hunches, fears?' Hoffmann asked, the dark eyes indicating no particular concern. 'Anything at all?'

'Always fear,' Brausch said softly. 'Our art is in choosing the precise moment to ignore it.'

Hoffmann smiled. Set his brandy snifter on the table. It was the motion of an interview come to an end.

This would not be the end, however. There would be a final afterthought. Brausch was bracing himself.

'I must tell you,' Hoffmann remarked in an entirely offhand tone, 'of Ritter's latest piece of hysterics.'

Hoffmann's finger traced the rim of his glass.

'Ernst commissioned some Gestapo research on Claire Jouvet. Uneasy about her from the first, he says.'

Brausch shook his head sadly.

'And he seemed such a trusting sort,' Brausch observed.

'Well, Ernst is a man of many parts,' Hoffmann conceded. 'Each of them paranoid.'

'I sleep more secure at night,' Brausch noted solemnly, 'knowing that Ernst is skulking nobly about.'

Hoffmann's smile faded very slightly. The dark eyes were still for a moment.

'He's quite distraught,' Hoffmann said. 'He's found a few drops of Jewish blood in the girl's family. Generations back.'

The shaggy brows lifted from their perch. They hovered above Brausch's tired eyes.

'Tullard Dossiers?' Brausch asked. This was the name given to files of Jews who had registered with French police stations at the beginning of the occupation.

'No,' Hoffmann said. 'Apparently, she never registered.'

This was, of course, a grave crime.

'Does Gus know?'

'Perhaps,' Hoffmann speculated. 'I doubt it.' Hoffmann sighed. He was weary of complications.

'Ernst,' he said, 'will insist that Gus break off with the girl. Says she is, by definition, unreliable.'

'What do you think?' Brausch asked blandly.

'I think that would be a damn pity,' Hoffmann answered. 'This girl is charming, a most useful diversion for Gus. And she is quite catholic into the bargain.'

'But you can't make Ernst see it your way?'

Hoffmann shrugged.

'I think things are going so smoothly with the work at hand, that Ernst just needs to look for trouble somewhere,' Hoffmann said. 'He strikes me as a man who cannot accept success if it comes too easily.'

And beyond his smile, Jürgen Brausch was a worried man. For that description applied to Hoffmann even more surely than to Ritter.

Brausch looked deep within his brandy glass.

'Nothing else?' Brausch asked carefully. 'The Gestapo finds no other evidence of this girl's . . . unreliability.'

'No,' Hoffmann lied. 'Nothing else.'

'In that case,' Brausch concluded, 'I would agree that Ernst has overreacted.'

Hoffmann nodded. 'Our ultimate concern must be maintaining Gus in good working order. Even the Gestapo protects Jews who are useful to the Reich. By the thousands. I should think I can prevail upon Ernst's pragmatism.'

Brausch heard. Brausch smiled. He was in no way comforted.

'At the very least,' Hoffmann grinned, 'I outrank him.'

This was true. It was, in fact, the principal reason that Ritter had reported the Croffts interview to Hoffmann, and to Hoffmann alone.

Hoffmann had then instructed Ritter to pursue Claire's Jewish ancestry, a task to which Ritter applied himself with considerable zeal. Hoffmann, however, assumed responsibility for checking out the lead on Armand Leclerc. After two days, Hoffmann advised Ritter that Leclerc was more than clean, a collaborationist of impeccable credentials.

Hoffmann's report on Leclerc was fully accepted by Ritter. It was not, however, entirely candid.

FORTY-THREE

Jürgen Brausch flicked on the light. It glowed, throbbed, a yellow-white pulse reflecting from the metal cabinets of the tiny room.

It was late. He was tired. His huge hand pawed at his eye sockets as his pupils contracted against the light.

He was operating now on something so far north of instinct that he could only call it magic. It was the tiniest atom of a thought. A fading radio beam launched from a distant star. And yet, he could not go to his bed. Could not sleep until he looked at the paper one last time.

He sat at the gnarled desk, his weight collapsing into the chair. Stared at the drawer, as if it would somehow open for him on command. When he pulled it open at last, he saw that nothing had been disturbed. The exquisitely arranged jumble of papers and objects remained precisely as he had left it.

His fingers went directly to the paper, as if he had plucked it from the chaos a thousand times. He placed the single sheet on the desktop before him. Pulled the chain of the round little desk lamp.

Brausch sat very still. His eyes were closed.

More than tired. He was weary from the weight of it. He had been carrying on so long alone now. He was old. He no longer knew who were more dangerous, the few he had trusted, the many he had not.

He sat in that chair, in that strange and pulsing light, and reviewed his life as if he were a dying man. A life so full, so rich in service and accomplishment. Richer still in the love of his family. It should all be a great solace to him. He should be ready to go.

Brausch smiled weakly at the thought. Was any man ever really ready to go? That was a poet's conceit. A man writhing in agony, tubes pouring from him in every direction, must still within him be breathing madly on the flame. While that spark burns, while it burns, nourish, cherish the fantasy it may burn forever.

He knew now that he would never see Helga again. Never lay eyes on her kind face, or fold his hand about her dear fingers. There would never be that last decent moment of good-bye, of thanking her for having been his other soul on the journey through it all. How remarkable, how wondrous, it had been to share. For it was the sharing that had made it human. Had validated it all.

There are some older men who cry quite easily. Brausch was not among them. Consequently, he was grateful to find that he had not entirely forgotten how.

His eyes clear at last, he turned them to the paper.

Standard cipher. Basic columnar transposition, based on a verse by Heine. Sent in the usual way at the usual interval to Group i of Branch I in Hamburg station.

There was nothing remarkable about the report. Any more than there had been in the opening hour of his visit with Hoffmann at the Ritz.

Why then were the bodies of unseen insects crawling up the back of his neck? Why were that visit and this paper the same?

The report had been sent from London by Treasure, the Abwehr's most glorified and productive agent in the field. The man had been reporting to Brausch for years. A hundred messages just like this one. Not like this one.

The security checks, the triggers, were all in place. The letter '*G*' in the eleventh and nineteenth positions. The misspelling of the thirty-fourth word. If Treasure had sent the message under duress, he would have intentionally omitted these.

There was no duress. This was a message Treasure had freely composed.

So Brausch just sat and stared at the paper. As if it would speak to him.

At last, it did.

As with Hoffmann, the sugar was a trace too sweet. The report contained perhaps one corroborating double check too many. A barely perceptible loading towards the type of detail Treasure knew Brausch preferred. There was the scantest whiff of overcompensation. Of defence against showing that one had pulled back somehow.

Overcompensating for what? What had changed within Treasure?

Brausch sat with his instinct in his teeth, his jaws gripping remorselessly at the shank of it. It did not concern him that the crack he had found was so tiny it might be invisible. Forty years, he had never seen a big one.

Could Treasure have been turned?

He was venal enough. Coward enough. If the English had him by the short hairs, he would whimper, he would crawl.

But they'd have to catch him first. He had been smarter than MI-5 for all these years. Smarter people do not stop being smarter.

More to the point, if MI-5 had turned Treasure, it would flow through Sir Geoffrey Macklin. What reason would Macklin have to deceive Brausch? They were allies. Scared as the devil of each other, but locked at the hip.

So Jürgen Brausch sat and thought some more. With the perfect confidence that this moment absolutely required, it never entered his mind that he was wrong. He was only sifting to find the way in which he was right.

The sifting began back at square one.

How did he come to be sitting here at this moment? He had heard some music in Hoffmann's voice. Heard it for an hour. And he had been right. Something in Hoffmann's words, in the rhythm and flavour of those words, had ceased to ring honest and true. And that was precisely what he was now feeling about Treasure.

Brausch listened once more to the music of Hoffmann's words. One last time now, he reread the report, straining for the sound of Treasure's music as well.

And at last he smiled.

It was a duet.

FORTY-FOUR

They were lying on their cots in the cell. It was May 24, and Gus had been told this was the last visit. He would never see Andy Wheeler again. Hoffmann was compiling the last of his material. He had set the end of the month as the date for issuing his printed report.

The book was about to close.

Andy, of course, had no notion that this was to be their last time together. He was only delighted that the visit had been such a long one.

They had been talking for eleven hours now. To Andy, it seemed twice that. He was exhausted, but nothing would induce him to sleep. Gus was Christmas morning. His presence was fulfillment of the promise that what you wait for, if you are very good, will finally and truly come.

So accustomed had Andy become to the secret protocol of talking in the cell that he shared his feelings fluently, unaffected by the hidden listeners. He and Gus had forged their own privacy. Own code, own club. Two boys, sworn in blood to each other.

To the death.

Andy had been talking about his first car. An old Nash jalopy that his dad had helped him fix up. It had been the only time Andy could remember Dad relishing the role of teaching Andy something. They would get out back with the tools and grease, and Dad's eyes would really light up.

Andy could remember the way Dad's fingers moved over the machinery. As if he could feel something that was speaking to him. Andy bet that Dad had never touched a woman that way, with that depth of understanding.

'Dad was sixty-eight,' Andy said, 'when I left.'

It didn't matter that this was three years ago. Home for Andy was a frozen snapshot of the way things had been when he saw them for the last time. Home would never change now, because Andy would never see it again. He had enrolled himself among the dead.

And hearing this in Andy's voice, Gus realized, with the terrible weight of the first time, that Andy was right.

'Y'think,' Gus wondered, 'the old guy can still get out in back and play catch with ya?'

The words drifted into outer space and were swallowed by the void.

'I mean,' Gus pushed it, 'he'll be, what, seventy-one when y'see him. Right? When's his birthday?'

There was silence. The real world, the future world, the place into which Andy Wheeler would not be welcomed, was of no interest.

Andy was off now in a different place. The only real place left. The past.

San Juan Island. The trip with Stephanie. The one trip. Illicit and golden and wondrous.

They had stayed at Roche Harbor, on the north side of the island. There was a grand and lazy hotel. The Hotel de Haro. Teddy Roosevelt had stayed there, and Taft. There were white picket balconies all along the façade, and a green shingled spire with the American flag.

And the people moved so very languidly. As if in slow motion. As if there were money and leisure to delight in whatever the world had to offer. He loved those people. They were Gatsby and Daisy. He loved their white dresses and starched shirts. The way they ate and danced. They were teaching him, by their very being, what pleasure in life truly was. Pointing the way to where he and Stephanie would surely go.

There was a flower garden. Big, crimson blossoms. Were they roses? The little boats tied in the harbour, their reflections shimmering in the water. The refracted images were so much more beautiful than the boats themselves.

Did that make them more real? Could anything lay greater claim to reality than beauty?

Stephanie's beauty.

Her eyes across the table, across the wine. Across the pillow.

The first and last and only love. The impossible, the most real. The move that was its own image shimmering in the water. That was beauty and reality. The love that filled him and made him whole.

'Stephanie was nineteen,' Andy said.

Gus waited, but Andy was silent again.

'That makes her twenty-two,' Gus said softly.

Quiet.

'By the time I get to stand up at your wedding,' Gus said, 'she'll be getting on in years. Maybe I should find you a younger one. You seem to like 'em young.'

'She had this cat,' Andy said, oblivious to the present tense. 'He was a fat, old Persian. She used to tell me I was like that cat.'

His voice was drifting, floating. A gauzy curtain was dropping between them.

'People thought I was a loner,' Andy said. 'But I was just afraid. It took someone to love me first, love me real hard, so I could love them back. Like that cat. Like that cat she had.'

Andy was staring at the ceiling, his arms folded protectively across his chest. It was the way they were folded when Gus had first met him.

Goddam you, Gus thought. Don't let go. Don't you let go on me.

The silence swallowed them.

'Hey,' Gus shouted, so sharply that Andy's head snapped around.

'Goddam you,' Gus shouted, tears suddenly welling. 'Don't you let go on me. Don't you ever goddam let go on me. I love you. I love you too much.'

Andy's eyes flooded. He was back. All the way back.

'There's one woman,' Gus said, 'I never told you about.

Claire. She's not at home. She's somewhere else. We really . . . love each other. And that was all I guess I ever wanted. All those years. Just someone who . . . where . . . we were good to each other.'

Andy's head was nodding now. Tears were flowing, but Andy was telling him he understood.

'So you know what I think?' Gus said. 'The first Sunday we're back. You and me and Stephanie and Claire. We'll all take a ride somewhere and have a picnic lunch. And we'll talk about everything there is. And we won't leave till we've had two hundred laughs. We'll count 'em.'

I'm going to make it happen for you, he'd said in the garden. Depend on it. Well, Claire had watched the door roll shut on Martin. And Gus had stared into the everlasting smile of Major Seitz, the moment before Madame Sainte-Juste had filled Gus forever with her screams.

Gus reached across the space between them. He shook Andy so gently.

'That's a firm date now,' Gus said. 'You write that in your little appointment book.'

Andy looked up and the lost expression became an Andy-smile.

'The first Sunday,' Andy said. 'First Sunday we're home.'

FORTY-FIVE

A sidewalk café in the busiest section of the Champs-Élysées. Broad, bright daylight. One Pernod, one gin on the rocks.

Walter Hoffmann could pick the damnedest time and place.

The afternoon air was palpably delicious. They had ordered another round.

'I've been having second thoughts,' Hoffmann said slowly, 'about finalizing our report.'

Gus' eyes indicated mild but appropriate concern.

'What would you think,' Hoffmann said, 'if I asked you to go back into the cell with Major Wheeler? Perhaps eight or nine more episodes over a four-week period.'

Gus shrugged slightly. 'Whatever is necessary,' he said.

Hoffmann's eyes registered their appreciation.

'I know,' Hoffmann said, 'that these long sessions . . . fifteen, sixteen hours . . . have not been entirely pleasant for you. Still, my hunch is that they are just beginning to pay off.'

The waiter arrived with their drinks. He seemed to flutter about them, cutting off the flow of Hoffmann's words. Hoffmann remained serene, smiling with good nature as the man fussily wiped up the sweat from the previous round.

After the man finally withdrew, Hoffmann smiled boyishly across the table.

'Let's see,' he said, 'I think we were discussing the war.'

Gus grinned.

'It appears,' Hoffmann said, 'that Wheeler's isolation is beginning to separate his mind from reality for comparatively long periods of time.'

'No question about it,' Gus concurred.

'I would expect,' Hoffmann said, 'that this will increase in frequency and duration. My thought is that you wait for moments when he is in this almost trance-like state, and take him once more through brief and carefully selected portions of his invasion story.'

Gus nodded. He agreed.

'I believe,' Hoffmann said, 'it's a check worth running while we still have this poor fellow in our hands. God knows what the Gestapo has in mind for him after we file our report.'

This was said in such offhand innocence that Gus was unprepared for the visceral impact of the words. He pictured a lake seething with piranhas, waters boiling with their frenzy as they waited for a living sacrifice to be flung from the banks.

Of course the Gestapo would tear Andy to pieces, in the

name of the final control check. Once Hoffmann's report was closed, the risk of cardiac arrest would become irrelevant.

Hoffmann was helping him buy time.

'There is,' Hoffmann said down into his glass of Pernod, 'a problem.'

He looked back up at Gus.

'Did you know,' Hoffmann said, 'that Claire has Jewish ancestors?'

In cold, absolute horror, Seitz appeared in Gus' mind. His smile now the dead and vivid rictus of a leering ghoul. If she were Jewish, Seitz sang eerily, she'd have been gone long ago.

Claire, standing where Madame Sainte-Juste had stood, the unheeded spittle of terror falling onto her nightdress.

Amy as Martin, in the freight car. Her little arms reaching to Gus, gasping for enough air to shriek her confusion and panic. Gigantic tears cascading down her reddened cheeks as she screams for him to take her. The train's irrevocable engine. The door rolling shut.

Hoffmann's smile was almost apologetic, but the dark eyes were direct. Reading, computing.

Gus shook his head very slightly, as if the motion were involuntary. He permitted the stabbing sensation in his chest to come straight up to his eyes. It was a reaction Hoffmann might as well see.

'Tell me about it,' Gus said softly.

Hoffmann offered a smile of reassurance.

'Ritter,' Hoffmann answered, 'has tracked sleuthed down Claire's great-grandfather. He was a Polish Jew. There is no more to it. And unfortunately, no less.'

Gus made his eyes add up the risks.

'I'm afraid for her, Walter,' he said at last. 'I love her.'

Hoffmann nodded sympathetically. His eyes were very wise. 'And I am afraid for you, Gus. Ritter is an animal where these things are concerned. I must know that you are willing to give her up. Only then can I promise her safety.'

Gus looked down at the hands around his gin glass. His own hands. They seemed so very far away, so alien.

'I don't really know that I can, Walter. I could lie to you. But the truth is, I don't think I can let her go.'

Hoffmann waited patiently until Gus looked up to meet his eyes.

'If Berlin finds out, they will see you as an unacceptable risk to the security of the project. Now that you know she is a Jew, under the law . . . it's miscegenation.'

That word. It conjured southern plantations. Red-faced slave owners taking frightened dark women to the Big House.

'For God's sake,' Hoffmann nearly whispered, 'technically, miscegenation carries a death penalty. I can handle that side of it, of course, but you'd still be cashiered. I can't afford to lose you. We can't let this thing take you off the project.'

Gus fought to keep the throbbing in his head under control. Hoffmann had built this trap. He would never have shown the trap to Gus unless he also intended to show him the door out of it. Hoffmann's door.

'You're Ritter's superior,' Gus said, trying to sound every bit as helpless as would be expected.

Hoffmann spread his hands.

'Gus, she's a *Jew*. A mission indispensable to Reich security. My key agent sleeps with a *Jew*? Can you conceive of Himmler's reaction? Berserk. He would be crazed.'

Say you'll do it. Open your mouth and say it. It's only the next step. Let him lead.

Gus began to nod slowly.

'I don't know how I'll do it,' Gus said. 'But . . . there isn't any choice. You've got to swear to me that she'll be all right.'

Hoffmann's eyes were never more human, yet never more opaque. He was offering tenderness and understanding. For the rest of it, he was keeping his own counsel.

'I needed to hear that,' Hoffmann said quietly. 'I hope it won't be necessary after all. I will tell Ritter that I need your concentration intact for this last phase with the Overlord.'

Hoffmann's smile was rueful.

'This, of course, will allow him to rationalize that he is stepping back in the greater interest of the Reich. The real leverage is that I am writing the report that will be crucial in evaluating his promotion. He needs me. Ernst would *marry* a Jew if she could make him an Oberführer.'

Gus' eyes were gleaming with friendship and gratitude. He had managed to summon up real moisture from somewhere.

'Thank you,' he said simply.

'I won't promise that I can keep you together,' Hoffmann said quietly. 'But I know what it means to you. I will do what I can.'

FORTY-SIX

The sisters of St Agonie are members of a Lazarite order founded in Jerusalem in the mid-twelfth century. The story of their order's service and sacrifice has reached across many lands, many years.

A key chapter of that history was taking place in Montparnasse, at 127 Rue de la Santé. For there, beneath the lunatic asylum of Sainte-Anne, the Convent of St Agonie had become a safe house for the *réseau* known as Jade Amicol.

It was six o'clock, on an evening turned unexpectedly raw and chilly.

A man hurried down Boulevard Arago – hands thrust deep into his pockets, his broad shoulders hunched against the cold. Armand Leclerc turned now onto Rue de la Santé, the small road leading to the convent.

He rang the bell. Stood, for what seemed to be several minutes. At last, the bolt was thrown and the mother superior, the legendary Henriette Frede, silently welcomed him.

Leclerc followed Mother Henriette through the nave.

They passed the sacristy. A spiral staircase led to the choir loft where Jade Amicol had hidden its wireless transceiver. The loft where Leclerc would later sit with a small oil lamp and relay this night's message to London.

For now, Mother Henriette brought him to a small room. Walls of stone, slow to warm. There were rough wooden chairs at a table with two candles. Mother Henriette smiled gently at Leclerc, offering the only real warmth in the room. She left him to his thoughts.

Six-forty. A young woman crossed Boulevard de Port Royal. She took small quick steps, bending her head against the chill wind whipping at her black hair. And as Jasmine walked, her mind endlessly replayed today's story.

The falcon had met with the badger. Had told the badger that his visits with the ferret had indeed not come to an end. The badger would visit the ferret at the lily pond eight or nine more times, and they would tell the story to each other again and again.

Jasmine turned directly into the wind at the Rue de la Santé. It stung her face and her eyes closed to slits against its force.

The badger was very happy. For the falcon had promised they would stay in the forest for one more month.

Jasmine, of course, had never met Gus Lang. Had never even heard of his existence. Nonetheless, it had been Gus who had selected her from all the candidates proposed by Claire.

Gus had known from the first that, once Hoffmann had the scent, the trackers would not follow Gus alone. There would surely be a team assigned to Claire. And although he had never seen them, although Claire did not know how to recognize them, Gus had indeed been right. Claire must never meet with Leclerc. Never go to the convent.

And so Jasmine had been chosen. Claire's courier.

She stood now, waiting at the convent door. Breath misting in the chill. Mother Henriette arrived and Jasmine was admitted.

And several metres down the road, a man reached into

the breast pocket of his warm woollen coat. He extracted a silver case. Shielding the flame against the wind, he lit a cigarette.

Walter Hoffmann seemed not to notice the cold as his eyes remained locked on the convent door. Locked for the longest of moments.

At last, he turned and headed slowly towards the river.

FORTY-SEVEN

In a green, wooded spot, as the Thames leaves London for gentler surroundings, an old canal barge bobbed beneath overhanging willows.

The barge had been converted to a restaurant called the Barque and Bite. Starched white tablecloths were in place for afternoon tea, but it was still a little early for the regulars.

Seated in a cosy spot, slowly thumbing his stack of afternoon papers, was a tubby little fellow dressed in heavy tweed. He had a balding dome and soft, round features. There was about him the slightly fussy, if good-natured, air of a certain brand of Oxford don. Which, in fact, he was.

He was also something else.

Under the code name of Treasure, this man had been the Abwehr's most effective British agent for more than seven years.

Treasure's product had more than justified his name. Had brought him a small fortune in cash from a grateful Reich. He was the only Abwehr agent permitted by Brausch to run his own sub-agents, and had long been in the comfortable position of having others do his fieldwork, usually the most dangerous phase of his craft.

All this had changed abruptly not very long ago, with a direct wireless from an unexpected source.

A large amount of money had changed hands, to be sure, but the decision involved the risk of one's life. It had therefore been made with some care and no little anxiety. This was slightly more than a routine change of employers.

And as he sat, and as he sipped, his small watery eyes contemplated the next few days with some misgivings. Why in bloody hell did he have to bring it himself? His word, his wireless, had been good enough for Jürgen Brausch all these years. What made these bastards so bloody different?

He had never been a rugged man. This was apparent from the very sight of him. The soft hands that had lovingly cradled first editions had never touched the flesh of a pistol or rifle. He was a gentleman mercenary to be sure.

And yet, to say the word *mercenary* and turn the page would be to miss the essential centre of the man. Would a man of his judgment and refinement turn against his native land for money alone? The truth was that this man would have done anything for money. But he would have done *this* without payment of a farthing.

There was no malice towards England in his deepest heart. England, for him, scarcely existed. From the earliest days of his seduction by the printed word, he had lived only in his mind. He was more than a citizen of the world. He resided in the timeless history of all humankind. The cobbled walks of medieval Córdoba, the sliding waterways of Quattrocento Venice, were his home as surely as the graceful tree-lined avenue of his Mayfair flat.

More than all of these, perhaps, the dusty and distant city-states of Greece in its Golden Age. For Treasure was a Platonist. From the age when most boys were wondering what made a combustion engine kick to life, Treasure had accepted the cult of the philosopher-king. Had known that the only true salvation of his species would be to place its collective soul into the care of the wise, the strong, the God-man with the vision and will to truly lead.

His path from Plato to Nietzsche had been a long and twisting road of growth and shrivelling and many detours. And so, if Adolph Hitler had been born in China or Colorado, this man, this man who considered himself the quintessential cynic, the ultimate pragmatist, would still have followed his ideal of the Führer off the edge of the earth.

Treasure would make the trip after all. Would risk his soft and fragile body, his life. And would tell himself that he did it for the money.

Gerhard Tessin, Brausch's pimp, arrived at the doorway. He was clutching his tweed coat in the chill. Their eyes met across the room, and Tessin received a warm smile of greeting from his old friend.

Treasure had placed a packet for Tessin on the seat beside him. Troop movements. Exercises. Changes in routes of supply. There was nothing extraordinary, nothing terribly useful. In time-honoured tradition, the packet would remain after Treasure had gone, while Tessin finished his final cup.

Their talk was business and politics. Fictional wife, make-believe mistress.

What their talk most certainly was not was anything that could reveal to Tessin that Treasure did not work for him any longer. That the Abwehr's most trusted mercenary had moved on to lusher pastures.

Tessin was instead told that Treasure would be taking a trip to Scotland for a few days' spring holiday.

Back next Wednesday. Same table, same time, same tired biscuits.

FORTY-EIGHT

Treasure had anticipated that his journey would be pure hell. It was not nearly so pleasant.

He had crossed the North Sea from Scotland in a bloody wreck of a twin-engine seaplane. They had ditched miles off the southern tip of Norway, and he had been taken the rest of the way to Stavanger by trawler.

From Norway, he had spent a lifetime of jarring rides and secretive shifts. Passed from one unsavoury thug to another. Why did these people feel you could put a uniform on an animal and call him an escort?

He was twenty years older when the last train hissed into the last station. From there, he was very much on his own. Only a pocketful of papers, mostly forged, and his own dulled wits to see him through.

The most ghastly joke of all was that he would be in Paris for exactly one night before the entire unsupportable journey would be repeated in reverse.

He found the rooming house somehow. A ratty little place in a working-class outskirt of town.

He sat now in the humidity of this filthy pit of a room and waited for three solid hours. Five minutes in the place would have been interminable. He was not a man slow to take offence, and he was using what little energy he had left towards the building of a trembling rage.

The precautions and security were fatuous. There couldn't be a single soul in all of Paris who knew, or gave a tinker's damn, who he was.

He had purchased a bottle of sherry from the neighbourhood bar. Considering the neighbourhood, he got what he paid for. He stared down into the greasy, tepid glass and let his misery billow about him. Too old for this. Too old for a great many things.

He had worked too many years for Jürgen Brausch to begin learning the idiosyncrasies of a new master. Brausch never would have kept him waiting.

A key turned in the latch and Walter Hoffmann entered the tiny room.

Hoffmann had little reason to smile these last days, but he couldn't resist a small one at the expense of the pudgy little man grimacing down at his sherry.

Despite Treasure's evident discomfort and self-pity, Hoffmann knew himself to be in the presence of the one thing he truly respected, a consummate professional.

Hoffmann bowed slightly from the waist.

'I am honoured,' he said in English.

'I am sweating like a sow,' came the response.

Hoffmann's playful smile made its appearance.

'I expect,' Hoffmann said, 'that you might have been somewhat more comfortable at the Ritz.'

'I would have been somewhat more comfortable,' Treasure assured him, 'in anything from a brothel to a rabbit hutch.'

As if on cue, a roach scurried for cover.

Treasure offered a low sound of pure revulsion.

'I think,' Treasure announced, 'that we can keep our life's acquaintance to five minutes. Your answer is in the parcel over there on the sideboard.'

Hoffmann settled himself into a spindly chair. He arched his brow expectantly. At these prices, he expected the courtesy of an oral report.

'And how,' Hoffmann said with extreme kindness, 'was your journey?'

'I wouldn't have wished it on your mother,' Treasure sighed.

Hoffmann nodded.

'I'm a busy man,' Hoffmann said with a very winning little smile. 'Suppose you tell me why you've dragged me out here.'

Even Treasure had to succumb, if only slightly, to the charm of the man.

'My countrymen,' Treasure said wearily, 'sometimes manage to slip beneath even my expectations.'

'Never underestimate the English,' Hoffmann counselled.

'Not only did they neglect to alter Wheeler's medical report in the hospital file,' Treasure continued, 'they actually clipped into said file a note from some imbecile named Peters.'

Treasure smiled at the idiocy of it all. He couldn't help himself.

'The note instructs the clerk to retype the report, adding the heart condition. It goes on to name a fictitious American cardiologist to be used as reference. It concludes by reminding the clerk to cross-reference the heart condition in any duplicate material forwarded back to Wheeler's American unit.'

And now it was Hoffmann's turn to sigh.

'Oh my,' Was all Hoffmann could say.

'Dear Mr Peters,' Treasure concluded, 'gave his orders and simply assumed that they were carried out. We Britons are an arrogant little breed.'

'Trusting,' Hoffmann corrected, in a sympathetic tone.

Hoffmann's eyes drifted off in quiet contemplation.

'There is nothing here which directly implicates Captain Lang in this deception,' Treasure said.

Treasure watched the handsome dark eyes. Eyes in which he had expected to find anything but what he saw. For there, unmistakably, was what Treasure could only describe as sadness.

Hoffmann's mind was even more of a puzzle to himself. Could he truly be sorry that he had come to the end of his search? His work was now completed. With one last loose end to tie, the dangling riddle of Jürgen Brausch, all would be in order. The secret report that had been forming in his mind would be written. The lies of the Overlord and his accomplice would be translated in reverse.

He would be Brigadeführer. Perhaps, no, probably, placed at the right hand of Himmler. More, he would go home now. Home to Anna and his sons.

Was he saddened, after all, that Gus had betrayed him? Hadn't he virtually known that this would be so from the first moment? Perhaps he regretted that it had been his lot to find Gus out. To destroy him. Perhaps he was saddened only by being alive in this world.

Hoffmann didn't really know. He clung now to the only part that suddenly seemed to matter. Home to Anna's love. To her bed. Rudi would make his morning coffee. Oskar would guess whether it was Monday or Thursday or the day Papa could stay home from the office.

'You are certain,' Treasure asked, 'that Captain Lang knew of this?'

Without even looking up at the man, Hoffmann simply spread his arms in a gesture of resignation.

'What can I say?' Hoffmann breathed into the dark world. 'The man is a helpless victim of coincidence. His lover meets twice each week with a girl who dashes off to a Resistance network. His immediate superiors in London falsify a heart condition that he then unwittingly passes on to us. Nobody tells this poor soul anything. A loyal servant of the Reich, he is surrounded by fiends who prey on his innocence.'

Hoffmann looked now at Treasure. There was no trace of the playful smile. There was no sign of pleasure or triumph or even relief.

'It is almost,' Hoffmann said, 'enough to make one suggest that the boy consider leaving this line of work.'

FORTY-NINE

Although he had no way of knowing it, it was the middle of the night. Andy Wheeler had been brought to the small interrogation room and left shivering in darkness and cold.

He did not have to wait long.

The light snapped on. Even blinking against the glare, Andy knew that he had not seen this man before.

Dressed in the gleaming black and silver of the SS, the man took his seat behind the desk.

Walter Hoffmann stared thoughtfully, waiting for Andy's eyes to adjust to the light. There were no colleagues behind the mirror in the next room. This was a most unscheduled, very private, interview.

'My name is Hoffmann,' he said at last.

He read Andy's eyes. There was recognition.

In that single moment, Gus' treachery was forever confirmed. Gus had never used Hoffmann's name in the cell. Wheeler could only have heard it in the garden. Only as part of a private warning.

He stood and walked to Andy. Reaching into his tunic, Hoffmann produced a photograph. The snapshot from the dinner party at Maxim's. It had been taken against the moment when Hoffmann might need to discredit Gus with Andy.

The dark eyes never moved from Andy's face as he stared at the photo.

'It's Gus,' Andy said, struggling mightily to imitate astonishment. 'I . . . I don't understand.'

It was pathetically clear to Hoffmann that Andy was lying. Gus, therefore, had told Andy that he was not a prisoner. That he had been posing as a German agent.

Hoffmann returned to his desk. He folded his fingers together and pressed them to his lips. Staring, always staring, directly at Andy's eyes.

Andy blinked, looked down at his hands. Already there was forming within him the terror that he could not prevent this man from raping his mind. And the dark eyes would be the instrument of that violation.

Andy looked back to those eyes for only a moment, then away again. This told Hoffmann everything. Told him Andy knew that he could never keep Hoffmann out.

There was no hostility in Hoffmann's gaze. There was only a relentless, penetrating questioning. As if Hoffmann were about to dissect Andy, slip a smear beneath a microscope, and learn some ineffable truth about disease.

'You are lying,' Hoffmann said at last. 'In these past weeks, Gus Lang has masqueraded as an agent of the Reich.'

Watching, reading. Confirming without question.

'He told you this,' Hoffmann said. 'He told you a great many things. And each one of them is true.'

He let this sink in.

'Gus Lang was,' Hoffmann added, 'in his way, an honest man.'

It was a simple word, the word *was*. Not said with particular emphasis or malice.

It sent the coldest stab of fear that Andy Wheeler had ever known.

'Captain Lang is dead,' Hoffmann said simply. 'He is dead and you are alone.'

This came an exquisite half-beat after Andy had realized it for himself. The effect was a finishing blow. It registered in every sagging muscle of Andy's body.

'I regret that,' Hoffmann added with obvious sincerity. 'I would have preferred having two of you to chat with. Unfortunately, some of my colleagues are not as patient, as rational . . . You have met Standartenführer Ritter, I believe.'

The dark eyes softened. For a moment, Andy felt the kindness and humanity he had experienced in his interview with Brausch.

'You do not smoke, do you? You tried cigarettes once when you were twelve years old. Decided they were not for you.'

Hoffmann extracted his cigarette case.

'Wise decision,' he said with a straight face. 'Undoubtedly added years to your life.'

Hoffmann lighted up ever so slowly. Slower still was the deep first drag that filled his lungs. The smoke billowed from his mouth, invading the meagre airspace of the cubicle. It seemed to Andy that his oxygen had been cut in half.

'Captain Lang was a good friend to you, Andy. I know that you will not want to let him down.'

The very use of Andy's first name irrationally brought tears to the brink of flowing. Andy was at the edge of sanity now. The edge of everything.

Why would this man tell him Gus was honest, a good friend? Why didn't he try all of the lies that Andy had waited for? That Gus had betrayed Andy, had sold him out.

'Right now,' Hoffmann said, 'you are planning to stick with your story about Calais and September right through to the grave. You're a brave lad, Andy.'

And now the silence grew long and longer.

Hoffmann carefully stubbed his cigarette into an ashtray.

'Your cardiac arrhythmia was his downfall, Andy. That is where we caught him. So you might say he died protecting you. All the more reason to cling to your loyalty.'

Hoffmann's face stopped cold. The penetrating eyes seemed to glow now, to heat the room.

'September in Calais,' Hoffmann said. 'Beautiful there in the fall. Personally, I have never been an apologist for torture. It's a point of philosophy. Question of style, really.'

And now the playful smile came suddenly. Came with a twist at the corners of the lips.

'We know now, of course, that it cannot be Calais. Cannot be September. Must be earlier. July? Even June perhaps.'

Andy shut his eyes tightly. Actually shut them. He had given himself over to the conviction that Gus was wrong. This man could use Andy's eyes as a perfect window to his thoughts.

He opened them to find Hoffmann's gaze. Waiting, absorbing.

'We have considerable information as to the scope of the Allied buildup in southern England. Therefore, the attack cannot come in Italy or the Balkans.'

The smile again.

'Biscay? Brittany, perhaps?'

Andy tried to stare blankly into Hoffmann's eyes. Tried to shut out the sound of his voice. Think of baseball. The farm. Never had another's words rung through so clearly.

'Less than ideal,' Hoffmann conceded. 'Andy, have you ever been to Normandy?'

Andy's heart pounded wildly against his ribs. The rush of blood in his ears must have been audible even to Hoffmann.

He tried to stare defiantly, dispassionately, at his enemy. He could do neither. There was not the slightest question. Hoffmann was reading the muscles of his face as if they were letters on a page.

'Normandy is exquisite in the early summer,' Hoffmann said easily. 'Even more so in late spring.'

Hoffmann looked down at his hands. For a moment, he had intentionally broken the spell.

Andy could feel the throbbing of every vein in his throat. He was suddenly aware that he was covered with perspiration.

'Do you begin to have a thought,' Hoffmann asked quietly, 'of the impossibility of your position?'

Andy had more than the beginning of a thought.

The voice changed register again. Became the kindness of Brausch's voice. Kinder still, became Gus' voice.

'I could have lied to you, Andy. I could have told you that we had extracted the information from Gus. That it would be useless to suffer, protecting data we already possessed.'

That was so. Andy had expected it.

'I haven't lied to you, Andy, because it is important for you to understand that everything I have told you, will tell you, is truth.'

Against all fear, against all defence, Andy had already begun to wonder if this could be so.

'The truth is, Andy, that I will have your thoughts. The only question is when. I am tired, Andy. I am tired of so many things. I want the truth from you *before* those butchers cut you to pieces.'

Something clear and sad in Hoffmann's voice rang out his revulsion in those words.

'It is the most pitiful waste,' Hoffmann said softly. His voice was not pleading, it was teaching. 'I can protect you as my prisoner, Andy. I can restore you to your family. To your Stephanie. I can do that if you will let me.'

And ringing in Andy's brain were only the words *cut you to pieces*.

Hoffmann's eyes carried the eloquence of incontrovertible fact.

'The heart condition is exposed, Andy. If you will not talk to me, can you honestly believe that there is a single reason in this world why they will not give you to Ritter?'

There was none. It would happen. The clenching, clutching of razor talons within him.

He had promised himself that he wouldn't be afraid when the time came. He'd never known it would feel like this. So physical, so instantly beyond any hope of control.

'Do you know, Andy, what the Gestapo will do with you?'

He did not. There was a fierce thrashing now inside him. A heat, a frenzied constriction of breath that kept tightening.

He sat, utterly unaware that Hoffmann was watching his chest heave.

'They will cut off your toes. One each session, at the end of the session. Unless they have heard what they want. Then, your fingers. One each session.'

Hoffmann again folded his hands before his lips. He stared so deeply, spoke so quietly, there was a protective caring in his voice that was unquestionably some form of love. Gus. Dad.

'Then they will take your ears, Andy. Then, your testicles. They will never stop taking parts of you until you are dead. And they are very practised at keeping you alive.'

Hoffmann reached for the cigarette case once more. He touched the flame to the tip of his cigarette most deliberately. Kept his eyes on the flame, letting Andy's panic rage through every part of him.

At last, the eyes returned to Andy.

'You don't believe me yet,' Hoffmann said, 'because it's too monstrous to believe of any human beings. But it will begin in exactly three days. Unless you decide that it shouldn't. Once it begins, you will believe.'

A deep drag on the cigarette. A smile of compassion and forgiveness. Of finality.

'It is over, Andy. You cannot hide your mind from me. Ten hours a day, twenty if need be. I'll find the truth. In your heart, you already know this is so.'

The cigarette was crushed. Hoffmann stood. He picked up his hat, turning it slowly in his fingers. The interview appeared to be ending. This was the moment most defences let go, so eager to believe that the ordeal is already over.

Hoffmann gathered himself for the final thrust.

'The irony is that your secrets have become irrelevant. You see, your people know that Gus is dead and that you are not. He did not kill you. He did not save you. They *must* now proceed on the assumption that you will be forced to reveal everything.'

A terrible light went on for Andy.

'The strategy that you and Gus fabricated together has come true. The only place they will *not* land is the place I must extract from your mind. I have told this to my superiors and I think they know that I am right. Still, my assignment remains unaltered.'

Hoffmann clasped the hat beneath his arm. He walked to the door as Andy's eyes followed.

'Think of one thing,' Hoffmann said, his fingertips caressing the latch. 'What would Gus Lang tell you if he were here? You know he would say, "Andy, it's over. We held them off for more than a month. We did our best. You are alive. Stay alive for my sake and for those who love you."'

Hoffmann turned away. Opened the door. Turned back.

'To suffer horribly and die without a purpose is not heroism, Andy. It is a waste. It is a *crime* against those who wait for you. Reach out to Gus with your heart, Andy. Let him teach you that.'

FIFTY

They were two very drunk men, sitting under a single lamp. The room about them was black. It was closer to dawn than to midnight.

They were drinking Scotch whisky tonight, although neither of them exactly knew why. Someone had given Hoffmann a case of Pinch. A random bit of plunder from God-knows-where.

For the most part, it was their warmest time together. The strained intimacy that Brausch had sensed in their last meeting seemed replaced by the genuine article.

At midnight, Greater Reich Time, they had paused to toast a death.

'It is June first,' Hoffmann had said, looking at his father's pocket watch. 'The Abwehr has ceased to exist.'

It was true. As of that instant, the Abwehr, the proud intelligence service of so many years of valour and genius, was gone. It had become the Amt Mil, the military department of the SD. Reorganization was now complete.

Hoffmann's right hand raised slowly. He extended his Scotch glass until it was held at the extremity of a Nazi salute.

'To the Abwehr,' he said softly.

Brausch, dry-eyed and not yet terribly drunk, had joined him. This kicked off a round of toasts that had now consumed more than three hours and by far the better part of the Pinch.

'To ideals,' Hoffmann said blearily, in what seemed to be his hundredth toast.

Brausch spread his palms and shook his head.

'Why drink to the past?' he murmured.

Hoffmann chuckled.

'Always the realist,' Hoffmann said. 'Your only vice.'

Brausch found this very funny.

'Realism is my luxury,' Brausch corrected. 'The only luxury I cannot afford to do without.'

Hoffmann nodded very seriously. He lifted his glass once more. It seemed heavy.

'To humanity, then,' he said quietly.

'Provocative choice,' Brausch murmured.

Hoffmann just stared at his glass. Turned it in his hand. His glazed smile disappeared.

'Did it ever exist, really?' Hoffmann asked.

Brausch's great head nodded sadly.

'Comes and goes,' Brausch said. 'Like the length of women's skirts. If you live long enough, you'll see it again.'

Hoffmann's smile was a remembering one. The reflecting lingered for a moment.

'Well then,' Hoffmann said aloud, 'as a shabby replacement for the past, let's drink to the future. To . . . national honour.'

Hoffmann struggled to his feet, snatching up the Pinch bottle in his free hand.

'This,' he said, holding forward his Scotch glass, 'is the Holy Bible.'

He cleared his throat.

'And this,' brandishing the bottle, 'is the flag of the Reich.'

Brausch understood, for there was only one ceremony he knew which required the grasping of those two objects.

The silence deepened, if such a thing were possible, and Hoffmann's eyes now cleared completely.

Hoffmann stared off into the distance and began to recite the Fahneneid. The Nazi corruption of the ancient blood oath of the Teuton knights.

'I swear by God this holy oath, that I will render to Adolph Hitler, Führer of the German nation and people, Supreme Commander of the Armed Services, unconditional obedience, and I am ready as a brave soldier to risk my life at anytime for this oath.'

The silence swallowed both men, as each remembered the day he was forced to take that oath, and what had coursed through him as he spoke it.

It took a moment for Hoffmann's smile to creep across his face. As he resumed his seat, his eyes held Brausch firmly.

'The Führer,' Hoffmann said, 'is not a man. He is not a force. He is not a devil or a god. He is only a context. He is the context in which we live and do our work. For now. Like a depression. Like a plague. You can feel about it as you choose. Beat your fists against it and weep. It is there. For now.'

A terrible smile lit Brausch's features.

He thrust his glass forward.

'To you, then, Walter. To all of you. You are the context that gave birth to his.'

Hoffmann thought about it for a moment. Was this the answer? It was. It was God's answer about Walter Hoffmann.

But much more, it was Hoffmann's answer about Jürgen Brausch. An answer to be confirmed very shortly, and one about which there should have been no surprise.

'To me,' Hoffmann said at last. He leaned forward and quietly clicked his glass against Brausch's.

'It is time for sleep now,' Hoffmann said, as if only just aware of the time. 'I promised Gus that I would take him and Claire and the baby for a day in the country.'

FIFTY-ONE

Brausch left the Ritz in the darkness of predawn. On the street, his driver was asleep in the car. The driver was a boy of twenty-three, handpicked by Hauptmann Trager. Like Trager, the boy was entirely trustworthy.

Brausch looked at the innocence of the sleeping lieutenant. During the night, the boy too had changed jobs. He would never serve the Abwehr, grow in its tradition, be admitted one day to its inner circle. Whatever the future of this new Amt Mil, this bastardized Abwehr remnant now enslaved by the SS, Brausch could only pray that such future would be mercifully brief.

Gently, he shook the young man, gave him a street and number. His caution was such that the address was nearly a mile from his true destination.

When they arrived at the Church of Saint-Séverin, Brausch sent the driver home.

Brausch was tired, but it wasn't a question of being tired. He had never felt older, but that too had become irrelevant. It was rather the weariness of being a few uphill steps from the end of a journey.

He hunched his shoulders against the predawn chill. Perhaps, he smiled to himself, some drunken policeman would ignore the uniform and shoot him for violating curfew. That would simplify matters.

Slowly, he headed up the Rue Saint-André-des-Arts. He walked east, towards the first light that would soon appear over the spire of the Church of Saint-Séverin. By the time he reached his destination, it was past five o'clock. Curfew was over.

Brausch pulled his body up the staircase. The same steps that Wilhelm Seitz had climbed in pursuit of his prey. Brausch arrived at the same landing.

He had to ring the bell several times. At last, Claire appeared, black hair flowing loosely over a thin robe.

He had never seen her before. How very lovely, he thought at once. Could little Katrina grow into this? Very old, he thought, to see a woman this beautiful and think only of one's granddaughter.

'I am Jürgen Brausch,' he said simply.

The grey eyes warmed at the sound of his name. Her soft hand reached for his, led him into the flat.

Claire vanished. In a moment, Gus appeared in her place.

'Please get dressed,' Brausch said. 'I would like to take a walk.'

They walked along the Seine, following the *quai* to Pont Neuf. They said nothing at all.

The silence seemed entirely comfortable to Gus, as if it were the most natural thing in the world to be awakened in darkness for a mute stroll across the river.

Whatever it was, Brausch would say it in his own time. Gus would use this time to ready himself.

Instinct alone told Gus that his preparation should not become the gathering of defences, of fears. Instinct said reach within, find the capacity to trust. This was, to be sure, against all training, against all conventional wisdom, against the inner voice of every mentor he had loved. Still, Gus knew with quiet certainty that he should follow none of these. Only the instinct. It was time to trust.

Light was beginning to give shape to the city as Brausch led Gus to Les Halles, the giant marketplace where the produce of all France was collected and sorted for sale to Paris.

Inside, the noise and smells and movement were overwhelming. Les Halles was the stomach of Paris, and Gus followed Brausch through its tubes and ducts, the roofed passages, the alleyways bursting with a kaleidoscope of foodstuffs. Huge stalls of live crabs, wheels of cheese, vegetables of all descriptions. They passed cabarets, where locals gathered at curfew's end for onion soup and snails.

The activity was so intense that the two men were swallowed whole and lost to the world. It was the most public, and therefore the most private, imaginable setting.

As they turned up an alleyway off Rue Baltard, Brausch finally spoke the words.

'Apparently,' he said, 'Walter knows.'

How very strange to feel the absolute shock of those words. They were words Gus had suspected from that first day, had virtually known were true for weeks now. He had gone to bed at night and wakened in the morning with that fear-knowledge for what seemed the last half of his life.

And now, shivering, paralytic shock. As if Brausch had calmly whispered, 'Oh, by the way, the angel of death is crouching in that closet.'

'I have had a premonition for the past few days,' Brausch said.

He spoke so softly into the din surrounding them. Yet each syllable cut through to the centre of Gus' brain.

'Something in Walter's voice,' Brausch said, 'combined with something in the tone of a certain wireless report.'

Gus nodded as they walked, concentrating every cell of his being on these words.

'So I had Walter followed. A most dangerous, extreme measure. I could trust only Trager.'

Brausch was quiet for a moment. Almost as if piecing it together for himself.

'Two night ago, Trager followed Walter to a decrepit

neighbourhood near Gentilly. Walter disappeared into a small rooming house. Trager was forced to wait outside in the cold. It was dreadfully cold.'

For some reason, Gus found Brausch's grandfatherly concern for Trager more than enchanting. It seemed to be the *leit-motiv* of a great truth. Brausch couldn't keep his essential humanity from seeping through the cracks. It was a sense of perspective Gus could only idolize.

'When Walter returned to the street, Trager let him go. Kept waiting.'

'In the cold,' Gus couldn't keep himself from saying.

'Yes. At any rate, in twenty minutes another man left the hotel. This man's clothing marked him as a man unlikely to be a guest in that fleabag. Trager followed him for an hour before losing him.

'Trager's description of this man was most precise,' Brausch continued. 'There is no doubt in my mind that Walter was meeting with an Englishman named Colin Desmond.'

They walked in silence for a full minute.

'This man Desmond,' Brausch said, nearly as an afterthought, 'has worked for me these last seven years. Under the code name Treasure.'

Full tilt into a brick wall.

'Treasure,' Gus said, 'is a woman. Her name is Worthy. A young blonde, quite attractive. As you well know, I've spent two years keeping track of her for MI-5.'

Brausch had stopped in front of a market stall piled with fruit. He picked up an orange and turned it slowly in his fingers as he spoke.

'That,' Brausch said, 'is what I had Gerhard Tessin tell you. That, in turn, is what you reported to your Colonel Nicholas. That, in turn, is what he shared with dear Sir Geoffrey.'

Gus stood, stupefied. He literally could not believe his ears.

And now Brausch turned to Gus and the tired old eyes seemed so matter-of-fact.

'There are two Treasures, Gus. The decoy you followed. And Mr Desmond. Mr Desmond was my . . . how did Nicholas phrase it . . . my ace in the hole.'

Gus said nothing. And Brausch, hearing Gus' thoughts, answered the question yet unasked.

'Because I am, after all, German.'

'And you're telling me now . . .?' Gus asked softly.

Brausch sighed. A weary smile travelled across his lips. It shouldn't even have been necessary to ask.

'For the same reason,' Brausch said.

Gus nodded. Brausch's time had run out. Hoffmann had seen to that. If the invasion against Hitler was to have any chance, Brausch no longer had any alternative but trust.

'Let me buy you a snail or two,' Gus offered.

They found a small cabaret, bustling with its early-morning regulars. They were father and son, sharing their soup and escargots.

'Treasure now works for Walter,' Gus said.

'Justifiable inference,' Brausch muttered, his fingers prodding their prey from its shell.

'But you don't really know what, if anything, Walter's actually found.'

Brausch nodded. 'It would, however, be gauche of us to ask him.'

'Then again,' Gus said, 'it would seem a long trek for Mr Desmond if the message were simply "no sale."'

'If he's come all this way,' Brausch said quietly, 'whatever he had to say has buried you. And since Walter hasn't shared this with me, it buried me as well.'

'Who has Walter shared this with?' Gus wondered aloud.

'No one,' Brausch said. 'I'd stake my life on it. Matter of fact, I have. Yours as well.'

'You're certain?' Gus asked, in one of those useless rhetorical questions that left him feeling instantly mortified.

'Walter,' Brausch said simply, 'is alone. Do you think he would confide in Ritter or his ilk before matters were fully sorted out and under control? In their scramble to share the credit, those cretins would make a total botch of it.'

Brausch nodded, agreeing with the sound of his own words.

'Walter left the human race and went to live with the SS,' Brausch said quietly. 'He is as alone as if he were on the moon. It is both the strength and the weakness of his position.'

And that was the answer. The thread that Gus had been groping for. He and Hoffmann were soul-twins, but the story would be told by one yawning chasm of a difference between them.

Hoffmann could not trust. Had placed himself in isolation from the first. It *was* his weakness, no one could help him. It *was* his strength, no one would fail him.

And Gus could not be alone. Had trusted Andy. Had trusted Claire. And now Brausch. And in the reversed mirror image of Hoffmann, Gus' trust would be his weakness and his strength.

The plan that had formed in his mind, the plan that could not be worked alone, was seen now as the inevitable course. The single difference between them became his only chance. His strength, all of it, hurled at his enemy's weakness.

Time now to peel away the final layer. To show his bottom card to Brausch. Information being, as always, the precise equivalent of power. When this story was told, Gus would have nothing left.

'There is,' Gus said with almost a shy smile, 'a two-step procedure I had planned. I hadn't intended to bother you with it until step one was already completed.'

Brausch's eyebrows raised, affecting injury at this wanton display of mistrust.

'And why is that, I wonder?' he asked.

Gus' grin tightened a little. 'Because,' he answered, 'you are, after all, German.'

Gus made his pitch. As he spoke, he watched Brausch's eyes. They seemed to droop ever so slightly. As if the old man were maintaining only the polite appearance of attention.

When Gus had finished, he hadn't the slightest clue as to Brausch's reaction.

'You are an intelligent and resourceful boy,' Brausch said at last. 'Under present circumstances, step one of your proposal seems altogether worth the trying. Why, however, would you risk everything on the second phase?'

Gus' smile was warm and open.

'We are a family,' he said simply. 'There is only one mentality when you are a family. Every one of us counts. Every one of us makes it through.'

FIFTY-TWO

Gus answered the door to find Hoffmann with his two bottles of Pomerol and his smile. They sat. They chatted. The weather was splendid, Hoffmann advised.

Claire appeared with a large picnic basket and greeted Hoffmann warmly.

'I'm sorry, Walter. I know you wanted us to bring the baby, but she's been driving me mad all morning. If I bring her, we won't have a moment's peace. I'll leave her upstairs with Madame Hedbert.'

Hoffmann understood.

As Claire left to collect Amy, Hoffmann stepped to the picnic basket.

'I suppose,' he said, 'the wine goes here.'

He opened the basket and began to rummage through it. Sausage, bread. Cheeses. Five, six pieces of fruit. A large tin of what was unmistakably duck pâté.

Hoffmann noticed one thing more. There was no pistol.

He raised his brows in admiration. 'Pâté, no less.'

Gus grinned sheepishly.

'There's an American tradition,' he said. 'We always try to impress the boss. At first, I thought I'd scrounge some extra coupons. Then I just figured, the hell with it. I've got all these crisp franc notes, generously provided by MI-6. So I went down to my favourite market. You know, the black one.'

Hoffmann was impressed.

'Your lack of scruples in this area is commendable, but sadly missing the flair of a true hedonist. Ritter, for example, would have brought a chef from Grand Véfour.'

Gus smiled. 'I knew there was a reason we should have invited him.'

Hoffmann returned the smile. Each man knew there were precisely no reasons why either of them would have wanted Ritter along on this particular day.

Claire returned with Amy in her arms. Hoffmann had never seen the child before.

'Say hello and good-bye to Walter,' Claire murmured, nuzzling the soft golden hair.

Amy tried to put her entire hand in her mouth. Finally, she settled for two fingers.

'Hullo an' goo-bye to Walter,' Amy said shyly, perfectly repeating her mother's inflection.

The men laughed.

Hoffmann reached out his arms, and in one of those unpredictable moments in which babies make such decisions, Amy reached her arms back to this stranger with the dark eyes.

Claire found this most remarkable, and said so as she handed Amy to Hoffmann.

Hoffmann held the child so lovingly that a sudden chill swept through Gus. Was this a story, a moment, they would live one day to tell Amy? If not, she would never know who the dark-eyed man had been, and what he had done to them.

'Do you like to speak French or English?' Hoffmann whispered to the child in his arms.

'Yes,' she said. In English.

'Do you know what's boring?' he asked.

'Yes,' she said, with no idea of what on earth he meant.

She liked the way he held her. He was like a papa, smelled like a papa. Like the fathers of other children. Like Gus.

'It's boring,' he said, 'when someone says, "You know, I have a little boy at home who is very much like you."'

'What his name?' she asked coquettishly, trying to fit a finger into her nose. She tried that a million times a day, but the opening was always too small.

'Oskar,' he said.

'Ossss-kir,' she repeated solemnly.

He nodded.

'Oskar likes it when I throw him in the air.'

She knew at once this was an invitation. She really thought about it for a moment. It was wonderful when Gus did that. But right now, her intimacy threshold seemed suddenly to have been reached.

'No,' she said firmly. Without even a smile.

The dark eyes stared at her for a moment. It was an honest and very intense look, meant only for her. The kind of look that children are rivetted by.

'Next time,' Hoffmann said, and handed Amy back to her mother.

Gus received a sweet Amy-kiss good-bye, and Claire left to drop the baby with Madame Hebert.

'Meet you downstairs,' Gus called.

Hoffmann's eyes swept quickly over him as Gus looked away. Thin pullover, close-fitting slacks. No place to conceal a weapon.

'Taking a coat?' Hoffmann asked, picking up the basket.

Gus' eyes indicated a leather jacket, lying across the arm of the sofa.

Hoffmann handed the basket over to Gus. It was quite heavy with the addition of the wine.

'You're young and strong,' Hoffmann said. 'Besides, I outrank you. I'll take the coat. Anything else?'

Gus shook his head. He stood with the basket in both hands, watching Hoffmann scoop the leather jacket under his arm.

'After you.' Hoffmann gestured towards the door.

As Gus turned, Hoffmann expertly ran his fingers along the jacket. There was nothing.

On the street, Hoffmann asked Gus if he would drive. He admitted to drinking Scotch with Jürgen until nearly four and didn't want to risk their lives on his reflexes.

Claire joined Gus in the front seat. Hoffmann lounged in the back with the picnic basket.

They headed out of the city to the southwest, past Sèvres and Villacoublay. Hoffmann gave directions and passed periodic morsels of Dutch cheese. Claire kept the banter flowing, well up to her usual standard.

They drove for more than two hours. At last, they reached a rolling green area with soft meadows and a brook. They pulled off the road and walked until they found an exceptionally beautiful spot. There was the unmistakable feeling that not a soul breathed within a hundred miles of this paradise.

Their lunch was sumptuous and lingering. They finished the first Pomerol and were well into the second before dessert. Afterwards, Claire curled up in Gus' arms as the talk continued.

Finally, Hoffmann's eyes fixed on Claire.

'I'm sorry,' he said. 'I'll need a short time with Gus. There is some business. Always business.'

Claire nodded good-naturedly.

'I brought a book,' she said, rummaging through her purse, 'against just such an antisocial eventuality.'

'Don't get up,' Hoffmann said, pulling himself to his feet. 'Gus and I will take a little walk. Be back in an hour at the most.'

She blew a kiss to Gus. He followed Hoffmann off the path and into the woods.

They walked for twenty minutes. Hoffmann in the lead, seeming to wander aimlessly. The sunlight slipped through the trees as they strolled, and Hoffmann's eyes appeared to surrender to the stillness.

A silence grew between them. Deepened. The last they would share.

They came to a clearing against a gently sloping hill.

It was time.

Hoffmann settled back against a tree, still enjoying the spring air. Gus sat cross-legged on the short grass, perhaps ten metres away, struggling to light a pipe in the soft breeze.

'I've changed my mind,' Hoffmann admitted. 'Again, I wonder if that's a sign of advancing age.'

Gus nodded. He'd almost got the pipe going now.

'Senility,' Gus agreed. 'I'd recommend immediate retirement.'

'Lovely thought,' Hoffmann ruminated, 'retirement. Look, I've decided to close the book after all. We have the truth. Why belabour it?'

Gus looked up to find Hoffmann waiting for a response. Friendly but professional.

'I'm a cautious guy,' Gus confessed. 'I always seem to opt for a few last double checks.'

Almost always, is what Hoffmann thought. 'Berlin is impatient,' is what he said.

Gus nodded.

'Rash, impetuous chaps,' Gus agreed. 'Don't tell me they demand an answer before the end of the war.'

Hoffmann smiled so benignly, his face ached from the effort. Never easy to smile properly at a betrayer.

'I have advised the Gestapo that they may have Major Wheeler by the end of the week. No problems with that from your end?'

Gus thought for a moment. Shook his head.

'Nope.'

Hoffmann took a small breath. He would begin.

'I was reviewing my files last night, for the report,' Hoffmann said easily. 'The arrhythmia. Were you able to examine the original medical reports firsthand?'

That was it. Treasure.

Deny fast, figure it out later.

'No,' Gus said, 'actually I never saw Wheeler's original files. Only copies.'

Hoffmann nodded, as if this were completely understandable.

'Then your report . . .?' he asked gently.

'I was in a briefing with Nicholas and a civilian named Peters. That's where I got the copies.'

'Oh.' Noncommittal, but not particularly thrilled.

'Can't remember,' Gus said in mild puzzlement, 'which one brought up the heart thing. Peters, I think.'

Hoffmann cocked his head slightly to one side.

'Your report,' he said, 'seemed to state the cardiac condition as an absolute fact. I suppose I just assumed that you managed to double-check the original files. As you say, you're a cautious guy.'

That bastard Peters. He'd screwed up the files and Treasure had found it. That arrogant, self-satisfied, priggish little moron.

Gus shrugged.

'Couldn't get to them. Anyway, I figured there wasn't much point. If they falsified the copies, they would have falsified the originals, too.'

'Ah,' Hoffmann said, 'deductive reasoning.' Definitely not thrilled with that little explanation.

'I told you the first day,' Gus said, as if defending the care of his labours, 'that I didn't believe the heart condition. Then when Wheeler started talking about it in the cell, I guess he sort of won me over.'

'Persuasive little fellow,' Hoffmann conceded.

'I'm not sure I see,' Gus said, 'why the heart condition is still an issue.'

'Well,' Hoffmann said, with a gentle imitation of Gus' tone, 'I'm a curious guy.'

Yes he was.

'When you give him to the Gestapo,' Gus said, 'you'll know soon enough.'

Hoffmann looked so thoughtfully at him. Reached to his inside coat pocket, as if to extract the familiar cigarette case.

The hand returned with a small pistol. Hoffmann regarded it almost as if surprised to find it there. He placed the pistol carefully in his lap.

'There are certain things,' Hoffmann said, 'that I'm afraid I already know, Gus. Unpleasant, unfriendly things.'

Gus looked at the pistol. Stared with thoughtful detachment, as if it were an object of abstract art.

Where was the fear? The acid, eating through his lungs? These could truly be the last moments of his life. He was watching his own death from a mountaintop far away. So desperately did he want the pistol, the moment, to be illusion. But it was the detachment that was unreal. Be *here*. Feel it.

'The first day we met,' Hoffmann said, 'I told you my professional philosophy. Give your subject all the rope he's willing to take. Observe him in all aspects of his humanity. Give him the freedom to reveal himself to you.'

Gus was looking at Hoffmann's eyes now, but his mind was measuring the distance to Hoffmann's lap. He was recalling the position of the pistol's handle. There was no question. He couldn't lunge halfway there before Hoffmann could squeeze off his first shot.

Hoffmann would have to be calm and reasonably accurate. He would have to be a killer.

Gus searched the dark eyes now for the answer he knew he would find. Hoffmann was fully capable of blowing his skull to bits.

'I hope,' Hoffmann said evenly, 'that you will forgive me for never having trusted you. It is a very wicked world and ours is a most corrosive profession.'

Apparently so.

'Through these past days,' Hoffmann said so quietly, 'something has troubled me. Deeply. Do you know what that is, Gus?'

He did.

'My mistrust,' Hoffmann said, 'of Jürgen Brausch.'

Hoffmann was reading now with a particular intensity. Then, just as suddenly, the searching was gone from his eyes. A truth confirmed.

'You do not know this man,' Hoffmann said, 'as I know him. Thought . . . I knew him. How could such a man, whatever his motives, finally betray his own people? What a dark mistake, I thought, to turn my paranoia on this man.'

Hoffmann was speaking now only to God.

'And yet, Emerald was his agent. Handpicked by him for this assignment. For you to be what you are, and for Jürgen Brausch to be innocent, would require that you had deceived him. Had outwitted him from the first to last. And with all respect . . .'

The voice trailed off.

'You were forcing me,' Hoffmann said at last, 'to choose between doubting his character or his intellect. And for me, both were unassailable.'

Hoffmann's eyes had gone cold and suddenly dead. It was the face Gus had never seen, but had dreamed so often.

And with the death of Hoffmann's eyes, Gus swung fully back to the slashing terror of this moment. His heart pounded violently. All moisture fled his mouth, his eyes. Turned to flame surging through him.

For Hoffmann's eyes were saying there were only seconds left.

'It was,' Hoffmann conceded, 'quite a dilemma. Until last night. I should say, this morning. While Jurgen and I were drinking.'

Gus kept his gaze locked straight ahead. Kept any muscle from the betrayal of a single twitch.

'I saw in Jürgen's eyes,' Hoffmann said, 'something I'm certain has always been there. Something I had simply failed to interpret. The vanity. The vanity of a man who believes he could truly play God. That he alone has the wisdom to see the right path for his nation, his people. He could see it, alone. He could feel himself free to act on that vision, alone.'

Gus' eyes still locked ahead. Only a few more seconds.

Hoffmann's eyes rekindled and the playful smile came one last time to his lips.

'That,' Hoffmann said softly, 'has always been the truly

distinguishing mark of Adolph Hitler. The saddest, deadliest flaw. And in that, Jürgen and the Führer are really one . . .'

Hoffmann stopped. There had been the barest flicker in Gus' eyes.

Hoffmann's muscles coiled before his brain could even begin to compute. And in that instant, he heard the voice.

Claire's voice.

'Don't turn, Walter,' said the voice. It was shrill, but very strong. 'If you twitch a finger, even slightly, you are very dead.'

There was the silence of a frozen lifetime. No motion, no sound. A moment that would never pass.

'The first shot,' she said, 'will pass half a metre in front of you. If you move, the next one will take your head off.'

An incredible noise split the silence. Split the world down the centre.

A bullet passed less than a foot from Hoffmann's forehead. The sound echoed and took an eternity to die away.

Gus could see Claire from the corner of his eye. Hoffmann could not. She was kneeling on the grass. Arms extended, elbows locked. The pistol was braced firmly in her two hands.

She had sworn to Gus that she could do it. He had bet their lives on it.

'Your arms,' she said, 'slowly to the side now, away from your body.'

And then the moment that Gus had feared. Had watched in his mind through the sleepless night.

Hoffmann did not obey.

Pistol in his lap, hands inches from it, Hoffmann was thinking.

And this, Gus knew suddenly, with a finality he had never experienced before, this is how it ends. It ends frozen between thought and action. It ends sitting, watching while Hoffmann thinks of the answer.

There was no more time. Gus would beat him or die.

The green eyes hooded over and the icy shield dropped in place. And Walter Hoffmann paused, stopped cold in the middle of saving his own life. For they were more than the eyes of a killer. They were the eyes of a man who would not lose.

'Claire,' Gus said. It was a voice neither she nor Hoffmann had ever heard before.

'When I count to four,' the voice said calmly, with such quiet authority, 'you will squeeze every shot in that pistol into the Nazi's ear.'

And there was no pause for thought.

'One . . .,' said the voice. 'Two . . .'

Perhaps it was the eyes. Perhaps the voice. Perhaps it was no more than choosing the word *Nazi* instead of *Walter*.

Hoffmann knew.

And slowly, Hoffmann's hands moved away from the pistol. They continued to rise until they were clasped behind his head.

Step one was over.

FIFTY-THREE

Jürgen Brausch was seated at the desk of his office in Vincennes prison.

A young officer entered. An SS lieutenant, one of Ritter's favourite lackeys. Brausch looked up from his paperwork with mild annoyance at the intrusion. He saw that the boy was clearly agitated.

'May I help you, Sturmführer?'

'Herr Oberst. Captain Lang is outside. He insists that it is urgent.'

'Then please show him in.'

The lieutenant's agitation increased. He scarcely knew how to say the words.

'He insists, Herr Oberst, that you come to the Pit. He says he wants witnesses.'

The heavy brows lifted.

'Witnesses?'

Brausch rose and followed the lieutenant to the Pit, a large common area shared by junior officers. It accommodated nearly twenty desks, plus telephone and wireless equipment. There was a long bank of dull green filing cabinets.

Brausch arrived to find that the normal bustle of the Pit had slammed to a halt.

All staff, a random mixture of SS and Abwehr officers, were staring at Gus Lang as he stood in the centre of the room. A single glance made clear that this was a different Gus.

Carriage erect and proud. His jaw was defiant, his eyes very cold and narrow. To all watching, he was a man only now revealing a personality long within him.

Brausch attempted to greet Gus informally, but Gus would not respond in kind. Using stiff, almost military movements, Gus took an envelope from his inside coat pocket and handed it to Brausch.

Brausch seemed at once irritated and puzzled by Gus' formality. He opened the envelope. There was a single sheet of handwriting, which Brausch read in silence.

Now Brausch's face reflected anger.

'This is a . . . joke, Captain?'

'You will tell your staff,' Gus said coolly, in very precise German, 'of the Oberführer's order.'

There was a strength and an edge to Gus' tone that seemed to stop Brausch cold. This was no prank. The hostility drained from Brausch's face, as his evident confusion increased.

'This is,' Brausch said slowly, 'or purports to be, a directive from Oberführer Hoffmann. It says that he has been ordered to Calais by Reichsführer Himmler.'

Brausch's eyes searched Gus' before going further. His voice sounded incredulous and more than a little frightened.

'It says,' Brausch went on, 'that Ernst Ritter is to be relieved of his commission at once and taken into custody, on the Oberführer's authority. It says that I am to return to Berlin immediately.'

The green eyes were stone. Coldest jade. There was no answer to be found there.

'It says,' Brausch concluded, 'that the American prisoner is to be given over to Captain Lang's custody, and brought by him immediately to Calais.'

'And what else?' Gus said evenly.

Brausch stared at Gus, as if desperately trying to piece this together.

'It says,' Brausch answered weakly, 'that, in the Oberführer's absence, you are to speak with his authority in these matters.'

Gus nodded slowly.

'If these matters appear preposterous to you, Herr Oberst, let me assure you that they are not.'

Gus' voice was rich and deep. The voice of an officer who has not only assumed command but who has seized a career-propelling opportunity.

The voice of a man who smells blood.

'We are dealing,' the voice said, 'with matters of treason. Against our Führer, our Fatherland. These matters will make themselves known within the next seven to ten days. For now, I need the prisoner.'

Gus turned. His eyes seemed to scan the room at random.

His arm shot forward like a ramrod. The finger pointed at Trager.

'You,' Gus nearly shouted. 'Collect the prisoner. You will accompany us to Calais. Get a driver and an unmarked vehicle. I want the prisoner here in ten minutes.'

Trager's eyes went only to Brausch.

Brausch looked at Gus for a nervous moment, then shook his head in the negative.

The tension level of the room screwed itself a full notch higher. There now seemed no air to breathe.

Gus straightened his spine. Seeming nearly to rise off the floor, he barked a four-digit number to Brausch.

'Seven-oh-one-three. That is the Oberführer's telephone in Calais.'

Brausch stood, as if still mesmerized by Gus' transformation.

Gus snatched a receiver from the nearest desk and thrust it towards Brausch. Slowly, Brausch reached for the receiver. Waited for the switchboard.

'Calais,' Brausch said clearly. 'Seven-oh-one-three.'

He repeated the city and the number. There was a long, anxious wait.

At last, Brausch's eyes indicated that a voice was on the line. He spoke in French. Waited. Then in German.

After what seemed an eternity, 'Walter, Jurgen . . . what . . .' Brausch looked towards the ceiling, as if concentrating on what he was being told. He was quiet for nearly a full minute.

In reality, of course, Brausch was listening to nothing in particular. The call had been placed to a Resistance operative in Calais. The man was silent now, permitting Brausch to concentrate on his performance.

'Walter, I'm afraid I would need direction from Schellenberg for . . . I see . . . I see . . .'

There was another long silence.

'Walter, surely you don't . . .'

Another silence. Brausch's face was reddening now. As if fighting his temper. At last, he began to nod towards the ceiling. He seemed to relax.

'I have your personal assurance on that,' he said. 'I will rely on that, Walter. Of course. Of course. In Berlin, then. Of course.'

Slowly, Brausch replaced the receiver in its cradle. He looked only at Trager. He nodded his head.

Trager glanced nervously towards Gus, then hurried from the room.

Ritter's young lieutenant did the same.

'Would you like a coffee?' Brausch asked Gus in English. 'You could wait in my office.'

His tone was formal, respectful.

'I am comfortable as I stand, Herr Oberst,' Gus replied in German.

Gus' voice was softer now, but quite correct.

The wait was three minutes.

Much of Gus' life passed behind his eyes as he stood. Claire and Amy were on their way to the safe house near Chamonix. He would hold that thought until Ritter arrived.

Ritter burst into the Pit like an enraged animal. He brushed passed Gus, storming up to Brausch.

'I am in command here,' Gus announced to Ritter's back, and Ritter wheeled as if he had been shot.

'You,' Gus barked, 'will address yourself to *me*!' And Gus' voice had become more than a gunshot. It was a slap across the face.

Ritter took a single step towards him, then caught the flash of the green eyes. They were glowing hot.

'Come on,' Gus said in guttural slang. 'Come on, you pig. Right here, right now. When you're rotting in prison, I won't have the chance.'

Ritter whirled back to Brausch, whose face was now ashen.

'I demand,' Ritter shrieked, 'to see the Oberführer's order.'

'You demand *nothing*,' came Gus voice.

It was a voice Ritter had heard before. A voice that came from only one kind of man. The man who held the cards.

There was too much certainty in that voice, and fear was stabbing now through Ritter's rage.

Ritter turned again and saw that Gus' smile was more than sadistic, it was positively demonic.

'I never trusted you,' Gus said slowly. 'Oberst Brausch will confirm that. You were too self-righteous by half. I warned him and the Oberführer about you from the first day we met.'

Ritter was dumbstruck. Every instinct was screaming at him to hold his tongue. He must not jump in any direction until he had more information. He was helpless without it.

Gus flicked his eyes to Brausch.

'Show him the directive,' Gus ordered Brausch, as if speaking to a servant.

Brausch handed Ritter the paper.

Ritter read and couldn't believe his eyes. He had seen Hoffmann's handwriting a thousand times. Whatever this treachery, whatever it meant, it came from Hoffmann.

Trager arrived at the door. His strong hand clutched the elbow of a manacled Andy Wheeler.

Andy had spent the last sixty hours since his meeting with Hoffmann in the blackness of a box five feet square. Too small to lie down, too low to stand up. Andy could only crouch with his face to the air hole.

In Andy's mind had been more than the clutching panic of his claustrophobic surroundings. More than the horror of the mutilation Hoffmann had promised. In Andy's mind had been Gus Lang in the garden of Vincennes.

Whatever they come and tell you. Whatever they use. There's a world full of people back home who will be counting on you, Andy. Counting on you to do one thing.

To trust me. And nobody else.

And that would be the bottom of it for Andy Wheeler. For in the darkness, he had decided. They could cut off his arms and legs. They could cut out his heart. Gus had given him Calais and September. That was all they were ever going to get.

All eyes in the Pit had turned now to Andy, wobbling on knees that were somehow holding him up.

But Andy's eyes had found Gus. For Andy, it was as if Christ had stepped down from the cross.

Everything inside of Andy welled up in his eyes. He tried to stop the tears. He had to. His brain was shrieking at him that he would screw everything up.

He had to stop the tears.

But he couldn't. Andy's eyes overflowed and his heart streamed down his face.

Gus looked at Andy's eyes. For Gus, there truly was no choice. He would have to stop his own tears. It was not the least, and not the last, of the things that Gus would have to do.

Gus' lips curled in unmistakeable disgust.

'*Schwachheit*,' Gus murmured, as if to himself. Weakness. 'A pathetic people. Look upon America, Herr Oberst.'

Gus started towards Andy, but Ritter stepped to block his path.

'I must talk to the Oberführer.' His voice summoned all of his remaining strength. 'I demand the right to speak with him directly.'

The green eyes narrowed with contempt.

'You? You are like that!' Gus said, thrusting his finger in Andy's direction. 'You will demand nothing. You will say nothing. You will hear the charges against you when the Reichsführer deems appropriate.'

Gus took one more step, but Ritter came forward to meet him.

The huge fists were clenched. There was no rationality to it. The man was fighting for his life now, and knew only one way.

And behind Gus' eyes, the film he had replayed since that first night in the dungeon. The light glinting from the collar button of Ritter's tunic, as in Gus' mind Ritter's body came across the table at him. Slow horrifying motion, the massive hands springing for Gus' throat. To snap Gus' spine in an instant. Like a twig. A twig. A twig. Before anyone could speak. Before anyone could move.

Gus smiled with bitter satisfaction.

'Hauptsturmführer,' he said to a nearby officer, 'take this man to the American's cell. He should find the accommodations suitable for reflection.'

Ritter's hand went straight to the pistol at his side. Unsnapped the holster cover. His hand closed slowly over the butt of the pistol.

His eyes were wild.

But Gus' smile never wavered. It was now cold joy complete.

'Thank you, pig,' Gus growled.

The green eyes shot across the room to Trager. He also wore a pistol at his side.

'Hauptmann,' Gus said to Trager, 'this man has assaulted an officer of the Reich. You will be so kind as to shoot him. Now.'

That voice. The voice Hoffmann had heard only hours before in the stillness of a meadow. It turned Ritter's soul to water. His mouth slacked open, and the fury of a moment before had been utterly replaced by terror.

The green eyes were burning with the light of insane calculation. Ritter knew in an instant that Gus had planned it just this way. And that he meant every word.

'That is an order, Hauptmann,' Gus said crisply. 'I expect it to be executed immediately, or you will share this man's fate.'

The room, the moment, were swaying. Trembling, as if time itself would shatter.

Trager's eyes once again looked only to Brausch.

Brausch stepped up behind Gus and placed a hand on his shoulder. Without looking back, Gus slapped it away.

'I am in command here, my dear Oberst. Will you kindly advise your young captain to do as I have ordered?'

The green eyes were aflame. They seemed at the outer limits of self-control.

Brausch's voice was soft and wise.

'That was not part of Walter's orders, Gus. He told me that Ernst was to stand trial. We have all seen the assault. It will be added to the charges, I assure you.'

Ritter's hand remained frozen on the butt of his pistol.

'I do not want your assurance, Herr Oberst,' Gus said coldly. 'I expect your obedience.'

Keep the fire up. Keep it there. Right at Ritter's eyes. Hold it, now. Hold it. You've got the power. Hold his eyes until goddam hell freezes solid. Show him who's the goddam Nazi in this room.

Ritter's hand slowly left the pistol butt. The hand fell to his side.

Don't lose it, now. Hang on. He's still got to step aside. Bully him, now. Pummel him. Run right through the sonofabitch.

Gus cocked his head to one side. A falcon, studying his prey.

The silence was excruciating. Hold it a beat. And one more.

'*Ungeziefer*,' Gus muttered low in his throat, '*schlammige*.' Vermin, slime. 'Hardly worth the bullet.'

Gus took a breath. Flexed his knees.

'Colonel,' Gus said to Ritter, 'you will make an appropriate apology and stand aside. You have five seconds.'

It was one more than he had given Hoffmann, but then Ernst was a little slower.

Their eyes locked for the last time, but the momentum had been established. Ritter's lips parted, but no sound emerged, From somewhere, he found the strength to take a halting step out of Gus' path.

With a last withering glare of contempt, Gus brushed past Ritter. He followed Trager and Andy out the door.

They passed down a corridor that seemed to extend for miles. Their footfalls echoed sharply.

Andy was between them, stumbling, being dragged by Gus and Trager with their strong grip at either arm. Gus said only one thing.

'Whatever happens, your legs keep moving. You're walking home now. You just keep walking until you're there. They blow your head off, nothing stops those legs.'

There was a staircase. Another corridor.

A doorway and blinding sunlight. They were in the courtyard.

Sixty metres away, or was it sixty miles, stood the car. Brausch's driver from the Ritz.

And Gus braced himself for the shout. The shout from a

balcony, from a window. The shout that would be followed by the clicking of a thousand rifles. One rifle. The one that would find him.

Gus slowed to a stately pace. The car was now two thousand miles away. The shout had not come. No matter, it would.

They began the sixty metres across the sun-flooded courtyard, in full view of four dozen men bearing their rifles at attention.

Gus wondered which of them it would be. Which had the reflexes, the steadiness of hand.

It didn't matter. He would pick up Andy and the whole damn car and go right through the wall. There was no way they could stop him.

They were at the car. The driver fumbled with the door. Gus' eyes swept across the courtyard of soldiers. Daring the shout. The shot.

They were in the car. Andy between them in the back.

It would come now. Let it come.

The gate of the château courtyard was rolled open. As the car shifted into gear, Gus reached for Andy's hand. He squeezed Andy's hand so tightly, so lovingly, that Andy was instantly convulsed in sobs.

The car lurched forward and passed through the open gate. It disappeared into the sunlit afternoon of June 2, 1944.

Less than four days later, in the grey dawn of Normandy, the liberation of Europe was begun.

EPILOGUE

Subsequent calls to Calais revealed that the number belonged to a private hotel. Walter Hoffmann was indeed on the register for June 2, and the cooperative young desk clerk (having been briefed by his superiors at Jade Amicol) described Hoffmann quite accurately. Unfortunately, Hoffmann had checked out rather abruptly.

A week later, Hoffmann's complete disappearance was finally acknowledged. The Gestapo tore apart his suite at the Ritz Hotel. They discovered a well-hidden and most interesting set of notes.

The notes, in Hoffmann's handwriting, revealed a conspiracy among Hoffmann, Gus Lang, and Ernst Ritter. A conspiracy to aid the American prisoner in his effort to conceal the true plans for the Allied invasion of Europe. It was not fully evident whether Hoffmann and Ritter were members of the Schwarze Kapelle.

It was clear that the confrontation between Lang and Ritter at Vincennes prison had been staged to exonerate Ritter, so that he could continue his treasonable activities from within the SD after Hoffmann and Lang had escaped.

Ritter of course, swore that he had been framed by Hoffmann, but Hoffmann couldn't be found. Ritter was imprisoned near Frankfurt pending completion of the investigation. He died shortly thereafter in what was officially described as a disturbance among inmates.

As to the others:

'Martin': Born Anton Woczyk of a Polish father and French mother, he was never to see his parents again after the morning of his internment at Drancy. The freight car of

Claire's nightmares deposited the child at Auschwitz. He was befriended and sexually abused by a young cook, through whose efforts he survived and ultimately escaped. After the war, he was taken in by an elderly couple who lived in the Baltic city of Gdynia. He never forgot the beautiful black-haired lady who had held him that day at Drancy. She remained in his thoughts and dreams. He remembered his Papa and Mama by keeping within him the image of their Sabbath dinners together. Eventually, he emigrated to the homeland of their prayers. Today, at the age of forty-four, the father of three strong sons, he is an artillery commander in the Israeli Army.

Jürgen Brausch: Spent the balance of the war in Berlin, continuing his invaluable reports to Lord Geoffrey Macklin (now elevated to the peerage through the triumph of Vincennes). Brausch ultimately retired to his country home in the Rhine Valley and the pleasures of visits from his many grandchildren. He died in his sleep in 1967 at the age of eighty-six.

Colin Desmond: Following D-Day, Treasure went completely to ground. Neither Tessin nor any of Treasure's former employers heard from him again. After the war, he was unable to reclaim his former post at Oxford. At the last available report, he was rumoured to have been in the employ of the British Secret Service.

Andy Wheeler: Returned home to Stephanie, awkward silences, and the realization that their love had not survived the separation. His disappointment was short-lived. Andy met and married Beth, who gave him two dark-eyed daughters, each raised in her mother's Jewish faith. Andy's genius for electronics was timed perfectly for his era. Surprising everyone, most of all himself, he ended up in management, retiring as a wealthy man at the age of fifty-five. He lives today with his family in Bellevue, Washington.

Claire and Gus Lang: Married in New Canaan, Connecticut, on June 2, 1945. Gus ran his father's business for a few years, until the restlessness took over. There followed a three-decade pattern of moving in and out of CIA and other American intelligence services on a project-by-project basis. Claire's diverse talents ultimately focused on sculpture. Her work is exhibited, sold, honoured. They had one child together, Andrew, who at thirty-four is an investment banker in New York. Andrew, the image of his father, has occasionally taken mysterious sabbaticals from Wall Street to 'work on one of Dad's little projects.' Neither Claire nor Gus has fully retired. Now in their late sixties, their principal residence is a small farm outside Aix in the South of France. There are pigs and a piano. Gus has learned to hammer out a fairly respectable ragtime.

Amy Lang: A brilliant student like her adoptive father, Amy preferred to follow her mother into the arts, where she had somewhat less natural talent. An indifferent painter, she is married to an excellent one, a gentleman seven years her junior who had escaped from his homeland of East Germany. They raised their children at the edge of Lake Como, in northern Italy. Amy is described by her mother as 'the only consistently happy person in the Northern Hemisphere,' a tribute that Amy required Claire to chisel onto a marble tombstone as a gift for Amy's fortieth birthday.

Oskar Hoffmann: Professor of ethics, University of Heidelberg.

Rudi Hoffmann: Went into business with his father. Papa's strong right arm, his able successor upon retirement.

Walter Hoffmann: A Resistance captive in Gascony until the liberation, Hoffmann was not included in subsequent war crimes trials. Jürgen Brausch and others saw to it that Hoffmann was presented with several opportunities to turn his genius to the reconstruction of Germany. All proposals for public service were graciously declined. Hoffmann focused instead on the private sector, in particular, the coal and steel industries. His success exceeded the expectations of his strongest admirers. At eighty, he lives today in Vienna with his Anna. He is one of the fifty richest men in Europe.